EMERALD SILK

PART TWO IN THE COIN FOREST SERIES

EMERALD SILK

JANET LANE

FIVE STAR
A part of Gale, Cengage Learning

GALE
CENGAGE Learning

Detroit • New York • San Francisco • New Haven, Conn • Waterville, Maine • London

GALE
CENGAGE Learning

Set in 11 pt. Plantin
Printed on permanent paper.

LIBRARY OF CONGRESS CATALOGING-IN-PUBLICATION DATA

Lane, Janet.
    Emerald silk / Janet Lane. — 1st ed.
      p. cm. — (Coin forest series ; pt. 2)
    ISBN-13: 978-1-59414-682-4 (alk. paper)
    ISBN-10: 1-59414-682-9 (alk. paper)
     1. Romanies—Fiction. 2. Chalices—Fiction. 3. England—Fiction. 4. Fifteenth century—Fiction. [1. Knights and knighthood—Fiction.] I. Title.
PS3612.A5498E44 2008
813'.6—dc22
                            2007041921

First Edition. First Printing: April 2008.

Published in 2008 in conjunction with Tekno Books.

Printed in the United States of America
1 2 3 4 5 6 7 12 11 10 09 08

This is dedicated to my pre-published author friends, those who have a passionate dream and great stories written and waiting to be published. Keep your dream, nurture it, and always believe in the talent with which you have been blessed. I applaud you and look forward to attending your first book signing.

ACKNOWLEDGMENTS

Thanks to my husband, John; our daughters, Jessica and Jalena; my wonderful mother-in-law, Dot, and all my family and friends for their support. It takes a village, and my village includes my wonderfully talented critique partners in the Alphas, Celestials, and Kay Bergstrom groups, and my gifted Story Magic plotting partners. Thanks to Margie Lawson and the KaizenWriters for the motivation and support.

To my lifetime friends, Pam, Laura, Carla, Carol, Jan, Rose— thanks for your unwavering belief in me.

To Jalena and Deirdre for the gorgeous book cover.

To Tina, Nancy, and the rest of my librarian friends at Bemis Public Library, Columbine Library, and Denver Public Library, thank you for your resourcefulness and help.

A tip of the hat to Dennis and Philip with the Poole Yacht Club for their information about navigating the prevailing winds and tides in Poole Harbor.

And special thanks to John Helfers; my editor, Alice Duncan; and Managing Editor Tiffany Schofield. You make the publishing experience a joy.

ACKNOWLEDGMENTS

AUTHOR'S NOTE

Over the centuries, Gypsies (Romani) have been romanticized, feared, tortured and expelled.

Yet these nomadic people for a brief time enjoyed a social honeymoon in Europe. In a time span of several decades, royalty, the church, and nobles in many countries not only welcomed the Gypsies, but willingly financed their journey through their lands.

Records of their travels suggest that India is their land of origin, but these nomadic people claimed Egypt as their homeland. During their exodus through Western Europe, the clever Gypsies discovered that nobility had its privileges. Always adaptable, they assumed titles such as "Count" and "Duke." Harnessing the popularity of pilgrimages, their story evolved: they claimed to be of noble blood, ejected from their lands in Little Egypt. They traveled on a pilgrimage of penitence by order of the Pope himself, who directed them to roam the earth for seven years without sleeping in a bed.

Dark-skinned and handsome, riding choice steeds and dressed in exotic clothes, the Gypsies dazzled peasants and royalty alike. Gypsies gained papers ensuring safe conduct from such dignitaries as King James IV of Scotland and Sigismund (1368–1437), Holy Roman emperor from 1411 to 1437 and king of Hungary 1387–1437.

While the first written evidence of Gypsies in the British Isles is dated April, 1505, it's probable that the Gypsies arrived at an earlier time. Official documents exist, along with stories which tell of Gypsies arriving in Paris in 1427, last seen heading toward England, likely enticed by the rich, powerful country that seemed to be finally winning the Hundred Years War.

Also during this time Roma were sold and traded, along with their bears and monkeys, in Bulgaria and Wallachia, and shipped to southern France. Thirteenth century records reveal that a young Romani girl was sold in Marseilles for nine pounds and fifteen solidi.

Tens of thousands of Roma were confined in slavery yet, with the right clothes and a convincing story, they could become Gypsies, noble pilgrims worthy of respect and sustenance during their travels. One would be hard put to imagine better incentive to reinvent oneself.

It is in this atmosphere of early social honeymoon that my fictional heroine, Sharai (*Share-EYE*), was shipped as a slave from Wallachia to Marseilles, fled France and ferried to England with a small band of fellow Gypsies, seeking freedom from slavery and a new beginning.

It is toward the end of this bubble in time that my fictional heroine, Kadriya (*Kah-DREE-yah*), half English and half Romani, fights the atmosphere of growing resentment and distrust in mid-fifteenth century England.

BOOK CLUB READERS' GUIDE: See ancillary material at the back of the book.

CHAPTER 1
THE EMERALD CHALICE

England's Applewood Horse Fair, September, 1448

Kadriya paused on the hill above the gentle valley where swarthy-skinned men groomed horses and children squealed with delight in a game of tag, their cheeks flushed with the breezy freedom of innocence. Their bare feet skimmed the earth. Watching them run, Kadriya's own feet yearned for escape from the tight English shoes and the confining life they represented. Soon she would feel the rich, earthy grass between her toes. She savored the aroma of fried apples and campfires, and the prospect of returning to a life without barriers, under the stars. The thought stirred the Roma side of her heart. It was here she belonged.

She hoped.

Shifting on her horse she spread her arms, palms to the sky, and inhaled the crisp September air. The sun had finally broken through and weeping willows graced the banks of the meandering Parrott River, sprinkling leaves of gold on the surrounding valley floor.

Below, her Spanish-bred stallions nuzzled and nickered in their corral amid scores of other horses offered by competing Somerset breeders. Her patron, Richard, Baron of Tabor, was away fighting in France, and she was handling the sale on her own. She would do Tabor proud and return with a good profit. Then she would begin her new life.

Her escort, Maude, pulled alongside her, reining her horse to a stop. She filled her saddle, a tall, stout woman with copper hair, ample breasts and a heart just as big. The skirt of Maude's gown rode up her thigh, revealing a collection of knives big enough to slay a dragon. Maude's eyes twinkled with good humor. "You look happy as a fox in a warren."

Kadriya smoothed her skirt, a light yellow wool, and adjusted her own dagger. "I am. Today Teraf will announce our intentions to break the tile together." Teraf, fiery leader of the Roma, was offering her marriage and a home. With him, and with her mother's people.

Maude's blue eyes shone. "Sharai will miss you."

Sharai. At the mention of her name, Kadriya's joy ebbed. "I wish she could be with us." A fresh ache grew in Kadriya's chest, a strain, as of a delicate web being wrenched from its mooring, forever breaking connections. Sharai had raised Kadriya from infancy. She was everything to her, mother, sister, friend. Kadriya adjusted her scarf, an airy linen weave of lavender, pink and yellow. "I can no longer abide the whispers, Maude." Twenty and unwed, unwanted by the nobility because of her mixed blood. "I must make my own way." Anticipation shortened her breath. She would finally be wed. At last she had found her place.

John Wynter peered through the sunset's gloom, separating the bushes enough to keep the heathens in his sight. Their campfire leapt higher, illuminating the frenzied swine as they danced at the river's edge, oblivious of the mud dripping from their feet. They had left the British section of the horse fair and gone to their own camp some hundred yards distant, a camp with several small fires and a community blaze where they all gathered. Two dozen tents, the larger ones flying colors of red and yellow. Gypsy flags. Devil's music leapt from their strange instruments, and they danced as if plagued with St. Vitus' disease, the women swaying their hips in an unholy bid for attention from all who watched.

John rolled his cross between his fingers, tracing the dent on the right crossbar, damaged during battle. The smooth surface of the gold reminded him of his faith, of his friendship with and duty to the abbot.

It had been two long, miserable days of riding from the monastery in a torrent of rain that had stopped just today. All because of the Gypsy thief, Teraf. He had stolen a priceless chalice from the abbey, a chalice with a history involving the most prominent bishop in England, a history that could cause his abbot embarrassment and loss of funding if it wasn't found, and soon.

These foreigners looked to Teraf as a king and he held court like a swaggering peacock, wild-eyed, his hair bound in a yellow scarf, flowing past his shoulders like an ink-stained curse.

Roger, one of the five knights who rode with John to seize the Gypsy thieves, joined him. "Still no sign of the other thief, Erol."

"The Abbot wants both, but by the saints, I will not let this one get away. Erol must not be here, and their ceremony is over. The Gypsy king has won his hen." John watched the beautiful Gypsy tart who stood so proudly at Teraf's side. Teraf had treated her like an ornament all the day, while she happily accepted any shred of attention he gave her.

He could not help but notice her large almond eyes with lively, expressive brows—none of that infernal plucking—and her full mouth. Her hand swept to her breast, a woman's enticement, but the gesture betrayed the hesitance of a girl. She covered it well with a delightful smile, but she was a maiden.

She had tied her scarf high, hugging her forehead and temples like a crown, tied in the back and flowing, fluttering from her movements, touching her neck, her shoulders. Her steps, sure and effortless, made her skirt seem to flow over the matted grasses. In spite of her excessive obeisance to the thief, she seemed to possess her own spirit.

Her hair was exposed; garish hoops of gold hung from her ears and her clothes swung shamefully loose, but never had he seen a more captivating woman.

An arrow of lust pierced him.

Leather sandals held her small feet and strapped up her ankles and higher, peeking out when the fabric rolled softly from her movements.

How high, he wondered, did the leather lacings climb?

Cease. He pulled his gaze from her, chipping a scale of mud off his armor with his thumb. He was here to serve his abbot, and she was nothing more than one of them.

Foreigners.

In moments she would learn her peacock was just a pigeon, and a black one, at that.

John turned to Roger. "Are their ponies hobbled?"

"Aye."

"Good. Now we strike."

Teraf offered Kadriya a broad, white-toothed smile. His cream-colored cotehardie hugged his chest, offering testament to his flamboyant nature. Who else, she thought, would dare to wear such a light hue when riding horses in muddy fields? The fine fabric was mud-stained and smelled deeply of male and horse sweat, though judging by his gaiety, it bothered him not. His raven hair spilled past his shoulders, framing untamed eyes that challenged, flashed and flirted.

Of all the tribal kings in Marseilles, Teraf was the youngest, just two and twenty. Though impetuous and sharp-tongued, he was respected among the tribe. She admired his intelligence and self-assurance—in spite of his limited command of English, he negotiated fiercely, relentless until he extracted the most coin possible for his tribe's horses. She appreciated the way he accepted her, as if she were a rare jewel, as if she were true-blooded, rather than the worrisome, mixed-blood woman she really was.

Teraf nuzzled her. "When I'm through with you, my queen, you'll spit in the eye of any nobleman you meet." He hugged Kadriya close to him, squeezing the air from her chest.

She coughed and pulled away from him. Teraf's laughter had grown steadily louder since their announcement, his normally gentle touch now more bold, more controlling. Her day, which had begun like a pleasant float on the river, had become a tossing ride on the unpredictable waves of the sea, with no sight of land with which to regain her bearings.

But she did not feel unwanted. Nay, if anything, he seemed ravenous. Likely the mead was pickling his brain, and he would be groaning come sunrise.

"I shall purge that dusty English blood from your veins." He kissed her, his lips hard and purposeful. "And fill you with pure Romani." His dark eyes flashed in the firelight, and he swung her, too forcefully, in a circle. He lost his balance and they fell together in the mud.

The wet earth soaked through her tunic to her spine. Kadriya gasped from the shock and pulled away from him. "Let me go, Teraf. You have drunk more than you should."

"Do not whine, woman."

A horse's whinny and gasps from the others brought Kadriya scrambling to her feet.

Three mounted knights rushed in on destriers. Two other knights approached from the riverbank, swords drawn, their horses' hooves plopping through the wet earth, then sucking free, adding to the confusion. The tribal dogs sprang from their begging positions near the fire, fangs bared. Several Roma rushed forward to protect Teraf.

The knights urged their mounts forward, one bumping Kadriya carelessly.

"Fie! Rein your steed," she said in reprimand.

The knight rammed her again, spitting on her skirt. His gaze settled on her chest and he reached for her.

She spun away and returned to Teraf's side.

Kadriya's mouth went dry. Since her childhood, she had been accustomed to Lord Tabor's protection, traveling with knights and escorts. But limited by law to carrying only daggers for protection, Teraf and his men were at the mercy of these heavily armed knights

Other knights approached from the riverbank, looming above them, swords drawn. "Stand back," the older one said.

She turned to Teraf.

The moment magnified, each man frozen, weighing his next move as the dogs rumbled threatening growls.

Dots of sweat glistened on Teraf's upper lip, betraying his fear and offering no reassurance. He signaled to the dogs. "Ho. Lie down." He nodded to his men. "Do as they say."

A sixth knight lunged out of the darkness, yanking Teraf's daggers from his belt. "You will come with us, thief."

Teraf's stout, muscular build offered no match for the burly, sword-wielding knight, so he did not fight back. "You make big error," he said in broken English. "I am Teraf. King." He gestured to include all the Gypsies. "Pope give papers of protection. Grant free travel. We—"

The largest knight urged his steed forward. "Papers," he interrupted, spitting the word out like bad meat. "Bring them with you." He wore armor but no helm. A gold cross stretched across his wide neck, held by a leather lanyard, its right crossbar bent at an odd angle. His dark blond hair lay flattened against his skull. The stubble of several days' growth shadowed his face, gaunt with high cheekbones, his blue eyes cold as a fireless night. "I am here on authority of the church," he said, "and we know who you are. A foreigner, a heathen. A thief. You availed yourself of work and coin at the abbey, and you repaid that kindness by stealing an altar chalice. A special altar chalice. You will bring it to us now."

Teraf struggled to free himself. "You are fool." He looked toward Kadriya. "These are all lies," he swore in Romani. "I have been to no abbey. I have been here, with my tribe." His scarf had been loosened in the scuffle, releasing his long hair and it fell, obscuring his eyes so she couldn't read them for truth.

Kadriya's heart pounded in her ears.

"Kadriya?" The moment grew heavy as Teraf waited for— what? Her confirmation that he had been here? But she had just arrived from Coin Forest. She didn't know.

But she must respond. *He's your betrothed. He's too smart, too dedicated to his people, to steal treasures from an abbey. He must be innocent.* Teraf needed her to support him. "It's a mistake. He is no thief," she said as much for her own reassurance as for the knight's. *Of course he's not. You would have seen signs of it.*

The large knight straightened, looking much like a metal tree, wide and hard, the firelight reflecting on his armored chest. Impossibly, his eyes grew even colder. "There is a reliable witness to his crime. An Englishman. A man of God. I am Sir John Wynter, here on order of Father Robert, Abbot of the Cerne monastery, to return you forthwith for hanging."

"Nay," Kadriya cried. Hatred burned hot in the knight's eyes, scorching her senses. It was frighteningly clear that he had no intention of learning the truth. She sensed then that Teraf must be innocent.

She approached the tall knight and lifted her chin to meet his eyes, still slitted in disdain. "He has no such chalice. Who is his accuser?"

The knight shifted in his saddle. "So you know a smattering of English, do you, heathen? Well done, but it will not save your thieving man." He tipped his head in the direction of a small wagon, signaling the other knights. "Tie him up."

Kadriya hurried to the wagon and approached a knight with several missing teeth, hoping he would have more compassion and wits about him. "Your abbot. Tell him Lord Tabor will speak for Teraf."

The knight dragged Teraf to his horse. "A nobleman would speak for this swine?" He laughed and bound Teraf's hands behind his back, tying him like livestock to the saddle.

Kadriya grabbed his arm. "Release him."

The toothless knight spun around and struck Kadriya, knocking her to the ground.

She landed on her hip in the mud. His horse pranced, nervous. She scrambled backward, away from the horse's hooves.

Sir John Wynter spurred his horse between Kadriya and the knight. "Sir Phillip. Strike no woman or child. We are here for the men and the chalice. We have found Teraf. Now find the chalice and Erol and we'll take our leave." He scanned the tents, his gaze resting on the largest one, Teraf's, a fine ash bender-tent dressed with red and yellow flags.

He rode to it, dismounted and bent to enter the round, low-slung shelter. He emerged moments later, grim-faced. "Erol must have it, but check the rest of the tents, just in case."

Two other knights pushed their way into the smaller tents, popping the wooden skewers that held the oiled linen taut over the support rods.

"Stop that. Leave us. We don't have your chalice," Kadriya cried, blocking one of the tents.

Kadriya's Romani friend, Bit, and her mother grabbed Kadriya's arms. "Get back. They'll kill you!"

The knights emerged from the last tent, still empty-handed.

Kadriya released the breath she'd been holding. *See, you knew it. There is no chalice here, and Teraf is innocent.*

The knights cursed, kicking the tent poles from the ground, and mounted their horses. They left, following the road bordering the barley field.

Sobered and wide eyed, Teraf ordered the dogs to stay and held out his free hand. "My brothers, I am innocent," he said in Romani. "Meet us at Blackwater Point and free me."

From the look on his face, the hateful knight John Wynter did not understand their language. He glared at Teraf and led his horse to the back of the procession. Regarding the Romas with drawn sword, he warned, "Follow us and we will kill you. You would do well to take your strange tongue and evil ways and get you back to Egypt, or whencesoever you came." He slanted a look of loathing at Kadriya. "All of you."

Kadriya watched, paralyzed as the knights and an anxious, tethered Teraf disappeared into the darkness, following the river to their left.

Children, evicted from the tents for the search, stood crying in the night air, their small feet lost in the mud. Women clutched their babes, worry etched on their faces, and the men huddled among themselves, some still holding their instruments and mugs.

Rill, wiry overseer of the dancers, signaled to his two large, light-skinned *gorgio* guards, and other men joined them, disappearing into Teraf's tent.

They emerged a moment later, securing their daggers. Murat, a handsome man with white hair and a greying mustache, was second in command after Teraf. He glared at Kadriya from under long, white brows. "We'll attack the knights and free Teraf. Stay out of our way, woman."

Kadriya faced his gaze, raising her chin. She would not let him dismiss her. She must help free Teraf. "I am not just a woman. I have been trained to fight since I was a child." Exaggerated a jot, but Sharai had taught Kadriya how to take down men twice her size, and she knew well how to use a dagger. "I have fought men bigger than you, and I am your future queen." She elbowed her way in front of him. "What are you planning?"

"To free Teraf at Blackwater Point."

Kadriya walked quickly, following them to the horses. In spite of her wildly beating heart she tried to use reason, as Sharai always did in times of emergency. "A dozen Roma with daggers against six armored knights? Mayhap you will cast a spell, then?"

His eyes flashed and he took a threatening step toward her.

She did not flinch or break her stride. "You will be cut down like wheat before the scythe."

Rill pushed past Murat. "What would you do, Kadriya?"

"They're mounted on warhorses sixteen hands high. Swinging swords." A scream knocked at her throat, wanting to surface. Teraf had been taken, Lord Tabor was not here to help her, and if she didn't think of something posthaste, she might never see Teraf again. "Our best hope is to unseat them."

She spied the metal props used to hold cooking kettles over the open fire. She eyed the long, iron rods, following the bend of the metal down to the end. The hook was curved wide to enable easy removal of heavy pots, the curl wide enough to catch a neck or an arm. Even a big one, she thought, recalling John Wynter's thick neck. She removed the pots of soup suspended over the fire and pulled three kettle props from the earth, holding them by the cold end. "These will help us pull them off their horses. Then the knights will be but half as powerful."

Rill's eyes lit in recognition. "Aye, and, you men, bring some long pieces of firewood. Hurry."

Wood and kettle props gathered, they mounted their horses.

Wet hoofbeats told of someone approaching. Maude rushed into camp, her red hair hanging on her mud-speckled cloak. She spied Kadriya and rode to them. "I heard what happened. 'Twill be all right, Sprig," she soothed, using her pet name. "They'll learn the truth at the monastery."

"Fie! With John Wynter, Teraf will be lucky to live through the night." She regarded Maude with determination. "We're going to Blackwater Point. To free Teraf."

Maude's eyes widened. "Have you lost your senses? This is a church matter and church law, Kadriya."

Kadriya understood the implications of attacking the knights. Death. But they were wrong. "He's innocent." She turned away from Maude and addressed the men. "Come. We must hurry."

They started down the river road and a thought occurred to Kadriya. She called for her friend. "Bit? Bit."

Bit, small as her name, popped up from behind a tent, eyes white in fear against her dark skin. "Aye?"

"Get Prince Malley from the cages."

"The monkey?"

"Aye." Teraf had bought him in Bath at Lammas. He was a questionable pet, just two feet tall and mostly trouble, but he might prove useful as a distraction.

Bit brought him forward on a chain, a daring creature with wine-colored fur, long whiskers, bright eyes and sharp teeth. Thankfully he was well trained.

With a grimace, Rill accepted Prince Malley and they followed the river toward the point. The horses labored through the mud, thick and congealed as blood pudding from the heavy rains, making their progress slow.

"The road turns left ahead," Kadriya said. "If we stay with

21

the river, we'll gain time."

Murat scoffed. "And sink in the mire."

"The knights face the same conditions as we do."

Murat's white brows furrowed. "Why should we follow a woman?" A derisive tone darkened his last word.

"Who other than she has a plan?" Maude challenged him.

Kadriya turned, alarmed to learn that Maude had followed. "Go back, Maude. If we fail, we'll be hanged with Teraf."

Maude straightened in her saddle. "Sharai said to keep you safe, and I will." Her determination rang clear in her voice, strong as the iron bars Kadriya had gathered from the campfire. There would be no sending her back.

Sweet saints, if something happened to Maude . . . Kadriya pushed the thought out of her mind. They must save Teraf. Kadriya shook her head at the complication and they continued to follow the river.

Rill caught up with her. "What do you know of Blackwater Point?"

"I took my morning ride nearby, in the valley. The hills converge on the path at a point, making it narrow." She wanted to urge her horse faster, but the earth was soft and slippery, and her mare was becoming fretful from the uneven footing. Kadriya checked the position of the moon. The evening was fading. If they failed to free Teraf, they would be trussed like their king and hauled to the abbey. She swallowed hard. To hang.

Kadriya prayed and crossed herself. Teraf had sworn his innocence and she believed him. He must be freed.

After a candle's inch they reached Blackwater Point. Three tall, sprawling hills surrounded them, opening onto fields devastated by the rains and dotted with feeble clumps of rye.

"They must pass here," Rill said. "Teraf is right. This is a good site for surprise."

Too perfect, Kadriya thought. The knights would have little

option but to thread through the hills on this narrow, muddied segment. "Aye, but there are no bushes large enough to conceal us. John Wynter will be alert for trouble, which will make it hard to waylay him. Let's ride ahead a little farther." They continued, following the road as it passed a final hill covered with short, hardy bir bushes. "Nothing here, we'd better—"

Rill reined his horse sharply and made a grunting sound, one of alarm.

"What is it?"

He shot his hand out, palm toward Kadriya in an urgent gesture to stop. "Don't move. Just to the right of the path, do you see it?"

Kadriya peered into the field, weakly lit by the moon. "What?" Stones from the ancient Roman road had collapsed, making footing unsure. The road had been graded high for drainage; with the support structure gone, nothing prevented an eight-foot slide into the field below. Kadriya backed up. "I think we've found our spot."

CHAPTER 2
BLACKWATER POINT

John Wynter led his knights along the Parrott River trail they had followed since leaving the horse fair. A half moon offered pale light, and the old Roman road sagged in disarray, signs of damage from centuries of wear and the unrelenting rains.

His destrier, Dover, picked his way over the wet hazards. The gelding balked at uneven terrain and had a surly morning disposition, but Wynter and Dover had shared five years of danger, and once in battle, a man could not hope for a stronger, more valiant steed.

Behind John rode Roger, second knight, his full brown beard spilling over his armored chest. Phillip followed behind him, guiding the horse that held the bound Gypsy thief. The knights Gilbert and Alwin brought up the rear.

"Sir John." Phillip's voice held a touch of pleading and a slight lisp because of his missing teeth. "Can we not stop for the night? We be hours from the heathen's camp and all's well."

"All's well so long as we continue forward."

"But the Gypsy camp is far behind us and—"

"We rest in Newberry, not before. Then continue south to the abbey." John wished he'd captured both thieves and found the chalice, but Teraf would lead them to the other, Erol, and, by the saints, John would fulfill his duty. It was his honor to serve the abbot.

John surveyed the terrain, noting the road several yards ahead, where the hills, black with forest, encroached upon the road, closing it in.

Under his armor and hauberk, fear chilled his skin. John had felt a similar foreboding in France, with Robert, Baron Brocherst, back before his good friend became a monk and, later, abbot. The night had been dark, the moon pale like this moon, this night. It had been quiet, stone quiet, and the French had burst from the trees like a covey of demons. John saved Robert's life, but couldn't reach the other men in time. He and Robert escaped by burying themselves in the blood-stained mud.

Aye, mud like this. To his right the rye and barley fields almost floated, patched with tall clumps of grasses sturdy enough to withstand the heavy moisture.

An itching sensation snaked its way between his shoulder blades, far beneath the armor where no hand could scratch, and John clenched his jaw, willing the feeling to vanish.

Willing these accursed Gypsies to vanish. He'd seen them in France, tribes of fifty to a hundred, here one day, gone the next. The heathens had good teeth, white as their eyes and bright against their dark skin. Called themselves kings and dukes, singing lyrics that stirred the blood. Collecting alms, then helping themselves to their benefactors' livestock and harvest. Naught but thieves.

Now a few of them had trickled over here like some bleeding infection, stealing altar treasures from Cerne. Bloody, filthy dogs. He would help rid England of them.

John eyed the congested road. If he were to wait in ambush, this would be a good place to execute it. "Teraf."

"Aye." The thief uttered the word with impertinence, fueling John's anger at the Gypsy's lack of fear.

"Is this where you told your heathen friends to meet you?" At his blank look John repeated, "Is this Blackwater Point?" It was the only portion of Teraf's parting speech to his people that

John had understood.

"No. I say Romani farewell, not filthy English."

John grunted. In case any Gypsies hovered he raised his voice. "If they dare attack us, each one that survives hangs."

They approached the menacingly narrow point. Small bushes grew some eight feet from the road. Was someone lurking behind them? He saw no movement. The road ended abruptly to the right, the land beyond it spilling several feet below to the wet fields. Perfect for surprise. "Phillip," John called out. "Put a dagger to Teraf's neck. Men, draw your swords." John checked his armor, deciding not to don his helm. The night gloom limited his vision enough without further blocking it with metal around his eyes. He pulled his sword, heavy and cold, its blade thin and true. His heart beat insistently in his chest, spreading heat and power through his body. "Forward, then."

John urged his horse through the narrow section, expecting a surprise with each step. Sweat trickled down his back.

Sensing John's nervousness, Dover danced and snorted in anticipation.

John murmured assurances to his horse and continued.

Roger passed safely, followed by Phillip, Teraf and the last two.

Relaxing in the saddle, John took a deep breath and released it. He sheathed his sword. The road opened up ahead, a hill on the left and more bushes, dense but short. He eyed a troubling section of the road. "The rains have collapsed the road to the right, men. Stay well to the left ahead."

They advanced past the next hundred yards and approached the turn in the road.

A movement in the bush caught John's eye. He turned toward it and began to shout a warning.

A chorus of screeching drowned John's voice. Bushes rose from the ground, revealing legs beneath them. A hefty man ran toward John, slapping a branch in Dover's face.

Dover stiffened, side-stepped.

John reined him sharply, forcing him from the crumbling side of the road.

Dover circled backward, away from danger, crying out.

"Whoa, whoa, boy." John relaxed his legs around the horse and spoke firmly, calming him.

A wiry Gypsy man waved a large metal rod, curved at the end. He thrust it at John, toward his neck.

John deflected it. The rod dented his armor and bounced off his arm. He caught a glimpse of a woman in lavender and yellow rushing by, her face grim with determination. The young wench from the horse fair, running toward Teraf.

Human and horse screams filled the air. To John's left, a tall, large woman jumped on Roger's horse behind him. *Red hair? Hell's fire. What manner of Gypsy tribe is this?* She wrapped her arms around Roger's waist, pulling him backward.

Another Gypsy appeared at Roger's right, waving a branch toward his horse's eyes. Roger's horse lost its footing and fell, spilling the woman and Roger.

Dover screeched in terror and reared.

A small, brown creature clutched Dover's face, biting it.

John slapped at the creature with the reins. Dover circled in panic and John swayed in the saddle, letting up on the reins.

Dover overbalanced and John rolled free, hitting the ground on his side. He struggled out of the mud and pulled his sword.

"Prince Malley." A female voice cried, followed by an uttering that sounded like a command in the Gypsies' strange tongue.

Ahead, Gilbert and Alwin flanked Teraf, but a bulky, white-haired Gypsy dodged them. He reached for Teraf.

"Phillip. Behind you!" John shouted.

Philip turned and swung his sword, severing the white-haired head. It tilted like felled wheat, slid off the Gypsy's body and rolled toward John's feet.

"Murat!" A woman screamed. More Gypsies rushed toward Teraf and Phillip.

John sank in the mud. "Philip," he shouted. "Take Teraf to the abbey. I'll follow."

Something crashed into John's head from behind. Fire seared his skull, white light flashed behind his eyes and he fell.

Kadriya winced from a sharp pain in her left hip and struggled to her feet. A knight had viciously kicked her as he passed with Teraf.

Teraf. Gone with the knights around the bend of the road. One of their guards was down, the bearded knight wasn't moving, and Prince Malley was perched on a tree stump, screaming and holding his foot.

Rill called to her from several paces down the road. "He's dead."

Her breath caught. "Murat. I know."

"And the knight called Roger. Horses trampled him."

Kadriya labored through the muck to Roger. His head rested halfway submerged in the mud, his helmet crushed with a hoof imprint. Dread froze her gut, and John Wynter's warning echoed: *You will all hang*. What had she done? "Sweet saints, save us."

Next to the dead knight, Maude awoke, moaning.

Kadriya ran to her. Maude's legs were beaten and bloody, her nose bleeding. "Maude, oh, Maude." Kadriya heard the fear in her own voice and gritted her teeth. She must be calm. "Let's tend to your leg. Rill. Bring Maude's horse."

"She cannot ride."

"I can." Maude struggled to standing. "Just some cuts and bruises. I'll be fine."

Kadriya stepped close to the white-haired man's severed

head, swallowing with difficulty. "Murat." He was second in command of their tribe.

Rill lifted the head, placing it with the body. "Murat. Pen," he said. *My brother.* Rill straightened. "He was a fine saddle maker and drummer. A loyal friend."

Dread seeped through Kadriya's bones. "We must bury him."

Rill gave her a pointed look. "He is no *gorgio,* to be planted in the earth like common peas. He is Romani."

Kadriya blushed, recalling the funeral fires she'd seen as a young child and part of the tribe. Unlike the English, Roma burned their fallen brethren, along with their possessions. She'd been too long in the English world. "Of course. I'm sorry. We have no wagon or tent for him. Mayhap a simple pyre of wood?"

"Aye, and a fine song to send him off."

Prince Malley jumped on her with a litany of nervous chattering. His amber eyes were wide, teeth bared, his jaw wobbling with each cry.

Kadriya rocked him until he calmed down.

Rill tipped his head. "What about him?"

A large, armored form lay near the bushes. She placed Prince Malley on the stump with a reassuring croon, pulled her dagger and gestured for Rill to approach with her, just in case. She ventured a wary touch. A poke. He didn't move, so she turned the knight over. His chest rose and fell. Thank heavens. Lifting his arm, she caught a glimpse of his face.

Like a nightmare that steals the sweetness of the day before it begins, his features drove a sliver of ice down her spine. She stared into the face of the man who had started all this. Bloodied, unconscious but lethal to them all, it was the formidable knight, John Wynter.

Rill turned to her. "What shall we do with him?"

Kadriya rubbed her forehead. "Bring him with us."

"Where?"

She unstrapped John's girdle to release his sword and handed it to Rill. Retrieving the knight's fallen dagger, she shoved it in her belt, further staining her yellow gown. In the church's eyes they were murderers. A chill to match the mud filled her stomach.

"Can we go to your castle?"

Coin Forest. Kadriya considered it. "Nay. John Wynter's knights will send help. Hunt us." She could never endanger Sharai by taking refuge in her village.

A kernel of panic lodged in her throat. By her own actions, her old life was now closed to her, and her new one as well, for attempting to return to the Romani camp would bring certain doom.

An image came to her: the forest just north of the castle, dense and protective. It stretched all the way to Marlborough Downs and it was not far. "I know of a place."

Rill tapped John Wynter's armor. "And him?"

"Strip him of his breastplate. God knows how many weapons he may have hidden there. And we shall give him a taste of his own treatment." She released him, letting him fall back in the mud. "Bind his hands, as they did with Teraf, and tie him on his horse."

A wave of nausea ripped through John and he turned to retch. He discovered his hands and feet were bound, his armor stripped, and he was tied to a tree. He rotated his shoulder, wincing from the pain, and wiped his mouth on his hauberk.

A fire burned close by, offering warmth. Daylight, but he was in a forest, the canopy so deep and dense it was hard to guess the time. The fire glowed with an unnatural halo. He closed his eyes tight and opened them again. Behind his eyes a devil blacksmith pounded his anvil, his steel mallet banging hard against his temples, and somewhere to his left a tortured soul screamed for mercy.

His vision cleared. That infernal monkey was screeching, and the red-haired woman rested on the grass on the other side of the fire. Her leg was wrapped in muddied yellow rags.

John remembered. Sir Roger had gone down with the woman.

The Gypsy strumpet noticed him and approached.

The yellow of her skirt had been all but stamped out with mud, and a large bruise colored her left arm. Her tunic was torn, revealing the smooth skin of her neck and the soft swell of her breasts. He pulled his gaze from them to meet her eyes but he stopped at her lower lip, which enticed him in spite of his effort to dismiss her for the heathen she was.

His roiling gut and the slicing pain in his head prevented a carnal response, and for that he was thankful. She was temptation incarnate.

Up close, her skin seemed to glow, notably lighter than the other Gypsies. She'd lightened it with ash, likely, just another foolish trick—or his eyes, failing him.

She knelt gracefully in front of him, extending a wet cloth.

He gritted his teeth and tried to withdraw but could not, and she pressed the cloth gently on his forehead.

"Where are my men?" His words sounded slow to him, slurred as if from too much mead. He felt full force the intensity of her gaze, hot with condemnation. As if it were he who had staged an ambush against the church.

"Gone," she said.

An alarm sounded deep in his skull. "All?"

"All but the bearded one. His horse trampled him, and he died." She averted her eyes. "I am sorry."

Roger. Though mentally dull and a swindler at dice, he was determined in battle, and a fellow knight. "You will hang. You will all hang."

Her eyes flashed. "Just as you will hang Teraf, an innocent

31

man? Doubtless you will be pleased to have us all dead."

"Certes you deserve it."

She stared at him, her hair, black and greased in braids, foul rings in her ears, and the garish, foreign scarf she had pulled across her forehead, a common criminal. He noted her delicate hands and wrists, her proud carriage and the gentle rising and falling of the swells of her breasts, so inviting a man's attention. Yet beyond the allure she possessed a presence. That, and she spoke with the smooth tongue of an English woman. He struggled through his punishing headache to make sense of it.

Then a sliver of sun shot through the trees, reaching the light flecks of green in her eyes, answering his unspoken question.

The abbot entered the chapel, still weakly lit by the waning sunlight. His back ached from an old battle wound sustained in France, before he'd taken his vows, back when he was known as Robert, Baron Brocherst. He strode down the aisle, his mind troubled and his patience tried. How could the Gypsies so easily steal the emerald chalice? The sacramental chalice, the very one that William of Wayneflete, Bishop of Winchester, the most powerful see in England, had bestowed upon them just last year.

Wayneflete, the very bishop who would visit in just two weeks and expect to see the costly chalice in service, just as Robert expected the bishop to grant funds for the abbey's new church.

If he could get the chalice back before the bishop's arrival.

He rubbed his ring, seeking comfort, but his problems were too big for such simple relief. He would need to get answers from Eustace, his sacristan, the one who witnessed the theft and identified the Gypsies responsible.

His knights had just arrived with the Gypsy, Teraf. His first knight, John Wynter, and Roger were missing, the rest injured and exhausted, and now the heathen thief refused to explain how he had gained access to the chalice, which had been locked in the chapel.

He would bring Eustace there to interrogate Teraf. Eustace was good at that.

Spying the treasurer intently carving a misericord, the abbot approached and tapped his arm. "Brother James. Where is Brother Eustace?"

James stilled his knife and looked up. "I have not seen him since None services, Father."

"Any idea where he might be?"

"He mentioned the infirmary."

Robert entered the cloister, through the abbot's lodge and the undercroft, forming new questions for Eustace with each step. How had the Gypsies gained entrance to the church? The heathens were forbidden to enter. With the chalice safely locked away between services, how had they been able to steal it? Passing the storage room, he heard muted voices. Unusual. The materials stored within the room were valuable, so the doors were always locked. Robert turned the handle. Locked. He heard another voice, softer. Mystified, he pulled his key and quietly unlocked the door.

Facing the inside of the wing, the storage room had no windows. Robert closed the door gently. His eyes adjusted to the gloom and he recognized newly forged barrels, the terrier's broken loom, stacks of linen to be sewn for the nobles' guest rooms. Dim candlelight burned behind a tall chest. More Gypsies? He should have brought one of his knights. His fingers tightened around his abbot's staff and he was glad that convention required he carry it when meeting the prisoner. Taking one last quiet step forward, he lunged past the chest.

Two men stood together. Geoffrey, the oblate, his blond, untonsured hair disheveled, his tunic gone, his young, muscular back bare. Eustace, his sacristan, fully clothed but rubbing

Geoffrey's back.

Eustace and Geoffrey jerked apart, guilt coloring Geoffrey's fair neck and face. Eustace could not meet Robert's eyes.

Robert crossed himself, and a moaning sound escaped his lips as he fought a wave of nausea. Their response was not innocent.

The men scrambled, knocking over boxes, and the candle went out.

Using his staff to find his way, Father Robert reached the door, blocking their escape, and opened it enough to let in some light but not so much that other monks in the infirmary might overhear.

Eustace approached, his face grim. " 'Tis nothing, Father. Geoffrey was collecting linens and tripped, wrenching his back. Punish him not."

"He tripped, and you just happened to be within earshot of the storage room? And you huddle together in the darkness, behind a locked door?" Robert gritted the last words out slowly, his vocal chords knotting as his voice rose higher, causing him to cough repeatedly from his lingering cold. Recovering, he swung his staff, striking Eustace, attacking the sin and shame that burned here, in the darkness of his abbey.

"Sinners. Fornicators." His staff struck Eustace on the side of the head. "You defile your office, your vow. Your God." He struck the unresisting Eustace again on the shoulders. "May God have mercy on your soul. You have corrupted an oblate, just days from his vows." He stopped, catching his breath. "Geoffrey?"

"Yes, Father." Geoffrey had slipped into his black work tunic and adjusted his hood, which now framed green eyes widened in fear.

Robert considered the oblate's punishment. In a little over a fortnight, Geoffrey would reach his religious majority and be free to decide between taking his vows or leaving the monastery. Mother of God. He had raised and trained Geoffrey from infancy, only to see him ruined by the unthinkable.

But he could still be saved. The Abbot struck him soundly in the neck. "Report to Father Brian at the scriptorium. You are to serve him exclusively. You will stand outside your cell, in the night air, without sleep for two nights. You shall forfeit your sandals for seven days and seven nights, and refrain from wine or ale at table. You will stay near the altar and pray for purity of mind and deed, and you may not see Brother Eustace alone, ever again. Is that clear?"

" 'Twas not his fault, Father."

Robert struck him again, harder. "You have sinned, and you will resist temptations of the flesh or be thrown out, back to the path of sin from whence you came. Get out. Go."

The oblate hurried out the door.

Father Robert tapped his staff in tune with the rapid beating of his heart. Evil had come to his abbey, and it had spread. He must smite it, one step at a time. He leaned into Eustace's face. "Do not think you will get off so lightly. Your punishment remains to be decided, but now there's another pressing matter." Overwhelmed with a new wave of anger, he paused. "The Gypsy Teraf has been returned."

His face hidden in the darkness, Eustace inhaled audibly. "And the chalice?"

"Two of my best knights were cut down trying to bring him here."

"Killed? Who?"

He would leave Eustace to fret about that. "The Gypsy talked to me."

"What did he say?"

Was that dread Robert heard in his voice? Robert had known Eustace for eleven years. The man was above . . . above what?

The cold vision of Eustace with Geoffrey slapped in his face. Robert cleared his throat. "Come with me. I have questions."

CHAPTER 3
THE MUSHROOM TREE

Kadriya strode on the forest floor, spongy with fallen leaves and fine grasses, each step generating a damp smell of vegetation. Rich earth, and a sense of safety after hours of fear and death.

She stepped past a massive fallen oak that sprawled in the spacious clearing, stained black with decay and blanketed with a dense cover of mushrooms. Felled many years ago by lightning, it split the clearing neatly in half. Kadriya was just seven when Lord Tabor showed her this lush sanctuary. Now she'd returned in the darkness as a fugitive from the church.

She had spent two days with the Roma and John Wynter here, deep in the forest by Tabor and Sharai's castle. She had settled them in this clearing with ample herbs and a bubbling stream, clear, cold and four hands wide. Maude and the knight rested at opposite ends of the fire. Rill had stationed the two *gorgio* guards at this end of the clearing to guard the horses. At the opposite end of the clearing, some ten yards past the fire, Dury, Teraf's older cousin, and the remaining three Roma stood guard.

Could more have gone wrong? Murat and the knight dead, hiding with five Roma she barely knew, Maude pummeled and sore; a hostile, violent knight held captive, determined to hang all of them at the earliest opportunity; and one hysterical monkey.

She needed to get them out of here, get to the abbey to free Teraf. *Impossible.* Above, a flock of blue tits sang, staking their claims on choice branches for the night, and the last rays of sunlight angled in low pinpoints through the leaves. Time was running. She paced, and when that brought no solution, she got busy.

"How's my Allie?" She checked her horse, running her hands down her horse's front leg, checking for signs of heat, which would indicate infection. She examined the ankle wound, a mended cut the length of her hand, and applied more healing leaf paste.

Allie snorted, as if understanding Kadriya's touch would help her. The horse breathed easily, her body heat warming Kadriya in the wet forest chill.

Rewrapping the wound with a strip of linen, she released Allie's hoof and ran her hands up the horse's knee and forearm, checking for more injuries. "Sorry, my lady. You're a racer, not a fighter." At Blackwater Point the short knight had reared his warhorse into fighting stance, swinging his sword. He had missed Allie by a sliver, and the sight of such a near strike that could have felled her loyal, trusting animal brought home the danger of her rash decision to help Murat attack the knights.

Rill approached. "Is she all right?"

Kadriya turned to the man who would most likely be next in command of their tribe, now that Teraf was away and Murat had died. Rill was short and stout, his skin tight on the muscles of his arms and neck, as if his body had not been made large enough for him. His face, too, seemed full, and a line had creased in his face from his nostrils to his jaw, framing his mouth much like a cathedral arch. His stern manner had also etched deep vertical frown lines between his eyes.

"She'll be fine."

Rill looked to his horse, brows furrowed. "And Thunder?"

"He's fine. His limp was caused by a stone, a sharp one that embedded near the frog. I soaked it in hot water and herbs earlier, when you were hunting." She moved to his horse, a black, compact stallion, and lifted its hoof, revealing the tender underside. "See? A mite swollen, but fine. Watch for any tenderness or favoring."

Rill grunted and gave a nod.

Trying to unfasten his leash from a tree near Maude, Prince Malley screeched and barked sharp yips of frustration.

Rill cursed and covered his ears. "Wretched monkey drives me mad. Let him loose."

Kadriya gave him a pointed look. "He fought courageously last night."

"Yes, but he brought the wrong man down. We wanted Teraf and instead we got this pile of rubbish." He pointed at John Wynter, who sat propped against the tree, sleeping after another attack of nausea.

"I'm famished," Rill growled. "Why haven't you cooked the rabbit?"

Kadriya's hand flew to her chest. "Me?" She shot him a reprimanding look.

He looked at her as if she had four eyes. " 'Tis your duty."

"Duty?" He'd never used this chiding tone with her before, when she was with Teraf. "I've been busy enough, nursing the men and the horses. Why not you?"

"Because you're a woman. You'll make a pitiful poor wife if you cannot cook."

"The guards are doing naught. Why waste my time watching a potful of soup boil when I can do more productive things?"

"Like planning a failed attack on the knights?"

"Murat was in charge, and he decided to attack them, not I. I gave my suggestions. Had we not brought kettle irons and Prince Malley, you would have been hacked to death or taken to the abbey along with Teraf. Had your men been quicker, my plan would have worked."

"We're not knights, Kadriya, and your plan failed."

She saw John Wynter's eye open. The knave was eavesdropping. Though the knight was distant and they spoke Romani, the *gorgio* guards near John could easily make out their raised voices. She gestured subtly to Rill. "We must stop arguing and make plans to save Teraf."

Rill shook his head. "The knights took him. He's gone. Good as dead, right along with Murat." He thrust the words at her, cold and uncaring as his dark eyes.

She reeled backward. "What?"

"We're returning to France. To Normandy, then home to Marseilles."

"You can't just give up on him."

"Be you deaf? We're going to France."

"He's not dead yet. I may have lived with the English, but I remember Romani honor. Why are you so eager to abandon your Romani brother?"

He turned away from her.

"Oh. Of course." Kadriya raised her voice so Dury and the others could hear. "With Teraf dead, you can be king. That's it, isn't it? You so covet his title that you're willing to sacrifice Teraf to get it."

He looked back at her, his facial lines drawing a scowl of anger. "I risked my life to save him, and I am now a hunted man, as are they," he said, pointing at Dury and the others. "Our whole tribe is marked for death, and this is our chance to escape. 'Tis your half-blood infirmity, thinking you can still save Teraf."

"My thoughts are clear. Like you, I'm scared. Worried. I wish Murat and the knight Roger had not died. We cannot go back, but we can explain at the monastery that their deaths were accidental."

"Such faith in the *gorgios*. You're going to not-so-accidentally *hang* if you set foot in that abbey. Teraf will likely be hanged before you get there." Rill pointed aggressively in her face. "Are you Rom, Kadriya, or English? I'll kill the knight before he can kill us. We can get out of here alive—if we leave on the morrow for France."

She looked from Rill's face, creased in determination, to the knight's face as he quietly watched her. Her sense of balance faded. Whether touring the fairs as a Rom or living among the nobility, she followed a standard of honor and respect. Fights were fair, won on personal strengths and one's wits. And family and friends deserved loyalty. "Let's take him with us. Release him when we sail."

Rill laughed harshly. "You heard him. He'll drag us to our deaths at the gallows."

She had no good answer to that. John Wynter had made it clear what he would do if he were freed. "The other deaths were accidental. What you plan is murder, and I will not live with death on my hands."

Kadriya spun away from him and walked across the clearing toward the knight. Her heart raced and she concentrated on slowing her breathing. Must not show fear, though it had settled squarely in her chest. She checked on Maude, who rested on the other side of the fire pit from the knight. Kadriya brushed the red hair from her damp forehead. "Maude, dear, how are you feeling?"

Maude moved her leg and winced. "Don't fret about me. What did he say? In all that Gypsy babble I caught something about the knight, and Teraf. And France."

Kadriya draped the blanket over Maude's shoulders and released a tremulous sigh. "He blames me for the failed rescue. Because I planned it, he says. Fie! He wants to replace Teraf as king, and he's given him up for dead." She glanced back at John Wynter. "He wants to kill the knight."

Maude grabbed her arm. "You must stop him."

She sneaked a sideways glance at the knight. Determined, brave, with a dark passion that belied his fair blue eyes, and muscles enough to lift a horse. A dedicated man, that was clear. But those blue eyes had swept her with looks of loathing oft enough that she knew no heart beat in his chest, and he had condemned them oft enough that she knew not much resided between his ears. "The thought of protecting that hateful man makes me ill." She dipped a cloth into the stream, held it to the fire to warm it, and washed a few remaining patches of mud from Maude's arms. "But he represents the church. He was sent by the abbot."

Maude captured her hand and squeezed it. "Aye, so you see. 'Tis his duty. If Teraf stole the chalice, the knight must deliver him to the abbey."

"But he did not."

She raised a red brow. "Forsooth?"

"Maude." She tried to dismiss it, but the possibility that Teraf might be guilty burrowed into her skin like a hungry flea. Kadriya scraped it away. "Teraf told me."

" 'Tis clear the abbot believes otherwise."

Kadriya knew defying the church was foolhardy. But for the urgency to save Teraf's life, she would never have done it. The flames of the fire, built low for cooking, danced free with occasional spikes, hypnotizing but bringing no solutions. "John Wynter is a knight, doing his job. I understand that, but not the hatred with which he regards us. 'Tis good for him to see the loathing his hatred has spawned in us so he learns that he reaps what he sows."

"But he does not deserve death."

A log collapsed and fell into the hot embers, giving itself to the fire, and Kadriya shivered at the memory of Murat's and the knight's deaths. Could she help avoid more? Sap bled from the fallen log, and the flames coughed and hissed. *Ssss. Shhh. Concession.* She swallowed hard. Compromise could avoid further death and aid her cause as well.

Lord Tabor's battle stories came to mind. "Of course. Prisoners are traded for gold, concessions of land or other prisoners. We shall trade Teraf for John Wynter."

Maude shook her head. "They'll as likely do that as kiss my bum."

"Why not?" Images of the horse and trade fairs flickered in Kadriya's mind, of the weighing scales, of the trading of coin for horses, of horses for merchandise. Heaven knows, she'd heard Teraf himself brag of his clever trades often enough, boasts that anything could be had for the right trade.

"I want Teraf, and my item of value is John Wynter. If he's as effective at battle as he is narrow-minded and mean, the abbot will yield to get him back." What else could she use to keep Teraf from the gallows? "Ah, the emerald chalice." She glanced at the knight, imposing, even bound as he was, hand and foot. "I shall claim to have it. I'm but a Gypsy in their eyes, and we're all thieves, yes? They'll believe me." Her voice caught, betraying the forced arrogance in her voice. "They'll free Teraf and we can leave for France."

"You would leave England a condemned thief, Kadriya? You'd never see Sharai again."

Panic squeezed her chest, making it hard to breathe. "I'm already condemned. At least this way, Teraf will not die for a crime he did not commit."

Maude grabbed her arm. "They'll hang Teraf and hunt you down."

Kadriya ran to her saddle and pulled out a small parchment, pen and bottle of ink. Securing the bottle in a cavity in the mushroom tree, she filled her pen. With her pen poised above the page, she started her letter but ran into a harsh wall that stopped her hand. Even if she freed the knight, she'd be hunted, too, because of her part in the assault. "If I stay to save Teraf, the tribe will abandon me. If I return home, Sharai and Lord Tabor will suffer for my actions." A gust of wind stirred her braids, sending a strange, new chill down her neck. Because of her decision to help free Teraf, her life had forever shifted. "All I have left is Teraf, and he's in grave danger. Which should I worry about most, Maude?"

She hugged her arms and blinked back tears that threatened. She must be strong, and she must hurdle this wall on her own power. "They will not hang Teraf if I tell them I have not only their injured knight, but also their precious emerald chalice."

John awoke to the grey of pre-dawn and the sensation of someone touching his arm, shaking him. He jolted upright, the ropes biting into his wrists and chest, holding him to the tree.

Kadriya withdrew her hand. "You were in pain."

Shocked anew that she spoke near perfect English, he met her gaze through the gnawing curtain of pain.

Her eyes were cold. "You were keeping us awake with your groaning."

He'd moaned like a babe in his sleep?

"Something about smoke. A fire?"

His neck heated, and he diverted his gaze. The nightmare again, the darkness of his past, leaking into his sleep.

Sorely aware of his lack of armor, he slipped a mental shield between them so she could not see his shame.

Or his fear. He'd heard the anger in the Gypsy, Rill's, voice, seen the look of dismissal he'd given John. He'd looked repeatedly toward the path leading out of the forest and heard no sound, seen no reassuring sign that his knights would make it in time to save him. John's instincts told him he would be dead before the Gypsies broke their fast. "Almost dawn," he said to her. "Any decent Englishman would be up by now, anyway," he said, glancing at the two tallest men still asleep by the fire, men who had skin as light as his own.

"They're *gorgio*—English, that's true. They chose to join our tribe," she explained. "We see past a man's skin," she said, giving him a pointed look. She examined his wrists and tried the ropes to be sure they were still secure. Her fingers were warm and smooth on his skin. She'd been washing with herbs, and he noticed a hint of oak moss and a pleasant spice he could not place. Her eyes were perfect, clear and gripping. He would fight with his last breath, but if this became his death day, no harm could come of lingering on her face, committing to memory the way loose strands of her hair followed the curve of her neck.

He chased the compulsion from his mind, recalling Lord Harbrough's observations about Gypsies in Marseilles: "They live among us, yet are not us. They touch us to entertain then take our coin, but keep such distance from our villages as some wild creature of the woods. They cling like bats to caves and pitch their tents in remote valleys, far removed from us."

Like this sneaky encampment, John thought, tucked deep in the towering oaks and pine.

Was there hope? John had seen her with the horses, rubbing them down, applying poultices. The horses were relaxed with her, even Dover, a significant fact to John, for the horse had proven to have a good gut sense about people.

He felt the pull of her eyes, large, expressive, and her full lower lip, her upper lip carved, as if drawn with an artist's sure hand into a delicate heart shape. But she had planned the ambush. An enchantress, heathen with no heart, no soul, no loyalties but to a branded thief who would soon hang in the disgrace he had brought upon himself.

Promising images nudged their way into his thoughts. She was learned. He'd summoned all his self control to feign sleep when she pulled parchment, pen and ink from her saddle. What manner of vile Gypsy could read and write? And she'd tended the men's wounds, and his own, prepared a tonic that chased much of the pain away, and her touch was gentle with the stitches to his scalp. Did she have the compassion to help him? He almost laughed at the thought. Even if she did, it would be her against five men. He should just make his peace with God and accept his fate.

She left him, walked back to check on the red-haired woman.

He recalled his words at the camp, ordering them to leave England. She despised him, as she should, he conceded. But the little wench thought she could bargain with the abbot. He recalled her eyes, a rich walnut hue, but bright with tantalizing slivers of green. It explained her easy knowledge of languages, and the confident way she handled herself with the men. She was a Gypsy, but she was also English.

He would work with these grains of hope and try to live past daybreak.

An hour later, Kadriya strung three rabbits on the kettle hangers and angled them over the fire. Crushing herbs to release their sweet, tangy aroma, she scattered them over the meat, but the tight ball of fear in her stomach killed her appetite. From the higher branches birds sang haltingly, cautiously, as if intimidated by the premonition of death.

Unless she stopped Rill.

She swallowed hard and tossed kindling into the fire. How could she? She'd exposed Rill's intentions to abandon Teraf to Dury and the others. Could she count on their help, or would they support Rill?

Prince Malley jumped up, eyes wide, arms needy, and she caught him on her hip and ruffled his fur. "You were very brave, weren't you, boy? You brought that huge knight down, all by yourself."

The words were no sooner out of her mouth than she felt his cold gaze. John Wynter sat, still tied to the tree, silent, observing. His fever had dropped, and he no longer slurred his words.

She stared without conscience. Locks of sweat-stained brown hair fell over his wide forehead, revealing lingering crusts of dried blood from his head wound. The fire highlighted the bridge of his nose, flattened from some long-ago fight. An advancing beard shrouded his features, and his mouth was set, brows drawn over his blue eyes in an expression of predatory observance.

Then something changed, raising the fine hairs on her neck, stilling her breath. The trees, Maude, the horses, the men blurred, and only his eyes were vivid, only a deep, unspoken message that flashed from the depth of his blue eyes—a question. Spawned from desperation, yes, but as basic as breathing, one living soul reaching out to another.

She wanted to spit in his eye, but though he stank with hatred, he did not deserve to die. She could not break their connection, and new hope replaced the question in his gaze.

She seated Prince Malley on a mound of grass and approached the fire. Rinsing a cloth, she wrung it out and kneeled at the knight's side.

He seemed twice the bulk of Rill and half again larger than the guards, who were tall and solid of their own right. Heat emanated from him, heat and restrained power.

She closed her eyes. Nothing had passed between them. This man had vowed to kill them. And Rill, just a stone's throw away, murder and conquest on his mind. *Teraf has offered me a home, a life with him and his tribe, and he may be hours from death. I must not wilt like a common English lady, hiding in the lace of a wimple. I am Romani.* Willing her hands to be steady, she parted the knight's dark blond hair and checked the stitches she'd sewn in the back of his head. They were clean, with no signs of infection. She pressed a cloth to his forehead, wiping off more of the dried blood. Her efforts revealed a thin four-inch scar running diagonally from his scalp to his left cheekbone. "Might you quell your hatred long enough to answer a question?"

He straightened. "I would hear you."

"Will Teraf have a chance to defend himself?"

His voice softened. "It is too late for him. You must think of yourself and your Gypsy friends, and Maude, who gives you sound advice. The longer you hold me, the more likely it is my knights will find you."

"Nay."

"You have a sense of honor, else I would already be dead at the hands of your tribe. I can offer you freedom." He paused. "Release me."

"What's going on over there?" Rill shouted in Romani from a distance.

She stood, still meeting the knight's gaze, and forced a laugh, making it hearty and loud. "Look at you, trussed like a pig, and yet you try to bargain."

She showed him her back and walked to the fire.

Rill approached, looking rougher than usual with another day's growth of stubble on his normally clean-shaven face. "Is your saddlebag ready?"

Kadriya noted the horses. While she talked with John, Rill and his men had packed and prepared the horses.

Rill gave her a penetrating gaze. "Get your horse. We're leaving." He turned to Maude, shifting to English. "Maude. You can come with us."

Maude raised herself on an elbow. "Thank you, Rill, but I—"

Kadriya waved her to silence and returned her attention to Rill. "To the abbey?" she asked.

His eyes narrowed. "France."

"Not yet. Teraf—"

"Is dead. You may mourn as we travel. We'll find another man for you."

"Teraf is alive."

"How can five men overcome a garrison of knights? He's dead, I tell you. And what of you, with the knight? I've seen you." He stood so close she could smell the mugwort she'd used to flavor his breakfast. "Having trouble choosing which end your bread is best buttered?"

"I made my choice with Teraf."

"And now he is gone, you'll stay with his people. I will care for you."

"You take Teraf's title and me, too? Nay."

"So be it. You and Maude stay. But this one cannot live." Rill strode toward John.

"Rill. No."

He pulled his dagger.

"No." If he killed the knight, he would end her last hope to rescue Teraf. She remembered everything Sharai had taught her, how to bring a knave down when he tried to steal her for a slave, how to fight off a man overcome with lust, how to dodge a drunken man's blows. She rushed in front of the knight and covered him with her body.

Rill's face slacked in surprise, then tensed in anger. He lunged forward.

She pulled a dagger from her belt and faced Rill.

Rill stopped.

Dury stepped forward, dagger pulled. "No, Rill. She is Rom. Teraf's betrothed. And she's under Lord Tabor's protection."

The words sank in and Rill restrained himself, his gaze darting from side to side.

"And mine." Maude had pulled herself up on her good knee,

Janet Lane

mouth set, eyes fixed on Rill, and in her hands a dagger cocked
to throw.

Kadriya stilled her with a gesture. "Think, Rill. Kill us and it
will be fruitless to run to France. Lord Tabor's there. He'll find
you—you'll be drawn and quartered as soon as you leave your
ship."

Rill kicked in her direction.

Kadriya turned her face away, throwing up her left hand in
defense.

Rill sliced at her right hand, punching her wrist.

Kadriya's dagger fell from her hand.

Rill made a choking sound.

Dury squeezed Rill's neck, choking him with his arm. "Stop.
The other knight's death was accidental. Let's go while we
can."

"All right," Rill rasped, and Dury released him.

Rill's fist shot toward Kadriya's face.

She dodged, but his fist hit her jaw.

She sprawled backward, knocking John over, and reclaimed
her dagger, facing him.

Rill laughed. "Warm the knight's bed, whore. You were never
Rom, and you're not part of our tribe." He leaned forward, spitting into her face.

She wiped the wet insult away and stayed ready.

He mounted his horse. "If he lives to kill us, the deaths will
be on your head, Kadriya. Remember that."

The men joined him and they rode away.

John blinked, not believing what he had just seen. The
wench . . . woman, he corrected himself . . . had the heart of a
knight. But women were frivolous creatures who embroidered
and whined and . . . what was he thinking? They were alone
now, he and she, Maude and the fiendish monkey. One detail

burned into his brain, making his soul shrink with the truth of it: this spirited woman with the compelling almond-shaped eyes had just saved his life. "Thank you," he managed. Daring to hope, he looked back at his bound wrists, then looked questioningly into those piercing brown eyes flecked with English green.

CHAPTER 4
COIN FOREST

John sat stiffly in his saddle, his skin burning from more than the hot sun. Kadriya had refused to release him as they neared Coin Forest with his hands bound, tied to his saddle, led by a woman. A woman.

She held Dover's reins as she rode her own horse, and her bruised friend, Maude, rode next to her.

He tried again to reach her. "Cut these ropes," he said. "I give you my vow, I shall not leave you."

"I can't trust you."

They entered the village, noisy with midday activities, and the villagers stared as John and Kadriya passed.

Unholy thoughts of revenge stirred through his mind. She must know of a knight's pride. Better that she had let him be killed, than this. He had no choice but to meet the eyes of the merchants as they passed them. Though she'd stripped him of all but his hauberk and lower armor, he was still a knight, by gad, and she but a woman. A Gypsy.

From the alehouse two whores ran out, their bodies and gowns the worse for wear. "Hey, Maudie," the old one shouted. "Which one's your fella, the big one in armor or the hairy beastie at your breast?" She pointed at the monkey.

Maude guffawed. "Neither. One's too holy and this one," she said, patting Prince Malley, "he's too smart."

John kept his eyes on Dover's mane, thinking of his small manor house and lands. He would return there after all this, resume the business of his harvest, which had been interrupted by the abbot's urgent call.

The village was lively with people. The harvest fields lay trim, dotted with abundant mounds of hay, and large flocks of sheep grazed in the fields outside the castle curtain, all signs her patron was successful. More importantly, this was no obscure country manor. A baron resided in that castle. Nobility. John would find allies.

He glanced at his captor, noted the gold swinging from her ears, saw her strong, straight nose and the full curve of her lips against the blue morning sky. A dark bruise shadowed her right jaw where Rill had struck her. She'd tended John's wounds with a gentle touch, and she'd risked her own life to save his.

Spirit enough for two, and the fairest woman he'd ever seen, with a strain of English blood in her. But she was still knee deep in the nest with them, a thieving exile.

"This is my home," she said.

"Indeed," he said. Not for long. She may not have the chalice, but she was the key to getting it. There was Roger's death to avenge. He would deliver her pretty-but-guilty hide to Cerne on the morrow to pay for her crimes, and get one step closer to recovering the chalice his abbot so urgently needed.

A horse galloped behind them. "Kadriya."

It was the Gypsy who had pulled Rill off Kadriya. Some years older than John, short, stocky, head jutting out, shoulders stooped, as with those who devote many years to craft.

Kadriya paused. "Dury." They exchanged words in their foreign tongue, excluding him.

"What?" he asked during a pause in their senseless patter.

"This is Dury, Teraf's cousin. He wishes to help and is coming with us."

Had Dury not intervened against Rill, they all might be dead. He picked at the coarse rope holding him, feeling the hard knot. A pox on the events that made him feel gratitude to those who defied the church and attacked his knights.

As they neared the gate, the guards spied them and horns sounded.

A contingent of knights rode out to greet them. A greying old knight with a mustache rushed from the drawbridge. "Mistress Kadriya! George brought word of the trouble at the horse fair and the Cerne knights."

Kadriya, welcomed as a lady? Astounding. This shed light, however, on the mystery of her almost noble bearing.

Kadriya introduced the knight.

Cyrill met John's eyes, then noticed the rope binding his hands to the saddle. "What in God's name is this?"

"This is Sir John, my prisoner," she said. "I'll explain, but I need to see Sharai."

Cyrill came beside John. "Your liege, Sir John?"

"Robert Foy, formerly Baron Brocherst, Abbot of Cerne Monastery," John answered.

"God's bones!" The knight produced a knife and cut the ropes.

"Cyrill, no." Kadriya leaned over to stop him, and another knight urged his steed forward, blocking her.

John rubbed his freed wrists and reclaimed Dover's reins.

"I crave your pardon, Sir John," Cyrill said. He waved in a gesture to stop Kadriya. "Whatever has transpired we will settle with Lady Tabor. Please, come with me."

Inside the bailey two sleek greyhounds rushed to Prince Malley, barking.

"Fang. Fool," Maude reprimanded them. "Someone, hold these dogs back."

Two young girls and a man still round-faced with youth raced to them. "Kadriya," they called. They had ink black hair, vivid green eyes and the same dark skin as Teraf, but were dressed in civilized clothes.

Kadriya dismounted and embraced them. "Faith and Joya. *Ves' tacha.*" A word of endearment, from the softness in her voice as she said it. "I'll visit you later, but I must go."

"Tell us what happened," the smaller girl said, grabbing Kadriya's muddied skirts. She spoke perfect English. Her bubbling innocence, her white-toothed grin and dimples tugged at John's mouth, urging him to smile. He resisted.

"Joya, not now."

"Momma's been frantic. That bruise," said the older girl. "Did he punch you?"

"No Faith. Let go. I—"

Faith eyed John with suspicion. "Who are you?"

"Look," shrieked Joya. "A monkey."

John dismounted, and the earth shifted slightly under him. His vision blurred, and he held the saddle to gain his balance.

"Are you all right, Sir?" Cyrill saw his head wound. "How deep is that?"

"I'm all right." John waved him off.

"He's dear," Faith said, fawning over the monkey. "Look at his little hands. Ouch!" Faith sucked her finger. "You devil. He bit me."

"Girls, please. Back away. Thomas." Kadriya turned to another knight. "Please tie the monkey outside the kitchen or he'll—"

"Kadriya." An old priest stepped forward. John had met him before, knew that deep, authoritative voice, but couldn't place where from. His heavy white brows furrowed, and he turned in question to John.

"This is Sir John Wynter," Cyrill said. "The abbot's first knight."

The priest inspected him. "Lady Tabor awaits you in the hall."

In the great hall, a fire burned off the damp morning chill. On each of the six massive support beams green and gold banners hung, fringed in gold, the fabric substantial. On the dais, the table was draped in white linen with green weavings and dressed with fine bowls and trenchers, and on the far wall a tapestry taller than two men graced the light stone wall.

That familiar feeling slid over him again, one of unease in the face of wealth. John had grown accustomed to the opulence at the abbey, understanding its links to worship and sacrifice, but outside of it, such displays reminded him of the gnawing hunger, disease and death that had marked his early life. It reminded him of his fortunate link with the abbot and his gifts, including John's first decent suit of armor and a small demesne near Cerne.

A small woman sat at the dais with three knights.

John approached, rubbing his fingers, which were still afflicted with moments of numbness and stinging. Three days of mud-sodden travel and two days of retching on himself had left him reeking, and he was keenly aware of being dressed in but half his armor, with a torn, bloodied hauberk and several days' growth of beard, here in this fine hall. But such was to be expected of a knight on the road. He drew himself tall and approached the woman.

Her keen eyes unsettled him, and she exuded power. Her skin was as dark as Dury's. *God's blood, another Gypsy. What's her role here?* Her blue gown was perfectly tailored to fit her small frame. The fine weave and soft sheen told him it was silk, as well. Her headdress flared fashionably wide, its noble effect diluted by large rings that cut garishly through obscenely scarred earlobes. The rings hung, swaying like wrought-iron merchant's signs in London. The woman glanced at Kadriya and gently tugged at the left earring as if it were too tight.

Puzzled, he followed her gaze. Kadriya casually turned her

head and pulled lightly on her left earring, as well. *A code between them?*

Seeing Kadriya's answering motion, the little Gypsy woman exhaled audibly. "Welcome back, Kadriya."

Kadriya gave a curtsy. "Please forgive me, Sharai, I—"

"And Sir John, welcome, on behalf of my husband and lord, Richard, Baron Tabor, who presently serves our king in Normandy."

Dancing devils! Lord Tabor had wed a Gypsy. However had the king sanctioned that, let alone the church? He'd hoped for an ally, only to land in a second trap where yet another Gypsy woman held him captive. Only this woman held more than beauty and compelling eyes. She also possessed wealth, a castle and a garrison of strong knights.

But he must give her her due. "Thank you, my lady." His gut knotted in protest but his head responded, bowing enough to demonstrate appropriate regard for her station. He straightened to stand but the rushes under his feet turned and twisted, and he stumbled. Small points of darkness grew larger, and, unable to regain his balance, he fell.

Sharai entered Kadriya's chamber. "Sprig," she said, calling Kadriya by her childhood nickname.

Kadriya rose from the bed, alarmed by the tight set of Sharai's mouth. "How is he?" The knight had collapsed in the great hall and Cyrill had taken him to the knights' quarters.

"Resting now. Oh, Kadriya, what were you thinking? They told me you dragged him through the village, bound like a criminal."

"He wants us all dead. Threatened to hang us. I couldn't—"

"What are you doing? First, you decide to wed a Rom. A *corturari!* You know what that means."

Kadriya knew. Corturari were the traveling Roma. Sharai was

vatrasi, Roma who preferred permanent homes.

Sharai threw her hands up. "He'll never settle. You had a home here, Sprig. A home."

"What good is a home if it means being alone? No one wanted my Romani blood. Teraf did."

"I didn't like it. How could I? Choosing a life with him meant you would leave. I would never see you again. But I agreed because I wanted you to be happy. But this. Have you taken leave of your senses, abducting the abbot's knight? And two men dead."

"I knew he'd tilt the story."

"Did you attack them?"

"They took Teraf. They—"

"Are two men dead?"

She swallowed. "Yes. But we thought they would kill Teraf for a crime he didn't commit. You should have seen Sir John. He's a cruel, hateful man. He despises Roma. Couldn't you feel it when you talked with him?"

"Remember Elias, the spur maker in Troyes?"

"What?" Images intruded in Kadriya's mind, memories from years ago when she was just six or seven summers. A table of spurs, a fat *gorgio* man with a facial twitch, an irregular spasm on the right side of his mouth. The twitch was distracting, but his oily way with women—fie! He had occupied a merchant's stall near the Romani peg-cutters where Kadriya had worked. At unguarded moments he haunted the peg tables, fondling the women, young and old, rubbing against them, violating them. Nimble and quick with her dagger, Kadriya had avoided him, but many of the older women were not so fortunate. Elias Gumbley. The name oozed like a foul discharge, a stinking relic from her past.

"What does he have to do with this?"

"After that year in Troyes, you developed a strong loathing to spurs, and to all men with a facial twitch."

"What are you saying?"

"Father Hugo at St. Giles has a twitch in his neck. Is he not a good man?"

"Elias Gumbley was a wretch."

Sharai smiled. "Yes. We need to remember it was Elias who was evil, not the twitch. Mayhap John Wynter struggles to separate the deed from the Gypsy."

"You talk in circles. John Wynter hates Gypsies, all Gypsies. Surely you saw it in his eyes."

"I saw a man exhausted. Weak. Wounded. A man of honor, devoted to his abbot, performing his duty."

"Sir John's knight killed Murat. Maude pulled Sir Roger off his horse and the horse stepped on him. It was an accident."

"Yes, you snared Maude in your foolishness." Sharai paced by the fireplace, shaking her head. "You've always been so rash. Why didn't you go straightaway to the abbey and clear up the matter instead of trying to free Teraf with force?"

"Looking at it now, in the light of day, it was wrong. If I could think quickly like you, I might have done otherwise, but it was so frightening, and this knight, so—odious. Beyond clear thinking. He swore Teraf would be hanged. Murat was leading them to attack, regardless of what I said, so I helped them." She looked to the woman who had raised her, hoping for understanding. "I am Rom."

"Fie! You are a lady. Educated. God-fearing Christian. Lawful, at least until now. What to do?"

"Ask Father Bernard to intervene, encourage more levelheaded thinking so Teraf can defend himself."

"You're too accustomed to our local courts. The church exercises its own justice, holds its own court. We have no say."

"I need to get there, but not under Sir John's thumb. I need food, coin—oh my grief, did the funds make it back from the horse fair?"

"Sir Thomas delivered them safely. You fetched good prices. Tabor will be pleased, at the least about that."

Shame washed over Kadriya. "I'm so sorry."

"You must let the church handle this."

"I must be loyal to my betrothed."

"Teraf is Count Aydin's nephew," Sharai said.

"He's not like Aydin. How could you think I'd judge Teraf based on his uncle's evil deeds? I, who have lived my life under the shadow of mixed blood?"

Sharai nodded. "Perversion through one's actions differs from the blood in your veins, or Elias's facial twitch. We should consider each man on his own merit. Do you know Teraf? While you do not condemn based on blood, do you trust him because of it? Are you not trusting him simply because he is a Rom?"

"He's our king."

"Then you trust him because he has a title?"

"I trust him for him."

Sharai's face softened. "Could it be hoping rather than knowing? Why would men of God pursue an innocent man? A golden chalice, with emeralds. Think of the markets in France. Teraf would fetch a fine price for the chalice there. It would bring many comforts for his tribe. Mayhap he didn't steal it just for himself."

"He would not. Fear is coloring *your* judgment, Sharai, making you trust strangers, based only on their titles as men of God. You wed Tabor and you have become one of them. You have abandoned your own kind."

"You keep making this a matter of skin. It's not. It's a matter of guilt or innocence. That's why you need to get to the abbey and learn more."

"It's a matter of loyalty, Sharai, and I see you have none."

Sharai drew her hand back and struck Kadriya on the face.

Stunned, Kadriya held her cheek.

"Of all people, you dare say that to me. You, who share none of my blood but as much of my heart as if we were sisters. I know you, Kadriya, but I do not know Teraf, and I doubt you do, either. Dare not burn bridges with those who care for you, and follow those who may not."

She strode to the door, her blue skirt billowing. "I'll send Mary up for your bath and a fresh gown. I trust you'll look more respectable for dinner." The door shut behind her.

John sat with Father Bernard in front of the church under the shade of a grand oak tree.

Father Bernard pulled patiently on the thin leather ties of his boot, unthreading them. He had just finished recalling the early days of the king's minority and the power struggle between the young king's uncle, Humphrey, Duke of Gloucester, and the rich, powerful Cardinal Beaufort. "Gloucester was a good strategist," the priest said.

"But unlucky." Gloucester's wife had been found guilty of witchcraft and it had politically devastated Gloucester. "So he was the one who granted Lord Tabor license to wed the Gypsy?"

"Sharai, yes," the priest corrected. "The king was but nine summers. Lord Tabor and Gloucester shared an alliance until his death last year." The priest banged his boot on a stump of wood to loosen the leather ties, and continued pulling.

"Shouldn't the cobbler do that?"

"He did. Always makes it too tight, hurts my corns." Father Bernard freed another loop. "Now Tabor is in Calais, heading to Normandy."

John shook his head. War carved strange partnerships. "So Lord Tabor offers counsel to the king. And has a Gypsy wife."

"Your tone reveals your aversion, but you're wrong. She's God-fearing, bright, capable. Well-loved here. Mayhap you've seen similar traits in Kadriya?"

John had. At first blush he'd thought her a simple heathen, but had quickly learned of her cunning, her courage and her kindness. Her sacrifice for his life. Like an arrow feathered by a careless fletcher, John felt out of balance, his loyalties tried, questioned by a nagging voice inside him that wouldn't be still. "We've been through this, Father. She planned the ambush. Drew weapons against us."

The priest cocked his head. "Doubtless she didn't think she could seriously wound a fully armed, mounted knight with just a kettle hook and a two-foot monkey."

John's neck grew warm. "Should I dismiss my knight's death?"

"Should you deem an accident murder?"

"I suppose you think Teraf is innocent, as well."

"What do you think?" the priest asked.

"I am but a knight. 'Tis not my place to judge."

"Forsooth?"

"What are you implying, Father?"

Father Bernard showed him his palm in a peace gesture. "I heard you were vocal, decisive about Teraf's guilt, so certain that Kadriya and the others worried that justice might not be realized, so they followed you."

John regretted his outburst at the horse camp and understood the Gypsies' actions. But, by the saints, he would not forsake his abbot for their cause. He would die defending the church and his abbot.

"The knight Roger's death was an accident, and you were still able to deliver Teraf to Cerne. You fulfilled your duty," the priest said.

"You know this?"

"We sent a pigeon to Cerne, and they to us. Your abbot knows you're safe." He paused. "But seriously injured."

"What?" John stood. "I'm fine."

"I explained the extent of your head injury. You must rest before traveling."

"I cannot. I—" He stopped himself. The abbot wanted as few people as possible to know about the significance of the chalice. "I know my abilities well enough. We're leaving on the morrow."

"Sit. Please. There's something you must know." The priest lodged a stick above the eyelets for give, and started re-lacing his boot. "Lord Tabor is familiar with Cerne Abbey."

John sat. "Yes?"

"I met you there the year of the Minterne plague. Just after the expansion of the tithe barn. Do you not recall?"

It came to him then. Lord Tabor was not just a benefactor to Cerne Abbey, but a primary one. John closed his eyes and could see, from his memory, Tabor's shield on the monastery's wall. With reluctance, he opened his eyes. The priest had abandoned his lacing and held his gaze, his white eyebrows curved like a hawk's talons.

It would be about money then. Did this priest have the authority to reduce or withhold endowments? John looked up, saw the grand oak against the sky, its leaves red as a rooster's wattle. He had no birds to send, no messenger to reach his abbot to learn if the old priest was misleading him.

"What can you hope to gain by detaining me?"

"Time."

Time he needed to find that chalice. "And what will time do?"

"I baptized Kadriya." The priest held his hand a yard above the grass. "Known her since she was this high. I want to give you a chance to think more clearly about this matter."

John stood. Even the priest held Kadriya dear. "All right. One day."

"Three." The priest stood, moving his hand to his cross.

"Two." His loyalties warred within him again. The abbot and his men. What would they say if they learned he was lax with the Gypsies after Roger's death? "But another day will make no difference. She must be tried and punished."

Chapter 5
Festival

Kadriya crossed the bailey, answering the horn signaling time for supper in the great hall. Golden dusk shone and the bailey was filled with field workers, freed from their labors. Heedless of their calluses and sweat, they laughed at their own jests and elbowed their way to the casks of ale. Joya and Faith chased their friends and tempted Fang and Fool with freshly baked bread. In the hall the air was charged with excitement: the three-day harvest celebration had begun.

But the merriment thudded, dull in Kadriya's ears. She'd passed the afternoon wishing back the words she'd said to Sharai. She needed to speak with her, tell her how sorry she was for insulting her honor and loyalty. The words had rushed out in the desperation of the moment. Saints knew, Kadriya owed Sharai everything.

She had dressed as Sharai wished. She wore her hair bound and veiled, donning a green gown, along with the Tabor coat of arms pin, a sword threading three silver circles.

At the dais, Sharai's seat was still empty, but the surly John Wynter was settled to Sharai's right, the place of honor. Kadriya's hopes faltered. Why would Sharai so honor him? Father Bernard sat to Sir John's right and the seneschal was seated to the left of Sharai's place, along with the harvest master, who was already slipping into his cups.

A murmuring erupted, and Kadriya followed the crowd's gaze. Sharai entered the great hall, escorted by Sir Thomas. She

65

wore a cream-colored houppelande with matching head dress, a stark contrast to her dark skin. With a warm smile Sharai acknowledged the servants and the ale master, the blacksmith and his wife and the butcher. She could mingle with as much certitude among the villagers as the nobility. Kadriya wished she possessed such grace and confidence.

She ventured a sideways glance at the knight. Sir John had cleaned up. His head wound was dressed and his hair, which had been pasted to his forehead with sweat and blood, was washed and combed. In the absence of all that grime it was a dark blond, the hue of raw oak, falling to his shoulders. She thought of touching it and a sense of fascination and fright overwhelmed her, just as it had years ago when she lit the cannon's pitched fuse during the feast of St. George.

She chided herself for such a daft thought and smoothed the table linen. She stole another glance, driven solely, she divined, by morbid curiosity. He wore one of Sir Cyrill's tunics, a copper-colored one that fitted him poorly, straining across his chest so that he could not finish the laces. His cheekbones were high and pronounced, leaving his face thin, almost gaunt, with a sharp jaw line. Had that stern mouth ever curved in a smile? His eyebrows were dark slashes, drawn into a perpetual frown. He was all angles, with a harshness that even his light hair could not soften.

Father Bernard had told her of their talk. John Wynter intended to make her hang alongside Teraf, all because of their Gypsy blood. Kadriya had felt rejection before, as a friend, as a potential wife, even as an acquaintance at the village or church, but never had she been so despised by someone that he wished her dead.

The knight tore at the chicken, gnawing it to the bone, and downed his wine in one motion. He scraped his bread over his trencher repeatedly, even after it looked clean, searching for one last morsel.

Father Bernard caught her gaze and raised a white brow. "Did you starve him out there in the forest?"

"Nay. He was ill. Couldn't keep food down."

"For four days? Well then."

Kadriya squirmed, not wishing to think he might have suffered under her care.

Father Bernard turned to Sir John. "Where do your sons squire?"

"I have no sons."

"Wife?"

"Nay."

"I'm sorry. Did you lose them to the plague?"

"Nay."

Father Bernard cleared his throat. "So you met the abbot in France. Where?"

"Le Crotoy."

"Ah, the Bergundian attack in Normandy."

"Aye."

So the knight had no family. But how could he, hateful as he was?

Walking under a sky of pre-dawn lavender, Sir John walked toward the stables.

A brown creature ambled past him, making sharp cries and trailing a heavy leash.

"Prince Malley. You come back here!" The little imp, Joya, hurried past John.

The monkey waited until she came close, then ran up the tree.

"Get you back here." Joya raced to the tree, hiked her dress up and started climbing, clutching the volumes of fabric and the narrow foot pegs that had been nailed in the tree.

"Be careful," John called to her.

Joya disappeared in the red leaves. She emerged, triumphant, dragging the monkey back down by his leash.

When she jumped to the ground, the monkey jumped on her shoulders.

"Get you off, you *dilli, dilli* monkey!" Joya dropped the leash and grabbed for the monkey's head.

John laughed. "He's a silly monkey?"

"No. *Dilli*. He's a stupid, slow-witted monkey. He peed on my gown!"

Prince Malley hopped off her shoulders and ran away.

"No! Come back here. Oh, Faith is going to get me if you don't come back." She hurried away.

Life shone in her big eyes, that and her dimples helped her live up to her name. A shame that she carried Gypsy blood.

He returned to the stables and picked his way around the bodies sprawled on the floor. Just in case the Gypsy Kadriya tried to leave during the night, he had slept at the stable entrance. As it was, neither she nor Dury had visited the stables, though many revelers had been drowning in ale, singing, dancing and stumbling into the stables to sleep.

She had not danced, though. She had retired after supper, her pace less certain as she climbed the steps to her chamber. Come to think of it, she had seemed less certain since they'd arrived here, a notable change from her sure strides at the horse fair and in the forest.

'Twas understandable. Despite Father Bernard's interference, she would be tried soon.

Passing the northeast tower to check the portcullis, John met the Gypsy, Dury. He approached from the north end of the stables, carrying his saddle.

John acknowledged him, keeping his distance. "I've been delayed. We leave on the morrow."

His eyes wary, Dury lifted his saddle. "Greasing," he said in his stumbling English. "To go monastery." He continued south to the worktables.

An uncomfortable sensation settled on John's skin, a gritty, abrasive impression that overwhelmed him whenever he heard a foreign accent, sweeping over him, leaving him feeling young and vulnerable. He gritted his teeth, burying the feeling and the memory.

He walked on, wondering at Dury's eagerness to reach the monastery. Surely he didn't think he could save his cousin or himself. Or her.

John passed the lesser hall and rounded the northwest corner of the castle, stopping at one of the two large fires from last night. It still smoldered, staining the morning with the smell of ashes and steaming pine resins. Bales of hay were placed nearby and the area was cluttered with stripped rib bones, half-emptied wooden mugs and three wasted revelers who lay snoring through their dirtied beards.

Amid the spilled hay two silver greyhounds slept, their stomachs bulging and their lanky legs sprawled immodestly toward the sky. For no particular reason John picked up a pebble and tossed it so it landed on the shorter dog's stomach. Fang jumped up, Fool joined him, and they ran to John.

Fang and Fool, harebrained names. His old childhood dog, Smoke, came to mind, his big paws and sloppy tongue, and his loyalty.

Those days.

His father's death at the mill and his mother's new husband. John's new half brothers and a new father, a clumsy wainwright who failed to shroud the rejection whenever he looked at John. Later, the blight, the pox, and the mind-dulling gnaw of hunger.

Fool jumped on him, jarring him back to the present. The wiry dog nigh jumped out of his skin with excitement, his butt swaying from the spasms of his tail. John smiled in spite of himself and scratched him behind his ear, finding the fur soft, smooth, and warm.

Jealous, Fang barked and sidled in, biting Fool's ear. Mayhap they had been named properly, after all. John retrieved a bone from beside the dying fire and tossed it toward the church.

Both dogs raced after it, Fang shouldering Fool into skipping a step and beating Fool back for another toss. Their antics nudged John to laughter.

"Don't go spoilin' them, Sir John." Maude shouted from the kitchen entrance.

John tried to dismiss the dogs but they held fast, following him as he neared the kitchen. He covered his smile with annoyance and brushed his hands on his hose. "Too late. They were so spoiled yesterday eve their guts are about to burst."

Maude practically reached the top of the doorframe, tall for a woman. Bruises covered her neck and arms, but she wore a fresh tan gown and her red hair was clean and curly, her blue eyes bright. A right fair face. He'd learned she had once been a prostitute, but she was God-fearing, and John understood the relentless need to eat.

She studied him now. "Heard you'll be staying with us while you heal."

"I'm fine."

"That's good," Maude said. "You'll be needing all your energy for the contests."

"What?"

"The festival."

Contests. A tournament would publicly demonstrate to all how hale he was, hale enough to travel. Hale enough to dismiss the priest's excuse to hold him, enough to return to the monastery. "A tourney?"

"Nay, just wrestling, and bowls. Archery, and dancing. If

you're up to it. Heard you were still swooning from that knock on the head."

"You bait me?"

"Just giving you notice. Certain people will be watching, and I'm putting my wager on you." Her smile faded. "I beg you, Sir John. Don't blame Kadriya. 'Tis me you should be blamin'. I unseated Sir Roger, not her."

Images of the attack flashed before him, Maude, jumping on Roger's horse, pulling him down. Kadriya, tossing the dark ball of fur that he later learned was Prince Malley into Dover's face. His assessments unraveled in his mind. "It's not my decision," he said, pulling away.

Time heavy on his hands, he retraced his steps to the smithy, its fire dead, the shop empty save a large black guard dog who gave John a growl of warning, its upper lip stretching over thick, sharp teeth. John scanned the blacksmith's worktables and shelves at a safe distance. He would get his armor repaired later.

He tried to sort the principles of right and wrong into neat slots, but they spilled out, grey and unruly.

The priest was right. It was not his duty to judge Kadriya's guilt or innocence. He must bring her in and let his abbot tend to it.

The church bells tolled, noting the passing of another hour.

Lured by the aroma of bacon and fresh bread, he headed for the great hall and spied Kadriya by the church. After seeing Dury earlier, he wondered. Why did she linger out here instead of breaking her fast? Were she and Dury planning to flee during the meal? He stopped at the stacked barrels outside the kitchen, a spot that afforded him an unobstructed view of her. She was dressed in a sky-blue gown, her small breasts high, her frame slender. Though her beauty was remarkable, 'twas the birds that caught his eye, three white doves, one perched on each of her shoulders and one poised fine as you please atop her head dress.

She approached the great oak tree, red as a Templar's cross in the early sunlight. Kadriya grabbed a wooden handle and climbed on primitive wooden steps nailed to the trunk. She and her birds settled on a fat, horizontal limb six feet high.

The tree had been trimmed over the years to keep all branches a safe distance from the wall for security's sake. From its unusual shape he guessed the left side facing the church must have suffered from a fire some time back, but the tree was still sturdy.

John came closer.

She settled on the branch and pulled off her head dress, shaking her hair free. It flowed to her waist, shining clean. Now free of oil and dirt, it was brown, not black.

A sensation of warmth entered his chest, unbidden, unwelcome. He leaned forward.

She sprinkled seed from her purse and the white birds jumped to their breakfast with enthusiasm. She spoke to them and lifted one to her face. The dove pecked lightly on her nose and she laughed, a sound that warmed the morning and softened the harsh realities of the day. She stroked the bird's feathers and it hopped to her shoulder and walked around the back of her neck.

She took it in her hands and held it to her cheek. Closing her eyes, she murmured something, and the bird leaned into the caress as if it were accustomed to such loving attention.

Her hands sheltered the little fowl. It cooed as she murmured, and they continued their extraordinary music together.

He had no right to watch, had no need of such frivolous displays that played havoc with his sense of right and wrong, with duty and lack of it. The moment lingered too bright to believe, too fragile to last.

Grunting from the effort, he remembered his commitments and turned away.

Kadriya climbed the steps to the solar and Joya came into view. Sitting on a rug by the fire, the little girl, Sharai's youngest child, sat in a snarl of ribbons. "Kadriya. I thought you would never come."

"Well, here I am. I desperately need peace and quiet away from prying eyes. The knight has been watching my every move."

Joya pouted. "Where have you been?"

Kadriya ruffled her black hair. "Doing the job I assigned you. I fed and exercised my doves. The falconer said they haven't been out of their cages much since I left. You're eight summers, old enough to fulfill your promises."

Joya grimaced. "I'm sorry. In all the excitement, I forgot."

"Forgiven, but only this time." Kadriya peered hopefully into Joya's lap. "How many bell rings have you sewn so far?"

"Three."

"Oh." The eve's harvest dance required bell rings for the women, circles of ribbon tied to a bell. "And how many do we need?"

"Momma said to make fifty."

Fifty dance circles. Kadriya groaned. She'd struggled for proficiency since her first sewing, but the skill evaded her. "Well, it gives me a chance to be with my favorite niece, so let's get busy."

Joya beamed. "I'm your favorite?"

"Aye, but keep it to yourself lest Faith's feelings be hurt."

They divvied up ribbons, threads and needles and fell into their work.

"You're in trouble with Mother," Joya said.

Joya was a little master at gossip. "What have you heard?"

Joya's needle stilled. "You surprised Sir John with Prince

Malley, and you're in big trouble now because you're irrepulsive."

"Impulsive, yes, I'm plagued with that. What else?"

"Teraf stole a chalice from the monastery."

"Joya, that's not true."

"Is, too. Father Bernard said Sir John said there's a witness. A monk who guards the relics saw him take it. Him and Erol."

Kadriya took a quick, sharp breath. Erol. In her fear for Teraf's safety, she'd forgotten him. Where was Erol? But Joya was still talking . . .

". . . thinks you should treat Sir John better. I think she's right. Sir John has a debt to pay the abbot. I heard Father Bernard say that. He's fierce because he's obligated."

"You're young, Joya. There are things you don't know." *Like how he thinks I'm a vulgar, lying heathen and wants me to hang.*

"At first sight I thought he was a brute. Stinking like a sot, and so mad. But he cleaned up and came to the kitchen and talked to us."

"Did he hurt Prince Malley?"

"Nay, but he kept his distance."

Kadriya had seen the knight visiting with Maude in the bailey. So he also spoke with her in the kitchen. "Probably digging for information."

"He's trying to catch thieves and find the chalice. Just so you know, he showed us a coin trick. He's not so bad."

Curse the man. He insulted her and all Roma, but found it acceptable to recruit innocent children as allies.

Joya patted her arm. "Worry not, Kadriya." Her little hand was warm, and it occurred to Kadriya that their roles had reversed, the child comforting the grown woman. "Mother sent word to Father, and he'll know what to do. He always knows what to do."

Kadriya swallowed hard. Tabor would not think kindly of her

bringing ill fortune to his house. Father Bernard had stalled the knight, but neither he nor Lord Tabor himself could prevent Sir John from ultimately taking her away. She had helped plan the ambush, and a knight had been killed. Kadriya stabbed at the ribbon with her needle, feeling ill of a sudden.

Teraf forced himself to remain still in his cell. If he did not find a way out, he would soon swing at the gallows.

Eustace, the tall Sacristan, arrived with a collection of guards behind him. There would be no bolting free. Teraf must convince Eustace to help him.

The monk entered, all meager eight stones of him. Oh, likely he weighed more, but he looked to be naught but skin and bones, like the unsold slaves in Marseilles, the ones Teraf routinely disregarded. After all, his hands were full with his tribe. The slaves could make their own way.

The monk's face pinched with worry, his haunted eyes locked on Teraf.

Over the years of horse fairs Teraf had developed a good vocabulary for French and English numbers and descriptions. He could still not master putting the words together right, but he could always get his message across. He met the monk's gaze and lifted his chin. "You have dirty secret." He spoke low so the guard who remained outside the closed door could not hear.

Eustace slapped him.

"Dirty secret, sodomite."

Eustace grabbed his silk cotehardie at the collar and struck him repeatedly, grunting his words out with each blow. "Heathen—filthy—godless—heathen-thief."

Teraf tasted blood and fought the impulse to strike back. Eustace would have already killed him if he could have done so safely, and Teraf would not foolishly give him a reason to do so now.

The monk's strength ebbed and he stopped his assault, holding his hand.

Teraf faced him. "You. Geoffrey," he said, naming the young, blond monk. "He told me. Free me, or I tell abbot. Geoffrey told me," he added with emphasis.

Eustace's face took on a lighter color. He paced back and forth in the little room, past the small desk, past the small bed with its rough, woolen cover and thin pillow, past the table with its holy inscriptions. He stopped, taking in enough air that he might have been preparing to scream his frustration across the cloister. "You are stained with sin to the depths of your soul." His voice was cold, flat, inflected with the privileged cadence of nobility.

Teraf smiled. He, a Rom, given none of the monk's advantages, could bring him to his knees.

Eustace lowered his voice to a whisper. "When you awake two or three hours hence, you will find your cell has been opened."

Teraf laughed softly and pointed to his temple. "Not stupid. I dead before I free, what you want. Chalice—remember? You leave out. No guard. No lock. Trap. Then try kill me." He smiled. "I too fast. Now help me." He drew out his words for emphasis and leaned into him. "Get me away past abbey, with horse—my horse. Saddle. Food."

The monk's eyes widened.

A shiver of pleasure rushed through Teraf, much like the sensation he felt when a woman put her hand on him, stirring desire. This powerful miscreant was at his mercy. Before the theft, Teraf had found reason to visit all the monastery's public grounds, taking stock of its treasures. He closed in for his final thrust, speaking low, calmly, betraying none of his excitement. "Also silver cross, infirmary."

"What of it?"

"I want."

Eustace's jaw dropped. "What? Never!"

Teraf pulled his chains to the limit. They clanked loudly and the monk flinched.

"You give, I not tell."

"You will burn in hell for eternity."

The fear in his eyes encouraged Teraf. "You rot here like fish. Lust eats you. You make big sins, bigger from me. You, loyal God man. Loyal men not win. Daring men win. Like me. What so bad of that? I dare. You, too, frisky monk." Frisky. Daring. Teraf had often heard those words used to describe the courage and spirit of young stallions.

The monk's face grew red with rage.

"What silver cross to you? Naught. Have many, I want one. I talk much when hang. Confession, you know." Teraf paused because he felt victory in his bones. He had worked enough fairs, broken enough men to know. "Abbot wants see me. I talk all? What I say, brother Eustace, you choose."

CHAPTER 6
THE CHALLENGE

The sun was already high and warming the cobbled path as Kadriya exited the main castle entrance into the bailey, deserted but for four sentinels posted at the towers and two more on the walkway and gatehouse. All able-bodied men gathered in the open fields past the mill to compete in or watch the harvest games.

Two of those sentinels leaned over the northwest walkway, laughing and cheering the action below. The late morning breeze wafted in from the fields, carrying the scents of fresh dough balls, cheese, and roast mutton.

The merriment escaped Kadriya. If he still lived, Teraf was waiting for help that would never come. She'd brought trouble to Tabor's demesne, and John Wynter would take her soon to the abbey.

The thought made her dizzy with fear. Just days ago, life had been so promising. She'd led her horses to the fair, looking forward to seeing Teraf again, to greet the one man who would take her to wife.

Now both of them faced death. The wall had grown too tall, too insurmountable.

She passed the oak tree where Joya and Faith worked with Prince Malley, reinforcing his tricks for this afternoon's show. The monkey would dance and tip his hat, or climb on a shoulder and kiss the braver folks.

She passed the entrance to the great hall. At that part of the bailey the kitchen maids had set up tables outside, in the shade between the kitchen and the castle. Worktables were full with maids washing and scoring eels, cutting onions, mixing eggs, grinding ginger and chatting eagerly about the games and evening dances to come.

Maude sat at an isolated table near the steps to the great hall, her skirt filled with fat bulbs of garlic and her table laden with a mound of peeled cloves. "Kadriya. My stars, you're finally up and about. I was ready to summon the physic."

"I had a fitful night's sleep," Kadriya said.

Maude looked closer. "My girl, your hair. Your eyes."

Kadriya pulled up a stool and joined her. "Sooth, my head's in a fog. Even my bones feel heavy."

"That bruise is looking a little better, at the least. Look at me." She straightened her arm, filled with purple blotches and scratches. "Have you broken your fast?"

"I don't feel like eating." She gestured to Maude's lap. "Pass me some bulbs and I'll help."

Made gave her a handful. "Thanks. Just do this." She split a bulb with her thumbs. Taking a few cloves, she rapped them on the table and rolled them between her hands briskly as if rubbing her hands dry. The paper-like husks broke and sprinkled off like wheat chaffs, and three skinned cloves dropped from her hands.

Kadriya attempted the same maneuver but one clove popped from the bulb and flew into the dirt.

"Here." Maude took her hands, showing her how to separate the bulb. "Ooh, your hands are cold."

Kadriya started to speak but stopped, worried about prying ears. She rose and checked the courtyard and great hall. Finding it empty save for dogs scavenging in the reeds, she returned to her stool. "He follows me everywhere."

"Sir John?"

Janet Lane

"He's made friends with you, I hear."

"Not friends, mind you, but he does seem to have calmed down since the horse fair, don't you think?"

"He's determined to see me hang."

Maude's blue eyes sobered to a look of motherly concern. "Nonsense. If it comes to that I shall stand for you. 'Twas my fault Sir Roger died."

"Maude. You came along to protect me. I showed them the way with the kettle poles and Prince Malley. I even picked the spot where we would surprise them."

"Enough of this. You're glum enough to sour fresh milk. Marie?" Unlooping a wooden mug from her girdle, Maude hoisted it to catch the scullery maid's eye. "Prithee fill this from the mead barrel, and pour one for Kadriya, as well."

Marie retrieved Maude's mug and returned with two full ones.

Maude lifted hers and pushed the other toward Kadriya. "Here. Drink it. 'Twill brace you." She lowered her voice. "You're not guilty. At the horse fair Sir John spouted off as if he was going to haul Teraf to the nearest tree and give him a swing, now, and you were scared out of your wits that your intended would die for no fault of his own."

"But I shouldn't have—"

"Listen. Sir John's got a burr in his armor about foreigners and it made his mouth run faster 'n a spring river. On the chance you didn't hear, the bishop is due at the abbey on St. Michaelmas, and 'twas the bishop himself what gave the Abbot that emerald chalice. For some reason Sir John owes the Abbot an arm, a leg and a sack of sisters, so he must needs find that chalice. Has to."

The mead slid down Kadriya's throat like sun-warmed honey. "How do you know all this?"

"The messenger from Cerne monastery, a'course. He was

mighty spent after his travel, but not so drained that he didn't wish to blow his horn," she said with a knowing half smile, "if you get my drift."

"Maude."

"What?" Her blue eyes twinkled. "I was an alehouse whore afore Lord Tabor rescued me, bless him. I know how to lead a man to drop more 'n his chausses, I do." She drained her mead and pushed Kadriya's back in front of her. "Drink it all. Saints know you need the courage 'cause you've lost it, Sprig, and you can't afford to lose it with a man like Sir John."

"I hate him as much as he hates me."

"So show it if you must, but don't lie down like a wounded duck waiting to be brought by the dogs to their master's table. Think of how you can use his pride to your advantage."

Kadriya selected a garlic bulb, divided it and managed to produce two clean cloves. "He's unfeeling." She looked up. "What about pride?"

"You know how the knights are, at practice and tourney. It's what they hate to lose above all else. What do you suppose he would never want you to mention to the Abbot?"

"That I'm an impulsive, reckless Gypsy who has the chalice?"

"He knows you don't, or he would have found it, and he'll tell the Abbot such. What would hurt Sir John's pride?"

"That I captured him?"

Maude smiled more broadly. "And how did you?"

"Oh." It was suddenly clear. She recalled Sir John's red face at the prior evening's supper when Father Bernard spoke of it. "Oh, Maude, I'm so dull witted. His pride. A big, burly knight is felled by kettle hooks and a monkey."

Maude smiled. "Aye, and a young woman's mettle. And do you think this hardened knight will be wary of a pudding-pie, sad-faced maid, or will he be cautious of a strong woman who was brave enough to fight for her man and even saved *him* from

Rill's dagger?"

Kadriya nodded.

"And here's one more piece to chew on. The mean, hard-hearted knight has a shine for you."

"Oh, Maude. Spare me your jesting."

"Forsooth. Saw him myself this morn behind the barrels. He watched you with your doves. Watched you with sheep eyes, he did."

"He hates me."

"He cares for you."

Kadriya rolled the thought around in her mind. If he did, she might still be able to sway him about Teraf and her. She hugged the big, warm woman who had looked after her since she was seven summers. "Thank you. I've been so weak."

"Fie. Just don't be scared. My brother died scared, and it broke my heart."

Kadriya put a hand on her arm. "Lord Tabor told me about it." Maude's brother had been severely crippled. He had been kicked to death at the alehouse where she worked. Maude had risked her life defending him, to no avail. "I'm sorry, Maude."

She nodded. "That taught me a lesson. Never give up. Think of the duck that squirms in the dog's mouth, quacking his heart out and pecking the hound's eye. 'I'm alive,' he's saying. 'I'm alive!' Right to his last breath. That'll be me, by gad. Give up and you're doomed, so what's to lose? Fight, Kadriya."

Later, warmed by the mead, freshly dressed for the festivities and bolstered with new hope, Kadriya strolled under the portcullis, across the bridge and down to the mill.

Maude's claims astounded her, but had she not sensed Wynter's interest herself? Still, in view of the knight's deep hatred for her, it seemed improbable. Yet in the past Kadriya had erred in reading men's intentions, thinking they were sincere, only to feel the pain of rejection. Maude was wise and experienced with men. Mayhap she saw what Kadriya could not. Maude's observations gave her hope. If Sir John could see past his image of a Gypsy heathen and view Kadriya as a woman, then he might even be able to see Kadriya for the person she was.

Kadriya passed a group of girls bent over a barrel top, playing Tali.

Faith saw her and jumped up. "Here, I'm done." She gave her sheep bone dice to another girl and caught up. "Kadriya. You're wearing your red houppelande."

Kadriya touched the fabric with a flash of uncertainty. Sharai had sewn it for the midsummer festival, crimson silk with a low neckline trimmed in white lace.

Faith grabbed Kadriya's hands and held her arms out, smiling approvingly. At only thirteen summers, Faith had taken after Lord Tabor's side of the family with height and stood head to head with Kadriya. She lifted Kadriya's hair, which hung freshly washed and loose to her waist. "Your hair. No headdress, but the scarf is beautiful. Did you make it?"

At that, Kadriya laughed. "You know how clumsy I am with a needle. I just folded it."

Faith aligned her forearm with Kadriya's, comparing their color, as she had done since she was a tiny squirt. As always, Kadriya's skin tone was decidedly lighter than Faith's, yet darker than Lord Tabor's—or Kadriya's father, who, if the tales were true, was blond with green eyes.

Kadriya took Faith's hand. "Is Prince Malley ready for his show?"

"He's in such a foul mood. He bit me, and jumped on the table and soiled it." Faith grimaced. "What if he does that during his tricks?"

"He's likely troubled by the large crowds of people. Give him an apple and take him to the withdrawing room so he can rest.

When he performs, keep the people back so he doesn't feel trapped."

"I'll get Joya to do that. I would that he be pleasant." Faith gave Kadriya a pleading gaze. "Though he bites and shrieks, we've grown fond of him. Can Prince Malley stay with us, Kadriya?"

Sweet Faith, on the threshold of womanhood, but her eyes still held the wonder of childhood. Loved swelled in Kadriya's chest and she hugged her, wishing she could shelter her from life's dangers. "The monkey's not mine to give, sweetling. We shall need to ask Teraf." And she would, because Teraf was going to somehow survive this ordeal.

Faith hugged her back and pulled on her hand. "Come. Let's play a game."

The field was crowded with a dizzying array of people: merchants from Coin Forest and surrounding villages, archers and fletchers, two nuns and pilgrims on their way to Winchester, knights and threshers and haywards and butchers, blacksmiths and alemasters, brewsters and their wives, wenches, and knights and guards to keep the peace. The various games were separated by the walls of people who milled about, surrounding the action like a living, shifting hedgerow.

Between the huddles of activity they found Stephen, Faith and Joya's older brother. He saw Kadriya and his eyes widened. "A right fair gown, Kadriya." He met her gaze. "It suits you better."

Like hers, Stephen's blood was mixed. Though his skin was darker, Stephen disavowed his Romani side and had been opposed to her wedding Teraf.

" 'Tis only for the festival," she said.

"Then let the festival last until Michaelmas. No, even Christmas," he said.

"Aren't you the charmer? Now off with you." Kadriya pushed

him playfully and she and Faith continued to the games.

As they passed men stared, lingering on Kadriya's neckline, and she adjusted her scarf and hair, discreetly covering herself from their stares. "Have you seen Sir John?"

"You slept most the day away and missed camp ball. Sir John played and scored three points for the Coin Forest team. We won. And you missed the foot race. Sir John is nigh as fast on his feet as the messenger."

"Messenger?"

"You know," Faith said, her mouth turning up in a shy smile, "the handsome young runner, Henry of Southampton, who came yesterday to confirm our wine shipment. Henry, Sir Thomas and Sir John were in the final race, and Sir John came in second only to Henry."

"Well. He's been busy."

"Aye, and look there. Now he's bowling."

Past the western field, shorn free of its golden wheat, a grassy meadow had been transformed for bowls. River rocks stacked four and five-high formed the perimeter of the dozen playing areas, each about the width of a wagon and the length of three. At the far end a large crowd had gathered, and the noise level rose and fell with each player's turn.

Kadriya and Faith worked their way back.

Sir John bowled with two other players, an armorer from the village and Sir Cyrill. The goal, a small, white feather, rested at the end of the grassy rectangle surrounded by two large, green bowls the other players had already rolled. It was Sir John's turn.

He knelt, his knees almost touching the ground, and turned the bowl slowly in his hands.

His hands were large, an angry red scar circling the base of his right thumb, as if it had been almost torn off. His long fingers ended with stubby fingernails. Might he chew them? She dismissed the thought. They likely annoyed him and got in the way of his work in the lists.

Those nubby fingertips explored the surface of the bowl as he turned it, as if memorizing any ridges and bumps to determine which way it would roll. He wore a tight-fitting brown gypon, and his hose revealed the shape of his thighs and calves, the muscles rippling, thick and brawny beneath the thin fabric.

He drew his arm back and with a motion that seemed too delicate for his massive size, he swung his arm forward. The bowl rolled off his fingertips, smooth as a whisper. It hit a tuft of grass in the middle of the lane. The clump of grass changed the bowl's direction so that it veered left, reaching its goal and resting squarely on the feather's barb.

"Not again," Sir Cyrill protested, and the armorer groaned. Grumbling, the men handed over their coins, which Sir John accepted with a smile.

The knight could smile. It transformed his face, softening the angles and stirring an unwelcome ripple of appreciation in her. She tamped it down. He deserved no measure of regard from her.

"Enough of this," a man cried. "Look at all the fair maids who have joined us. Is it not their turn to play?"

The women looked at each other in surprise and, suddenly wary, backed away from the men.

"Aye. Time for stool-ball."

The men grabbed and pushed and the women shrieked and laughed. In the social game of stool-ball, women perched on one-legged milking stools. If they didn't keep at least one foot on the ground they would fall. Their challenge was to avoid being struck by bowls rolled by the men, while still keeping their balance. Those men who could strike the women's foot or ankle won a cake or a dance.

The crowd moved to the barns where five stools had been

positioned in a row and, some ten yards away a line of boards ran, behind which five men lined up, each holding a bowl.

"All right, ladies," Will, the seneschal, barked. He was missing half his left arm, but had a certificate to show it was lost to battle and not as a punishment for theft, so Lord Tabor had retained him last summer. "Time to show us how fast you are. You know the rules. Men can't cross the line, can't bowl to their own women and must wait their turn. Women can't get off the stools and can't run with 'em, either."

With the players identified, the women whispered among themselves and five women selected stools in front of a crowd of men.

"Such a silly game," Faith said.

"Wait until you're older," Kadriya teased her.

Laughter and hoots filled the air, and finally, the tall fletcher hit his mark first. Cheers rose and the winning fletcher and the girl he bowled for won apple cream cakes. They left together, laughing and holding their cakes. Two more rounds were completed.

Faith grabbed Kadriya's arms, a smile on her face.

"What?" Kadriya asked.

"There," Faith whispered. " 'Tis him. Henry."

"Ah, the fleet-footed messenger." Maybe Faith was old enough for this game after all. Kadriya stepped behind Faith, waved to catch the messenger's eye, and pointed down at Faith over her head where Faith couldn't see the gesture.

Henry nodded in appreciation and stepped up with his bowl, and Sir John followed him. Three women from the village saw Sir John approach the playing field and became interested in the game, moving toward the stools.

Faith saw Henry lining up to play and grabbed Kadriya's hand. "Play with me," she pleaded with a hopeful smile.

Kadriya glanced at Sir John from the corner of her eye. "With him? I'd sooner muck stables. Without a shovel," she added for clarity.

"Who knows when I might see Henry again? It could be weeks. I beg you, Kadriya," Faith whispered.

Her heart-felt plea wore away Kadriya's resolve. A public game would do no harm. She'd make sure he didn't win. "Oh, all right."

"Thank you. Make haste," Faith urged, striding past the men to the stools.

They took the two stools farthest left, sliding in just before the other women. Faith was in front of Henry, and sure enough, when Kadriya had secured her seat she glanced up and met Sir John's gaze.

Yes, black-hearted knight, Kadriya thought. *You're stuck with me for this round.* She had frustrated many a player with this game. He would not win a cake this day.

Sir John's eyes were brooding and unreadable but his mouth was relaxed, not drawn in a thin line of disgust or hatred as it was so often when he looked at her. The sunlight shone on his hair, drawing golden highlights as it brushed his shoulders. He was ruggedly beautiful, like a saint's statue, its fine lines gnawed by a century's worth of wind and rain.

She dropped her gaze to his hands to better concentrate.

He held his bowl, turning it over this way, then that. From the way he bowled before, she knew he was determining every bump and detour the bowl would take in its journey to her feet. Would he deliberately lose to avoid her? He had strength and a sharp focus, but she possessed good timing, quick reactions. She would not wither before him.

The intensity of his gaze brought a spell of dizziness about her. Defiance flowing through her veins she bent forward, scooping up her skirt to reveal her feet and ankles and tucking the fabric under her. She straightened and shook her head so her hair fell forward, covering her shoulder. "I've seen your horsemanship," she taunted, raising an eyebrow as she reminded him of his unseating at Blackwater Point.

That got him. His eyes darkened, and his grip on the bowl tightened.

"Now show me your aim," Kadriya challenged, stirring his anger to decrease his accuracy.

"Lizbeth," Will hollered to the woman on the third stool, "Raise your skirts like the other ladies so we can see your feet and ankles. Okay, everyone, watch carefully. The first bowl that touches a woman's leg, it's a tag. Begin. Bowl one."

Sir John wound up as if he would hurl the bowl directly at her face.

Quack, quack, she thought, remembering Maude's speech, becoming determined not to flinch.

He rolled the bowl briskly at her feet.

She watched its approach and resisted the urge to pull both her feet away. She raised her right foot at the last second. Lifting it casually, she avoided the rolling bowl and crossed her right leg, swinging it in a mocking challenge.

He stepped back, his expression neutral while he waited for the assistants to return the bowl.

Kadriya started to uncross her legs to return her right foot to the ground for balance.

"Do not move." His voice was rich but rough at the edge, like dried leather scraping silk.

Her leg froze.

"Keep it there." An evil smile curved his lips, making his high cheekbones more pronounced, softening his blue eyes, which were so often slashed by angry brows. "I dare you."

He'd challenged her.

His smile revealed strong, white teeth. It lit his face, brought a liveliness that made him somehow more approachable, pulling

Kadriya into his gaze. He wasn't the biggest man she'd ever seen, but without doubt the tallest, and muscular, making him graceful, fluid, all chest and arms and legs and . . .

His power leapt across the distance that separated them, touching her. Her breasts tingled, and she fought the urge to cover them as she struggled to find her breath.

The crowd had grown quiet.

"Well, well." Will strode between them, his eyes lit with knowing, as if he had sensed the jolt of excitement that had passed between them.

An unwelcome heat radiated in her face.

"This game becomes more interesting." Will faced Kadriya. "The prize has grown. The victor will not get cake this time. Instead, this fair maid will give him a kiss."

"Fair maid?" Stephen laughed. "That's Kadriya."

Many laughed, and Kadriya shot an arrow of anger Stephen's way.

Will raised his arm and dropped it. "Bowl two."

Sir John's intense stare bore down on her. He committed the depressions in his bowl to memory again with his hands and drew back, much further back this time. The bowl would come at her faster.

She swallowed and dropped her gaze to his hands. Pride kept her from lowering her right foot for better balance.

He swung the bowl wide out to his right and prepared to release it.

She guessed its trajectory and moved her left foot to her right, away from where he was aiming the bowl, sliding her bottom around to keep balance on the stool.

He held the bowl a second longer than she expected, then released it.

He'd anticipated her adjustment. She tried to jerk her foot out of the bowl's path, flailing her arms to keep her balance.

The bowl hit her ankle. "Ow!" She cried out, grabbing her leg. She lost her balance and toppled off the stool.

Will helped her up, pulled her toward John and hoisted his arm in the air.

"Sir John is the winner. He wins Kadriya's kiss."

John's smile grew wider, and the gloom that hung perpetually at his ears lifted. He looked years younger. Pleased.

Her throat tightened and her heart hurried in her chest. She imagined this must be how a deer felt when cornered, when capture was imminent. But this heat, would it feel such heat?

Will pushed them together and a crowd circled around them, shouting encouragements and ribald comments, ready to witness the prize.

He came closer, filled her view with his masculine bulk. He smelled of smoke and sweat and fresh grasses, so close to her she could see the individual brown hairs of his brows, the forehead she had cleaned and cooled after his injury, and his eyes, sea blue and heavy-lidded with hunger. A spike of excitement made her shudder, and the air grew heavy with a mist that spun only between them.

He cupped her face and when his lips were nigh touching hers, he turned her slightly, just enough to kiss her cheek.

His mouth was soft, warm. Her skin tingled, as if faerie's wings had touched her.

One fluttering moment and it passed.

The crowd thinned, some booing, some cheering. She spun away from him and strode toward the mill.

"Kadriya. Wait." Faith caught up with her. "He kissed me. Henry kissed me," she whispered. A glow of happiness flushed her face. "On the mouth. And your knight only kissed your cheek."

Kadriya searched for her voice. "He's not my knight." Sir John had behaved honorably.

Faith's happy chatter seemed to be coming to her from a distant tunnel, and she nodded, though she hadn't discerned her words.

Kadriya walked carefully, her steps uncertain, as if she had become so tall she couldn't quite locate her feet.

Sir John flicked a rib bone to Fang and another to Fool.

The silver hounds lay on their sides by the fire in the bailey, barely moving their eyes in the direction of the bones.

John laughed. "Well, then. You've finally reached your limit."

Sir Cyrill laughed along with Sir Thomas and several other knights who surrounded the fire. The games and the minstrel songs were over, the dances were danced, and the ladies had retired to the solar for their sewing and whatever else women did in the evening shadows of their chambers.

Sir Cyrill helped himself to a fresh mug of mead. Walking past John, he poured half of his drink into John's mug. "Drink up, Sir John. You won at every sport today. I salute you, Sir."

"Thanks." John tipped back the mead, sweet and rich in his throat. A warmth hummed through his body, and he felt better than he had in months. Mayhap it was the thrill of competition and victory, or just from being with fellow knights like this again, sharing stories of battles, the miseries of travel, and the glory of cheating death.

These men knew this, and loyalty. And duty. They didn't go traveling from country to country, stealing along the way, like Gypsies. Damned Gypsies.

A movement caught his eye, a window opening above the curing room. Kadriya's chamber. He had chosen to sit by this fire so he could keep an eye on her.

It was his duty.

The side entrance below her chamber had been closed after a long-ago siege. Was there a way to open it? He could not have her slipping away.

He stood. "Excuse me. I need to walk."

"Probably you need to think about that kiss you squandered," Thomas teased, the fire dancing off his chipped front tooth.

"Foolishness." John left their laughter behind and headed around the northwest tower to the main entrance.

He passed the great hall, its fire dwindling, its lower tables set as beds for the scullery maids and kitchen servants. He pulled a torch and climbed the steps above the curing room, feeling like an intruder. He should not be here, but some corner of his soul beckoned, carrying him up each stone step. He was passing an open door when she appeared in the doorway.

"Sir John." She held her torch, and in the spotty lighting he could not read the expression on her face. She still wore the enchanting red gown from earlier at bowling. He forced the thought away. He would maintain control in the face of this woman. He must.

"What are you doing, sneaking around the hall at this hour?"

"Just checking." He would forego the pleasantries and pretensions.

She stepped out into the hall. "Search to your satisfaction."

He entered her room, casting torchlight in the chamber, noting the luxurious objects. Her bed was draped in red silk, mayhap her favored color, her bed linens thick and shining in the candlelight. An image flashed like distant lightning, her brown hair against the red silk of her pillow, her face relaxed, smiling up at him . . .

Idiot. You're here to see if she might bolt. A reading desk held a book, ink and pen, and a dressing table held a generous collection of combs and a dainty box of jeweled finger rings. He saw no evidence of impending flight, and felt of a sudden like a lumbering draft horse, too big for her chamber. "Forgive the intrusion. I shall leave you now."

"Not just yet. I would have a word with you." She passed by him and the air sweetened with that same fragrance of spring flowers and spices that had drifted to his senses after stool-ball. She crossed the hall, placed her torch in a wall sconce and folded her arms in front of her, causing her breasts to rise higher from the bold neckline. Her skin was smooth, lush. Perfect. A bolt of lust slammed into him, caught him unaware. Light flashed off her earrings and he swallowed, willed the desire away.

It refused.

"Where's Dury?" Her voice had a silken edge, like her linens. It echoed in the narrow hall, surrounding him.

John hesitated, trying to recall her question. "Dury. At the fires, I suppose."

"You don't know?"

He didn't. He tried to step away, but a trap had just snapped closed at his feet.

"Do you not fret that he will flee? Why do you plague only me?"

He cast about for an answer, but found none.

"I was foolish enough to think you might shed your hatred long enough to see me as a person, yet still you look at me as you would a worm in your apple after you've eaten half of it. You despise me."

"I do not." He had at first, perhaps, but no longer. Now he could not keep his gaze from her. She was a delight to the eyes, like dew sparkling on the grass in the morning, or a touch—he tried stopping the thoughts that would be best left unthought, but, as if he wished to be cruel to himself, they only grew more vivid.

Kadriya regarded the man who would have her hang, the man who regarded her as his prisoner. She thought of what Maude had told her about Sir John watching her with her doves, and saw his eyes now, shining dark with desire in the torchlight.

Was she the object of his disgust or his desire? Mayhap both, an unhealthy attraction. Was he righteous, or did he harbor lust for what he deemed a murderer? Fresh anger swirled, anger and a sudden urge to expose his hypocrisy.

"Dury was at Blackwater Point, too, but you do not follow his every movement."

For once uncertainty showed in his eyes.

"I'm awearied of your constant condemnation." She paused. "You watched me this morn with my doves. Am I so wicked that I cause you fascination?"

"This is a most improper discussion, Kadriya. In reply to—"

He dared to deny it. "Do you like the taste of the worm? Is it the forbidden that stirs your blood?"

"You speak nonsense." He raised his eyebrows, as if that would better enable him to look down on her, judging, dismissing, disdainful.

"Do I?" She stepped forward, so close she could feel the warmth of his breath in the chill hall. "It must be difficult, guarding me, watching me, being so close to a . . . Gypsy." She pushed the word out, charged it with the same disgust and condemnation he'd used at the horse fair.

She touched his left shoulder, an invasive tap, his muscles hard under her fingertips.

He shrank back, his face a mask.

She enjoyed his discomfort and poured the disease of judgment in his cup, for a change. "You worry that my hands might stain you?" She placed her other hand on his right shoulder, but she didn't tap this time. She skimmed her hand over the thin, dark orange fabric, over the laces that strained to hold the tight tunic stretched across his chest, feeling his muscles tense as she touched him, responding to her. "Afraid some of my color may rub off on you, mayhap? Make you weaker?"

An alarm sounded in the back of her mind. She was moving dangerously close to the edge of a steep, rocky cliff, and she would do well to step back.

But he would escape if she did, and anger had been building in her, provocation at his stubborn way of thinking, at the cold censure with which he regarded her and the heat in his eyes now.

She moved closer so he could not look away. "Do you fear my evil eye might catch you, deliver you into the devil's arms?"

He swallowed audibly and tried to back up, but the stone wall prevented it. "Some people may fear that, but not me."

"You're not afraid of me?"

"Nay."

His protest sounded raw and strained. "Liar. You hate me, you fear me, and you want me."

She pressed herself against his chest, as if she could push him through the wall, through his wall of hatred, so he could see himself for what he was.

His eyes darted like a trapped buck.

Satisfaction warmed her, and something else, a dizzying awareness that she had pushed her entire body against his. She felt his tight muscles against her breasts, his heat.

His blue eyes grew heavy-lidded with desire.

A thrill raced to her stomach and heat flashed to her core.

His arms engulfed her, his big hands pressing at her back and waist, bringing her closer.

Air rushed from her chest and her arms worked of their own accord, wrapping around his neck, bringing her closer until she was clinging to him.

His mouth covered hers, warm, wet, crushing, as if he'd come to the well after days without water.

He tasted of honey mead and smoke. He had surrendered

and the avowal overwhelmed her—that and his closeness and passion.

Her nerves screeched with resistance for a moment, then, to her horror, her body surrendered to him, and she returned the kiss in an earthy, hungry way. Like a flash fire to dry kindling, she explored his skin, the contours of his neck.

What demon possessed her? Her hands swept the rough stubble of his cheek and the curve of his ear. Her fingers, long wanting, dove into the dense mane of his tawny hair.

His tongue moved hungrily in her mouth and his heart beat strongly against her breast.

Nothing delicate. Raw. Hot.

Desire leapt and danced to the rhythm of his tongue and she fell into the flaming turmoil of his soul, into the spell of his masculine passion.

Her hands skimmed the width of his chest, so wide, he so tall, so much taller than Teraf . . .

Teraf. The thought of him snuffed her desire down a notch and she regained her senses.

She withdrew and turned away from him, desperately trouncing at the flames that still licked inside her. "You see? I was right." She grimaced at the huskiness of her voice. She had proven her point, but at what cost? Before he could condemn her again, she hurried to the safety of her chamber.

CHAPTER 7
THE PROMISE

Father Bernard clenched the stone banister on the stairwell where he stood, his head just clearing the first floor landing, high enough to see without being seen. The abbot's knight held Kadriya in a heated embrace. Father Bernard started forward to stop him, but at that moment Kadriya pulled away, said something and disappeared in her chamber.

Sir John approached the stairwell and recognized him. "Father." His expression was guarded, his movements slow, as if he were in a fog.

Fog, indeed. If the priest had a bucket of cold water, he would have splashed him with it. "I would see you in the church."

Minutes later the front door of the church swung open, causing the candles to flicker, and the knight entered, looking slightly hesitant.

Father Bernard gave him an appraising look. "What possible reason could you have, Sir John, for being in Kadriya's private quarters at this hour? With her alone?"

He possessed at least the decency to look guilty. "I feared she might try to escape."

"From her chamber? Would she not first have to pass by the great hall, stop at the stables for her horse and clear the gate before doing so? Why would you deem it necessary to go abovestairs? Or think you have that right?"

Sir John opened his mouth to speak.

"Before deception corrupts you further, knight, I saw the two of you. Embracing. How dare you taint her with scandal, when no man would have her as it is?" The words rushed out before he could stop them.

The knight's brow furrowed. "What mean you?"

Father Bernard ignored the probe. "If you cannot find it in your heart to help her, stay you away from her."

"What do you mean, no man will have her?"

"We have made you welcome. If you cannot comport yourself with the dignity your station demands . . . Zounds, man. What of your vows?"

Sir John's eyes flashed. "What of them? I am here to protect the church."

"I've sworn knights to service. I know the vows. You vow to protect widows and orphans, and who could be more orphaned than Kadriya, losing her mother in the year of her birth and unclaimed by her father?"

He raised a brow. "Poor Kadriya? Raised in the comforts of a nobleman's castle? I have known poverty, father, and that woman bears no scars. Her eyes are clear, her bones are even, her hands soft."

"So we get to the crux of it. You deem her mollycoddled and selfish, playing pranks to fill her hours?"

"Is it not true? She claims loyalty to Lord Tabor then runs off with the Gypsies and brings shame to those who harbored her, educated her."

Father Bernard hesitated. The facts did place Kadriya in a poor light. Closing his eyes, Father Bernard prayed to master his anger and help this man find compassion. "That young woman," he began, and, hearing his voice break, he checked his emotions and started over. "I have known this dear girl since she was seven summers. She came here in wide-eyed innocence, eager to accept Christ as her savior, sharp-witted and willing to learn our language." He pointed to the small apse. "See that narrow section of stained glass, above? And there, that small patch to the left of the cross? Kadriya was just ten when she climbed the ladder and repaired that panel for me."

Wynter's expression softened for a moment. "But where Teraf is concerned, she'll betray you, too, Father."

"Since she reached her terms, many self-professed gentlemen have pursued her for her beauty. Their motives proved shameful. None saw her good heart and soul, only her mixed blood. Teraf was the only one who spoke for her. The only one. For that she's thankful and loyal. Yes."

Father Bernard traced a section of the stained glass, running his finger over the lead outlining the tunic of St. John the Baptist. "She came to me a young heathen, and she donned the white robe of baptism and received the light of Christianity. She has been worshipful since. She has brought joy."

The knight frowned.

"She's troubled, and with good reason. We all have our good and bad stretches, don't we? In her seventeenth year I saw her so sick I administered last rites. I almost lost her then, and I won't lose her to you now, with your short-sighted fears about her Gypsy blood."

The knight raised a brow. "She chose Teraf. Her future is in France with the Gypsies. She cares not for the education and faith you've given her. She forsakes it all to be with him. She is not yours to lose." His tone was cold.

Father Bernard nodded. "You're right. She is not mine." He pointed at him, speaking deliberately. "Nor is she yours."

John closed the door of the church, strode past the portcullis and bridge on his way to the stables. Just as the headaches had passed, this new headache plagued him, this bewitching woman with many allies and many more problems. The half moon floated high in the sky, a haunting reminder of time passing, time which should be spent finding the chalice. He rubbed his shoulder muscles, taut as a dulcimer string. The night was all but spent and sleep would be futile.

He found Dover and gave him a pat of greeting. "How fare you, friend?" The horse moved forward as if friendly but nipped at his hand.

John jerked his hand from danger and thumped Dover on the nose. "Don't bite me, you devil."

Failing to claim flesh, Dover turned away.

"Grumpy again. But I've been occupied. We travel soon and you'll have more of me than you want." He pulled a brush from the hook and started grooming. Gentle circles, a few kind words, more firm brushing by the shoulder, where he liked it, and the horse was leaning in to him for more, all forgiven.

Giving, receiving. Trusting. So unlike the temperament of a certain perplexing woman.

Sweet saints. What an evening. What a day. That infernal stool-game. Her eyes flashed in his memory, her tiny foot fluttering in the air like a squirrel's tail, teasing him. Her arms crossed, her hair, flowing over the tops of her breasts in that red gown.

Desire slammed into his veins again and he clenched his fists, trying to regain control.

What had he been thinking? Egad, and what was she doing to him? Sweet savior, he'd kissed a Gypsy. And it had been thrilling, her mouth warm and responsive as it was beautiful, her body strong. Rich with an appetite fit for a man's dreams. He'd heard stories about the Gypsies, the enchantments, the magic. Certes it must be true, for in the span of a few days she'd rendered him senseless. She was so skilled at it, she had enchanted Sharai and Lord Tabor. None the mystery he'd run off to France, likely to clear his head from the two of them. Even Maude had slipped under her power, and the priest had fallen hopelessly to her sway. And Teraf?

Nay. John had seen him at the monastery before the theft, and again at the horse fair. Teraf bore charm and a keen eye for valuables, but he hadn't treated Kadriya with respect and love, as these people did. Teraf had treated Kadriya like a finely bred pet.

Did she love him? Likely not. He was just a last resort for her. She could not love Teraf—John licked his lips, remembering—and kiss him in that manner.

And what of himself? He'd responded all right. He'd done all but bray like a hart in heat, and with the good father there, watching. Sweet mercy. Would the priest mention that to the abbot, along with his litany of praise for Kadriya's virtues, and deliver a full report of how Kadriya had felled John and his knights with kettle hooks?

John smacked the brush on a support beam. He must focus on his duties. He would deliver her to the abbey and get on with his search for Erol and the chalice. And in all cases keep his distance from the woman from here on.

Just after matins the next morning, John visited the market. He needed to catch the merchants before they abandoned their stalls for the harvest games. Not that John would partake of any game or frivolity this day. He was done with games and intrigue and heated caresses in the night. *And bewitching foreigners.* He stopped at the armorer's stall, where the young craftsman straightened the dents in John's breastplate. He moved on, selecting cheese rounds, dried strips of mutton, fresh ale and hard bread for the trip. They would leave today for the abbey.

John paid for his provisions, gave instructions for delivery to the knight's quarters, and strode toward the bridge to the castle.

Tall, half-woman, half-child, half-Gypsy Faith raced up to

him, tearing at his surcoat. "Sir John," she cried. "Help me. It's Joya."

Joya, the little imp with the twinkle in her eyes. "What's happened?"

"Her arm. It's stuck in the lift that raises the wool to the storage loft."

"Have you told Sharai?"

"There's no time. Hurry!"

The sun rose higher. Morning was burning away, but fear glittered in Faith's eyes. The images of gears, mangled arms and a helpless child flickered in his mind. "Which way?"

Faith pointed and they ran past the cooper's shop, turning left at the alehouse.

"There," Faith said, breathless, pointing at a tall stone building.

John dashed to the door and entered, searching for a sign of Joya. The earthen floors were packed and clean, no young girl in sight. A tinge of hay and horse-dung odor lingered in the air. Scanning the walls, John noticed feed stalls and windows for ventilation, the area large enough to shelter two dozen horses, but still no evidence of a trapped little girl.

In the center of the room a large winding gear had been installed to lift the wool bales to storage. A raised platform locked into a large opening to the first floor. He thought of the dimple-faced Joya and a flash of anxiety needled him. "Is she in there?"

"Nay. Upstairs." Faith led him to a narrow stone stairway and fumbled with the door.

"Make haste."

She grunted and struggled with the handle. "I'm trying."

John grew impatient. "Step aside." He pounded the handle down and punched the door open with his leg. The door gave easily.

Faith wedged past him. "Joya? Joya, dear we're here."

John hurried past a wall of barrels and scanned the rest of the area, mostly empty at this time of the year save for stacks of eel and rabbit traps and partial bales of wool that rested in the far corner. "Joya?"

John heard footsteps on the stairs. Kadriya and Henry, the messenger Faith had taken a shine to after stool-ball, rushed in and promptly disappeared behind the barrels.

Kadriya's face was pale, her breath rushed. "Where is she?" She saw John and her eyes darkened. "What are you doing here?"

"I came to help."

"You are not needed. Leave us."

"If her arm is caught in the gears you will need me," he insisted.

"A shame we can't be as all-wise and all-knowing as you, Sir John. No, we don't need you." She spun around to speak with Faith. "Where's Joya?" Her brows furrowed, and she looked behind the barrels. "Faith? Henry?"

John looked behind the stack of eel traps. "Faith?"

The door slammed. From the other side, a metal bolt clanged into position.

Their eyes met.

Realization widened her eyes.

They rushed to the door, trying it.

John cursed. "Locked."

"Faith, open the door," Kadriya demanded.

"Nay. Not until you make peace." Joya's voice lilted from the other side of the door.

Kadriya pounded on the door. "Joya. You cried wolf again. Your mother will hear about this, and you'll be tied to your chamber for the rest of the festival. Is that what you want?"

" 'Tis you who are confined, Kadriya." Joya giggled, and

Faith and Henry laughed.

John nudged her away. "Let me deal with this. Henry. I am a knight in service. Punishment for detaining me will be dear to both you and your family. Open the door now."

"He cannot hear you, Sir John," Faith said. "He's not here. Never was," she said with mock innocence. "He's at the games playing camp ball."

A horn sounded.

"Faith, listen," said Joya. "The games have begun. Kadriya, we're going to get Prince Malley ready for his show."

"No. Joya!"

"This is what momma does to us when we fight. Solve your problems," said Faith. "We'll be back."

Sir John pounded the door. "Open this door!"

The sound of their footsteps faded.

"The little churls. And Henry. He'll suffer for this."

Kadriya put her hands on her hips. "You dealt with that quite smoothly."

He ignored her and walked past the barrels. He should not have been so easily tricked, but his fear for Joya had distracted him. He studied the lift. Loath to ask Kadriya's help for anything, he eyed the workings. It appeared to be a simple gear design. Thinking he might be able to lower the loading platform manually and exit that way, he tugged at the chain but it wouldn't budge.

"It unlocks from below," she said. "Even so, the release is secured by another lock, and only Will and Lord Tabor hold the keys."

Remembering what her anger had led to the night before, he disregarded her. He would not look at her, engage her in argument, or in any way fuel her aggression.

She bent over and reached through the small knee-high window by the wool bales, waving to anyone who might see.

"Help. Let us out." The thin fabric of her orange gown afforded a tantalizing outline of her bottom, and each wave of her arm caused a spell-binding motion.

He tore his gaze away, focusing his attention on the storage hooks on the north wall. "Cease your yelling and listen."

She paused. "Stop ordering me. Listen to what?"

He gestured out the window. Cheering, barking dogs and laughter floated up to them from the nearby fields, where a couple of hundred souls had gathered for camp ball. A large wave of shouting rose. "Someone has taken possession of the ball. They're running to the river to score. They can't hear us."

She nodded. "And with all that activity I doubt we'll be missed."

She pulled a short barrel from the stacks and sat down. "Why did you come? Why did you not just enlist the help of Will or Sir Cyrill? Had you minded your own business—"

"Do not harp," he interrupted. "I was concerned about Joya."

"Why? She's naught but a thieving Gypsy."

"Are you going to sing that song again? She's just a young girl."

"But still a Gypsy."

"She has English blood."

"Hah." She pounced on that like a hound on a soup bone. "So she's a diluted Gypsy, is that it? Only half as bad?"

"You're like a stubborn mosquito. Feed, or be gone."

"What's that supposed to mean? You need to be bled? Methinks so, bled and purged of your stubborn ideas."

"Such as?"

"Such as your idea that I'm half heathen, half human. That I deliberately attacked you and killed your knight. That I deserve to hang." Her voice caught on the last part.

The collar of his tunic seemed suddenly tight. He adjusted it. He must not engage her. The outcome would be a calamity.

The moment hung heavy. It would be wise to find a more neutral topic.

He scanned the walls searching for an escape he knew didn't exist. Leaning against the wall, his eyes fell on the lift mechanism. "This lift, this storage building, is most canny. The wool is stored high, away from the moisture. The windows are small so thieves cannot steal it when the gear is locked down. The stones cannot be burned by enemies. Your Lord Tabor is resourceful."

Her full lips began to curve into a smile.

It was as if a spring breeze stirred his heart.

But her smile was strained, her expressive pensive, as if her thoughts carried an edge of pain.

He could not ignore the woe in her eyes. Though terrified of heights, he swallowed and took the plunge. "What is it?"

"You see all of life in this way, don't you? Vulnerable or defensible. Fortified or breached. All based on power. So strong, but you battle constant threat." Her eyes narrowed in an expression of fresh awareness. "You're never at ease, are you?"

His collar chafed again, but he could not adjust it under her watchful gaze. Truth be told, he was never at ease with her. "You speak in riddles."

"You admire Lord Tabor's ingenuity. He's a fine man. Finest I know. He often saw possibilities like this . . ." She gestured to the lift. ". . . when none others did. Possibilities in people, too. He used to come to the St. Giles Fair every summer and he always visited Etti, the Gypsy woman who took Sharai in. Sharai was an escaped slave, did you know?"

So Sharai had gone from slave to noblewoman. The story grew more impossible, and Kadriya wandered, directionless, with her words. He shook his head. Women.

"Don't you see? It's where Lord Tabor met Sharai. He noted the color of her skin, of course, but he had seen dark skin before, on slaves in France, on merchants in Navarre, and even on the nobles of Castile, so it did not startle him."

"You infer that your skin color startles me?" *Or that I am not as worldly as your noble patron.* He made a scoffing sound.

"Maybe 'unsettle' is more accurate. To Tabor, it was just part of Sharai's beauty, something to admire. 'Twas not her skin that he loved, but the woman beneath it."

So the priest was right. Beautiful as she was, Kadriya had been rejected by men because of her Gypsy blood. "Life is not fair. I could tell you tales of battle that would make you weep. 'Tis best to forget them."

"Aye. If you can."

She fell silent and the laughter and noise of the distant games filtered in through the windows.

After a time she rose. Drifting around the room, she spied a bracing wood used to bundle the wool bales. She fanned herself with it to stir the air, which had become stifling in the day's growing heat. She stopped, strolled, then stopped again, as if working up courage to speak.

Curiosity welled in his mind. Unlike most women, she was not loose with her tongue, rambling about rugs or fashion or gossip. He inspected the barrels, noting the skill of the coopers who had shaped the staves and secured the bands. Giving her time. The more he thought on it, the more he realized she wasted words on no one, and words were ready to burst from her.

He paced to release the worry building inside him. Moving to the next barrel, he ran his hand along the top.

Her small hand covered his and stopped his motion.

The sensation of her flesh, warm and soft against his, shivered through his hand, up his arm, into his chest. Her green-flecked eyes made astonishingly direct contact, revealing a delicate vulnerability he had never seen before.

His mind splintered like old wood and his feet seemed to lose firm contact with the floor beneath him.

She started to speak, but hesitated. Straightening, she began. "I must ask something of you."

By the look on her face, 'twould be no small matter. The air he'd just taken into his chest lodged there, unwilling to leave, suspended in a strange, unspeakable hope he had never wanted to feel again. "Go on."

"I need your help." She coughed the words out like tenants offered their tithes in years of drought, grim and out of sheer necessity. Still, she needed him, and something deep inside his chest slipped into a better place. He wanted to help her.

"You made me a promise in the forest," she said. "I have decided to hold you to it."

"What promise?"

"You said, 'Release me, and I can offer you freedom.' "

John jerked his hand free from hers. She asked for the unattainable. "Nay." He'd feared for his life when Rill was set on killing him so the Gypsies could escape. "I made that promise out of desperation. Your priest released me, not you."

"I never released you from my care. Are you not indeed still in it?"

Still nourished and sheltered by her household. By the saints, she was right. After all these days, he still felt a need to escape. Even now, he was held captive in a sweltering storage building. "Forsooth." A dagger of suspicion pierced him. "Were you in on this scheme to trap me here?"

Her mouth puckered in annoyance. "Do you really think I would choose to spend the day sweating in a wool house? Just to be with you?" She raised her hand to him. "Never you mind. Don't even answer."

"Why should I offer you freedom?"

"Because you vowed you would."

He recalled his quiet despair when Rill made it clear he would kill him. "I mumbled nonsense."

"But you must have had some reason to think you could," she pressed. "With your friendship with the abbot, are you in a position to offer someone freedom?"

"Why must you carp like this?"

Her eyes flashed with sudden fury. "Curse you! Because it's my life. You're intent on hanging me, for God's sake. Do you think I don't lie awake through the night, thinking about it? Hearing every word you've said since you first took Teraf? How can you offer me freedom?"

"I could speak to the abbot on your behalf."

"He trusts your judgment?"

"Aye."

"So you can. And since you promised, I'm asking you to do so."

"What? Because of you I almost died. And you did not release me."

"I released you the best way I could. I saved your life."

"After you almost killed me."

"As did Dury," she persisted. "And Maude took up arms to protect you from Rill as well."

He saw her bruise, still swelling part of her right jaw, the bruise she suffered defending his life in the forest, and a queasy feeling tugged at his stomach, the same sensation he suffered when sailing to France. Father Bernard would make his case known to the abbot: Kadriya, a God-fearing Christian woman who saved John's life, only to be ravished by him in her private chamber. "You speak the truth, but twist it to suit your need." *Whose need? Who's twisting the truth here?* John fought to still his conscience.

"Is it not so with your logic? Think. You believe the thieves to be Teraf and Erol. Teraf is at the monastery, awaiting trial. Erol is somewhere with the chalice." She paused for a moment. "Once we're charged with murder you cannot help us. More important, we cannot help you then. But you can spare us the charge by deeming the deaths at Blackwater Point accidental, which they were."

"You overlook one vital point. 'Twas you who planned the ambush."

Her jaw dropped. "What?"

"I heard you say so yourself to Maude, in the forest. I can overlook the others who joined you, but someone must pay for leading them to attack our knights."

"All this time you've thought I was their leader? A woman?" She shook her head. "Murat led the tribe that night. He was second in command after Teraf and the one who made the decision to follow you and attack. He ordered the other Gypsies to join him. I suggested using the kettle hooks and Prince Malley. We wished only to distract and unseat you and, in the confusion, free Teraf." She frowned. "Don't look at me like that. Ask Dury. He knows."

"You expect me to believe a Gypsy?"

"Fie. You may think me many things, but come now, do you seriously think I can domineer a tribe of stubborn Gypsy men?"

"I saw you in the forest. Forsooth you're capable of accomplishing anything you set your mind to doing."

Her frown changed to an expression of pleasant surprise, and she blinked. "Why, thank you." A soft smile played on her full lips, and John realized the gift he'd given. In spite of her bloodline, he felt no wish to take it back.

"But I vow," she said, "I did not make the decision. Murat did, and he paid for that decision with his life. Justice has been served." She took a deep breath and paused. "I hear the bishop is coming to the abbey for Michaelmas, which leaves you just a sennight to find the chalice before he arrives."

"How do you know this?"

"No matter. You need the chalice, you need my help, and I need yours. Speak for me to the abbot and I will help you find Erol and the chalice."

She had placed his life in peril, but she'd also saved his life. He could not deny that. "How do I know you will do this?"

She laid her hand on his forearm and squeezed it firmly. "Because I give you my word."

Her eyes simmered with determination.

And what of Teraf? He could not voice the question for he knew the answer. He covered her small hand with his. "Then I give you mine. I will speak for you, and I will take you to him."

Giggling, Joya tossed another piece of apple toward Prince Malley's opened mouth.

Prince Malley caught the wedge of apple in his mouth and ate it. With a hop and a squeal, he tossed a slice to Faith, who waited, open-mouthed. It landed on her eye, and the girls laughed again.

In spite of their prank with John, Kadriya had to laugh, too. She sat at the front table before the fading bonfire with Father Bernard, the girls, the monkey and, at the other tables, some high street merchants and their families.

Joya approached, wrapping her small arms around Kadriya and kissing her neck. "We love Prince Malley. Can we keep him? Please?"

Kadriya pulled Joya's arms forward and kissed her hands, keenly aware that this little girl could melt her heart and resolve. "Yes, you naughty girl. You may keep him."

Joya and Faith cried out with excitement, and the monkey screeched and smashed a handful of apple slices on Joya's head.

Unsuccessfully suppressing a smile, Kadriya swept Joya's hair clean. "But you must use the commands he's been taught. Keep him obedient. And you can only have him until Teraf and I return from Cerne. Prince Malley is his, remember."

Firelight flickered over Father Bernard's smile.

"Also remember," Kadriya cautioned, "that you promised never to pull a trick like that again. You left us locked in that storehouse for four steaming hours."

"We're sorry," Joya said.

"It worked out well," Kadriya conceded. "But it might not have and you must swear to it."

The girls gave the Romani fist-to-heart gesture that sealed their oath. "We promise."

Kadriya hugged them. The ebony sky pulsed with the mystery of endless stars, and an uncertainty filled her, a dread for what they might find at Cerne Abbey.

A maid circulated among the outside tables, pouring last year's harvest mead. She poised the pitcher over Kadriya's pewter chalice. "More?"

"Thank you, no. We leave at first light and I must sleep."

Sharai circled the table, gathering Michaelmas daisies into a hand bouquet, a secret smile lighting her oval face. "Kadriya, I would see you in the solar."

Kadriya caught the quiet excitement in her eyes and bade Father Bernard and the girls a good night.

In the solar, Sharai seated Kadriya at the window. "Before you leave, Sprig, I have a surprise for you. Now, sit you there and close your eyes."

Kadriya did as told, excitement growing, as if she were young again and it was time for gifts of the new year. She heard the creak of a trunk being opened, a rustle of fabric, a step toward her. "Open," Sharai announced.

What magic had she wrought with her needle? Kadriya wondered. She opened her eyes.

"Your wedding gown, Sprig."

By the saints! In all the difficulties, Kadriya had forgotten about it. 'Twas a vision from sweet dreams, a shimmering ivory gown of the lightest whisper of silk, sewn with tiny stitches of gold at the neckline in a delicate statement of English fashion, and covered with a surcoat of crimson satin and black sleeves trimmed in red, the perfect Romani frock portending good fortune. She released a large sigh. "It's beautiful, Sharai." She scooped up the fabric, smooth and cool, so fine it was almost liquid in her hands.

Sharai pointed to two forest-green buttons, on which two triple circles of silver were sewn. "The Tabor coat of arms. And here, on the tip of the left sleeve, four French deniers from the fairs in Troyes, and on the right sleeve, four English coins, so you'll not forget your heritage." Her voice dropped, thick with emotion.

Kadriya draped the dress on the window seat. Tears slipped without warning. "I'll never forget my heritage, and I'll never forget you." She hugged the one person who had cared for her since birth, a friend, a sister, a mother, the only family she had ever known.

Sharai stroked her hair. *"Ves tacha."* My beloved, she crooned.

Kadriya lingered in the safety of her arms. "France is so far."

Sharai gently disengaged. "You know Lord Tabor and I will visit."

Kadriya wiped her eyes and retrieved the dress, admiring it. "It's everything I could have hoped for. Thank you." She pulled away. "Let us hang it in the cedar wardrobe."

Sharai bit her lower lip. "Nay, Sprig. I would have you take it with you."

"To the monastery? Whyever for?"

Sharai studied her nails. "In case you have to leave, um, abruptly, I would that you have your wedding gown."

"You think him guilty."

"Fie! If I thought him guilty, would I send you to him with your wedding dress? I hope he's innocent, but at his release he may be so angry that he will have nothing more to do with English traditions or people, and wish to leave straight for France. If he does, so must you, and you will have your gown."

"Oh, Sharai. Such turmoil. And the wedding. Cannot Father Bernard come, too? I would that he wed us."

"We have been through this. Teraf refuses the faith, so Father Bernard cannot."

Kadriya touched the prayer beads in her purse, rolling the smooth beads through the fabric. "Teraf does not deny me my faith, but I wish—"

"You will face many challenges. So long as you love each other, you will find a way."

Kadriya held the dress to her body and swirled, watching the fabric sway, shining, in the candle light. "Do you miss it, Sharai?"

"What?"

"The laughter of the tribe? Cooking and cutting pegs together—bathing the horses in the river? Falling asleep to the nicker of horses, under the stars? And especially the music."

Sharai smiled. "Aye, the busy roads, people from faraway places. We had wonderful times together, you and I. Winchester, Troye, Marseilles. But you forget. I'm of the *vatrasi,* the settled Roma. Teraf is of the *corturari,* the travelers." Her expression grew wistful. "I miss the music. But we have our minstrels."

"Not the same."

"Aye, Romani music touches the soul. And the closeness, the devotion we shared in the tribe. But there's no Tabor in that world, Sprig." Her eyes sparkled and her face softened. "I had no world when I met Tabor, so it mattered not which one I chose. If Tabor were a Rom, so would I be, but he's here so I'm here. You cannot force love. It simply . . ." She raised her shoulders and palms, searching for the word. "It simply comes." Her eyebrows lifted inquiringly. "You do love Teraf, don't you, Sprig?"

Kadriya traced the triple circle coat of arms on the wedding gown. "It's not the way it was with you and Tabor. It's like a spell, you with him and he with you. With Teraf I'm always happy to see him. I feel safe."

"Do you feel safe now?"

"Nay, but not through any fault of his." She thought about the young man who had shown her honor, the man she would wed. "When I close my eyes I see Teraf the way I first met him, riding, his black hair flying, his head thrown back, laughing. He has this joy about life and an easy confidence, whether he's settling disputes or dancing or fighting in the mud over a dice game."

"Perchance you'd like to be more like him?"

Kadriya thought of the weeks last fall with Teraf, with the buyers, at fireside, at council. His tongue never faltered as hers did. His words always flowed, entertaining and sure, no matter the person he met. Even with Englishmen he managed to communicate his enthusiasm. She admired how capable he was at selling bidders on a certain horse's strength or intelligence. The way he lived his life in precisely the way he wanted rather than yielding to others. When Kadriya was with Teraf, she believed it possible that she could do the same. This belief brought an intoxicating happiness. She wanted to be herself. But how could she tell this to Sharai, who had always been so like Teraf in this way? Sharai would think her weak and foolish.

"I'd like to be free like he is. Not tied to all the rules of life."

"Do you love him?"

Kadriya held the gown between them, focusing on the fine weave of the silk. "I love his spirit, and his—"

"Kadriya." Faith appeared, Father Bernard behind her. "A

messenger just arrived. He said Teraf—"

"Stop, Faith," the priest reprimanded her, stepping ahead. "Our messenger just returned from Cerne Abbey."

He spoke too evenly, too calmly. Kadriya reached for Sharai's hand and found it. "What?"

"Teraf has been found guilty. He is to hang on the morrow."

CHAPTER 8
FAREWELL

Maude stirred from her bed on the kitchen floor. "Kadriya? What are you doing up at this hour?"

Kadriya nestled her torch in the wall sconce and tightened the belt on the green wool traveling gown she had hastily donned. "Shh, Maude, stay you there. I'm here for bread and ale. We're leaving for the abbey."

Maude rose, her red hair matted on the left side from sleep. "Now? Why?"

The leather flasks would not cooperate, and Kadriya's fingers shook as she hurried to open them. "A messenger came. Teraf is to hang on the morrow."

Maude struggled up, straightening her tunic. "Fresh ale is in the barrel to the right," she said, nodding at the casks in the north corner of the kitchen. "I'll pack bread, dried herring. Want some figs, too?"

"Yes, thanks."

She helped Kadriya fill the flasks and swept her away with a gesture. "Go ready your horse. I'll bring the food out."

Kadriya threaded through the empty tables in the bailey, past the church to the stable. Inside, Dover was saddled and Sir John was adjusting Allie's saddle blanket. She met the blue calm in his eyes. "You heard?"

"Aye. It's as I told you."

"Be not smug. He may die."

His eyes darkened. "But for your priest I would have left two days ago. Are you packed?"

She tied the flasks on the saddles. Regretting her outburst, she touched his arm. "Thank you. My bags are ready."

Kadriya visited the girls' chamber, rousing them from their sleep to bid them farewell. "Joya, I trust you will care for my doves. Do not forget."

Joya hugged her. "I'll remember this time. And Prince Malley, too."

"Especially Prince Malley. He gets grumpy if you neglect him, and he can be very naughty."

Faith's green eyes grew wide. "When will you be back?"

"As soon as I can, *ves' tacha.*" She kissed them and assumed a stern position to ward off tears. "Now back to sleep. Morning comes early, and monkeys and doves need tending." She kissed them and hurried to the bailey.

Maude brought the food and gave Kadriya a sound hug to her ample bosom. "Godspeed, Sprig. And remember." She tapped her cheek affectionately and lowered her voice. "Be strong."

Kadriya strapped her bag on the saddle. It held two gowns, personal items and her pouch of poultice and herbs.

Sharai draped Kadriya's wool cloak on her shoulders and handed her an oblong leather bag with a brass handle. "Tie this in with your others," she said, handing the bag to Kadriya.

Kadriya looked at the bag and met Sharai's eyes. Was it the wedding dress?

Intuiting her question, Sharai nodded. "Just in case."

Would she ever wear it? Kadriya blinked back tears. "Thank you, Sharai." She hugged her, aching as the moment of parting loomed. "I don't know when I'll see you again."

"Shush. Send word as soon as you can." She withdrew, wiping away a tear and lowering her voice. "I believe the knight will speak for you as he vowed, but I'm sending Father Bernard and

Sir Thomas, should you need them. Fare thee well, Sprig. Now go. Go!"

Kadriya mounted Allie and urged the horse into a fast canter, following Sir John, Father Bernard, Thomas and Dury past the gate and drawbridge. On the road, she prompted Allie to a gallop. Over twenty miles remained, a journey across meadows, forests, and hills scarred with deep veins of wash-off and wagon ruts that made for perilous travel. She imagined the distant abbey, praying they would arrive in time.

They crested the hill past the village and she slowed, sparing a glance back at the home she'd known for the last dozen years, but the hill obscured the castle. A sense of loss pricked her soul. It was too late for last looks.

Cloaked from the moonlight by a cluster of bushes, Teraf covered his stallion's nose to keep him quiet and waited for the brigands to pass. The back of his neck stung with the knowledge that he had no dagger, and his muscles tensed for flight should the strangers sense him hiding in the bushes.

Speaking in hushed tones, the men passed.

Waiting a safe amount of time, he emerged from his shelter. He had just followed the gentle valley past the abbey and into the village Cerne, surrounded in the distance by towering hills. On the shores of the wide river just outside the village, campfires of the bridge masons and their laborers became visible. Some tents were still lit, and occasional bursts of laughter erupted amid the temporary settlement of a dozen tents.

He tethered his horse, removed two bags from the saddle and stashed one in a dense bush growing out of the ruins of an ancient stone wall some distance away. He continued silently on foot until he spied it. On the back of one of the darkened tents a yellow scarf had been tied to the top grommet. He laughed softly, gloating at his cleverness. The scarf identified Erol's tent.

The monks would never think to look for their precious chalice so close to the monastery, amid a crew of working men. They would never think of the laborers, the nameless, faceless wayfarers who pursued work from village to village, building god palaces and bridges. They would never look here for a thieving Gypsy.

He approached the tent entrance and whistled the call of a forest warbler.

No response. He whistled again.

"Teraf?" Erol's voice. He approached, carrying a torch. The light revealed his ill humor and soiled clothes. Dried crescents of sweat stained his tunic at the chest and underarms and he smelled of toil, mortar and fish. " 'Tis been a sennight. I thought you dead. Where have you been, you dog?"

Teraf silenced him with a gesture. "I have something to show you."

They entered the tent and Erol planted the torch in the dead fire pit. "What do you have?"

Teraf regarded him. "Where's the chalice?"

Erol nodded. "Under the fire."

"Show me."

Erol's eyes flashed. "Do you not trust me?"

"Only as much as you trust me."

At that, Erol laughed. "All right." He shoveled just outside the fire pit and dug into the soil a foot deep, unearthing a canvas-wrapped package. The soot sifted like flour away from the fabric, and he opened it.

The chalice shimmered in the torchlight, a splendid, wide-bellied goblet of pure gold, a foot tall and adorned with eight emeralds, smooth and radiant, their generous size testament to their value. 'Twas a treasure.

Excitement danced in Teraf's veins, and he thought of the fine stallions he would gain with this. His wealth would rival noblemen. But other eyes might see it. "Cover it."

Erol did so. "Where's the tribe? Wait until they see this."

"They won't. They're gone," Teraf said, guessing. He had seen Murat's head roll, and he'd expected to see Rill and Kadriya and the others at the abbey, but they had never come. With the chalice secured, he didn't care. He could catch up with them later, or find another tribe, but for now Teraf had no wish to share any more of this bounty than necessary. Seeing the greed in Erol's eyes, Teraf quickly calculated the price of his next risk.

"But what . . ." Erol stopped, tightening his grip on the chalice. "What do you plan to do with this?"

"Sell it, of course."

"I want my share."

"It's mine. Remember, Erol. I was the one who found it," he lied. He had never told Erol how the Sacristan had left it ripe for the picking. "I risked my life for it, so I'll take it."

"Damn you. Do you know what I've gone through? Look at my hands." He showed his right hand, raw with broken blisters and scrapes. "I've been working like a slave, waiting for you. A stonecutter's son stole my horse, and I have been shut up in this tent like a mother hen, guarding this."

Teraf fought an urge to wince. Erol's stallion was light and fast. "I'm sorry for your loss, but I have something for your suffering. A real prize." Teraf unstrapped a cloth-covered bundle from his leg and unwrapped the cross from the infirmary. "A gift from the sodomite monk."

The silver cross, twice again as tall as Teraf's hand, had been devotedly polished by Eustace's monks, the silver gleaming in the firelight. Sculpted olive leaves swirled the length and width of it, with an embossed circle in the center surrounding four smaller leaves arranged to make a cross within the cross. 'Twas the fine craftsmanship that had initially caught Teraf's eye.

Erol accepted it and hefted the treasure, more intent on its weight than any craftsmanship. His eyes widened in appreciation, but he checked himself and sobered. "But the chalice is worth much more."

"Erol. Think. I was the one who got both of these pieces. I'm sharing one with you. 'Tis fair."

Erol hesitated, playing the game they both as Roma knew so well. One never accepted a first offer, no matter how fair.

"I have no time for parleying, Erol. Take it. The monks and their knights are just a stone's throw away and daylight will come soon."

Still Erol hesitated.

Teraf sighed heavily, making an effort to look annoyed and trapped. "All right. Curse it. Take the cross and take my horse, since you lost yours."

It was a large concession, but Teraf had thought it out carefully and, with his offer, some of the stubborn lines in Erol's face eased. "What else?"

"What in greed's name else do you want?" Teraf glanced down at his rings, one a heavy gold serpent and another a gold cross. He met Erol's covetous gaze. "You want the cross?"

"I want both."

"Die in hell. I keep the serpent."

Satisfied, Erol handed him the chalice.

Equally satisfied, Teraf took it and gave him the ring and the cross. "There. Two crosses. You're twice blessed, my son." Teraf laughed at his joke, swirling his hand in a figure eight in front of his chest, mocking the monks. He stuffed the chalice in his bag.

"Now how do we get out of here with our heads?" Erol asked.

"What? You rob me then ask me to help you escape?"

Erol grinned. "You expected it." He pulled a flask from his belt and offered it. *"Pen,"* he said. *Romani brother.*

"Pen," Teraf echoed, drinking from the flask. The wine

bordered on sour, but he covered his distaste. "The abbot's knights are looking for us, but I have, ah, convinced one of the monks to send them north, toward the horse fair. To get out of here safely, cross the river and go south, away from the big hill. Sail from Poole. It's safer than Weymouth, and you'll find jewelers at High Street who will buy the cross." Teraf paused. As if having an afterthought, he added, "And don't forget your yellow scarf on the tent."

Erol busied himself packing. "Aren't you coming with me?"

"There's one more piece I want from the monastery."

"Fie. You would not dare return."

"They didn't find you, now, did they, right under their noses? And you were so worried. They won't be missing the cross," Teraf said truthfully, "and their knights are chasing after us toward the fair, so the last place they would think to guard would be their own chapel, now, would it not?"

Erol exited the tent, laughing. "You're a madman. Fare thee well."

Teraf stayed in the tent, only touching the threshold to shake his hand. "And to you, my friend. See you in Marseilles."

The half moon lit the narrow, winding trail that led over a series of hills toward the abbey. Kadriya followed Sir John, encouraging Allie as she navigated the ruts and cavities of the well-worn road. Lagging behind due to his horse's timidity was Father Bernard, followed by Dury and Sir Thomas.

Sir John stopped, giving her time to catch up. He sat tall, his broad chest covered with armor, his light hair brushing his shoulders. His every movement conveyed certainty and masculine power. Fortified by his promise, she allowed herself to hope.

"We will get there in time," he said.

"How do you know?"

"I know the route, the abbey schedule, and I know the abbot. Matins at two bells, Lauds at five, and they always run long because the abbot enjoys the hymns. Prime follows, and the abbot never skips his daily meeting. Never. We will have time."

"Thank you."

The briefest of smiles touched his lips and he took the lead, his pauldron plates rubbing against each other in rhythmic, metallic whispers. "Is Teraf a Christian?"

"No."

"Are his parents in his tribe?"

"They live in Boulogne. They can no longer travel."

"Does he have brothers or sisters?"

At the string of questions, she tensed. "No." She would not remind him that Dury was Teraf's cousin. It could be a risk to Dury's life.

"I thought Gypsies had large families."

"So you think we're like so many bees in the hive. Do all nobles have large families?"

"Nay. Some are not blessed with any children."

She glared at the scarred surface of his armor and the back of his opinionated head. "So it is with Gypsies. Or do you think we have spells for everything?"

The moon cast long shadows and they rode in silence, following the curve of the primitive road cut in the side of the hill that towered over the valley, curving down to their left like the sides of a deep bowl, the slope velvet black and treacherously wet with dew.

"Have you known Teraf long?"

Suspicion needled her. "Why all these questions?"

"If I am to help talk him out of the noose, it would be useful to have some information about him."

"You would do that? Speak for him?"

He did not respond.

She wanted to bite her tongue to make it more socially graceful, but her back hurt so from the uneven riding that she was loath to deliberately create any more pain, and his questions were tying her stomach in knots.

"I would not speak for him," the knight said. "But I might present some of his attributes—should he have any—if it would help you."

Overcome, she touched the neckline of her gown. His concern for Joya had given her pause and she welcomed his newfound respect for her. And now this gesture. Under all that metal and ferocity might rest some dignity and honor.

"From what I know about him thus far," he continued, "I would not have much good to say. He's a heathen tribal king who puts his people at risk, and he has parents in Boulogne." He turned so she could see his profile. "And he owns a noisy monkey."

She smiled. "Thank you for your help. Teraf is a good king to his tribe. His uncle, Count Aydin, first brought the tribe here for the fall fair at St. Giles. Teraf has developed a better route for us so we can attend more fairs."

The knight grunted. "A score this year, twenty score next. I saw it in France. They don't belong here."

They. It warmed her that he no longer thought of her as a heathen foreigner, but she had cast her lot with the Roma and felt guilt that she would be even momentarily happy to be distinguished from them. "You'd be pleased to know, Sir John, that Teraf has protected your borders. He guards the English market from other Gypsies in France."

"How so?"

"When the tribe is in France he forbids them to speak of the lucrative fairs across the sea."

"Not as a favor to England. 'Tis a favor to himself."

"And his tribe. He thinks of his tribe. He also finds good

summer markets so we can earn our passage here in the fall. He provides for his parents and can train a horse without breaking its spirit. He is canny at assessing a horse's value at first glance."

"So they make their money with horses?"

"Breeding. Selling. Racing."

"And gaming." He uttered the word with the same venomous judgment he had shown when first she met him.

She would not elaborate on Teraf's ability to profit from men who knew little of horses but loved the thrill of a gamble. "Some," she admitted.

"Then pray tell what was he doing at the abbey?"

"He was never at the abbey. Teraf told you."

"He stayed at the fair?"

"Aye."

"You were with him? You know this to be true?"

Kadriya rubbed her arm, feeling a chill. "Need I remind you that you found me there?"

"But I checked with the fair master. You didn't arrive there until Friday. The chalice was stolen on Thursday morn."

Her heart beat faster in her chest. "I trust him, Sir John. 'Tis something I fear you have difficulty doing with anyone, but believe me, people do trust each other."

The trail opened up and the stands of trees to the left grew more dense. Sir John stopped. "Let the others catch up."

Father Bernard, Dury and Sir Thomas joined them, forming a circle.

"The road has been blessedly clear," said Father Bernard. "I had feared highwaymen."

Dury looked to Kadriya. "What did he say?"

"The road," she said. "He's relieved the road is clear."

"They call this a road?" Dury laughed and spat neatly over his horse's right shoulder. His hair, like Teraf's but greying, fell in undisciplined streams over his shoulders. "This is a path.

One wrong step and we're headed to hell in the valley."

Sir John frowned. "What did he say?"

Kadriya interpreted and Father Bernard glared at Dury.

Dury glanced at the priest. "Sorry."

Father Bernard nodded, shifting uneasily in his saddle. "It is one of the less pleasant paths I've ridden."

"Really." Sir John's voice lilted in challenge. "You whimper like women, yet the woman among us has no complaint. Mayhap you should follow her example." He spurred his horse neatly away, the muscles of his legs flexing in the moonlight, the horse and man moving together effortlessly. "The footing is more sure from here on, but we'll need to cross the forest to reach the bridge over Chase River." With a touch of his rein, he and Dover disappeared into a dense stand of oak and pine.

Kadriya pressed Allie to follow. The sharp, silver light of the moon became obscured under the leaves, faded but for small patches that broke through the canopy, lighting the trail.

Padding softly through the carpet of old pine needles and freshly fallen leaves, Kadriya weighed the risk of trust. Sharai had always been there for her, as she had been for Sharai. As a young girl, Kadriya had trusted no one else. Who else was there to trust? Dangerous men who slashed each other with swords, drawing blood and death? The Romani men with a peculiar fire in their eyes who tried to lure Kadriya away from Sharai? Or the knaves and shadowy strangers at the fair who drove Sharai to give Kadriya her own dagger and teach her how to use it.

When she first met Lord Tabor, she'd feared him, too, but his eyes were sincere and in time he'd proven himself worthy of trust. And Father Bernard. And Teraf.

So many thought her foolish to trust him. And now, God help her, she was trusting this knight's word. Did she dare trust them both?

Fear of the unknown chilled her spine and she pulled her

cloak tighter. They reached a clearing, the site of a recent fire. Black corpses of once mighty oak and linden trees pierced the mist, their branches twisting toward her. Were they snaring her, entangling her in death at the monastery, taking her to the end of her dreams?

She heard a scream in her ears—but no, it was just fear. She urged Allie onward into the shadows.

Eustace foraged in the bush at the base of a crumbling old wall. He'd broken his vow to the Gypsy and from a safe distance he'd followed Teraf from the monastery. The secret the scheming thief carried was too dark, too threatening, to risk setting it free. He spotted a canvas bag. Pushing a branch clear, he lifted it. There on the bottom was a permanent stamp of a cross and St. Augustine's spring. The symbol of the abbey.

He slipped the loop free and glanced inside. Aye. It contained the provisions he had given Teraf.

A soft whinny sounded to his right. It was a horse, tethered nearby, a tan horse with three white socks and a light tail. Teraf's horse.

Just fifty yards away, a temporary camp had been pitched by the masons while they repaired the Cerne River wall and bridge. Teraf was hiding in one of those tents. What a fool, taking refuge so close to the abbey. Teraf was not as smart as he pretended to be.

He rubbed his eyes, burning from several sleepless nights. Each day he'd suffered through hymns at Lauds and passed the sacrament storage wardrobe, thinking of the emerald chalice, how the theft that Eustace himself had invited now threatened the abbot's friendship with the bishop and in turn the funding for the new church, as well as future endowments.

With each sun's rising, he wondered if this was the day he would be found out, disgraced and banished from the abbey.

Self-loathing heated his neck. Fooled by a witless, Godless Gypsy. He removed the bag. The Gypsy would not leave with food. Indeed, if Eustace wished to maintain his reputation and position at the abbey, Teraf could not leave with his life.

He took refuge behind a bush not far from the horse, where he could see the masons' tents. He huddled, gripping a sharp scythe, broken into a makeshift sword. When Teraf came out to claim his horse, Eustace would put an end to the Gypsy's adventures.

They stopped for water at the Sheplet River. Impending dawn turned the surrounding meadow and trees a silver blue.

Sir Thomas and Father Bernard had stopped several yards upstream, tending to their business.

Dury lingered with Kadriya and John. He glanced at Sir John. "Do you wish me to stay?" he asked her in whispered Romani. "You're the only woman here." His eyes lowered and his voice trailed off.

Touched at his gallantry, Kadriya summoned a casual air to prevent any further discomfiture on Dury's part. "Sir John is honorable. If not I have my dagger." She tapped it to confirm her words and touched his arm. "Thank you. If I need you, you'll know."

Dury nodded. "After Blackwater Point, I believe so." He left, heading upstream toward the other men.

Kadriya dismounted and strode to Sir John, who was bent at the riverbank, refilling his water flask. The grasses, cold and glistening, soaked her leather shoes. "Why do we stop now? The horses are still fresh, and we must be close to the abbey."

John rose and looked down at her. "Just a mile. I—" He paused. "I needed to talk with you before we get there."

She gave him a gesture of dismissal. "Let's go, before it's too late."

"Have you thought more about Teraf leaving the horse fair before you arrived? That he might have been at the abbey when the chalice was stolen?" His manner was gentle, which disturbed her more than if he had been his usual, dark self.

"He swore to me he was not."

"I'm sorry to tell you, but—"

"I trust him."

"Kadriya, he was there. I saw him there, several times, with Erol. Before the theft."

"You lie."

His brow creased in concern. "I swear by Saint Christopher it's true." His blue eyes met hers with no hesitation.

His certainty further bruised her hopes. She spun away from him, jerked the flask from her saddle and dipped it in the river, watching the water bubble into the container, trying to wash the significance of his words away.

"I'm sorry, Kadriya."

She swallowed. "You're mistaken."

"You don't know him. He's clever, but deceptive."

"He's my intended."

"You cling to him as a last hope, but you do not love him."

She jumped to her feet. "I'm trying to save his life. He may be dead before we get there, and if he is, an innocent man will have died because of you."

"Innocent? He was found guilty in court."

"Ha! Found guilty by the shade of his skin."

"He's a heathen and a thief. I cannot fathom your charitable attitude toward him. He's part of the rabble that needs to leave England."

"I'm part of that 'rabble,' too."

"Nay. You have English blood in you, you're God-fearing and learned. Why do you insist on allying with them?"

"I am to wed him."

"Wed a man you don't know? You were raised back there, in Coin Forest. You said yourself they're here just for a week or two during the autumn fair. You've known him a couple of weeks. At most. Hardly enough to know him. His true character."

"Two weeks at St. Giles, two weeks at the horse fair. And you forget, I grew up with them."

"Not him. And what can you possibly remember of the Gypsies? You were just seven when you joined Lord Tabor's household."

"Oh. So I haven't known them long enough to form a judgment. And what of you? You have no problem judging them, but how much time have you spent with them? Or me? Yet you don't hesitate to judge both."

He pulled back as if attacked. "What of Sharai? She knows you, and Gypsies. Does she approve of this marriage?"

Kadriya hesitated. *She had not given her blessing.* "What does that have to do with Teraf?"

"He has no land, no reliable means to support you or your children. Does your patron, Tabor, approve?"

"We don't need land. Now, stop. We need to get to the abbey."

"Do you love him?"

Stunned with his blunt question, she hesitated.

"Then why do you want to marry him?"

She hated him then. A dull pain throbbed in her chest from his stripping her bare and judging her, a pain quickly displaced by anger, and she lashed out. "You! A hired killer for a monastery in a sad, poor village. You, all alone, hiding behind your armor, licking your trencher as if it were your last meal."

His face grew ashen.

Fear rang in her ears, dread that he was right, that the dying

132

hope she held in her heart would soon be crushed. "What would you know of love?"

CHAPTER 9
CERNE MONASTERY

Kadriya shifted in the saddle and rubbed the small of her back, sore from hours on the road.

Sir John rode just ahead with his usual, infuriating certainty, his golden hair brushing against his armor, his big hands light on the reins and offering an occasional glimpse of his profile. From time to time he talked to Dover, giving the animal brisk pats of affection. The gentle undertones of his voice reminded her that beneath the armor and accusations, the fierce knight had feelings. And she had hurt him. She'd seen it in his eyes.

Shame gnawed at her. He had been concerned, and she'd lost her temper at his probing questions. Her words had been harsh. She wished she could take them back, but it was too late for that. She would apologize at first opportunity.

They cleared a hill and the valley stretched out before them in the early morning light. The river and surrounding hills cradled the small village of Cerne. It snuggled like a bird's nest amid the green fields and lush stands of red maples and oaks, wrapped neatly with a sturdy wall of stone. Was Teraf still alive within that wall, or was he—

She pushed the thought away and urged Allie ahead.

They passed a cluster of tents curtained with lazy threads of smoke rising from several dying campfires, and neared Cerne's old city wall and bridge, where dozens of laborers loitered near high heaps of sandstone being cut to make repairs. A section of the four-foot-thick wall was being replaced. She wondered why the bailiff allowed his workers to dawdle, and why the bridge carried no other travelers.

Several guards hurried from the gatehouse. "Sir John." Four other guards approached.

"We thought you dead," said an armored knight with missing teeth on the right side of his mouth.

It was Philip, the knight who had struck her down at the horse fair. Kadriya stiffened.

Philip whacked John on his armored thigh. "We thought you dead, then we heard you were still at Coin Forest. Good you're here now. We need you. The Gypsy thief has escaped."

Kadriya gasped. Allie, unsettled by Kadriya's surprise, side-stepped.

Her movement caught Philip's attention, and he recognized her. "God's blood! Look you there, 'tis the thief's woman. John has caught the thief's whore." Philip lunged toward Kadriya. "Where is he?"

Sir John's face steeled and he wedged Dover between Philip and Kadriya. "Leave her be."

A cluster of monks climbed up from the riverbank below and hurried toward them. A tall, dark-tonsured one moved more purposefully than the others. His pale skin stretched over a hawkish nose, his brows drawn in a severe frown. His black tunic was belted and anchored with a chain of many keys, and he wore a gold ring with a large red ruby.

The abbot.

"What goes here?" he demanded.

All dismounted and knelt. All but Dury.

Kadriya met Dury's eyes and pointed subtly to the ground.

Dury dismounted.

"Father Robert," John greeted him. "We have just now arrived. I bring with me Father—"

"Bernard. I can see," the abbot interrupted, his eyes narrowed, his manner ill-tempered. "And Sir John, how surprising that you look as hale as ever I have seen you. I received a message that you were seriously injured and desperately needing rest." He faced Kadriya, suspicion narrowing his eyes further. "And who is this?"

"This is Kadriya," John paused for a moment, "A ward of Lady Tabor."

The abbot's expression softened. "Mistress Kadriya. We appreciate Lord Tabor's support over the years, and we are in debt to you for the care afforded our knight. I bid you welcome."

Philip tugged on the abbot's sleeve. "Welcome? She's the wench with the monkey. She's the thief's whore."

"What?" The abbot's voice rose with incredulity. He glanced at Father Bernard.

Father Bernard's heavy white brows drew together, deepening his wrinkles. "She is of good repute, a Christian, and has pledged to wed Teraf."

The abbot turned to Kadriya. "Is this true?" He pursed his lower lip and released it. "You are betrothed to the thief?"

The moment hung, heavy with anticipation. She thought of the brazen Englishmen who had unfairly judged her for her mixed blood, saw the change of expression in the abbot's eyes, as if a whip had been snapped in his face, changing it from warmth and acceptance to suspicion and fear. If she said, "Yes," it would be a public confession that she was as evil and corrupt as they thought Teraf was. They would disregard the whole of her life in the English world under Lord Tabor's sponsorship, and she would permanently ally herself with her Gypsies.

They wore it on their faces, all of them save Father Bernard, Dury and Sir John, who looked at her with sorrow.

They wanted to hear her clarify it, condemn herself with the truth of it.

But she wanted justice. This was her chance to use reason to help Teraf. "You do not know him," she said. "You do not know of his guilt. You need someone to blame, and he is an easy mark. If he had stolen the chalice, you would have found it in his tent or on his person, but you didn't. Yet still you condemn him and talk of hanging. If I were him, I would run, too."

Philip regarded her with smug hatred. Sir John shifted on his horse, his mouth set in grim displeasure, and the other men watched with a mix of fascination and revulsion.

The abbot took a deep breath and exhaled, shaking his head. "You have committed yourself to a heathen. A heathen thief. What evil has settled in your soul? What have Lord and Lady Tabor done to make you shame them this way?"

His disgust drifted over her like a dark disease, taking her breath away.

"Give me your reins," the abbot ordered, his voice cold.

Kadriya did so.

The Abbot handed Allie's reins to a guard. "Your thief has forfeited any chance for freedom," he said. "Yet even if he escapes my knights, you'll not join him. You are a Christian, and I would sequester you as a nun to save you from such a Godless life."

"Nay!" Kadriya turned to her priest. "Father, help me."

The abbot's eyes narrowed. "He cannot. Not even your Lord Tabor can save you from the web of trouble you have spun for yourself." He nodded to the tall, overpowering knight that stood beside her. "Sir John, take her to the upper chamber and assign two guards to watch her. She is not to leave the chamber. Father Bernard, you and your companions will wait for me. I have some questions about your assessment of Sir John's condition."

"And Hugh." The abbot pointed to another guard. "Return to the abbey and have the prior dispatch messengers to the surrounding villages and seaports. Tell them who we hold here.

We'll be ready when the thief comes for her."

Kadriya sat in the armored circle of John's arms as they rode together to the abbey.

She pulled her cloak tighter against the wind that stirred the iron grey clouds, releasing brief waves of sunlight on the earth. Cerne Abbey sprawled before them, golden stoned and three stories tall.

"Father Robert can be harsh," he said, breaking the silence. "Curse Philip. I had hoped to have private audience with Father Robert first."

"Not your fault." She turned to catch a glimpse of his face. "I regret my harsh words. I wish I could take them back. I crave your forgiveness."

"I've wished back some of my own words of late."

A patch of sunlight fell on the window of a stone building next to the abbey. "Will I stay there?"

Sir John followed her gaze. "Nay. That is the guest house. You will stay in the abbot's compound." He paused. "We have little time left to talk, Kadriya. I'll try to find Teraf before the other knights do. Which direction do you think he went?"

"Can you not just let him go?"

"He is safer here, believe me."

She remembered the gate, and the hostility in Philip's and the other knights' eyes. "I do."

"Will he try to sell the chalice here or in France? Where is the tribe?"

"God's blood! He doesn't have the chalice, John."

"If he did. If he did. We're nearing the inner gate. Tell me now."

"Rill intended to gather the tribe and return to France directly. I don't know. Portland? Poole?"

"So he'd head south?"

"He would know the tribe could not stay at the horse fair, and he saw Rill at Blackwater Point. He would expect Rill to lead them back to Marseilles. Yes, south, I think."

They crossed the drawbridge and Sir John dismounted. He took her by the arm and they approached the gate house. John knocked on the wooden window. "Brother Samuel?"

The window tilted open and a tonsured head and freckled, round face appeared. "Sir John. Thank the saints, you're safe."

"I'll be in the south cloisters. See that the guest master helps Father Bernard and Sir Thomas when they arrive. The Gypsy, Dury, will be staying with them in the guest house."

The monk's brows furrowed. "A Gypsy?"

"He is under Sir Thomas's guard and cannot leave him."

That would keep Dury distanced from the hostile monastery guards. "Thank you," she whispered to John.

They passed the inner gate and the front of the monastery loomed before them, laden with shields of various coats of arms, supporters of the abbey. Lord Tabor's shield was at the upper left. An ornate porch loomed above the arch where two oriel windows jutted out like elongated eyes of judgment. Eyes of danger.

Inside the abbey, a monk named Alfred escorted them to a fortified chamber, dim and sparsely furnished with a straw bed, a writing table, a wash basin, and a window the size of a bible.

"Thank you, Brother Alfred." Sir John dismissed the monk.

The monk departed, leaving the door open.

Sir John offered a smile of reassurance. "You will be treated well," he said, his deep-timbered voice holding the gentle tone he afforded Dover. "I will find Teraf before they do." He reached his hand out as if to touch her face, but stopped.

Kadriya grabbed his hand, wrapping hers around it. His hand was warm, callused and strong between hers. She held it like a lifeline, heedless of revealing her growing desperation.

He took her hands in his and squeezed them. The brittle smile dissolved and his expression deepened with an intensity that darkened his blue eyes and left no question of his caring.

Something potent and uplifting passed between them, as the flutter of wings inside her heart, making it lighter. His image wavered in tears that threatened to spill.

He pulled free and strode from the room.

"Thank you, John," she called to him, failing to keep the tremor from her voice. "Godspeed."

The iron door shut by unseen hands, and the lock clicked in place.

Sir John left the abbot's wing and entered the courtyard. He neared a point on the north side of the abbey where the earth had been dug down in a large rectangle and anchored with four large corner stones that would serve as the beginning of the foundation for the abbot's new church, a church with ample light and a clean, simple design, much like the abbot himself. John had seen the plans. A square tower would dominate, with octagonal turrets at the top.

He kicked a stone. Or it would never happen. It would remain a cavity of dirt because the bishop would be so angered at the loss of the chalice that he would withhold the building endowment and deny the abbot's dream. A church for a chalice. It seemed an astonishingly outrageous link, but John had witnessed similar mysteries when power clashed with dreams.

Curse Teraf. He wondered if he could resist strangling the scheming, filthy ferret when he did find him.

He approached the tithe barn, where the chamberlain said John might find the abbot gathering harvest numbers for his meeting. John shook his head. Even in the strain of Teraf's escape, his friend would not dismiss his daily meeting.

The tithe barn loomed, its three-storied sandstone structure buttressed and more grand than many country manors. The entrance was choked with wagons and farmers anxious to deposit their annual share of grains and corns and be back on the roads to their fields, where they would plough and sow wheat and rye before winter.

He glanced at the expansion made possible by Lord Tabor's generosity, and chased the thought away. He needed to speak for Kadriya, as he had promised. He would explain that she was a victim of misplaced trust and had naught to do with the theft—or the tribe, for that matter.

He spied the abbot, gesturing at a farmer who stood, hat respectfully in hand, nodding. The abbot dismissed the farmer and greeted others with a warm nod, revealing none of the inner turmoil he likely was feeling. His black gown flowed as he strode past their wagons, lifting it as he approached a pile of horse dung.

"Father Robert," Sir John called across the ten yard distance.

The abbot turned. "Sir John," he acknowledged, his voice cold.

"I would have a word with you, if you please."

The abbot nodded and crossed the courtyard, following the millstream north toward the abbot's lodge. "What say you?"

"It's about Kadriya and her promise to Teraf. 'Tis true, she's guilty of bad judgment, but she is not—"

"Up to her neck in it? Of course she is. Father Bernard praises her virtues, but she's still a Gypsy and publicly loyal to Teraf. She's a fool, but she can be useful to lure the thief back."

At least the abbot knew she wasn't directly involved with the theft. "If you please, I will join the others in the search."

"A sennight. That's all we have to get that chalice back, John. Seven days, and the bishop will be here."

"But the chalice was stolen. It was not sold or given away. If we can't find it, surely the bishop will accept that."

"No. There are—unseemly circumstances surrounding its theft that—" He stopped himself. "You must find it."

What kinds of unseemly circumstances, John wondered. "I understand."

"Do you? You spent three days lazing at Coin Forest. I thought you were seriously hurt."

John straightened from wounded dignity. "My departure was delayed. I was held."

The abbot raised an eyebrow. "Against your will?"

"Father Bernard threatened reduced endowments if I didn't respect his concern about my head wound."

"Did he?"

"Obliquely. Only obliquely," John added. In truth John had seen the look in the priest's eye and hadn't wanted to cause a shortage of funds at the very time the abbot was trying to build his church. "I was knocked unconscious." He pounded the metal covering his chest. "Look at my armor."

"I've relied on your loyalty for years, John, but reports about you make me question your judgment."

"Reports?"

"Shows of affection in quiet chamber rooms."

Alfred. The monk could only guess what passed between them. He could not know the bittersweet joy of seeing trust in the eyes of a woman who made his heart stir, of knowing she needed him desperately, this woman of courage and grace who foolishly loved a thief, a woman who had sealed her doom by speaking for him.

For it was true. In spite of her courage and loyalty, a lifetime of respectability and God-fearing worship, it was, in the end, as if she had stood under a rain, the rain of her people, the Gypsies, with their odd ways and sins. She had stood under a tainted rain that would separate her from her English roots and her Gypsy roots, following her like a curse, staining her dreams and thoughts and, much as she might wish, she could never escape that rain.

"She is a good person, Father."

"Heed this: Teraf needs to be caught. He cannot escape. The chalice must be found before the bishop's arrival. And you must put your vows above any misplaced feelings for this Gypsy girl." He gave John a penetrating look. "Do I have your word?"

What secret was behind the chalice that the abbot could not share? The bishop was from Winchester, site of St. Giles Fair, where Lord Tabor met Sharai. Gypsies. A connection? John met the abbot's gaze, could almost see his mind racing, searching for any circumstance where John's loyalty would be compromised.

He was more than willing to bring Teraf back to justice, and he would devote all his efforts to find the chalice in time and return it. "Yes," he said. "You have my word."

Kadriya stepped past the door of her gloomy chamber and into the hall. Resisting the urge to jump and sing in joy at being released, she nevertheless hugged Father Bernard, and his fur-trimmed collar tickled her nose. "Thank you, oh, thank you, Father. 'Tis so lonely in there, and dark. However did you convince the abbot?"

"I volunteered your services. A horse is injured, a fine palfrey. A bad gash that could damage the eye. The wound is too bloody to tell. The stable monks joined the knights pursuing Teraf, and the infirmary monk fears horses. I told the abbot how well you tend our horses. So long as you're watched by two guards, he has asked that you help."

They joined her two guards, Herbert, with his pox scars and Gedwin, with his sagging jaw, and left the abbot's hall. Outside, she touched the priest's arm. "We'll need poultice, clean linen and needle and thread to close the wound, if need be."

"I'll get them from the infirmary," Father Bernard said.

"Thank you. Oh, and if stitches are needed, we'll need something for the pain, cowbane or, better, mandrake."

The young palfrey was already down in his stall, tan with a dark mane and a nasty three-inch tear just above the left eye. "There, there," Kadriya soothed. Blood had drenched his face all the way to his jaw.

The horse was restrained by a young monk. His blond hair had not yet been trimmed into the tonsured haircut of a monk's station, so he probably hadn't taken his formal vows yet, but he wore the black Benedictine tunic. "Is it mortal bad?" the young monk asked.

Kadriya bent down. "I worry about his eye, but it will be hard to tell until we can get him cleaned up. What happened?"

"I was in the village to fetch ink for the scriptorium." He nodded to a tightly bound canvas package as proof. "I tethered him soundly, but someone—green lads likely—took him for a ride and found some kind of trouble. I reported it to the reeve, but he cannot leave the outer gate for the lack of guards and knights looking for Teraf." His delicate mouth twisted into a threat. "They will suffer, whoever did this."

Father Bernard entered. "Here you are," he said, handing her a linen bag.

"Thank you, Father. This is Father Bernard, our parish priest from Coin Forest," she told the young man. "And I am Kadriya."

"I'm Geoffrey," he replied. "This," he said, returning to the horse, "is Falcon."

"Nice name," Kadriya said. "Here, hold Falcon firmly, like this."

They immobilized the horse's head and poured the pain-killing brew down his throat. After cleansing, she found no more damage than the tear above his eye. After checking to be sure the mandrake had done its job, she worked the flesh gently together and decided where best to begin.

"Herbert," she addressed the guard with the scarred face. "You may as well sit down. This will take a while. You, too, Gedwin." The guards settled at both ends of the barn, blocking the exits.

"I'll take my leave now, Kadriya, and see if there's any news about Teraf," said Father Bernard.

"Please let me know if there is."

"Of course. I'll visit you later." Father Bernard left, and Geoffrey remained close to his horse, holding his head. Glancing around to be sure no one else could hear, Geoffrey leaned forward and lowered his voice. "Can you get word to Teraf for me?"

Her needle paused, along with her heart. "You know him?"

"Aye," Geoffrey whispered. "We became friends when he and Erol were here, last fortnight."

The words scraped her heart. Sir John had spoken the truth. "What were they doing here?"

"They helped break two horses they'd sold to the abbey," he said. "In the evenings, they danced and sang with the minstrels." Geoffrey's small mouth curved in a smile. "They showed me another kind of life." He lowered his voice. "A better one."

She swayed, losing her balance, and put her arm out to steady herself. "When did you last see him? Teraf, I mean."

"Before all this trouble about the chalice." The youth's voice fell to a whisper. "I want to leave. Teraf invited me to Troyes. Can you tell him?"

The harsh reality of his words pushed against her chest, making it hard to breathe.

"Did you hear me?" Geoffrey whispered. "I can't bear another day in that scriptorium. Do you know, we cannot even speak? Whole days of silence. I can leave the scriptorium tonight when—"

"Geoffrey." A grey-haired monk strode in. "Do you have my inks?"

Geoffrey held Falcon's head closer to him. "Aye, all that you asked for, Brother Brian. There was trouble with my horse."

"Then get you back and to work while there is still light." Brian ignored Kadriya, but stopped to speak to Herbert at the front of the barn. "Did he see Eustace? He is not allowed to speak to him. Did he?"

Herbert scratched his head. "Nay. I have not seen Eustace all day."

Brian turned to Geoffrey. "Good news for you. Now, come on."

"But my horse," the young monk protested.

"Now." The vexed monk pulled Geoffrey away.

Herbert slipped in to hold the horse. "Are you about finished here?"

Kadriya fought to keep her voice steady. "One more stitch. I'll need to watch him for a time to be certain it doesn't begin bleeding again."

Falcon struggled to get up, to escape the pain of her needle and get to his feet.

Kadriya placed her hand on his neck, feeling his distress. She felt one with the horse. Fallen. Injured. Bleeding from Geoffrey's words. *Teraf had been here. Teraf stole the chalice.* Like the horse, she wanted to rise and run, run far away from here and not face the ruin her life had become because of Teraf's duplicity.

Pain centered in her chest, as if Falcon was standing on her, his hoofs crushing her heart. Teraf's selfishness had caused Murat's death, the knight Roger's death, and crisis for his tribe. It had brought untold anxiety to the abbot and Sir John. Even now, the abbey placed itself in peril by dispatching scores of its best knights and guards to the surrounding villages and forests to find the thief. Teraf, the thief, the liar.

He had used her.

The enormity of her mistake echoed in her mind. She had destroyed her reputation, making a good marriage impossible. Had brought scandal and dishonor to Sharai and Lord Tabor, after all their support and love.

She pulled the thread taut and tied it off. Her fingers moved as if rusty around the needle; indeed, she wondered if those were her hands that were giving the horse a reassuring pat and bracing herself to a standing position. All movement seemed detached, painfully slow, meant for nothing because nothing meant what it seemed to mean any more. After all she thought she knew, she'd known nothing. After all the good she'd meant to do, she had only harmed.

Vision blurring, she nodded to her guards. "I'm done."

Eustace crept closer, staying behind the cover of the five-foot hedgerow. Saints help him. Limp with exhaustion, he'd fallen asleep behind the bush and Teraf had left while he slumbered. The sun had risen, a cruel awakening, and he'd been reduced to instinct and guessing which way Teraf had taken.

He'd traveled with purpose, hoping he had chosen the right path, and now his faith was rewarding him.

What he saw before him made his heart sing like Brother Williams' falsetto at Lauds. He resisted the urge to cry out with joy. Just twenty feet away a fine stallion grazed. The end of its reins dragged, as if it had been tied but had worked the knot loose to forage on the sweet trefoil. The horse had three white socks and a white-tipped tail, revealing the identity of its owner.

A few feet past the horse Teraf rested, his legs sprawled over the root of a gnarled oak and his arm draped over his eyes, shielding the late afternoon sun. He had picked a fine place to hide, here in the wooded corner of a neglected field gone to

147

weeds. Had it not been for his horse being tempted to mischief, Eustace would never have spotted him.

Eustace advanced slowly in a haze of fear. Years of commissioning, cataloguing and guarding sacramental treasures had done little for Eustace's physical strength. There was his height, but in a struggle he wouldn't trust his strength or speed. With this wiry, slippery Gypsy, he must use surprise.

Working his way to a break in the bush, Eustace crossed the barrier. Inching closer, he considered his options. He had never killed anyone before. His hand found the improvised sword and gripped it tightly.

Teraf rolled over on his stomach, resting his forehead on his arm.

Eustace fell flat to the ground, hiding himself in the tall weeds. His heart thudded against the cool grass.

The Gypsy didn't move and his breathing grew more shallow and rhythmic.

Eustace' throat constricted. It had to be fast. He was taller, but weaker. What if he stabbed Teraf and he fought back, took the scythe away? Eustace could not endure a long struggle. He rose soundlessly. A few large stones hid under encroaching grasses, stones long ago pulled from the fields during plowing. He spied one four hands wide and two thick. Rocking it gradually from its earthen cradle, Eustace finally freed it. Sweat dripped in his eye and he wiped it away.

Moist beneath his feet, the earth gave silently as he stepped closer to the sleeping Gypsy. Teraf's gold ring, a cross, shone softly. Filthy heathen had no faith. Nothing could save his soul. Eustace lifted the stone above his head and, aiming with trembling muscles, he chose a point and slammed it on the back of Teraf's head.

The stone landed with a wet thump, sounding like wash day

at the river when the monks thumped their soiled linen on the rocks.

Teraf did not move.

Moments passed.

He had to be dead.

The wind blew, drying the sweat on Eustace's face, and his heart boomed like cannons in his chest. He dared a brief touch on the Gypsy's shoulder.

Nothing.

He grew more bold, shaking him, and still no response. He turned him over.

Sweet Virgin! It's not Teraf. Eustace fell backwards into the grass.

Thunderstruck, he looked at Teraf's horse, the Gypsy's long, black hair, and recognized him. It was Teraf's friend, Erol.

But what in God's name was Erol doing, wearing a yellow scarf, riding Teraf's horse, and wearing Teraf's ring?

Eustace sat on his haunches, rocking, and after a time the thought entered his brain that he might be discovered. He had murdered a man, and it had been the wrong one, and he would die for it.

His head cleared. Teraf had tricked him again, this time making Erol a decoy. If he returned with Erol's body the Abbot would still want Teraf and, because Eustace had fallen asleep in the bushes, Teraf had escaped. He checked Erol's travel bag and found the silver cross Teraf had demanded in return for his silence. If he left Erol here, all he had accomplished was to restore a silver cross that no one knew had been removed from the abbey.

He studied Erol's build, and a thought occurred to him. This Gypsy was younger than Teraf, but roughly the same size. Teraf knew it. That's why he'd given Erol his horse. Or mayhap Erol had murdered Teraf and stolen his horse and scarf and ring.

What did it matter? Erol could serve him now.

Crossing himself, Eustace uttered a fervent prayer for his soul. He raised the silver cross and brought it down on Erol's face again and again, battering his features beyond recognition.

He swung the cross until his strength left him. Using his flask he rinsed the cross clean, wiping it with his black tunic. He tied Teraf's horse loosely to the tree and returned to his own horse some hundred yards away, slipping the cross into his bag.

Walking to the river, he slid down its steep bank and immersed his body in the fast-flowing stream, gasping from the shock of the cold water, and cleansed his hands and tunic of the blood. He accepted the convulsions that wracked his body and retched into the stream, purging his stomach. All strength had left his body; he trembled as he mounted his horse. Weak but hopeful, he guided it in a wide swing away from the river and northwest, back to the abbey.

CHAPTER 10
THE BELLS

John and Thomas followed the river Frome, a wide, swift river that led to the shipyards and large, shallow harbor of Poole just a day's ride ahead.

Thomas guided his horse over a broken fence to avoid uneven ground. "Do you think the tinker can be trusted?"

"Shh," John said, gesturing for Thomas to keep his voice down. They had met two tinkers and a buckle peddler outside Dorchester who said they had seen a lone, dark-skinned man following this river, riding a horse with distinctive white markings similar to the coloring of Teraf's horse. "He looked honest," John said quietly, his pulse and senses stirred by the new lead. Teraf's horse was agile. No need to give him advance warning of their approach.

John noted the hedge, wildly overgrown, with a dead section so wide a sheep could easily escape. "These hedges have not been plashed for at least two seasons."

"Abandoned, do you think?" Thomas asked.

"That, or contested in the courts." A movement caught John's eye. A brown horse grazed just fifty yards ahead, a horse with three distinctive socks. John reined Dover to an abrupt stop and signaled Thomas. Some yards past the horse, at the north corner of the field, a small island of large oaks towered over several hazel trees.

John's gut tightened. Now was the time to bring the heathen in, return the chalice and end this chain of misfortune.

He drew Dover to a tall alder and tethered him, and Thomas followed suit. Working his way along the bank, John made his way closer, two pledges echoing in his head. One vow he'd sworn to the abbot to capture the chalice and the thief, and the other to Kadriya to catch Teraf before the knights did.

A gentle afternoon breeze swayed the sweet clover that had tempted Teraf's horse into the open. *Where's Teraf?*

Dagger drawn, John neared the hazel trees, getting so close he could see the woody shells of the fruit, already coaxed from green to brown by autumn's cooler nights. He moved slowly, watching for any movement of the branches, but could sense nothing but the breeze.

A tan leather travel pack rested against the trunk of one of the hazels. Grass had been trampled here. He caught a glimpse of a bloodied red tunic.

The wind shifted and the black smell of death tainted the air. The hairs on the back of John's neck raised. *I'm too late.*

A short male lay face down in the grass. John kicked the body over. John had fought in too many battles to blanch at the sight of brutality, but a sliver of pity wedged in his throat at the sight of the corpse's mangled face. This man had been beaten boneless.

"Is it Teraf?" Thomas asked.

The corpse was Gypsy, all right: short, slight, muscular build, ebony hair. "This is his gold cross ring. I recall seeing him wear it at the horse fair." The skin was cold to the touch. "He's been dead several hours," John said. "Bring me that travel bag by the tree."

Thomas handed John the leather bag, left open.

John noted the abbey's mark on the bottom of the bag and lifted the flap. "See how the clothes and food have been crushed in the bottom and sides?" John asked. "Something has been removed."

Thomas released an exasperated sigh. "The chalice."

John nodded. "Kadriya was right. Teraf was heading for Poole to rendezvous with Erol."

"And this is the way to Poole," Thomas said. "So it is he."

John brought Teraf's horse in. "No injuries. Why would a thief leave this fine horse behind? Unless the thief knows Teraf, and knows he's being chased, and the horse could be easily recognized."

John walked around the grove of trees. "Here." He gestured Thomas over. "Looks like a deer wallow, but see these two indentations, as if someone kneeled," John said, fitting his knees into the depressions, "waiting for a chance to surprise Teraf."

God's nails! He'd found the thief, but not the goblet. He fulfilled his promise to Kadriya to find Teraf, but how could he face her with the corpse of her intended? Or face the abbot empty-handed? Looking to the sky, he crushed the bag in his hand.

Terce bells finished ringing at the still-distant abbey. Nine. The morning was well on its way as John and Sir Thomas rode abreast, followed by Teraf's horse, draped with Teraf's body.

They arrived shortly thereafter at the abbey and knights rode out to meet them.

"Sir John." Gilbert greeted him, looked at the body and whistled. "What a slaughter. Deserved every bit of it, too."

Alwin pushed ahead, his young face animated. "Is he dead?"

John nodded.

They entered the gate. Residents from the guesthouse gathered for a closer look.

"The Gypsy is back," said a farmer.

"Sir John has the thief and he's dead," said a merchant.

A young lad ran close. "Someone really pounded him."

Sir John and Sir Thomas rode among the growing crowd to

the abbot's lodge and dismounted, stopping in the shade of trees by the porch. The abbot emerged with his miter and staff, followed by Kadriya and her guards.

Her gown, the color of honey, made her stand out from the monks' black tunics like a delicate flower in a field of drab mushrooms. She had tucked her long hair under a simple head-dress with a short white veil, and her captivating eyes shone with welcome.

Her gaze worked its way to his heart. She was glad to see him. He realized that, with all the people crowding around, she had not yet seen Teraf's horse, or the sad shape of its rider.

Tension pulled at his heart, and he wished he could take her in his arms and shelter her from this moment.

From the cloisters Eustace ran with the almoner and the cellarer.

The abbot approached John, giving a reluctant glance at the corpse. "The chalice?" he asked quietly.

The word was too difficult to utter. John shook his head.

The abbot's face fell, and he examined Teraf. "Where did you find him?"

"South and east, just before Wareham."

Mathias approached, clad in chest armor. "South? Why did you go south? We were told to look north."

"Why north?" asked John.

"Because Eustace saw him escape," said Mathias. "He saw him leaving that way."

John regarded the tall sacristan. Remarkable, how Eustace was always around when Teraf was escaping.

Eustace stood with the almoner, his face unusually pale.

"Are you ill, Eustace?" asked John.

"Nay." Eustace stared at the body. "He left riding north, toward his tribe. We heard they were in Trowbridge."

"Is it Teraf?" the abbot asked.

Dreading it, John met her eyes. "Kadriya?"

She read his pity and blinked back tears. Squeezing her prayer beads in her hand until it hurt, she regarded the dangling hand. His skin was dark like a Rom, but he might not be one.

She approached the body and put her hand under the chin, preparing to turn his face forward.

Sir John dismounted. "Do not," he warned. He spoke forcefully, his deep voice edged with a quality she had never heard. Worry.

She froze.

"He has been beaten. Viciously."

But she had to know. She turned his head.

A nightmare of wounds stunned her. She released the man's head and swooned.

Sir John took her arm, steadying her.

She recovered, standing on her own. " 'Tis not Teraf. His hair is too short."

"Mayhap he cut it as a disguise," John said.

She swallowed the bile rising in her throat. Something caught her eye, a distinct indentation at the dead man's right temple. Looking closer, she could almost make out a pattern, a circle the size of a coin. She blinked. She was seeing things in the horror of his pounded flesh.

Her hand sought the comfort of her prayer beads again and she rolled them in her fingers. "Why would someone do this?"

"His bag was left, opened. Thievery, I suspect," said John.

The tall man they called Eustace stepped forward. "Justice, I would say."

She touched an unbloodied section of his scarf. "This is Teraf's scarf." Her voice sounded flat to her and muted, as if it were coming from a distance. She lifted his right hand and a strangled cry escaped her lips. "His ring."

She held the hand that had once held hers, the hand that he

had offered, welcoming her to his tribe. But was it Teraf's hand? She closed her eyes, trying to conjure a memory of his hand on the reins, or holding her hand. Saints help her, but she could not form a clear image. She could see John's hand clearly, the angry scar that circled the base of his right thumb, the long fingers, and the nails, chewed to the quick. Why could she not remember Teraf's? She shook her head in confusion.

The tall man they called Eustace stepped forward. "It is Teraf's horse, is it not?"

"Yes."

"And Teraf's scarf, and his ring?"

"Yes."

"Then it must be Teraf. The thief is dead."

Cheers rose.

Caught in a fog of sorrow and loss, she withdrew, standing alone amid the monks and knights. "Where is Father Bernard?"

"The guesthouse, with Dury," Eustace answered.

The abbot turned to Kadriya. "We will hold the ring, his horse and any other articles of value. With the return of the chalice, they will be given to you."

"No. They must go to Dury. He is his cousin," Kadriya said.

The abbot signaled to his monks. "Dig a grave for him outside the village walls."

Kadriya shook her head. "My thanks, Father, but he is a Gypsy. By your leave, we will give him a Gypsy funeral."

Kadriya sorted the clothes, food and daggers she had found in Teraf's pack, not recognizing them. He had probably stolen the provisions after escaping from the abbey.

She washed his tunic and scarf, scrubbing away the blood stains as best she could, and hung them to dry in the sunlight. She had not known Teraf well, she allowed, and he had betrayed her, but he had paid for his mistake with his life. She had pledged to him and he needed her now for this final duty to set his spirit free.

They selected a field past the village, distant from the abbey, as Father Robert had specified. John and Dury built an elevated pyre of wood twice the size of a wagon bed and lay Teraf in the middle. They spread pitch around the edges and propped additional dried wood on the side and underneath for fuel.

Kadriya arranged Teraf's pack of clothes and food at the right of his body. The infirmary monk had provided clean linen for his face, and she secured it by tying the yellow scarf at his temple, as he had worn it, covering the eerie circle impression that still unsettled her.

Dury placed Teraf's stirrups, reins and blanket on the pyre to Teraf's left.

Kadriya sprinkled oil on the body and scattered salt, lavender and a handful of daisies.

Removing his own scarf, Dury held it to his heart.

Following his lead, Kadriya removed the strip of linen she had tied around her head for the ceremony and pressed it to her heart. "Teraf, our king," she said in Romani. *"Pen. Our brother."*

"A fine horseman," Dury added. "A fearless risk-taker."

Her throat became unbearably tight. She recalled the esteem Teraf's tribe held for him, that she had held for him, but that reckless courage had robbed him of needed prudence, and his duplicity had left her depleted. She took his hand one last time. His ring was gone, the skin of his hand rough. Turning it over, she noticed a white powder under his fingernails and traced the broken blisters and scabs on his palm. Raising his hand to her lips, she kissed it.

She stood and turned to John, finding comfort in the gentle understanding in his blue eyes. She drew strength from his presence and nodded.

Dury lit the fire. Flames leapt on the platform with a whoosh, as if a fiery blanket had been billowed over the pyre. It blazed to three times a man's height, hot and clean.

Raising a flute borrowed from minstrels who had arrived at the monastery the night before, Dury played, making light notes, a tune of celebration. He snapped his fingers and Kadriya listened, catching the rhythm, and joined him.

One of the minstrels, a florid-faced man of years, added the strumming of his gittern to the song. The light notes of the flute lilted, unfettered and irrepressible, and the gittern's strings vibrated like a brash version of heaven's harps, too bold to be saintly and proud of it.

She danced, her feet bare for the occasion, moving in a pattern that reminded her of the spirit of a stallion on a cool spring morning, like Teraf's unfettered spirit.

He had promised to love her, to be with her for all his tomorrows, and now he had no tomorrows to give. She remembered lively horse races across the meadow and evenings by the fire when he would tell stories under the stars. Pain wedged its way into her heart. What yesterdays they had shared were now sullied by his lies. *Did I know you at all, Teraf?*

She remembered when Teraf had presented her to his tribe, his brown eyes warm, his smile engaging, his arm wrapped protectively around her. "This is my Kadriya," he had said. "Honor her as you do me, for she is to be your queen."

Tears grew cold on her face. *So I honor you, Teraf, you who would have been my king.*

John tossed the last logs onto the pyre. The songs had faded, the dancing had ceased and still she stood, her eyes haunted, watching the flames. He signaled to the distant abbey tower and a single bell tolled. To keep the evil spirits at bay, Dury had said.

He waited until the echo of the bell faded in the breeze. "It is done," he said, though he knew for her it was not.

At the city wall Father Bernard approached, taking Kadriya's arm, and led her away toward the abbot's hall.

Dury watched her leave. "Needs rest."

"And you?" John asked, speaking slowly. "What will you do now?"

He pointed to himself, then the road. "Free?"

"I will ask the abbot."

"You will?"

"You defended me in the forest," John said. He pointed to Dury. "You helped," he pointed to himself, "me."

Dury nodded and re-tied and positioned his scarf. John could see Dury's long hair and, beyond Dury, the flames from the pyre. But for the greying hair, from this angle Dury bore a strong resemblance to Teraf.

John shook off a fleeting premonition and walked toward the abbey.

Dury joined him and Sir Thomas, still fulfilling his duty as guard.

"Now look chalice?" Dury asked.

"Yes."

"I, too. I, too, look chalice."

"Why?"

"Two sisters, brother in tribe." He gestured toward the glowering knights in the distance. "Gypsies. Trouble. Knights kill Gypsies." He made a slicing gesture, as if cutting of his head.

"Knights did not kill Teraf. If knights found Teraf, he would have been brought back safe."

Dury raised his brows. "You think?"

John remembered the hatred in Philip's eyes, in the eyes of some of the other knights. Had he not been anxious himself to find Teraf before others did, for fear of what they might do to him?

Dury's face was earnest, his gaze direct. "Talk abbot. I help get chalice, he let us go to Marseilles."

Reasonable, John thought, but that familiar feeling of distrust settled in again. Dury was a Gypsy, one of "them." John wondered if the abbot would even consider his request. One could only trust one's own kind, certainly not a foreigner.

John dried his face, wiping small beads of blood from his neck, and sheathed his shaving knife. He combed his hair, noting its length. It rested on his shoulders. He should get it cut, but the morning had been spent with Teraf's funeral. He must see the abbot and depart while daylight remained. He left the laymen's quarters, passing the cellarer's office and refectory on his way to the Abbot's hall.

Eustace emerged from the refectory and caught up with John, matching his stride. "Unholy practice that, burning the dead. But of course he was just a heathen."

" 'Tis their way."

Eustace lowered his voice. "Is that how you found him?"

Anger flared. "You would imply that I killed him?"

"No, no. Of course not. What I meant was, was he dead when you found him?"

"You saw his face, Eustace. What think you? That he could live through that beating and still share last words?"

The sacristan touched a thin hand to his mouth. "I was hoping that he might have, um, given you some clue so we could find the chalice."

Annoyed, John stepped up his pace. Most times Eustace floated in his own stream, aloof, self-important as he jangled his big ring of keys and hoarded the relics and altar silver as if they were his own. He could understand Eustace's frantic reaction to the chalice being stolen, but why all the questions? If Teraf had spoken last words, John would have told the abbot. He glanced at Eustace, whose thin features were drawn in intense concentration. Why?

Eustace kept pace with John's long-legged stride, seemingly determined to stay with him.

Something smelled. Odd that Eustace had witnessed the theft *and* both of Teraf's escapes. How involved was he in the unholy dealings?

John remembered the distinct, circle-shaped impression on Teraf's battered temple. He had looked closer and made out a cross inside the circle. A religious symbol, and Eustace was the sacristan. It was pure stab-in-the-dark, but John decided to fish.

He rubbed his forehead and sighed, as if this was a trial in which he would rather not partake. "Before he died, Teraf did speak."

The quick intake of breath was skillfully cloaked, almost inaudible. Eustace looked straight ahead, striving so hard to appear removed that the effort was transparent. "What did he say?"

John stopped, waiting for Eustace to look at him so he could see the sacristan's reaction. "Teraf said something I didn't understand." John shook his head. "Something about . . . a cross."

As if a branch had smacked him in the face, Eustace' features spasmed. He recovered, but not fast enough. "That makes no sense," he said. "He was a heathen."

"Exactly what I thought. It was likely just a dying man's groan." John stopped under the abbot's porch. "I must see the abbot now, Eustace. He has summoned me," he said, dismissing him.

John climbed the stairs with even more questions. Eustace

was somehow involved in Teraf's death.

The abbot's mouth thinned in grim determination. "We have but five days to find the chalice." He turned from his writing desk and leaned forward. "I put my trust in you, John."

Warmed by his friend's belief in him, John met Robert's eyes. They had shared tense moments in France when survival seemed doubtful, but he and the abbot had relied on each other and prevailed. So they would once more, he hoped. "When the knights went north, did they find any trace of Erol?"

"None."

Ten days had passed since the theft of the chalice. The challenge of finding it now threatened to overwhelm him. John paced, banishing his doubt by stating facts. "Teraf didn't have the chalice at the fair, so he must have given it to Erol. Teraf risked his neck for it, so he'd definitely find Erol and get it back. He likely had it when he was killed, and whoever murdered him took the chalice."

John chewed a piece of his fingernail that had dared try to grow. "We seek a thief and a murderer," said John, "who may or may not be a Gypsy."

The abbot shook his head. "Of course it's a Gypsy."

"Teraf was hurrying to the sea when he was killed." John seethed. Teraf had no intention of finding his tribe, or Kadriya. He was on his way to a seaport to sell his treasure and leave for France without a thought to the woman who so valiantly defended him and ruined her life trying to free him.

"And?" the abbot prompted.

"It can't be Erol. No reason for him to give Teraf the chalice, then kill him for it."

"They're thieves. Clever ones. Erol might want us to think just what you're thinking, so we don't look for Gypsies," the abbot said.

"Whoever he is, the thief will want to sell the chalice quickly. On foot or on horseback, he's just one day ahead of us. We must guess his path, one that will lead to a major town with jewelers sophisticated enough to know the value of the chalice and wealthy enough to give him the coin for it. He will avoid Weymouth Bay, I'm thinking, because it's so close to the abbey."

"I'll send Mathias and Philip to Weymouth, to be sure, and knights to Lyme Bay, as well."

John nodded. "I'll take Sir Thomas with me. And Dury."

The abbot's eyes narrowed. "He cannot be trusted."

"He has asked to go. He wishes to help."

"More proof he cannot be trusted. Why would he want to help you?"

"To right his cousin's wrong."

"Gypsies have no honor."

"He feels responsibility for his tribe and wants them free to leave England." Dury hadn't asked for a pledge, but John felt he deserved it for his sense of duty and willingness to help. "He asks, if he helps return the chalice, will your knights allow them safe passage through the seaports?"

"Perhaps."

"He needs your word."

"His kind does not deserve it."

John thought of Eustace. "Some of our kind do not deserve it, either, Father. If he does as he vows, he deserves it."

The abbot's eyes flashed. "Has she softened your thinking, Sir John? They are Gypsies."

"I faced death by the hand of the Gypsy, Rill," John said, "and Kadriya and Dury defended me. Their actions reveal that some are better than others, and 'twas you who pointed out we have just five days."

The abbot hesitated, sighed. "Give him the confounded assurance." Robert's eyes narrowed. "But until that chalice is returned, Kadriya stays here."

The words hit John unaware. "You do not trust me."

The harsh look in the abbot's eyes softened a little. "I know how you suffered with Gelsey, yet you do not heed my warnings."

John steeled himself for another lecture. He taken Gelsey to wife years ago and she had suffered from his long absences, pleaded with him to forsake his duty. When he would not, she had left, running away to parts unknown in the middle of the night when he had been lying, left for dead, in France. "Women have their place in the world, with men who can tend to them." Only then could they make suitable work partners in life, shouldering duties of the hearth and family.

"I know well the nature of men who have not taken the vows. There are three things, John, that, if taken in paucity or excess, become evil: the tongue, righteousness, and women. Avoid excess, John, and mind your fealty."

John had no need for a wife. He could not, however, stop thinking about Kadriya. He could still see the highlights in her hair from the sun and the fire, the green flecks in her eyes, laden with tears that had burned through his armor.

He stirred in discomfort from a peculiar tension near his heart and a sensation of vulnerability under the abbot's knowing gaze. "I am taken by her beauty and her sorrow," he admitted. " 'Tis merely fascination, I vow. It will pass." Words spilled out of his mouth as he tried to restore the armor she had somehow dislodged. He could not afford to be judged weak. "I will not sway from my duty, Father. You will see your chalice."

"Then go while there is still sun. Godspeed, my friend. Godspeed."

CHAPTER 11
THE JEWELS

John's feet dragged as he climbed the steps to the first floor of the abbot's lodge. If Kadriya was sleeping, he would not disturb her.

It had ground his nerves raw to hear her singing Teraf's praise during the Gypsy funeral. Teraf, their king, indeed. The swine. He had stolen for greed, betrayed his tribe and abandoned the woman who defended him. Men reaped what they sowed, and Teraf had received his fair share.

What would he say to her? A temporary farewell and a meaningless reassurance that all would be well? But he must at the least try to offer comfort. Why did this compelling need to soothe her gnaw at him? The closer he came to her chamber, the quicker his steps came. He needed to see her.

He reached her quarters but her guards were gone. John tried the door and it opened. Her room was empty. He checked the trunk. Her bags were gone. The silence quickened his heartbeat and he rushed back through the hall, hurrying down the steps. He found the prior at the entrance. "Where is she?"

"In the south fields. Riding with Father Bernard."

Riding? "And her guards?"

"Dismissed. She is free to come and go within the grounds now the thief, Teraf, is dead."

Why would she take her bags if they were just riding? Would she dare travel alone with just a priest? He rushed to the stable where Dover was already saddled and ready for his trip south.

He pushed Dover to a gallop out the gates and across the bridge. He spotted them in a harvested wheat field beyond the river. A huge sense of relief swept through him, and his heart pounded as if he had been running on foot. He had come close to losing her, yet she was not his and he wondered at the mad possessiveness that coursed through him.

She had changed to her green wool riding clothes and covered her hair with a travel hood. Her bags were tied to her saddle and Father Bernard had brought his bag, as well. "Kadriya. Father. What are you doing?"

Kadriya's heart jumped when she saw him running Dover full speed toward her, his light hair flowing in the breeze, revealing the strong jaw, the battle-blunted bridge of his nose and a fierce expression. He was fully armored less his helm. As he neared, relief shone in his blue eyes. He was happy to see her.

His closeness brought an unsteady beat to her heart. She swallowed convulsively and warmth coursed through her body. He seemed like the calm after the storm to her, yet something more made it difficult to breathe.

"Kadriya," he said, his voice thick with emotion. "Where are you going?"

"We're just riding. Allie needs exercise."

"I came to bid you farewell for a few days while I fetch the chalice."

Fear chased the warmth away. She had come to rely on this strong, fierce knight, and the thought of his leaving her alone brought slivers of panic.

He glanced down. "You ride with your bags?"

She would tell him straightaway and calmly, state it as a fact and hope he would agree to it. "We are coming with you," she said. "To help in your search."

"Nay. Sir Thomas is coming, and two knights from the abbey. I have sufficient help and would have you wait here."

"I do not belong here, and there are many who wish me gone. My Gypsy blood offends them."

" 'Tis too dangerous."

"It's dangerous for me to stay."

Father Bernard came forward. "Is it so risky, traveling with six men, four of whom are knights?"

"I speak Romani," Kadriya said. "I can—"

"Dury is coming. The fewer in our party, the faster our progress."

"He can't interpret as I can. Besides, you will need someone to help with the horses. Prithee, do not leave me." She spoke the fear in her heart and her voice broke. She touched her throat in an attempt to calm herself.

His blue eyes softened.

"She can ride as fast as any man," said Father Bernard. "And I may be old, but I can keep up. Let us help you."

"I will not go back there," she vowed, looking back at the abbey and beyond, where smoke still rose from the funeral pyre. She turned Allie around to face the road. "You wanted me to hang for what happened at Blackwater Point. I cannot undo what took place that night, but now that I know Teraf was involved in the theft, I must do something to redeem myself."

"Nay."

"These are difficult times for Lord Tabor," she began, laying open her deeper guilt at the harm she'd caused her patron because of her involvement with Teraf. She hoped he would understand. "Tabor's political position has been tenuous."

He nodded. "His alliance with Gloucester. I know."

She recalled the summer seven years ago when Gloucester's wife, Eleanor, was charged with witchcraft and Gloucester was stripped of his Protectorate and died in disgrace. "Tabor suffers from that alliance, and I've only added to his trials. If I can help find the chalice, I can right some of the wrong before the bishop comes."

John leaned back, crossing his arms, and a scant smile tugged at his mouth. "Sprig," he said, using the nickname Sharai had given Kadriya years ago, and her heart skipped.

"How do you know that name?"

"I heard Maude and Sharai use it just before we left Coin Forest. Somehow the name suits you," he said. "Wait here while I fetch Dury and the knights." He reigned Dover away, his blond hair whipping under his armor.

Kadriya loosened Allie's reins and settled into the rhythm of her canter as they rode south from the village Cerne. Sir John and Father Bernard led, Dury and Sir Thomas flanked her and the two abbey knights followed. They crossed a harvested oat field, dotted with fluttering sparrows.

Hoofbeats sounded from behind. Two knights hurried from the village, their galloping horses stirring the orange and crimson leaves covering the path. "Sir John. Wait." They caught up and reined to a stop.

The lead knight was Philip, the toothless knight from Blackwater Point. He was followed by another knight and, behind them, Eustace, the Sacristan.

Philip regarded Kadriya, his gaze dark with loathing. "Father Robert has sent us for the Gypsy whore. She is not to leave Cerne Abbey."

John's lips thinned with anger.

Philip advanced, pushing Kadriya's horse and grabbing for her reins. "The abbot sent me. Give me your reins, woman."

Kadriya retreated.

John held up his hand in a gesture meant to stop Philip. "Tell the abbot this is not a matter of excess. She has offered her help, and I have accepted it."

Philip smirked. "Her help for what, exactly? These are my orders." He grabbed Kadriya's reins.

"Nay." John nosed Dover between them. "She stays with me."

A chill hung on the edge of his words, leaving no question. John's face was not visible under his helm, but the knight's eyes widened.

A glimpse of steel shimmered in the afternoon sun, and Philip's sword arced in the air.

John's mirrored the affront, and their blades clashed. They rode the confrontation to the hilt, where the blades came to a shuddering stop.

"She rides with me." John's words rang hard and clear under the falling autumn leaves.

Philip met and held John's gaze and carefully withdrew his blade, sheathing it in the sudden quiet. "I shall tell the abbot of your resistance."

John's blue eyes narrowed. "Tell him I will hold myself personally responsible for her."

Kadriya walked the bank of the Cerne River, stretching her legs after two hours of riding. Deep and narrow, the river flowed like bubbling glass, sparkling under the afternoon sun. A group of willows had claimed the spot, casting cool shade at the river's bend, and sunlight bathed a cluster of daisies hemming the opposite bank.

The men had filled their flasks and returned to their horses.

Sir John emerged from the stand of willows, stepping down the hill and stopping an arm's length away. He stood tall, his broad shoulders covered in armor, a vision of force and power. "You look weary. I should not have agreed to your coming."

"I'm fine." She lowered her gaze, swallowing. " 'Tis been a long day."

Coming closer, he lifted her chin, his blue eyes soft with understanding. "I'm sorry."

Remembering how he had helped her through Teraf's funeral, tears welled. "I know."

He pulled her to him and held her gently against his chest.

Finding sanctuary in his arms, she let the tears flow.

He lowered her hood and caressed her hair, lightly rubbing the back of her neck and shoulders.

She cried for Teraf. His moment of temptation had started all these problems, but what a dear price he had paid for his weakness. She cried for herself. She had been so weak, so concerned about her own life that she had not come to know her intended. "I could not even remember his hands."

But I remember yours. All that once made sense no longer did. A veil had been cast on her life and she struggled, unseeing and hopelessly tangled, trying to free herself.

His strength comforted her. Tears finally spent, she looked up into his eyes, seeing a tender side to this hardened fighter.

He pulled away and turned to leave.

She wanted to thank him. She wanted to tell him how she relied more and more on him, how his mere presence gave her strength and . . . *pleasure,* her soul whispered, but she could not acknowledge that.

Too confused to voice anything, she touched his armored shoulder, drawing him back to her.

His eyes darkened with emotion. He closed his eyes and let out a ragged breath, as if he were waging a battle inside himself and losing.

Standing on her toes she wrapped her hands around his neck and touched her lips to his. They were soft against hers, neither resisting nor willing.

He moaned in surrender. Cupping her face in his hands he brought her to him, caressing her mouth with his.

Sweet desire surged within her. She pressed against him but the armor hindered, hard and unyielding.

He deepened the kiss, brushing her lips with his tongue.

She opened her mouth, welcoming him, and ran her fingers through his coarse hair, finding the softness underneath.

He ended the kiss and buried his face in her hair.

Her heart pulsed quickly and they stood, breathless, sustaining the sensual bond.

Pulling free, he brushed the hair from her eyes. "The others wait for us," he said, his voice husky.

She climbed the bank to the road where Dury stood, arms crossed, his dark features made darker by the look of condemnation in his eyes. "Shameful behavior for a fresh widow," he said in Romani.

She met his gaze. "I am no one's widow," she responded. "I belong to no one. Only to myself." She could not explain what was happening inside, how she could move from loathing to longing, but it was her own affair. She brushed past him and mounted her horse, and they continued south. Father Bernard caught up and gave her a pointed look but said nothing.

While their judgment meant little, John's opinion mattered to her, and her sense of discomfort grew with each hill they cleared. *What must he think of me?* she thought, *being so forward, and just after Teraf's death.* Why did her wits abandon her whenever John came close? He was just extending sympathy, a shoulder to cry on.

She'd cried on his shoulder. She had never cried on any man's shoulder. She had cried and sobbed, and he had strived to preserve her honor but she had stopped him, nay, grabbed him and kissed him. And she would do it again.

But he hates Gypsies. He was just feeling sorry for her, yes, decent enough to show compassion.

She watched him spur Dover over a crevice, noticed the

muscles of his legs tense as they hugged his horse's side and moved with such agility. With great effort she looked away. *Whatever instincts I am following must be curbed. I could not bear rejection from this man.*

A short time later two churches became visible, surrounded by a compact oval of many dozens of buildings, some three and four stories tall, continuing over the hill.

"What village is this?" asked Kadriya.

"Dorchester," John answered.

A stone bridge spanned the wide Frome river that flowed by the village. At the end of the bridge guards blocked the gated entry leading to the village. "Your name, and state your business in Dorchester," the taller guard asked.

John gestured to the banners his knights displayed, banners bearing the cross and St. Augustine's well, emblem of Cerne Monastery. "I am Sir John Wynter, in service to the Abbot of Cerne Monastery, and this . . ." He gestured to his side. ". . . is Father Bernard of Coin Forest. We are here to procure salt and spices."

The guard studied Father Bernard, his gaze lingering on his red belt and silvered purse. Apparently satisfied, he turned to John. "And how is Father Henry?"

"Father Robert," John corrected, validating his claim. "He is well. From here we will visit the Kingston quarries to select stone for the abbey's new church."

Wise, Kadriya thought. A credible answer.

The guard looked Dury over and his eyes narrowed. "What is this heathen doing with you?"

Dury held his head high, making no attempt to conceal the sleeve of his tunic, torn and blood-stained from the ambush at Blackwater Point.

"He is our translator," John said. "And a good one."

"You may pass," said the guard.

They crossed the bridge and entered the village. To the left, colorful signs hung in front of the crowded buildings. The streets to the right were dotted with smaller houses huddled in a random pattern. A breeze stirred a distasteful odor into the air, evoking the same sense of attraction and revulsion she had experienced when Lord Tabor had taken her to London. The activity—fish merchants, bakers, jongleurs, rope makers and bustling townsfolk—made for excitement, but unlike the open-air fairs that diverted sewage from the merchant stalls, the village's cobbled streets reeked from trash and night soil.

They took the streets straight south and the air grew cleaner.

John stopped at a sign bearing a white arm with red stripes and signaled the man who stood beneath it. "Excuse me, is there a jeweler here?"

The surgeon-barber cleaned his knife on his apron and wiped his brow, wet from the afternoon sun. "Bear north to the square and turn left at the cutler's shop." He regarded John more closely. "And see me after for a trim and shave, if it please you, Sir."

John touched the hair at his shoulder and laughed. "Forsooth, I need it."

Following directions, they found a red sign with a white unicorn, symbol of the goldsmith. It hung at the front of a two-story building. Two children played outside, boys, bouncing a blown-up pig's bladder on the cobblestones. John reined Dover and dismounted, and the boys scattered a safe distance, watching them.

John tethered Dover and helped Kadriya dismount. He turned to the men of his party. "Mayhap you will find the cutler's wares of interest," John suggested. "While I look for a present for my lady." He crooked his arm for Kadriya, offering her a playful smile.

Her heart skipped, but she chided herself. *Cease. It's just an excuse to search for clues to the chalice.* Still, his words echoed like soft music in her ear: "My lady." Enchanted, Kadriya accepted his arm.

He leaned down, as if to whisper an endearment. "The chalice is gold, this high," he said, gesturing almost a foot high, "and has eight emeralds."

"Emeralds." *That large, and gold? Sweet saints!*

They entered the jeweler's shop. A large, square wooden desk sat next to the far wall with a shelf of metal bowls and plates. An open door led to a back room, where a large, dark-haired man pounded metal on an anvil.

A squarely-built man greeted them, his hair greyed, his features dough-faced with age. "I am Gordan Sampford. How may I serve you?"

"I am Sir John Wynter of Cerne Abbey. I seek a pin of gold as a token of the esteem in which I hold my lady," John said, squeezing Kadriya's hand.

His lady. Butterflies flitted in her stomach. She hated loving the game, felt as young and foolish as Faith that she enjoyed it because it was so far from the coarse truth. But touching his hand and seeing the warmth in his eyes felt like running through warm rain in the sunshine, fleeting and rare. She willed the hoax to last, forever thankful that thoughts could not be heard.

Gordan nodded. "And a beauty she is, too," he said, regarding Kadriya with a smile. "We will find something worthy of her. Sit, please." He moved two stools out from the wall, positioning them in front of the desk.

He doesn't know I'm Roma. 'Twas no surprise. Her hair was brown, and her skin was of a color that could be seen two ways. If people didn't know her heritage, they saw her skin as light but carelessly exposed to the sun. Those who knew she was Roma noted how dark it was. Her only strong Romani traits were straight teeth and a lack of height. Even her eyes reflected her English heritage. She could have pretended to be English, but she had long ago dismissed that option as a silent lie that would eventually catch up with her. For now, however, it was a convenient cover.

The jeweler rang a bell. The distant hammering ceased and the sturdy young man appeared. As he came closer, his resemblance to Gordan became noticeable. "This is my apprentice. James, bring me the swan, the dove and . . ." he turned to John. "Coat of arms, Sir John?"

"Ermine stripe with a black lion rampant," John said. "But as a servant of God, I carry the arms of Cerne Abby."

Black lion and ermine, Kadriya thought. That suited him, light in color, like the ermine, fierce at heart, like the lion.

Gordan glanced at Kadriya's hands. "You are not yet wed?" he asked John.

John released her hand as if caught stealing a kiss and recovered before he abandoned the game completely, concealing his sudden reaction by placing her hand between both of his, lightly stroking her left hand with affection befitting a besotted young man. "No, not yet."

"Then bring them the lover's knot. Her hands are petite, so bring the smallest ones."

With his index finger John traced Kadriya's fingers from the tip to the palm, igniting trails of arousal that shot up her arm and set Kadriya's senses to spinning. Was it a nervous distraction, or did he know what devastation his touch was wreaking? A glance at his profile lent no clue.

Gordan closed and bolted the door to the street, and James returned with a black velvet display pillow. He placed a swan pin in the middle.

"This is a fine pin. Etched silver." The proportions of the

swan were off, creating a rather stumpy looking bird with a fat neck.

John shook his head. "What else do you have?"

At Gordan's signal, James removed the swan and placed the second pin on the pillow.

A dove, white enamel against gold, seemed poised to fly from the pin's base. Unable to resist, Kadriya traced its delicately engraved feathers.

"And finally," Gordan said, "we have the lover's ring."

James removed the dove pin and placed a ring on the velvet. Its gold bezel featured an engraved blessing hand above two joined hands.

"I should like the ring," John said.

"A pound, two crowns," said the jeweler.

"Too dear," replied John. " 'Tis silver, and there is no jewel. Three crowns."

"Silver with a gold bezel. Look you at the workmanship." The jeweler pointed out qualities with his tweezers, enjoying the negotiations. "A pound."

" 'Tis a treasure, but I am no nobleman, and look at the thin weld on the side, by the man's thumb. Three crowns and two shillings."

"Agreed." Gordan slipped the ring on Kadriya's finger.

It fit perfectly. *It means nothing. Nothing.* No matter how strong their attraction or how fervent his kisses, her blood was Romani blood, something she could not change. She forced a smile. "Thank you, John."

John patted her hand and stood. "The abbot has asked me to look for something on his behalf. For sacraments. Have you made any worthy acquisitions of late, a fine plate, perhaps, or a cross?"

Gordan's brows rose with renewed interest. "James, watch the front." He nodded to John and Kadriya. "Come with me."

They rose and entered the back room, and Gordan locked the door behind them. Here the windows were barred with ironwork, which provided security while letting sunlight in.

A long worktable supported by wrought iron bases ran down the middle of the room, which, warmed by the furnace fire, was considerably warmer than the outer room. An array of hammers, tongs and bellows hung on the wall by the fire. Along the opposite wall, locked caskets ornamented with enameled medallions, ivory rosettes and carved angels were stacked chest high behind a table, holding unspoken treasures. In the sequestered quiet Kadriya imagined plates of gold and priceless gems, and her skin tingled.

The jeweler slid stools out from beneath the wooden table and they sat.

With appropriate flourish he showed them a silver plate, jeweled robe clasps and reliquary pendants that opened to reveal small compartments for storing such saints' relics as teeth, bone fragments or hair. He also produced a free-standing gold cross.

John asked to see it and ran his hands over the smooth surface, as if looking for something and not finding it. He admired the pendants, opening and closing them. "Have you any chalices?" he asked casually.

Gordan showed them a dozen, none with emeralds.

Erol may have sold some of the jewels rather than the whole chalice. "What of gemstones," Kadriya asked. "Do you have any rubies, or emeralds? I have a pin from my mother and the stone was lost."

"How large?"

She looked to John. She did not know what the emeralds looked like.

"Two fingers high and half that wide, I think it was," he offered.

The jeweler looked at her skeptically. "That large?"

"It is an heirloom," Kadriya said, casting him a look of warning.

Realizing he might be jeopardizing a sale, Gordan nodded. "I crave your forgiveness, miss." He unlocked a small chest and showed her a fine ruby, an amethyst, and an emerald.

John leaned forward, inspected the amethyst first, then the emerald. "This is good," he said, nodding.

"Hard and durable, and look at the vivid green. A beautiful stone." He offered John the glass loupe.

John held the stone to the light and positioned the loupe. "But flawed. There's a wisp of white there, on the lower left corner."

"Flaw?" The jeweler's voice rang sharp with indignation, and he pulled his loupe to his eye to examine it.

"Do you see it?" John asked. "Those lines on the left side of the stone. White, filmy."

"Oh, that. It's not a flaw. It's a feature of the emerald."

"It's a flaw," John said. "And that's why I know . . ."

"Show me, please." Kadriya interrupted and slid her stool in closer, plucking the stone and loupe from Gordan. From her years with the French fairs she recognized the stone as a cabochon cut, oval, highly polished, not faceted. She turned it in the light, falling into the spell of its rich, earthly beauty, like moss in a spring forest, made bright by the morning sun. The gem shone clear but for the wisp in the corner, like a tiny, soft swirl. "Yes, I see it. It is a flaw."

"Some features are flaws and some are simply properties of the gem." Gordan smiled indulgently. "Just like us. We all have our strengths, don't we, our individual ways that stamp us as singular. So it is with the emerald." He turned the stone in the sun. "The feather-like lightness you see is known as *emerald silk*. Some call it a flaw. They say it diffuses the intensity of the green, but in fact, these are considered part of the character of the stone. To my eyes, it enhances its value. It softens the gem. Gives it depth and makes it entirely one of its kind."

"Indeed it does," John said. He pulled the loose gem from the jeweler, holding it firmly in his fist. " 'Tis because of the emerald silk that I know precisely where it came from."

The jeweler dropped his glass loupe. "What mean you?"

"How many of these have you?"

The jeweler stared anxiously at John's fisted hand. "Two."

"Who sold them to you?"

The jeweler swallowed visibly. "That, sir, is my personal business."

"You would not want word to reach your guild that you sell stolen goods."

"I do not!"

"You may prove it by telling me who sold these gems to you, and when." John stood, looming over the jeweler. "Or would you prefer to face the guild's prevot for an investigation and punishment?"

Gordan's face lost all color. "If I tell you, you will not breathe word of this to the prevot, or any others?"

"To no one. You have my word."

He looked to Kadriya. "And yours as well?"

"Verily."

Gordan returned the other gemstones to his chest. "Yesterday afternoon. A young man, well dressed. Dark skinned, long hair and dark eyes. I speak limited French and he spoke but a handful of English words, but we managed. He was from Marseilles. His horse and luggage had been stolen and he needed funds."

John scoffed. "You never doubted his story?"

Cold dignity hardened his features. "No."

"Or noted the setting marks and wondered why they were separated from their mountings?"

"Loose gems are not uncommon. He was in no hurry. After

our business, he lingered at the alehouse, trifling with the whores. He left just before sunrise, I heard." He held out his hand. "Give me the emerald now."

John held it between his thumb and forefinger. "I would buy this and the other gem back for what you paid for them. And yes, I will want to verify that by looking at your books."

Gordan's mouth thinned. "I am a goldsmith, not an almoner."

"Aye, a goldsmith who relies on his good reputation in the guild."

The jeweler drew back. "How do I know you won't take them for your own?"

"Because unlike your dark-skinned stranger, I come to you with authority. I am the abbot's first knight. I have served him since Normandy, six years ago. If you have doubts you may contact him about this matter, though that will delay us, which I assure you Father Robert will not appreciate."

Gordan gave him a long, studied look. "Who is your sacristan?"

"Eustace. He came to us from Weymouth seven years ago."

"James," he called to his apprentice.

"Yes?"

"See to Sir John's banner and describe it to me."

James exited and returned. "There are two other knights there and a priest, and the banner they carry is Cerne Abbey's, sir, a cross and St. Augustine's spring."

Gordan pulled the second emerald from his purse.

"Settle accounts with Sir John. He has chosen the ring at three crowns and two shillings. He will buy these two stones at cost."

The young man turned his ear as if he had not heard correctly. "At cost, sir?"

"You heard me," Gordan barked. He handed the second gem

to James and turned an angry glance to John. "Settle with James," he spat. "Then go."

Chapter 12
Seven Stars

They left the Dorchester gate behind them, Kadriya following Sir John, then Sir Thomas, Dury and Father Bernard. Kadriya guided Allie beside Dover. "Here is your ring," she said to John, preparing to remove the lover's knot.

He turned to her, his tawny hair waving in the breeze and shining gold in the low sunlight against his armor. His blue eyes caressed her with welcome and a touch of playful flirtation. "I would have you wear it."

A warm thrill flickered through her, and she tried without success to dismiss it.

John glanced at Father Bernard, dignified in his white hair and black silk toga, and inordinately attentive.

"It will ward off suspicion," John said.

Of course. Kadriya absorbed the sting of disappointment, chiding herself for bearing impossible dreams. Such wishes caused naught but trouble.

"When people ask our purpose in traveling, we will say we are headed to Poole to be wed," said John. "A priest is with us, so 'tis quite believable, eh, Father?"

Father Bernard regarded him. "You should not speak lightly of matrimony, Sir John. 'Tis one of the most important sacraments."

"I meant no affront, Father. Traveling to Poole to be wed is a good way to be discreet with our true purpose. Should the bishop visit Poole after Cerne Abbey, my abbot would not wish it to be common knowledge that we were chasing about the countryside looking for his chalice."

"What of the Dorchester jeweler? He knows."

"He's not apt to make it known he was duped by a thief. He has his reputation with the guild to maintain." John met Kadriya's eyes. "You were helpful with the jeweler, getting him to show us the emeralds without drawing suspicion."

"Thank you." His favor warmed her more than the unusually mild afternoon.

He rode ahead and she gazed at the gold and silver ring. She tipped it so the sun shone on the bezel, highlighting the engraving of the joined hands. *That's love. Hands joined as the hearts are.* 'Twas what she yearned for.

She recalled the tingling sensation that overcame her when John put the ring on her finger. She barely knew this man, despised him just days ago, but the more time she spent with him, the more she was becoming drawn to him. His virility was obvious in the span of his chest, his height and the muscles that defined his body. But he had treated her with tenderness, and she had seen him with Joya—he was a man of compassion and honor. His mere presence altered her heartbeat. It was as if he could draw her soul from her, heat it with desire and send it back to her through his eyes.

In the distance lush willow branches, still green amid the autumn reds and golds, wept onto the riverbank. *This man. Is it too much to harbor hope?* He desired her; that was clear. *But what if that's all it is?*

Recalling her poor judgment with Teraf, she clenched her jaw and tamped her wishes. With Teraf she had made the rushed, unsound decision of a desperate woman. She would not repeat the mistake. John himself said as much on their trip to the abbey. She should not force herself to fit in the narrow confines of a nobleman's world, or in the borderless, unconditional life of a

Rom. She thought of Maude, much older than Kadriya, twenty-seven summers and never wed, but Maude was happy. If Maude could be happy with her lot, so could Kadriya. She would repay John's kindness and help the tribe by finding the chalice, then she would resign herself to spinsterhood.

"Our visit to the jeweler revealed one thing," John said. "We know it's Erol, and we know he's headed toward Poole."

"We must take nothing for granted. We don't even know it's a Gypsy," Kadriya corrected. "Gordan said he had dark skin, black hair and spoke broken English. That could be most of the Gypsies in the tribe. He could even be from Spain. He spoke French. He could be a French Moor."

"It's a dark-skinned young male, selling emeralds unique to the stolen chalice," John said. "It has to be Erol."

"If it is, he won't be moving very fast," Dury said in Romani. His face was drawn with pain, and he seemed to droop even more in the saddle than usual.

"Your back," Kadriya said. "It's troubling you again."

" 'Tis nothing," he said. "Tell John that Erol's horse has a toe crack. Raced him too much the first week of the fair, so Erol's horse will be slow."

Kadriya interpreted.

"Good news," John said. The thought of Erol riding a tender-footed horse lifted his hopes.

Truth be told, the look of trust in Kadriya's eyes had already brightened John's day.

Why had he suggested she wear the ring? His brain and his tongue had become erratic. The invitation had simply come out, unbidden. Forsooth, the ring shone like a small star on her dainty hand, winking in the sunlight.

But it was not merely that comment that unnerved John. He always stumbled in some way in her presence, as if he were in a dim forest and the trail, once so familiar and easy to follow, had become filled with surprises, both pleasant and not.

While Teraf still lived, his guilt and deceit and Kadriya's unswerving loyalty to him had frustrated John and he had wished ill to come to Teraf. But when he found Teraf's body, John had gained no satisfaction in her sorrow and pain.

Her eyes, vibrant and alive, the hue of dark honey and flecked with green. She seemed at once the innocent, trusting Teraf as she had. Innocent, yet not without faults.

Flaws. The thought swirled in his mind. She was flawed like the emerald. Aye, that was what he saw in the depths of her eyes, that lusty, rich green of late summer. The same hue of the chalice stones.

Her judgment was flawed. She had played a part in the attack at Blackwater Point and her interference had mistakenly caused a knight's death, all of which caused turmoil for her patron's family and her priest, a man who never failed to defend her.

Her blood was flawed. Her passion was wild, untamed, unpredictable. Because of her heritage, dangerous.

Would that her Gypsy blood could be let from her veins.

Suddenly conscious of Father Bernard behind him, John dashed his thoughts. Here he was again, veering from the path, contemplating gems and Gypsies when he was supposed to be fetching the chalice. He shook his head as if to clear it. *Be not daft. 'Tis only a physical attraction. Until this morning she was intent on wedding Teraf.*

Dover balked at a narrow bridge and John urged his horse on, patting him low on the shoulder where he knew the horse would be most reassured. *The chalice. Erol.* John considered the Gypsy he knew little about, other than he was Teraf's closest friend. What if, after all this unfolded, Erol turned out to be the thief and Teraf the innocent go-along? Mayhap that would bring Kadriya comfort, that she had judged Teraf accurately.

John mentally slapped himself. What was he thinking? She

was affecting his judgment, just as the abbot suggested. Teraf had been a scheming, selfish thief who, tempted with a substantial treasure, could not resist it and impetuously drew his tribe and Kadriya into his web of trouble.

Was that the way it was? And if Teraf was tempted, who'd done the tempting? What was Eustace's role in all this? What secret did he fear Teraf had revealed with his dying breath? Mysteries. They would follow him to Poole, but hopefully not beyond. John would live with the anxiety so long as he could deliver the chalice before the bishop's arrival.

Five days. What if you can't find it in time? He pushed the thought from his mind. He would! Erol had to sell the chalice before he reached the seaport. It was much too valuable to keep on one's person.

Look what it had done to Teraf.

They crossed an expansive down, treeless, with low-lying bushes and acres of lush grass. In the heat John had removed his breast and back plates, and Kadriya discreetly watched the way the muscles of his forearms worked, how the light hairs covering his skin shone in the sunlight. His padded hauberk concealed the flesh, but not the way his powerful muscles moved beneath.

He had a commanding manner, yet showed tenderness with Dover, stroking him, talking softly to him, and when he would turn and afford her a glimpse of his craggy profile, with that firm, sensual mouth, she had to force herself to turn away or become obvious.

These thoughts are vain. Foolish. John Wynter was a knight, not clothed in the finery of a nobleman, but still, encased in armor that shielded his body and his heart. He hated who she was, pitied her as he would a wounded animal. Why torture herself with hope?

Like an impulsive child stealing marchpane from Sharai's

186

kitchen, she stole another glance. She could not stop. Fine. She would have her moments of madness, of fantasy. They would find the chalice, John would fulfill his duty and be gone from her life. A dull pain grew in her chest. She would enjoy his presence until then.

They neared a village and the knights once again straightened in their saddles, alert for trouble. The gatehouse and wall were made of wood, offering meager protection at the west side of its borders. The manor house was modest, just wattle and daub, bricks only at the base and affording barely enough room to shelter their animals. This was a poor village, but John wanted to check to be sure Erol had not thought this humble little settlement a good wayside refuge.

The church, boasting a modest bell tower, sat at the east end of the village, which held some three dozen small homes.

John and Sir Thomas visited with the two gate guards and they were granted entry.

Passing the blacksmith's shed, they saw the ironworker hunkered over his fire, working with two young boys of about eight and six years of age. They were hammering pieces of iron, and by the sound of the blacksmith's rising voice, they were not learning quickly enough. "Hold tight on the head," he growled, "hold it tight, I said."

They continued to the butcher's shop, where they learned that no dark-skinned man had visited recently. Father Bernard visited with the priest, who reported the same. The ale master had seen no one, nor had the miller, who advised that the Fowler Inn, a mile downriver could not house all of them. Five miles farther, however, an inn known as Seven Stars, where the River Shufflebottam flowed into the Frome, had more rooms and a larger stable.

They passed the blacksmith's space again as they were leaving. The smithy's face was bloated and had grown red with anger. He stood tense behind the older boy as he worked at the anvil with the hot iron.

The young lad clenched his mouth, scratched at his grimy, coarse tunic with the handle of the hammer, and swung down on the anvil again.

The blacksmith boxed his ears. "Harry, you stupid oaf," he said, cursing. "Look you. In your haste you have broken the pintel. The hinge will not work now. Come you here. I told you and told you," the blacksmith growled, dragging the boy to his feet. "Now it's the bucket again."

John reined Dover in sharply. His face blanched, stricken, as if he had made the mistake instead of the young lad.

"Nay!" Harry cried, dropping the hammer and scrambling off the stool.

The smithy grabbed Harry's hands and yanked them behind his back, locking them with his big hand, and dragged the boy to a cooling bucket resting on a work table. The bucket was filled with water upon which a black, bubbly residue floated. He shoved Harry's head into the soiled water.

Harry struggled, digging his feet into the dirt and trying to back up, but the blacksmith was stocky, at least fourteen stones to the young boy's seven.

Kadriya started to get out of her saddle to intervene.

John put his arm out, stopping her, though it was clear from the set of his jaw that he disapproved of the blacksmith's brutality.

Her stomach churned. The oaf was within his rights, but the boy had been trying his best. She wanted to see the blacksmith placed in the stocks, and she wanted the first throw.

The blacksmith pulled Harry up for air. "Are ya goin' to listen now and do it right?"

"Aye," he gasped.

Dunking him again, the blacksmith repeated. "Speak louder.

I didn't hear you."

"No," Harry choked, confused. In his fear, he soiled his breeches.

Furious, the blacksmith dunked him again.

John's breathing grew more labored. The scar running from his scalp to his left cheekbone darkened and his face twisted in anger. Stripping his sword belt off, he let his sword drop and looped the belt. Moving with cat-like swiftness, he dismounted, rushed behind the blacksmith and snared his throat with the belt. "You devil. Leave him be."

The blacksmith released Harry's head and he emerged from the water.

Choking and vomiting the dark water, Harry collapsed.

John grabbed the smithy by his hood, held him at arm's length and struck him with his fist.

The smithy's head jerked back and he staggered.

"What kind of animal are you?" John struck him again.

The man grabbed his nose, looked at the blood in his hand. "You whoreson!" He lunged at John.

John dodged, taking the blow on his shoulder, and countered with another punch.

Reeling, the smithy retreated. "He broke three pintels today. He's clumsy and stupid," the blacksmith said.

"God's nails!" John's voice came out in a shouted strangle, as if the boy had died. " 'Tis no reason to drown him."

The blacksmith held up his hands. "Get thee gone. Guards. Guards!" he called for help. When none arrived, he retreated. "He's my son. I can do with him what I wish."

The fury left John's face, and his features grew frighteningly calm. He released the man.

If I were the blacksmith, Kadriya thought, *I would apologize and retreat.* But the cast of the blacksmith's eyes suggested he was by nature ill-tempered, and he said naught.

"Have you found this punishment effective?" John asked.

"Aye. Keeps the little whelps working when they would be idle or slipshod."

"No. I mean, have you ever tried it yourself?"

Wary, the blacksmith backed up. "What mean you?"

Contempt hardened John's features. He grabbed the brute's arm, twisting it viciously so the blacksmith had to turn his back to John to avoid breaking it.

John used his knees to kick the blacksmith's knees forward. The blacksmith stumbled, waving his free arm for balance.

John captured it, looped that hand with the other and bound his wrists together with the sword belt, capturing him just as the blacksmith had done with Harry.

"Let me go!"

"In due time." John gripped the big man's hair just behind the ears and shoved the blacksmith's head in the bucket.

The blacksmith used his powerful legs, trying to regain his balance and freedom, but John seemed a man possessed, driven by some inner demon that twisted his features in rage and grim determination.

John used his fury and his own weight for leverage and held him there. When large bubbles surfaced on the water, John pulled him up.

The smithy's dark hair hugged his head like a black rag.

"None too pleasant, is it," John growled. "Care to have another turn at it?"

The blacksmith struggled. "Nay."

"What? I could not hear you." John mimicked what the blacksmith had said to Harry and dunked him again.

The blacksmith emerged again, drenched and gasping.

"These boys will work hard for you," John said. "Won't you boys?"

The boys rushed to the corner of the shop, crashing into

themselves in an effort to back away from John, their eyes wide in terror. "Aye, sir. Aye."

"Good. And you." John shoved his forefinger on the blacksmith's chest. "You won't be using this method of punishment again. If I get word you do, I'll return and we'll discuss this again." He released his wrists and gave him one last shove.

Water from the blacksmith's hair dripped into his eyes, and beneath the lashes pure venom glowed. He strained forward as if to attack, but checked himself.

John turned his back on him and strode back to Dover and remounted. His hands shook as he held the reins, and he avoided Kadriya's eyes. "Erol is not here," he said, his voice still tremulous. "Let us find the Seven Stars Inn."

Erwin, the inn master, unlocked the door leading off the kitchen. "This and the room above the stable are all we have," he said. Circular scars the size of fish scales covered his cheekbone. Remnants of the pox, John guessed.

The inn master jiggled the lock and wrenched it free from its bolt. Once inside, he lit candles so the room could be seen in the darkening gloom of night. The small hearth was dark and, in addition to a bed, a small table nestled in the corner with a wooden wash basin.

Kadriya inspected the bed while John paced the room, considering security. Ground floor offered less protection from break-ins. He opened the shuttered window and dust motes floated in the final rays of sunlight. The courtyard was large, surrounded on the other side by more rooms, a barn and the stables, where John and the other men would sleep. No trees would obstruct his view of her window.

He shuttered it closed and secured it with an iron bolt on the inside. "Good. It's secure," John said. "Is it sufficiently clean?"

Kadriya replaced the covers she had pulled back to inspect

the linen-covered straw mattress. "Aye."

A far cry from the luxury of her own room at Coin Forest, John thought, but she made no complaint. He nodded to the innkeeper. "We should like to stay."

"Good. Prepare for supper," he said, "and listen for the serving bell in an hour. The fare is chicken and pigeon pie."

John slid into the wide river, the cool water taking his breath away but soothing his skin, rubbed raw from his armor. Repairs from the damage at Blackwater Point had been thorough, but the back plate chafed at his arms. He dove under the surface, and the water flowed over his eyes and chest. What had he told the abbot about Kadriya? *Merely a fascination. Taken by her beauty.* Oh, he was. Her body tempted him, but it was the spirit in her eyes that gave him pause, that drew him in.

He had seen the look of outrage in her eyes from the blacksmith's brutality. She had been as concerned as he with the boys' safety. Forsooth, she was tenderhearted with Joya and Faith, even when they locked her in that hot barn. She would be a gentle mother to her children.

And loyalty. No woman possessed such fierce loyalty as Kadriya.

He floated, watching the overhead curtain of leaves and branches drift slowly by. *She's a Gypsy.* Mayhap he had said it to himself too many times, for, like an insect bite that at the outset flares and itches, then fades with time, it seemed less important now than it had before. How much did it matter to him?

When he held her in his arms, naught. Naught.

But the abbot. John's standing at the monastery and among his fellow knights.

The current pulled him harder, and he checked the shore. How far had he drifted? He edged toward the shore where the current was weaker and swam back to the inn.

Dining was under way when John and Kadriya entered the hall. Three ten-foot tables ran the length of the room, with ale and wine kegs to the left and, to the right, a small fire in the hearth. Two large, brown, flop-eared hounds begged at the tables, one a new mother with puppies whose tiny tails wagged as they scampered to her stomach for a meal of their own.

John had visited with some of the inn's guests earlier. Four wool merchants traveling to Southampton to finalize a shipment to Flanders, a burly stonecutter looking for work and two Dominican monks were among the guests. Besides Kadriya and the innkeeper's wife there were only two other women, an older one—wealthy, judging by the fur trim on her hood—and a fragile, sallow-faced girl, her eyes sunken from illness. John searched the full tables, looking for a dark-skinned face, and saw none. Dury had not yet arrived.

John felt a wave of interest flow toward them. His size and armor often attracted interest, even alarm, when he entered a hall, but his years with the abbot had provided many opportunities to observe the outpouring of reverence and respect when Robert entered a hall.

With Kadriya on his arm, the men appeared not even to see him. They turned to her, staring openly, pleasure and admiration lighting their eyes.

Forsooth, she was beautiful. John could feel the heat of her arm on his, and she had washed with the spices and herbs that reminded John of spring moss and flowers. She filled his senses with a humming current of excitement.

The short, balding merchant rose, shamelessly staring. "I am William, fair lady," he said, "and this," he said, gesturing to a merchant with embroidered sleeves, "is Mark. This shabby dining hall is made brighter with your presence."

Mark, the merchant with embroidered sleeves, laughed. "And your tongue is so honeyed the bees are swarming."

Anger flashed through John, tensing his muscles, tightening his gut. His hand itched, wanting to punch the slimy-mouthed merchant in the face for wooing her, jumping like a hot hare in spring, when she was clearly John's woman.

Your woman? Have you lost your senses? He blinked as if to clear his mind of such folly.

Kadriya thanked him for his compliment and lowered her gaze, a gesture that oozed charm and naiveté.

The tall one gave Kadriya sheep's eyes, and the long-haired merchant looked as if he would swoon.

John's hand formed into a fist, and he feared he would lose control. What was wrong with him? He must need rest, get some distance from her so he could think more clearly.

He tightened his grip on her arm and led her to the table farthest from the men and close to the wealthy woman and her ill daughter, who, they learned, were named Paulina and Emma. They were on their way to St. Swithun's shrine in Winchester, where they hoped Emma would be healed by the relics.

"The chicken smells delicious," Kadriya said, serving herself from the large platter.

"A jot dry," said Paulina, "but filling. Too much in my case, but at my age, who's looking?" She laughed. "From whence do you hail, Mistress Kadriya?"

"Coin Forest," Kadriya answered.

"We're from Weymouth," Pauline answered. "My husband is a weaver." Her chin rose slightly with pride. "A master of his guild."

"Perhaps he's met my patron, Richard, Baron Tabor? He has visited Weymouth for woolens."

"I'm sure he has."

Father Bernard, Dury and the abbey knights entered the hall.

The shortest wool merchant stood, glaring at Dury. "You. Gypsy. You are not welcome here. Go you out with the horses to eat."

Dury looked to John.

"Never mind him, Dury," John said. "We have a seat here."

The short merchant rose and approached Dury. "I said get out."

John excused himself and walked between Dury and the merchant. "Your name, sir?"

"William. William Pounder. I make auncels. Weights," he added.

"I'm John Wynter, first knight to Robert of Wayneflete, at the Abbey Cerne. You may put your fears to rest, sir. He is my translator, and we are paid boarders."

"I do not fear him. I find his breed offensive."

John took a step closer to the merchant, his jaw tight with purpose. "Then take your own meal to the stables," John said. "He is in my employ and he eats here."

The merchant's friend, a wiry-haired young man, joined William. Noting John's height and size, he backed up a foot. "I'm Mark. We don't abide Gypsies. They speak to the devil and steal from honest merchants. Do not look him in the eye. I say he goes, too."

Hell's bells. Every worm that could crawl out from under a rock was doing so. John raised a fist and stepped forward.

"Wait." Kadriya rose from her table and joined them, facing the merchants. "Would you send me to the stables to eat, as well?"

They both assumed expressions of chivalrous shock. "Why, of course not, my lady," the short one said. "We would welcome you at our table."

She tipped her head, flashing a demure smile. "Certes?"

"Indeed. Your eyes light the evening," Mark, the wiry-haired merchant said, bowing with an engaging smile. "Prithee join us."

"I heartily thank you." Kadriya lifted the hem of her gown and stepped closer to them until she was eye to eye with the short one. "Then Dury is welcome, too," she said, gesturing to him, "because he is my cousin." She uttered the last words with precision and purpose and held her green eyes wide, feigning innocence and challenging them to throw her out with Dury after they had made such gallant speeches of welcome.

The merchants' smiles faded, and the shorter merchant's eyes blinked quickly as if Kadriya had spat in his face. Mark backed up into the bench at his table and fell backward onto it.

The merchant, William's, eyes simmered with hostility. "You cheap, fil—"

John rushed forward, grabbing him by the throat, blocking the offensive words. "Honor her, or answer to me. Is that clear?"

William choked something unintelligible and nodded.

John escorted Kadriya back to the table, and Thomas, Father Bernard and Dury joined them.

Pauline took Kadriya's hand. "I can't abide foul tongues, my dear. So you're a Gypsy? How wonderful! We met some of your kind in Calais. Such handsome people, though you are the most fetching Gypsy I've ever met, Kadriya." She tipped her head and sighed. "The dancing, the singing, the horsemanship!"

A young merchant leaned over from a neighboring table. "I'm Henry of Lyme Bay. I visited the fairs in Troyes last summer. The Egyptians, they call themselves there. They're fine coppersmiths, and make good saddles."

"They work hard," the merchant next to Henry said. "Well, when they're not playing their instruments. Recall you when that old woman took my hand?" He shuddered. "She knew my fortune before it came to pass."

Pauline clapped her hands in excitement. "How thrilling it

must be to see the future, to travel and delight people with your many talents." She pulled her purse from her gown and lowered her voice. "Do you need funds for your travels, dear? I'd be pleased to help." She offered coins under the table.

Kadriya closed Pauline's hands over her coins. "How kind of you, but I haven't traveled since I was seven summers," Kadriya said. "I have lived in Coin Forest as a ward of Lord Tabor most of my life. And thank you, yes," she said, meeting John's gaze, "the Gypsies are a people of many talents."

The merchant, William, stood, yelling above the din of voices. "Their talent," he said, slurring the word, "is thievery." He raised his chin, making a presentation of sniffing the air. "What's that foul smell? Ah yes, I recognize the stench." He glared at Kadriya. "Gypsies." He lifted his travel pack from the floor and led his friends out the door.

The noisy dining hall had become quiet but for the whimpering of the puppies.

John struggled to find a comfortable position on his hay-stuffed mattress above the stable. His exhaustion should have sealed his eyes to restful sleep, and his body was more than cooperative, but his mind kept spinning with the day's activities. Finding the emeralds, the jeweler's confirmation that Erol was just ahead, the captivating presence of a certain woman and her surprisingly strong spirit in spite of the daunting circumstances, kept playing out in his mind. He tossed and turned, trying to get comfortable, but like a monotonous day of threshing wheat, the same visions passed again and again in his head, keeping him awake.

Rising, he peered out the window, checking again to be sure her shuttered window was still safely closed.

Behind him Dury slept, and Father Bernard, mouth yawning wide as the caves at Cheddar, slept to the tune of a rumbling, squawking snore.

Worry needled him. The merchants had angled hateful glances at Kadriya through the meal and after, during the minstrels' music. She had humiliated them, and now they slept in a room near hers. What if they sought revenge in the night? Would John be able to clear the courtyard and reach her quickly enough? What if, in his state of exhaustion, he didn't hear her cries for help?

God's teeth. His bones ached from hours in the saddle with armor rubbing at his neck, armpits and thighs. His hands hurt from hitting the blacksmith and ramming his hand on the rim of the bucket, and now this. With a sigh, he gathered the drooping, hay-stuffed mattress and slung his wool traveling cloak over his arm. He would sleep in the hall at her door. If those men wished to seek revenge, they would have to go through him.

John tossed, dreaming, on the floor at Kadriya's door. He was running in a field of wheat, with heads heavy and ready for harvest. In a wink he was no longer running, but riding his destrier, Dover, full out, relishing the sensation of the wind in his hair. It was spring, and they raced through the fields, fairly flying over the earth beneath them. The breeze carried the fragrance of lilacs, and the grasses grew tall off the path. The sun's rays warmed his face and back, and everywhere birds sang, chirping, nesting. After a year of darkness and frigid cold, the earth was alive again.

John's legs didn't reach the stirrups. He was short, and small, a child again.

Clouds rolled in, stealing the light and the warmth, and the spring breeze grew to a vigorous gale, then a frightening storm. It blew Dover backward, broke great limbs from the trees and tossed the jagged wood at them and lifted John and Dover into the air.

Dover screamed in alarm, his eyes wide with terror.

John clung to Dover's mane, wrapping his legs tightly around the horse.

Dark night fell suddenly, as if they had been covered in a heavy cloak. The wool scratched his skin, and the wind tossed them to and fro.

A huge gust came up and threw John to the ground. The earth shifted beneath him. John gasped for air but found none. Dover was gone. He was alone.

Smoke, John's beloved childhood dog, ran up to John, barking with excitement.

"Smoke." Joy filled his chest and he hugged his dog. "Smoke, you're alive."

The dog's eyes were bright, his coat shiny and healthy, his tongue warm and wet on John's face. John hugged him. "Smoke. I've missed you."

The earth rumbled beneath him, and John cried out. He grasped Smoke, but his fur came out in large clumps and he was left clutching nothing. The luster left Smoke's eyes and they became haunted and dull. The last of his fur fell and he wasted away in front of John's eyes, his spine and ribs protruding obscenely from tight, dry skin.

"Smoke." John sank slowly into mud. The mud covered John's face and he could not breathe. A knife pierced his side and he tried to cry out in pain but mud filled his mouth and no sound came out.

He could hear Smoke's whimpering, then yelps of pain.

Anguish gurgled up John's throat, and a pain spurted through him like a dark, fetid evil, and all his affection for Smoke was ripped from his chest.

He cried out again and again, and a hand yanked him from the mud.

John wiped the mud from his eyes. A huge man stood above

him, his small, closely set eyes devoid of any feeling, his dark face wide, his eyebrows slanted, with a small, stingy mouth like none John had seen before. He smiled, showing big teeth, and he held John's bleeding heart in his hand.

It was the foreigner.

Chapter 13
Smoke

The sound of anguished moaning awakened Kadriya. Disoriented, she felt the prickles of the straw mattress and saw the shuttered window and the flames of the warm fire the inn master had built for her. Another groan sounded, just outside her door. Her heart skipped and hurried. Had someone been stabbed? She tried to calm herself. Mayhap it was just the mother dog with her puppies.

Securing the ties on her linen gown, she rolled from the bed and pulled her dagger, gripping its ivory handle carved with a bird in flight.

Kadriya stood at the door. "Who is it?"

The creature moaned again.

Kadriya hesitated. "Answer me."

A word mumbled by a familiar voice made her heart stop. John. She opened the door.

He lay on a thin mattress of straw, clutching his cloak to his chest and face. In the firelight from her open door his light oak-hued hair covered only half his face, revealing a tortured expression of loss and pain. Seeing him collapsed and suffering took her breath away. "John."

She knelt on the floor, looking for blood, and found none. He was dreaming again, just as he had dreamed in the forest, after Blackwater Point. She sat next to him and lightly stroked his hair, lifting it from his face.

Tears wet his eyelashes.

"It's all right, John." He was in a deep dream and did not respond. She cradled his head near her breast, rocking him slightly and humming a tune that calmed her doves when they were startled.

His temple pulsed under the light scar that ran from his scalp to his cheekbone. He had likely come close to losing his eye in whatever battle had given him that wound.

She knew so little about him. An air of violence and mystery swirled around him. As a knight, he must kill to survive. The mystery about him must be dark, very dark. She tried to muster fear and could not. She trusted him, and knowledge of that made her more afraid than any unknown shadow in his past. For in trusting came risk, something Kadriya, still raw from her disappointment with Teraf, was not prepared to take.

John heard music. It was Kadriya, crooning to her doves. He moved closer to her soft warmth.

Soft warmth? He jerked awake. *God's nails!* Her brown hair cascaded around his head and he was nestled at her breast. His head was resting in her lap.

She stroked him like a puppy. "You were having a nightmare and woke me. It's all right," she said, her voice soft and maternal.

A rash of embarrassment spread over his skin, itching, burning. He freed himself from her sheltering embrace and sat upright. "I need no coddling."

Her brows knitted in concern. "I wasn't coddling you. I was offering comfort."

"I have no need of comfort, either."

She cast him a dark look. "Forsooth. You were the one who woke *me*." Her voice chilled with indignation. "I thought you had been stabbed, many times by the way you were moaning. Just like you did in Coin Forest. You woke me then, too."

Egad, had he been moaning again? She must think him an overgrown boy. Beyond speech, he just stared at her, caught like a fool in his own protests.

A crashing sound came from the kitchen next door, followed by drunken laughter.

He rose quickly, pulling her up along with him. "We must preserve your honor. They cannot find you out here at this hour, with me," he said, pushing her toward her door. "Get you back inside."

"With a knight camped outside my door?" She lowered her voice. "Come in with me." She gestured as if wiping a tear from her eye. Looking downward at his arm, she tapped her sleeve.

He touched his eye and found it wet, and in checking his sleeve, he saw that it was wet with tears. Sweet saints, he'd been crying. He jerked his head toward the kitchen, where more than one man was brawling. Should they enter the hallway and see him here, like this . . .

He seized his mattress and followed her into her room.

With the door safely shut, she assumed an air of efficiency. "Put your mattress there by the fire and warm up."

He looked at her, but for the first time since he had met her, she avoided his gaze and turned to her travel bag, from which she drew a flask and handed it to him.

He pulled the stopper and sniffed. Mead. The aroma of ginger, cinnamon and nutmeg drifted to him, dear spices that reminded him of the wealth to which Kadriya was accustomed. The mead flowed over his tongue, sweet and fresh with apple. "Exceedingly good," he said, handing it to her.

She took a drink, too, shivering as it went down. "Thank you. We stand it three full months. Maude poured it just before we left."

The honeyed mead warmed his stomach and spread through his limbs, relaxing him. She made no more comment about his blubbering and didn't mention his howling like an infant in the hallway, waking her, or about why he had camped outside her door. He wanted to strew pearls at her feet for her gracious tactfulness. For her understanding.

She handed him the flask and he took another pull and passed it back to her.

Accepting it, she sat down cross-legged in front of the fire, content to share his prickly seat. He looked at the beautiful woman before him, her hair shining with golden highlights at the fire's side, and he could have sworn he saw a halo.

His gaze moved from her face to her long, graceful neck, and the light linen gown she wore, the tops of her breasts rising and falling with her breathing, the skin of her arms smooth and naked in the firelight. She took a drink, licking a drop that spilled past her full lips. Catching his gaze, she regarded him with those remarkable eyes, colored with the earth and the grasses, dark, clear and penetrating. "Was it the blacksmith?"

"What?"

"Did the blacksmith's brutality provoke your nightmare?"

She would not let the matter rest. Her halo faded slightly. He took another drink, the mead tasting progressively smoother.

"Was your father cruel to you?"

"Nay." He knew the nightmare well. 'Twas not about his father, nor his stepfather.

She regarded him, her mind working, as if she were playing a game of chess and had his queen in jeopardy. "Does it involve a woman?"

What did I say? "Nay."

She spent a full minute playing with the love-knot ring, as if waiting for him to tell more, but she gave no sign of disappointment when he did not speak.

She handed him the flask. "Tell me about Smoke."

She was a fine chess player, this woman with half a halo. The mead had worked a spell on his head, and his cares seemed more distant, the dream less devastating. She twirled a long tress of her golden-touched hair around her finger, and the motion, so feminine, so sensual, was spellbinding.

Suddenly he needed to tell her, to release the pressure of the burden, wanted the words to spill out, to join the disorderly pile of pearls he had already strewn at her feet.

"Smoke was my dog," he said, swallowing convulsively from the memory of the animal he had loved so much. "A big, long-haired dog, dusty black, like the color of spent firewood." He could not tell her about his father's death, or his stepfather, who accepted John as an unsightly growth on his mother's arm when he wed her, the stepfather who never cared a jot for him. Nor would he tell her about his moment of shame.

"It was bitter cold that whole year," he said, and the dark terror unfolded, distant but alive in his memory. "The leaves on the trees budded dark and small from the harsh cold, but they could not form fruits. The horses and cows fed on the meager grasses until there were no more. Finally they stood so gaunt you could count the bones of their spines and ribs.

"Months went by and the harvest was poor. We slaughtered our last cow, our last pig. Somehow we made it through the winter."

He stopped, overwhelmed by the memory of the smell of death that spring day.

She took his hand, a simple gesture, but it gave him a bond with someone he had grown to trust.

Her closeness encouraged him, and he continued. "Eventually the rivers were stripped of all fish, the lakes of all eel. The rabbits dwindled. We boiled bark for food. Simon the Cheeseman dared to hunt the royal forest, and brought a thin deer home to the village. We shared a good dinner and for that one day, we had hope. Some whispered of ancient gods who were angered, but my family never swayed to that line of thinking. That night, we gave special thanks to God."

He sighed. "Word traveled, and Simon lost his right arm as punishment for hunting the king's forest. He might have lived out his life as a beggar, but God spared him and he died."

She kept her gaze on the fire. "Trying times. I'm sorry, John."

"With each week Smoke grew as gaunt as we were. His fur fell out in clumps and he grew bald in large patches about his chest and back, but he never failed in his duty to warn us, protect us. Brigands roamed the countryside, and we fought for the few possessions we still had. As hunger grew, the thieves grew more bold, too.

"So it was that morning. My mother had taken my sisters and brother to the stream for water. They stayed, hoping to catch a stray crayfish or two, and I helped my mother carry the buckets back. Water was boiling on the fire, and Smoke barked. Three men approached.

"My stepfather went out to stop them and they slashed him down right there where he stood. My mother screamed and tried to bolt the door but they forced their way in. We had nothing." A ragged edge had grown on his voice. He cleared his throat. He could not finish the story, and stared at the fire. The fire burned steady, and from the fresh, sweet fragrance it put forth, he could tell the wood had come from an apple tree.

He would not tell her of the three strangers, one just a boy, maybe nine, his skin mottled, his teeth loose in their gums and three fingers missing on his right hand, the brand of a convicted thief. He would not tell her of the father, or the other man. The one immensely tall and dark-skinned, with eyes black as night, wearing a scarf, flashing a long dagger.

"Give us your food," he had said, speaking with a heavy accent John had never heard before.

His mother had turned her palms up to him. "We have none." Fear made her voice waver, and she backed up to the wall.

The foreigner advanced. "Then we shall have you, woman."

John grabbed the scythe from the wall and drew it like a sword, and the foreigner stopped, surprised at the challenge. He looked at John and started laughing. "Your little knight has wet himself." He pointed at John's feet, where urine puddled. In a flash the man reached out, and his iron grip paralyzed John's hand. He squeezed until John dropped the scythe, then picked it up off the floor. He grabbed his mother's breasts but pushed her away in disgust. "Skin and bones," he slurred, walking away from her.

"What happened then?" Kadriya asked.

"Outside the foreigner looked at Smoke."

"The foreigner?"

He would not tell her of his dark skin. "He had . . ." He paused to think of a careful way to say it. ". . . unusual features. He came from somewhere far away. He said to the other stranger, 'Take the dog.' I yelled at Smoke, 'Run. Run, Smoke!' But he wouldn't run. He came to me instead, and the foreigner took him. I cried out, and Smoke bit him, so he slit Smoke's throat and threw him across the back of his horse." He swallowed. "And they left."

"I should not have cried out. My weakness doomed him." John's emotions warred with one another. A strange sense of peace settled in his bones for having spoken of it, as if the black memory had less power now. Still, it was weak of him and he tensed, bracing himself for her pity.

But she made no move to soothe him.

He quietly exhaled.

Collecting a handful of wood chips, she pondered one at a time, slivering some with her thumbnail and spinning them in the fire. The pieces caught ablaze and landed in small balls of fire onto the larger logs, half spent in the late evening hours. "Was this foreigner a Gypsy?"

His dream was about Smoke, not the stranger. She had missed the point. Even when she meant not to, she somehow managed to complicate things. Other than hatred, he had never given the foreigner any thought. He picked at a corner of the mattress, pulling bits of straw through the coarsely woven fabric and wishing desperately he hadn't moaned in his sleep and had not come in and shared this story. Nightmares were private pains. He had always thought himself mad. Now she would, too. "I miss my dog. 'Tis all it is."

She shot him a cool glance. "I think you've devoted enough hatred to the Gypsies that you would know. Was he a Gypsy? Or was he just someone with unusual features, from another place?"

"I'm sorry for the way I treated you in the beginning. I did not know you. I—"

Her eyes became moist, drawn in reluctant awareness. "Every time you look at me you see this man, don't you?"

"Don't be mad. You are none of the things I thought you were. I misjudged you."

Pain filled her eyes. She braced herself to get up.

He put a hand on her shoulder. *I must tell her how I feel.* He met her gaze. "When I first saw you dancing with Teraf, I was taken by your beauty. You were like a flower in a field of weeds, but you were his, and you were with them."

"The Gypsies."

"Aye. And I thought you were like them, but you're not. You're honorable. Loyal. All the things Father Bernard said." His throat tightened, but he forced the words out. "Pray forgive me."

Her eyes were unreadable, but her strength shone in them, an invincible spirit that would carry her through whatever life cast her way. Of course she would not accept his apology. He had condemned her, insulted her. The air chilled in spite of the fire, and he looked away. Her rejection carved an unseen wound, and his chest ached from the loss. He should never have revealed the darkness of his dreams. Taking a deep breath, he released it and rose from the straw mat.

She stood and reached out, touching his arm.

He pulled his arm away. He could abide her anger, but not her pity. "I am fine."

She took his arm, this time more forcefully. "Do not go."

He dared to meet her gaze.

"I accept your apology. You are a fine man. I misjudged you from the outset, as well."

Kadriya held his forearm even after he turned her way. She could feel his pulse beneath her fingers, and the connection, and the look in his stunning blue eyes stole her breath. He was fiercely handsome and proud, and yet she sensed his uncertainty, which made him endearing, more approachable. He seemed ready to bolt, and she tried to read the signals of his body and the look in his eyes, trying to know when to hold back and let him talk and when to step forward herself.

"Your words bring me happiness." Somehow, over these past several days, his opinion of her had come to mean so much. She swallowed, hoping her courage would last. "You have been my strength. I have hoped that you would see me for who I am."

He regarded her with an intense gaze, his breathing shallow. "And do you see me for who I am?" His voice was husky.

"You are judgmental, but also kind. Honorable." The memory of being locked in the hot storage barn brought a smile. "You are patient with wayward little girls. And skilled at stool ball."

His mouth curved with the memory of their flirtation. It lit his face and gave a glimpse of his brighter side, causing a fluttering thrill to shoot down her body, all the way to the floor beneath her toes.

An unseen spark danced between them, and she swallowed again, overwhelmed with emotion. "I see you, John Wynter." Her voice had dropped to a whisper.

His blue eyes darkened with passion. He drew closer and his

scent, earthy with a hint of fresh grasses and leather, filled her senses.

"Kadriya." Her name resonated, rich and colorful on his tongue.

Her womanly instincts heeded the rough timbre in his throat. *He wants me.*

Fearful of his rejection, she stepped back. "I am not who you think I am."

His blue eyes never wavered. "I lacked good judgment in the past, but not now. Trust me." Laden with emotion, his voice deepened, the request like a plea to her heart. He extended his hand to her, his light brow raised in question.

The moment hung heavy in the firelight. Sharai had enlightened Kadriya of the ways of physical love and had shielded her from men who might force her against her will. Kadriya had guarded her virtue; surrendering to her passion now would make her an even less suitable bride than she'd been before.

Virtue had brought her nothing, though. She thought of Murat and Teraf, on the burning pyre. Life was fleeting and she had never felt like this before with any man. She was drawn to his strength and assurance, to the dark mystery of him and the mesmerizing invitation in his eyes.

She moved closer.

He touched her face, his fingers tracing magic, like the flutter of the dove's wing on her skin, and the passion in his eyes set her body to a slow hum.

"I should leave." He spoke softly.

Her pulse fell into the rhythm of his and she touched his face, the stubble from half a night's growth rough on her palm. "Stay." The word escaped her before she weighed it, but it seemed right as breathing to her. "I trust you."

He brought her into his arms, his chest muscles hard against her breasts.

A ragged sigh escaped her lips and a thrill rushed through her, as if her doves had lifted her into the air and she were floating. His mouth covered hers, his lips soft and moist, and his tongue rushed in to join hers.

He tasted of sweet mead and salt, and she returned the kiss. Held in the powerful circle of his arms, she embraced him. No matter what the future might bring or however short her time with him might be, she had come home to her heart. She ran her fingers through his thick hair and caressed his shoulders, feeling his muscles moving under her fingertips.

His hands slipped low on her back and he pulled her to him.

He was hard and eager against her, and the sensation sent a spike of fresh desire into her swollen breasts. She threw her head back.

Taking advantage, he kissed her neck, working his way down to the base. His big hand covered her breast, his fingers seeking her nipple, rubbing it, teasing it.

Overcome with pleasure, she cried out.

He lowered his head and covered her nipple with his mouth, soaking her gown. His tongue danced across the tip, and the sensation of his tongue and the fabric brought a new, throbbing ache from between her legs.

Her knees weak, she held tight to his broad shoulders. She hungrily sought his mouth and found it, kissing him, heady with the sensation of their tongues joining in an irresistible swirl of desire.

With an effortless motion he gathered her in his arms and carried her across the chamber. He held her suspended in his arms, and kissed her again and lowered her to the bed.

He pulled off his doublet, unlaced his tunic and slipped off his travel boots. Watching her, he released his points and slipped out of his hose. His face dropped to the task and his light hair fell over his eyes.

Fascinated, she watched his muscles work as he disrobed. Every part of him was sculpted and strong. Firelight danced on his back as he worked out of his hose, and she saw more evidence of battle. Her warrior carried angry scars across his chest and shoulders, deep scars in his soul. But his heart was pure; she knew it.

She glanced below his waist and seeing his arousal, her confidence wavered, but he came to her, looking through his loose hair with a reassuring smile. He kissed her soundly, and desire claimed her again. He worked the gown over her head, his hands skimming over her body. "Kadriya," he murmured. He kissed her breasts, and she arched her body to him, growing desperate for him. He kissed her knees, working his way up her thighs until she cried out for him.

His fingers skimmed between her thighs and roamed between her legs. He found the point of her desire and stroked her slowly, bringing waves of hunger she had never felt before. She clung to his shoulders, too weak to cry out for relief, but always seeking his mouth, a wet, rhythmic caress that urged her to greater heights.

He supported his weight over her, his chest muscles bulging from the effort.

Acknowledging the growing need that melted her, she raised her hips, but logic made her wonder if she was being inviting or lewd. "John, please." Fear mingled with the excitement and she sought his closeness to dispel it, stroking his back, pulling him toward her.

He moaned in deep pleasure, as if she had answered his secret wish, and a deep pool of desire swirled inside her, heat and moisture and need. His fingers stroked her again and slipped inside her, bringing a rich, new sensation that pleased, yet made her even more needy for him. She moved against him, clinging to his shoulders, moaning through their kisses.

She gasped and her body shuddered in relief. Her tremors embraced him, and he ended the kiss and met her eyes.

"Kadriya," he breathed.

His big hands cupped her bottom, raising her to him.

A pressure increased inside her, a sharp pain as he entered.

She gasped.

"I do not mean to hurt you." His voice was raw with need, but he stopped moving and held her.

He kissed her and traced her eyebrows with his forefinger, caressing her face, trailing kisses on her neck and stroking her body, patient and gentle.

She took a slow breath, willing the pain away. Desire returned, and she ventured moving her hips, and a rich sensation overruled the pain.

"Relax, my love. If it's too much I will stop. Just tell me."

He kissed her and moved slowly, and his fingers found her spot again, caressing with purpose, causing the throbbing to increase, a pool to form inside her.

His eyes, liquid blue, locked with her gaze and she saw desire transform his face, the reaction in his eyes when he recognized the passion that must have shown in her face.

All her troubles, all her fears melted away and she saw the blue passion of his eyes, and after a while, his desire was hers, and hers was his, and they moved as one. She savored his labored breathing and the moans of pleasure escaping his throat, and wondered that she could have that effect on him.

The rhythm of his thrusts increased, and a stab of desire pushed Kadriya higher. She was in pain and on fire, and he was the torch inside her, heating her. "Love me," she cried. "Love me, love me." She chanted in desperation, and he responded, touching her, kissing her, stroking her deeply.

A calm swept over her, and just as suddenly a breathless invigoration overtook her, as if she were racing Allie, and her horse had taken a huge leap in the air.

She reached the top and fell, pulsing with pleasure. She was vaguely aware of her breathless, wordless expressions of delight.

He made a sound, an exhaled sigh of ecstasy, and he held onto her bottom as if he would fall from a cliff, thrusting faster and deeper, then withdrew and released a shuddering cry.

He rested against her, his heart racing at the same fevered pace as hers.

Kadriya lay in his arms, her shapely legs wrapped around his. John checked the candles. They had burned about an hour's worth, and the fire had died down.

He stroked her peach-smooth shoulder, closed his eyes and nuzzled her neck, savoring the sweet closeness of her embrace. Recalling her wide-eyed reaction to his touch brought a bolt of fresh desire flashing through his body. He could love her again and again and never get enough of her femininity, of the womanly mystery of her and the gripping, breathless desire she stirred, just by whispering his name.

She had given him her purity. He recalled his first judgment of her as a Godless heathen, and a pang of regret stabbed in his gut. He had been so mistaken.

Kadriya had given him her body, but the deeper gift she shared stirred his heart, and he trailed kisses down her arm and onto her dainty hand and kissed her fingers, lingering on each one. *She trusts me.*

The sound of splitting wood woke Father Bernard. He jerked up from his straw mattress in the room above the stables. The quick movement pulled a muscle, but he swallowed the pain. It was well into the night and it took him a moment to see the broken door in the predawn gloom. "Who is there?"

The four merchants they had met earlier in the dining hall

stormed in, pointing at Dury, who sat up, confused, behind Father Bernard. "Get him." They ordered two heavily muscled men forward.

The priest scrambled up, struggling with his clothes. "Leave him be."

Sir Thomas rose, cursing, and pulled his dagger. "Get out."

Groggy with sleep, Dury scrambled to his feet.

The tall merchant pulled his dagger. "We mean no harm to you, Father. We only want the Gypsy."

Father Bernard refused to move. "Are you mad?"

"They drove us to it," another said. "Gypsies robbed us at the hot fair in St. Jean."

"Bloody filth. Lured us from our wagon," said the younger one.

"They diverted us from our route to Calais with a story of an outbreak of the plague near Seine village," the tall trader said. "Then stole our horses and our entire wagon of tapestries and Greek vases. This heathen was there."

"Are you certain?" asked Father Bernard.

"Of course."

The priest tested his story. "Who was with him? Can you describe them?"

"They all look the same, now, don't they?" the tall one said.

"He is the one," insisted the younger one. "We'll mount his head outside Poole. If he has any friends in Dorsetshire, they will see what happens to thieves in this realm." He pushed Father Bernard aside. "Get back, Father. We have no issue with you."

Sir Thomas lunged for the leader.

From the darkness, a large man grabbed Sir Thomas from behind and pulled him off balance. A second man struck him with a club.

There were seven of them now that Father Bernard could

make out. They fell on Dury, disarming him and dragging him to the door.

Father Bernard turned to the corner where John Wynter had been sleeping. "Sir John!" Neither he nor his bed was there.

The priest felt a blow on the back of the head and fell.

CHAPTER 14
DANCING FAERIES

Dover's loud neighing woke John. Boneless from lovemaking and peaceful sleep, he jumped up, throwing on his clothes.

Kadriya slipped into her gown. "What is it?"

"I'll see. Bolt the door." John rushed across the courtyard and through the open door of the stable, tripping on a fallen pitchfork obscured in the bleak light before dawn.

His horse was skittish but sound, and John gave him a couple of gentle, reassuring slaps. " 'Tis all right, boy, I am here."

Upstairs, the sound of voices, strained and raised in urgency, made John's heart falter. He took the stairs three at a time.

Splintered wood from the broken door bolt littered the floor, and Kadriya's priest lay in an awkward position on the floor, his black toga immodestly revealing his knees and thighs.

A delicate pattering sounded on the wooden steps behind him, and Kadriya rushed in. "Father Bernard!" She ran to him.

Recovering, he straightened his toga and waved her away. "I'm all right, child."

The stonecutter, Lucas, had come from his room in the main building of the inn and knelt before Sir Thomas. Paulina, her greying brown hair unbound and tousled from sleep, propped Sir Thomas, revealing his bloodied shoulder.

John ran to him. "Thomas. What happened?"

"The merchants, they—." He cried out in pain.

Kadriya circled the room. "Dury. Where's Dury?"

"They took him," Thomas said. "We tried to stop them."

217

John's guts clenched. He could have prevented this, had he been here. Robert was right; being with her had softened him. He had lost all sense of duty, left a fellow knight alone to face—"Who were they? How many?"

"The merchant, William and his friends. The four we saw in the dining hall, along with three others." The priest turned his head gingerly. Suspicion shadowed his face. "Where were you through the night, Sir John?"

The question burrowed under John's skin. He suffered the shame of knowing he could have prevented this. "Guarding Kadriya. I thought the merchants would take out their wrath on her."

"They wanted Dury," Father Bernard said. "They think he was part of a band of Gypsies who robbed them in France last month."

Kadriya gasped. "They'll kill him."

"Aye, they said they would," Thomas said.

"Sir Thomas?" Kadriya knelt before him.

"I'm all right," he said.

She looked at John. "We must help Dury."

He checked Thomas, noticed the unnatural angle of Sir Thomas's right shoulder, and the blood. "You're injured."

"John, we need to go for Dury."

"Thomas needs help."

"But Dury—John, please."

John pulled his dagger and cut Thomas' sleeve from his tunic, revealing the misshapen joint, swollen, bruised and gashed.

He touched Thomas' good shoulder, and nodded to the injured one. "Can you move it?"

"No. I felt it pop out. I—"

"John, Paulina can help Thomas," Kadriya interrupted.

John drew her out of the room and down the stairs for privacy. "Had I been here, this might not have happened. I have a duty to help Thomas."

"There are others here who can help Thomas. Dury—"

"I grow weary from your misplaced faith in these people."

"These people, John," she said, her voice strained, "are mine."

"They are not yours. These people," John persisted, "have brought trouble upon themselves. You more than anyone know of their thieving ways. Why do you think more and more people are refusing Gypsies passage through their lands? It's no coincidence. They steal. Get caught. Why persist in defending them? Teraf fooled you, and now Dury. Do you know of his innocence, or is it just more blind faith?"

"How dare you judge him so harshly? Dury's helping you find the chalice. He has honor, yet you condemn him based only on the accusations of strangers. Strangers you saw for yourself are so blinded by hatred they condemned me, as well. Unless you think I, too, am a thief?"

The thought spooked him, and he shoved it in a dark corner. The orderly borders of his life had crumbled, churning like a river's whirlpool, and he had brought it on himself. "Sir Thomas needs my help. I will not abandon a fellow knight for a common thief."

Her lush mouth, so recently soft and sensual against his own, thinned, and her eyes flashed in anger. "Oh, I see. You think there are no good Gypsies. That we are all thieves. That makes it easier, does it not?"

He could attest to only one Gypsy. *Kadriya.*

"Consider Dury and the honor he has shown you. Does a thief act with honor?" She studied his face, hope lighting her eyes.

John shook his head. Hell's flames, her logic plugged his brain like a log in a mill wheel. "If Thomas does not receive good care, he may lose use of his arm. His right arm. He is a knight! You know what a useless right arm will mean." He reached out to touch her.

She pulled away.

"I cannot leave Thomas." He left her on the steps and returned to Thomas and Father Bernard. "Bring us mead. Strong. I'm going to re-set his shoulder."

Behind him hasty foot falls sounded down the steps. She would be angry with him, and he was sorry about Dury and would help him later, but by the saints he would not forsake a fellow knight in his time of crucial need.

Kadriya hurried down the steps, but at the last step she hesitated. Hope would not leave her, even in the face of John's refusal. How could he refuse her? Dury had helped her defend John from Rill. Had he not seen for himself the hatred bubbling just below the surface with those merchants yester eve?

But Sir Thomas was hurt. Sweet saints! Had it not been for her, Sir John would have been above the stable with Dury, and the merchants would never have been able to take him. Dury could not die because of her. She must help him, but what could she accomplish, alone, against seven men?

A sturdy, dark-haired young man descended the steps, a laborer, judging by his leathered skin and the considerable size of his forearms. She'd seen him last night at table.

She stayed on the steps, blocking his way. "Your name, sir?"

His grey eyes were direct. "Lucas Stonecutter," he said.

"Lucas, will you help me? Some men—merchants staying here—took my cousin. I need to help him—"

"I saw them. I'll not face them alone."

She chose not to waste time being insulted that he did not count her. "I have coin to pay you. I will make it worth your while."

"How much?"

"A week's wages for an hour's work. But we must find Dury

before serious harm comes to him."

Lucas raised his eyebrows in doubt.

"I have coin. Lord Tabor is my sponsor. They are simple merchants, weak and unfit compared to you. And I have a plan. But we must hurry. Please."

He hesitated, likely thinking of the value in a week's wages, and she took advantage. "Quick. Saddle your horse."

They mounted their horses and galloped toward the sun's first rays. After an hour's travel they met two knights and five monks driving ox-driven wagons of salt and dried fish.

"We seek seven men, merchants, with a dark-skinned man," she told them. "Have you seen them?"

The taller knight spoke. "We saw four men, wool merchants they were, with a Gypsy man. Grey hair?"

"Yes." She turned to Lucas. "Just four now, better for us." She faced the knight. "When did you see them?"

"They're about a half hour ahead of you."

Kadriya looked ahead at the sunny, open fields. These merchants were not armed knights as at Blackwater Point, but this time she had neither the cloak of darkness nor Prince Malley as a tool of surprise. "Come on, Allie." She urged her horse to a run, thankful to hear Lucas' horse's hoofbeats behind her.

The early morning air chilled her face, and their speed whipped Kadriya's hair away from her face. A part of her brain numbly realized she had not even taken the time to plait her hair. To the merchants she would look just as they thought her to be: a shameless heathen. *Never mind that. Just get me to Dury in time.*

They came upon them at the confluence of two wide rivers that snaked through the valley like a tumbling spool of Sharai's fine ribbons, flowing forcefully as they neared the sea. The rivers ran this way, then that, flooding a field then turning again, at times narrow and at times wider than the length of the lists

221

and dotted with fishing boats.

Kadriya recognized William, the short, balding merchant who made weights, the one who had invited her to his table; and Mark, the one with the embroidered tunic. Dury rode with his hands bound, following the tall merchant. His face was bruised and his clothes bore marks of muddy boots as if they had kicked him on the ground. She slowed Allie. "Halt."

Lucas rode beside her, tense and no doubt re-thinking a week's wages worth of trouble.

They approached the merchants together. Shows of weakness would only encourage them, so Kadriya sat taller in the saddle and assumed a mask of firm resolve. "We have come for Dury."

"William, get him closer," Mark said.

The tall merchant pulled Dury's horse in.

The other two joined Mark's side, blocking the path.

"We're taking him to Poole," said Mark. "Get you gone."

Dury met her eyes. "They think I stole from them in France. I did not," he said in Romani.

"I know," she answered him and regarded William. "He is innocent." Kadriya moved closer. If she could just snare the reins . . .

William regarded Lucas. "And who are you? Another of this Gypsy whore's men?" His grip tightened on the reins. She would not be able to yank them from his grasp.

She wished she had a warhorse, but still, Allie was swift-footed, and together they had worked enough horse shows that Allie knew her signals.

Frowning as if to hurry over to Mark and argue, she passed Dury's and William's horses. Just past William, she kicked Allie's flanks and pulled her reins. Allie jumped high in the air, kicking at William's horse.

William's horse whinnied and back-stepped. William dropped Dury's reins.

Dury leaned forward. He grabbed his horse's mane with his bound hands and kicked. His horse bolted away from Allie.

"Follow us," Kadriya shouted to Lucas and urged Allie, pushing Dury's horse forward.

"Stop them." Mark raced to cut them off. The other three followed.

His natural balance hampered by his bound hands, Dury struggled to stay on his horse. Kadriya hurried to the side, trying to snare Dury's horse's reins. They rode away from the path. They were fast approaching one of the rivers. She would have to return to the path to cross the bridge.

Hoofbeats pounded behind them, and the merchants' shouts filled the air. They closed in.

Kadriya slowed. She must get those reins. She reached for them and missed by an inch.

Must get them. She slowed and reached again, but in her desperation she overbalanced. In a sickening, slow moment, she slid from Allie and landed on the ground.

The impact knocked the wind from her.

Ahead, Allie stopped.

Lucas whirled around, alarm and uncertainty widening his eyes.

"Go!" she shouted to Dury, scrambling to her feet.

William overtook her and jumped off his horse, grabbing for her.

Kadriya fled. "Run!" she screamed at Lucas, who hesitated on the other side of the bridge. "Go back to Sir Thomas."

William caught her arm, gripping it tight. "Got you, whore."

Kadriya smacked him in the face.

He cried out and lost his grip.

Kadriya ran, lungs screaming, vaguely aware of sharp stones through the soft leather of her shoes.

Mark loped after her, gaining ground.

Another merchant ran ahead, cutting off her access to the bridge.

Allie had followed her. "Allie! *Come! Av!*" But the men were too close. She couldn't wait. Desperate, she ran toward the river and slid down the bank.

A fisherman from a boat stood up, waving his hands wildly.

She stopped, turned, and saw the merchants just five feet behind her.

Frantic at the thought of their catching her, she jumped into the water.

She went under and the river grabbed her, sucking her downstream into its racing current. A whooshing sound filled her ears. She stayed under for a moment so they could not by chance grab her. When it seemed safe she struggled against the weight of her saturated gown and came up for air.

Allie had followed the shoreline and stopped, ears pricked, waiting.

". . . long-lines out there," the fisherman hollered. "Get out of the river." He pointed behind her.

She looked down river and his warning made sense. Taut rope ran from the fisherman's boat to the shore. She recognized them and gasped, swallowing water. Long-lines. They weren't nets, but lines of hemp yarn stretched across the width of the river and anchored at the bottom. From each of the ropes ran a series of vertical lines that disappeared into the water. Each of those ropes ended in barbed hooks.

Her heart raced even faster. She choked again. Should she dive deep to avoid shallow hooks, or were the snares sunk well below the surface? *I must decide.* "Allie! Stay!" She watched the shoreline, estimating the swift current and, saying a quick prayer, she dove deep.

The current carried her under the hooks. They flashed, reflecting the sunlight, and a dozen trout and sunfish shimmered like silver leaves fluttering in the wind as they struggled against the sharp barbs that snared them.

She bobbed above the surface, relief filling her. At the shoreline, the merchants were nowhere to be seen and Allie was still followed her at the shoreline. She followed a bend in the river and saw more boats in the distance. More lines.

Sweet saints!

On shore, clumps of flying mud followed a man on horseback who raced past Allie, trying to keep up with her. A warhorse, a rider with a head full of long, wheat colored hair.

John. Her heart hammered with hope.

Kadriya started swimming, aiming half upstream, half to the shore, struggling to reach her knight. She tried to scream for help but her lungs were too needy. She clawed at the water, saw a new line strung across the river just ahead, and stroked with new urgency.

Exhaustion setting in, she glanced at the shoreline again. The destrier had no rider. The next line approached and she dove deep, hoping to avoid the hooks again.

The water churned under her, dark green and cold, hissing in her ears. Harsh fingers reached out and clutched her. Terror flooded her bones. A net.

Her heart raced faster than the current. She fought the urge to scream. The current relentlessly dragged her downstream and the net closed in around her like a devil's claw, trapping her in a flexible tomb. Fish wriggled against her face and arms. Just four feet above the sun shone, casting a watery ray of light down to her.

My dagger. I can cut my way free. She reached for it, but the yards of fabric in her gown had swirled into a cocoon and her right side was pointed downstream, where the net's pressure bound her the tightest.

Her heart banged against her chest. She would die and be

hauled in with the fish and dumped on shore.

No. No! Finding footing in the net, she took a step up. The current was strong, flattening her against the net. She tried again, pulling more than pushing. The coarse net scraped against her face and slick creatures slid across her skin.

Her lungs burned and she pulled for her life, grasping for hope with each square she could conquer.

She took another step and broke through the water, gasping for air. The sun faded and everything went black.

"My love. Come back, Kadriya. Come back!"

A warm glow surrounded her, and she heard John's voice, sweet words of endearment, his voice cracking with emotion. She was in heaven.

Something rained heavy blows on her back, heavy thwacking that hurt her lungs and chest. She was lying on a log. No, it was a big, solid leg, and people were slapping her legs and arms.

"Wake up, Kadriya. Please."

She rolled over, tried to focus, met John's brilliant blue eyes, his face surrounded by a halo of light brown hair, shining gold from the sun. They were sprawled in tall grasses, sunshine overhead. The net was still wrapped around her, and a score of fish flopped against her skin.

"John?"

He crushed her to him, laughing in relief. "Thank God!" He framed her face with his big hands and kissed her again.

When he was certain Kadriya had recovered enough to travel, John led them away from the monastery and back onto the road to Poole. They had visited the monastery's guesthouse for a bath so Kadriya could banish the smell of fear and fish, and a change of clothes, made possible because John had hastily packed her bags and brought them from her room when he left the Seven Stars Inn. They enjoyed a mid-day dinner, thanked the monks for their hospitality and left.

John mentioned nothing to the monks about the chalice, or about the merchants or Dury, who was likely back at the Seven Stars Inn with Lucas by now. Time was running. In just four days the bishop would arrive, yet John was finding it more difficult than ever to concentrate. He had almost lost Kadriya in that fisherman's net. *By the saints!* His fingers still shook. It had taken all his strength to pull her from the river's grip, and the desperation he had felt when he thought he was losing her shattered any hope he might have had about his life ever being as it was before he met her.

She might have Gypsy blood, but she was precious to him. It was just her relationship with the Gypsies that troubled him, a relationship that made her loyalty waver. She had shown loyalty to Dury over loyalty to Sir Thomas, her own knight. *Or to him.* She had left John to save Dury.

Did she care more for her Gypsy roots than for him? And if so, now that she had given him her virtue, who would have her?

You would. He jerked in reaction to the thought, pulling Dover's reins up sharply, and the horse came to an abrupt stop.

Beside him, Kadriya stopped. "What is it?"

"Nothing." John looked at her trusting eyes and the blade that was gnawing at his gut plunged deeper. *What are you doing?*

Father Bernard suspected what John had done, and he knew the difficulties it could bring in Kadriya's future. And Dury. He wanted her to acknowledge her Gypsy roots and leave England.

John remembered the trust in her eyes, and the passion, and an ache built in his chest. *But by gad, she's English, too.*

By mid-day they caught a glimpse of the seacoast waters far below, shimmering dark blue against the lighter blue of the sky, a bold contrast to the lush greens of the land.

Kadriya jumped from her horse and ran to the hill overlooking the sea. Her brown hair tossed, unbound, in the cool breeze as she ran.

John left Dover and followed her.

Below, the coastline meandered east, dipping in to form a wide harbor a few miles ahead. He pointed toward it. "See that harbor, there, where the coastline recedes?"

"Is it Poole?"

"Aye. And can you see the land that juts out in the middle of it?"

"Where?"

"We are still too far away to see it clearly, but that's Brownsea Island. Cerne Abbey has a chapel there, dedicated to Saint Andrew. The monks produce salt there. The island sits right in the middle of Poole Harbor, a fair sight for the eyes."

She scanned the waves east to west and her mouth curved into a smile of wonder. "See how the water sparkles. It winks, as if a hundred faeries dance upon its surface. 'Tis how I feel, like a dancing faerie." She took a deep breath. "I'm here. With you."

John looked at the water, as if seeing it for the first time, populated by wispy, tiny faeries. Her rapture became his and he laid his mission to find the chalice aside for the moment. The way she held her hands, so child-like, and the wonder on her face was as fresh as the sea breeze. The green in her eyes contrasted with her gold gown and her hair, washed once from the river water and again with the monastery's rainwater, stirred gently, the short wisps at her temple dancing like her little faeries.

John's heart swelled with a quiet joy to be with her, to enjoy the way she saw life, as if it were new and bright, as if no pain or shadows could touch them now. He rested his hand on her shoulder and skimmed his hand down her arm, weaving her fingers into his.

Her fingers, warm and delicate as they curled around his,

created crests of excitement under his skin.

Her tongue moved enticingly across her lips and they shone like the sea, inviting him. He accepted the invitation and covered her mouth with his. She returned his kiss and he relished a delicate, new sweetness and joy.

She pressed close, and desire swept over him. He caressed the soft, smooth skin under her arm, trailing down to cup her breast. The hitch in her breath kicked his desire into a full gallop, and he took her firm bottom in his hands and pulled her to him, savoring the feel of her body, the softness of her curves against him.

Her tongue danced, eager, with his, but they were on a well-traveled road. He summoned self-control to end the kiss. "We must go, or we will never find that chalice."

She sighed, sending another bolt of desire into his arousal.

Giving him a half smile, she returned to Allie and mounted, poised to close the distance to Poole where, God willing, the chalice waited.

Eustace settled into his room at the inn with the sign of Seven Stars. He had just missed John Wynter, but knew Lord Tabor's knight lay wounded above the stable. He toyed with his belt, sorely missing the abundant collection of keys that usually hung there, keys that now hung during his absence from the belt of his assistant, James, the revistiarius.

Keys Eustace should be holding. He was, after all, the Sacristan. The *only* sacristan.

Hungry for something concrete to touch, he opened his prayer bead pouch, extracting the parchment message he had intercepted. He unfolded it:

Father R,
Recovered two stones. Following E. to Poole. Mud.

It hadn't been hard to decipher. Eustace had often overheard John Wynter and the abbot reminisce about that time in France when they had escaped some battle by hiding in the mud. So Eustace had determined it was a message from John Wynter to the abbot, one the abbot had never had the chance to read. John Wynter, that taunting, arrogant knight and his Gypsy woman. What had Erol told him before he died? "Something about a cross," Wynter had said.

He knows I did it. He knows Teraf is alive.

Images flickered in Eustace's head. Pools of Erol's blood in the grass. Peaceful sleep would never be his again, he knew this, and dread crept into his veins. He watched his fingers tremble, and his lips convulsed as a new wave of fear washed over him.

He had found a way to lessen the guilt. He released the breath he had been holding and left his body again, floating above himself, escaping the dark thoughts and unbearable tension. Below him, his poor, miserable, aging self stared at the parchment, the muscles of his face drawn in a grimace created by days of worry.

So lucky. So fortunate for him that he had learned how to escape and could watch from a distance. He could think more clearly this way.

So the Gypsy bastard was selling off parts of the chalice. Like ripping feathers from the wings of an angel, this heathen bastard was dismantling the emerald chalice, the exquisite treasure he had stolen.

Eustace had tried to kill him before, but the dark-skinned worm had been too clever, offering up his own friend instead. And Eustace had taken the bait and swallowed the hook and killed Erol instead of Teraf.

Eustace should have killed Teraf when he was being held prisoner at the monastery. Should have killed him when he demanded that Eustace help him escape.

The man below was weak. He had made serious mistakes, and Eustace must clean up the unsightly mess he had made.

The fire was warm, welcome after his time on the road. Eustace removed his sandals and aimed the soles of his feet at the fire. They had been here the night before, John and Teraf's heathen whore. She had slept in this very bed, mayhap John, too, given his lust for her.

Wrapped in serenity, Eustace hovered by the ceiling and watched himself below. The emeralds might even have been in this very room.

If he had arrived yesterday, it would be he who possessed the gems now instead of that Gypsy-loving knight, John Wynter. The removed Eustace pointed at the seated Eustace in anger, cursing his failure.

The seated Eustace became frightened and tried to move his feet from the fire, but the overseeing Eustace made him move them closer still, closer and closer, until the flesh turned red and the poor wretch cried out in pain.

You will find Teraf before John Wynter does. You will kill the thief once and for all, and bring the chalice home.

CHAPTER 15
THE MUSIC

John and Kadriya neared Poole under the noontide sun, following the path that led to the eastern entrance. Though tall and mounted on Dover, John could not see over the twenty-foot sandstone wall protecting Poole, but he knew what lay beyond: a vibrant town of ships and commerce. From Poole and her teardrop harbor sailed large ships carrying fine English wool, and in times like these, ships laden with warhorses, knights and archers crossing the channel to France.

He thought of the Gypsy thief, Erol. Would he risk another full day's ride to reach Southampton on the southern coast and sail to France from there, or would he take a chance and leave here? Kadriya had told him the tribe typically traveled to and from France from Southampton.

Nay. Erol was clever to have made it this far, but he would not know of the monastic influence in this harbor town. He would see this town as a faster way home.

He would be so wrong. Erol could not know the Cerne Abbey monks possessed Brownsea, the island nestled in this harbor. He wouldn't know of the monks' sole rights to hunt deer and other wildlife there, or their right to claim any spoils washed ashore from wrecks but, more importantly, Erol would not know the monks were empowered to punish poachers and thieves. If Erol came anywhere near the little island, he could not hide behind manorial or city courts.

Erol's trail was still warm. Excitement stirred in John's chest.

The chalice was here. He sensed it. John would find it, soon, and return it and the thief to Father Robert.

The road widened and traffic increased as people on foot, in wagons and on horseback joined the road from other paths.

Riding beside him, Kadriya had bound her hair and covered it with a white veil. Her light cinnamon skin glowed in contrast, her beauty breathtaking. The veil's delicate hem danced in the slight breeze, brushing her neck at just the spot John yearned to kiss.

He pulled his gaze from her skin and followed instead the lines of the city gate archway, trying to salvage his wits. Duty called and, attached to that, his honor.

Poole's wall was sturdy, fifteen feet thick, but not well manned. The overlooking guard windows were empty and only two guards were stationed on the street level.

John needed to glean information from them but he would be discreet, as the abbot requested. Knowledge of the chalice theft was to remain limited to the abbot and his guards.

John dismounted and helped Kadriya off Allie. One of the guards, angular with even features and friendly brown eyes, greeted John with a smile of recognition. "Well, look what rolled in with the seaweed. John Wynter."

It was Buck Penhale, John's friend. What good fortune. Buck most often worked in the high street merchant area. John slapped Buck's arm in jest. "That's *Sir* John Wynter to you." He pointed to his friend's head. "What happened to your hair?"

Buck laughed, rubbing the short, waving brown locks at his neck. "Your abbot is more lenient than Councilman Deeves." He bowed to Kadriya. "I am Buck Penhale, lovely lady," he said in a honeyed tone. "Overwhelmed at your considerable beauty. Wondering why in heaven you're keeping company with this lout."

Her full lips curved in an enticing smile, her teeth perfect and white in the full day's sun. "Good day, sir."

Possessiveness flared in John's chest and he controlled the urge to slap Buck's hand away from Kadriya's. "This is Kadriya of Coin Forest, ward of Richard, Baron Tabor," John said, catching Buck's gaze with a pointed one of his own. "We are here to be wed at the chapel on Brownsea Island."

"Wed." Buck's eyes widened and his mouth split into a grin. "What of your alehouse speeches about love's encumbrances?"

Of what did Buck speak? John was an intensely private man and would give no speeches about love. He caught Kadriya's eye. "Pay him no heed. He's jealous."

"Methinks it's catching." Buck's brown eyes twinkled as they did when he knew he held a captive audience. His easygoing friend could always turn every ear, even in the most crowded of alehouses. John admired his smooth, polished manner.

"So you've come to Poole to be wed?" he asked her.

"Aye." Kadriya gave Buck an easy smile. "And it's my pleasure to meet one of John's friends."

Buck jabbed John with his elbow. "As it is mine." He gave Kadriya an appraising glance and cocked his head. "That accent. Are you from Spain?"

"Nay," said Kadriya, rubbing her arm lightly.

"I'm well acquainted with this man, Kadriya," Buck said, changing the subject. "Between us, John and I have killed some several hundred mugs of mead together over the years. He's a good man." He shot a rogue's glance at John. "Even if he is overbearingly opinionated."

Kadriya laughed, a bell-like melody that danced down John's spine, generating a ripple of pleasure. "I'm familiar with that side of his character," she said.

An uncomfortable heat burned at John's ears.

"Enough about him," Buck said. He spoke briefly to his fellow guard and returned to them. "My duty here is done. All I have yet to do is check the beach and I'll be free. My sister, Prudence, has been hoarding a fine burgundy worthy of toasting a wedding," Buck continued. "Come walk with me as I check the shoreline, then come sup at our home and I'll catch you up on news about Poole and the tax fines that have the merchants sweating farthings."

Buck put out his arm, blocking John's progress, so he could sweep Kadriya away. "Then I can tell you all about me, an enormously more interesting topic than this crusty old knight, John Wynter."

They passed the gate, found stalls for their horses and wound through the crowded streets. The merchants' shutters were lowered for business, offering hats, shoes, tailor's services and, at the next street, oil merchants, wine criers and fish mongers offered their wares.

They neared a goldsmith's shop. "Give me a minute," John said to Buck, wanting to check for emeralds.

Buck made a subtle hand gesture, stopping him. "Just keep walking, John. With haste."

John caught the urgency in Buck's gaze, and veered away from the shop. They approached steps leading to the beach, and John took them two at a time, catching up with Buck. "What is it?"

Buck released Kadriya's arm and fell back a couple of steps. "The tale sounded too far-fetched to be true, but sure enough here you are with a Gypsy. You've angered the abbot. We have orders for your arrest. Have you lost all your wits?" They reached the beachfront, where dozens of ships in various stages of construction sprawled in the sand, their skeletal cage work waiting for a skin of outer planks and pitch caulk to make a viable hull. Buck waved at workers building a three-mast ship, then ducked between two smaller ships and stopped. "You're in trouble fit for a king," he said. "What in blazes are you doing here?"

John stalled. The abbot wanted secrecy, but he'd dramatically changed the rules by ordering John's arrest, and years of friendship made him trust Buck. "I'm looking for a Gypsy. Your age or a little younger. Long black hair. Carries a fat purse of coins. I must stop him before he books passage to France. He may be with other Gypsies." John took a deep breath. "He has something I need." He paused. "Desperately."

Buck's brows raised. "A wealthy Gypsy. That should be easy to spy." He looked over his shoulder. "But you're an inch away from capture here. The abbot wants Kadriya as well as you. He has ordered her to be taken to Brownsea and held."

Buck's fist shot out, connecting with John's jaw. John fell backward into the sand.

"No." Kadriya jumped on Buck, legs wrapping around his hips, trying to tackle him.

John struggled to his feet.

Buck swung her off like a discarded cloak. "John. Hit me. Hard. Then run. Meet me at Poole Quay, ten tonight. Now." He pushed John hard on the chest.

John grabbed him by the collar. "Thanks, friend." He punched him in the eye, guaranteeing a visible wound and swelling.

Buck went down.

They ran ten yards, and a hard blow battered John's lower back, knocking the wind out of him. He fell, landing on his side.

"So. The peasant John Wynter." A square-shouldered knight hovered over John, his jaw shadowed with stubble and eyes narrowed with ill temper. "No virtuous woman will have you, so you settled for a Gypsy." He laughed, ridicule staining his coarse words.

"Henry Miller," John said, forcing a laugh. "Your accusations don't hurt me." Pulling his fighting dagger, he swiped it at Henry in one smooth movement. "But don't slur this good woman's name," John growled.

"Gelsey was mine." Henry pulled his dagger.

"Gelsey chose me, but she left me for another. We were both cast off. Lay it to rest."

"Let's take a boat ride to the island. And when you hang, you'll go to hell."

"Unholy thoughts for such a nice afternoon." Invisible knives cut into the small of John's back where Henry had kicked him.

Henry dodged to avoid the blade. John spun and kicked Henry square in the chest.

Henry fell onto his back.

Small hands tugged on John's arm. "They're coming. Let's go," Kadriya cried.

"Not yet. He's been asking for this for years." John pounced on Henry, pounding his face, sand flying as Henry struggled.

"Look out!" Kadriya cried.

A large brown object swung into view straight ahead and John rolled out of the way.

Henry rose to sitting.

Kadriya stood spread-legged, her feet dug into the sand for balance, the muscles of her short, slender body taut. From behind Henry, she swung a section of deck railing at his big head, making solid contact.

Henry fell soundlessly into the sand.

"Come on," Kadriya begged.

Several guards raced toward them from the market streets.

John took Kadriya's hand and they ran, scaring black-backed gulls that scattered, crying in protest. John's legs kicked long but his feet sank into the soft sand, making progress difficult.

Kadriya's veil sagged and her hair flew around her shoulders, unrestrained. "One of these ships?" she asked.

"No. First place they'll look." He panted, sucking air. "Head for those trees." They forged through the thick underbrush, crawling to penetrate the wild growth, running where the path cleared. Kadriya proved fast and agile, and the sound of the guards' pursuit slowly faded. Finally they stopped, catching their breath in the shade.

She filled her lungs with air, her breasts rising and falling, her eyes wide with fear. "Come here," John said gruffly, wrapping his arms around her. Small, almost fragile, he remembered her swinging that railing at Henry and laughed softly into her hair. "Thanks for getting that ox off my back. You're one strong fighter," he said, pride and affection warming his chest. "And you didn't even need the monkey."

She swung playfully at him, striking his forearm. "No, but I will be needing to know more about this Gelsey woman."

"Old story."

"How old?"

"As old as Joya."

"Oh. Good, or I'd have to call upon Prince Malley." She warmed to him again. "Thank you for defending my honor."

"And thank you for getting us moving along." He sobered. He'd been so smug about the monastic power in Poole that he forgot it could be turned on him. "I can't understand why the abbot would order my arrest."

"They have Allie and Dover," Kadriya said, worry straining her voice. "Will they be safe?"

"I know the stable master. They're fine," he assured her. "For now we'll travel by foot. We just need to bide our time until we can meet Buck." John said.

"Why is the abbot doing this? I thought he was desperate for the chalice."

"I defied him." *God's teeth.* Still, why would the abbot stop him after he had found two of the emeralds? Surely he had to know how close they were to regaining the chalice. What was he thinking? How could they search for the cursed thing when they couldn't be seen in town?

A new, chilling thought passed through his brain: he would not let his abbot take Kadriya. He would never let him or anyone else take her. He recalled her passion at the Seven Stars Inn, the warm trust in her green eyes, and warmth surged through his veins, filling his heart. He remembered his stark terror when he cut her from the fishing net, limp and unbreathing, and the joy he had felt, as if it were his own life's renewal, when she opened her eyes.

He had thought earlier that his attraction to her was only physical. He almost laughed at that, but he had long passed the point of amusement. He could never bear to lose her. *Sweet Mary, mother of God, I love this woman.* He wanted to lift her willowy body in his arms and dance with joy, but the abbot's eyes intruded in his mind, equally trusting him to find the chalice. Robert, Baron Brocherst, who had fought alongside him in France, the man who had risked death with him in battles. The abbot was a man of generosity, a man of God who had raised John from poverty and restored dignity to his life, the man John thought of as a father.

A pressure built at his temples and a sense of imbalance overwhelmed him, as if he were standing on a deck rail in a storm-tossed sea.

Find the chalice. Evade capture. Please the abbot yet somehow, some way, keep hold of this special woman.

A black thought chewed its way into his heart.

Her breasts, pressing soft against his chest, and her dainty hands behind his neck holding him close, made his heart ache with happiness. He held her closer, rocking her, needing to calm himself as much as her. He stilled his thoughts, breathing deep the hint of the monastery's lavender and rainwater in her hair and trying to will the menacing thought away, but still it seeped in like a broken bottle of the finest scripting ink: *I must choose.*

Autumn leaves fell on John's shoulders and carpeted the damp ground as he and Kadriya walked on the banks of the sunken creek bed. A soft breeze stirred the more stubborn leaves, twisting them as they clung, creating a sparkling pattern of late afternoon light on the sodden bank.

They had walked perhaps two miles inland when the faint sound of music reached their ears.

Kadriya squeezed his forearm with a small gasp, her lush lips curving in pleasure. "Gypsies."

The drums pounded, the deep, low-pitched sound of vibrating skins pulsing in what at first seemed random but as it continued, thumping through the autumn air, John felt it, connected with it. Thump, pause, thump-thump. Thump, pause, thump-thump. It beat to the rhythm of his heart.

Transfixed, John continued walking, one step followed unthinkingly by another, and they grew closer. The drummer's sequence changed and thin steel vibrated, sounding to John's ear like a sword being unsheathed, singing a metallic whisper, one that touched his knight's heart. Two brash, swift clangs followed, as if prancing in defiance of standard musical measures.

A flute and a deep-toned horn joined in, equally garish, followed by a woman's voice, singing words that held no meaning to him, yet they passed his defenses, touching him. Sensuality hung on the edge of her voice, stirring the blood in his veins.

Next to him, Kadriya hummed the bewitching tune and began singing the same exciting, carnal intonations.

A chill shuddered down his spine, as if the air itself had grown defiled with an unseen illness and his breath caught. He stopped walking.

Her singing ceased, dying along with her smile. "What is it, John?"

He swallowed, but the overwhelming lump that had grown in his throat persisted. Was she more Gypsy than English? "Naught," he said dismissively. "Do you recognize the voice?"

"Aye, it's Bit. I'd know her voice anywhere, and I recognize the pattern of the drummer." She nodded. "It is my tribe."

Her tribe. The otherworldly music continued, haunting him now with its alien sound. John pulled his hand from hers and felt for his dagger. "The chalice." *God's bones.* He should have had Dover beneath him and a dozen monastery knights behind him, yet here he was, mere yards from the chalice, and he stood there, on foot with one fighting dagger, captivated against his will by their music. *By her music.*

She glanced at his hand, fingers curled around the dagger's handle. "We won't need that. I'll talk with Bit. She's my friend."

They advanced to the camp and waited for the infernal music to cease. Darkness fell. When Bit finally left the other musicians and entered her tent, Kadriya whispered to her through the heavy greased linen, and Bit appeared moments later in the woods by the river's edge.

Kadriya's heart skipped at seeing her friend. They shared a warm hug. Bit's skin was cool and extremely dark. In the edges of the large campfire, the whites of her eyes seemed to glow. Her jet hair was loose to her waist, and her tiny neck was draped with a new gold chain.

"*Li' ha' eer!* By the gods, Kadriya. Your dress, your hair—you look wild," she cried in Romani. "And the filthy church knight. What are you doing with him? You must not let Rill see you here."

Kadriya turned to John. "I'm sorry. She can't speak English.

She says we must not let Rill see us."

Kadriya took Bit's hand. "Sir John is not to be feared. He seeks only the chalice." Kadriya glanced toward the fire. "Rill is here?"

"Aye," said Bit. "He's our new king. And we broke the tile together. I am queen now," Bit whispered.

"Bless your union, Bit. I'm happy for you." Kadriya hugged the small woman again. "Is Erol here?"

Bit grunted. "That *choro*. We'll kill him."

Kadriya turned to John. "She says Erol is a thief."

"Rill said he would leave posthaste for France," Kadriya said. "Why are you still here?"

"Teraf stole the tribe's money from the horse fair. We've been working to earn passage back to France."

"But he couldn't. Teraf had no time to take the money when the abbot's knights came for him."

"Erol," Bit said, cursing. "Erol had the funds, and Erol was gone when Teraf was arrested, remember? The two are back in France by now with our money, and his chalice," she said, pointing at John.

"I'm sorry to say, but Teraf—"

The aggressive shouting of several men interrupted Kadriya, the shrieks coming from all directions. Shadows moved quickly in the dark. Several hands grabbed Kadriya's feet, pushing her down.

"Oh. Let me go." She fell face forward. Knees gouged her back.

Her hands and feet were quickly bound with rope. Her dagger was ripped from her hand. Her skin burned, and she felt the warm pulse of blood on her skin.

Nearby, John growled and struggled. He was down and several of Rill's men pushed, leaned and sat on him. They disarmed him, tied his ankles and bound his hands behind his back.

"Drag them to the fire." Rill's stout body appeared, silhouetted against the large blaze behind him.

Men dragged Kadriya on her stomach to the fireside. Rill lifted her up by the hair.

Her scalp burned from the assault. She cried out and cursed him.

"You. Half English, half whore. Not Rom," Rill said in halting English.

"You witless bastard," John growled, his voice hoarse with fury. "Leave her be. Untie me and we'll see what kind of man you are, you coward."

Rill kicked him. "Shut up. I'll knock teeth out." He turned to Kadriya, reverting to Romani. "Where's your bastard thief, Teraf?"

"He's dead," John said.

Rill turned his back on John, addressing Kadriya in Romani. "I should have killed him when I had the chance, but my patience has rewarded me. Now I can turn both of you in and get a good sum for my efforts."

Kadriya's heart raced. "We are worth naught to you."

"Isn't that amusing, Kadriya?" Rill reached down and pinched her face. "Someone finally wants you. You can be certain that we do not," he said, gesturing to take in the dozens of Gypsies watching in the firelight. "You are not welcome here." He got up and strode to the horses, unfettering his stallion. "Put them in my tent and watch them," he said to a cluster of men who stood nearby.

Bit ran to him. "Where are you going?"

"To market," he said. He gave a crooked smile, but the vertical frown lines between his eyes rendered the expression null. "I have a healthy boar and his sow to sell."

The men near Rill laughed dutifully.

Encouraged, Rill continued, speaking louder and more dramatically for the benefit of his tribal fellows. "Who will pay the best price for them? The guards at Poole? They want them. The grey-haired monk at Brownsea Island? He wants them, too." He put his hands on his knees and bent down toward John, as if taunting him because he could understand nothing of what Rill said. "Or maybe that tall, nervous monk from Cerne Abbey who came snooping here. We will see." He mounted Thunder and rode off, whistling.

Two men dragged John to Rill's tent, which used to be Teraf's. A young man hoisted Kadriya over his shoulder, carrying her like a bolt of carpet into the tent. Tying their wrists and ankles securely, the men left.

The tent was spacious, an ash bender tent fitted neatly with oiled linen and pulled weather-tight with wooden pegs. A bed was positioned in the far end from the fire pit, which held a small, young fire, and three locked chests were stacked next to the bed. A collection of pegs and whittling knives hung from the side of the table.

As if reading her mind, one of the men hurried in. "I'll take these," he said. He snatched the knives and for good measure took the pegs, as well.

Kadriya rolled on her side. "I'm sorry, John."

" 'Tis I who failed," said John. "I should have been more alert. I was so certain Erol was here, that the chalice was here. I thought only of getting it in my hands." He shook his head. "Witless."

"What will they do to us?"

"Who?"

She remembered Rill had spoken his news in Romani. "Rill is riding to Poole to see who will pay the most for us. Guards have come here, looking for us, and monks from Brownsea Island,

and some tall monk from Cerne Abbey, he said."

"Eustace. Curse the man, he keeps elbowing his way into our business. Why?"

"He wants the chalice. He must feel some responsibility for having failed to protect it. That's his job."

"Yes, I suppose, but something gnaws at me about him. He's worried that Teraf said something to me before he died."

Her heart stumbled. "Did he?"

"No. This is a strange time to start doubting me."

"I don't, but you might keep something from me if you thought it could hurt me."

"Not something like that. But Eustace. He seemed afraid of whatever Teraf might have said, had he still been alive."

"A puzzle, but what about now? We won't meet Buck in time. We'll be caught, and the chalice will never be found."

John crawled to her. "Don't give up hope. Just rest. I'll think of something."

Outside, fish roasted in the fires, fish and fried biscuits. Kadriya swallowed, her stomach grumbling.

The music resumed, but Bit did not sing. The Gypsies' laughter grew louder.

"They're drinking."

"Aye," responded John softly. "Good. May they drink more, and may Rill's horse be slow and fitful."

He struggled to stand, but could get no leverage from his arms because they were bound behind his back.

Kadriya remembered the sharp, rough spot on the outside of the lover's knot ring. She wriggled to a sitting position with John behind her. "Put your wrists near my ring," she said.

John positioned himself so they were back to back, with his bound hands next to hers.

She snagged a few fibers of his rope and started sliding it back and forth. The threads broke. She worked more threads in, repeating the action. A few more broke. Encouraged, she continued.

John tested it.

"Anything?"

"The rope is too thick, Kadriya. Good idea, though," he added to spare her feelings.

Frustration rose in her throat. She thought of the reinforcing stitches Sharai made when sewing points. A stitch by itself, not so strong, but many threads together made a stress point sturdy. She resumed her patient rubbing.

" 'Tis no use, Kadriya."

"I've nothing better to do. I'll see to just one thread at a time, not the whole rope."

She continued through two songs and a heated argument between the Gypsies about how the bounty would be split. Her wrist and shoulder ached from the monotonous task.

"Wait." John shifted his weight and grunted, trying to twist the rope free of his wrists. "Glory to God. You've loosened it." He struggled with renewed enthusiasm, bumping into her. "But I still can't work it loose. Cursed big hands."

"See that top chest by the bed," he asked. "There's a loose hinge there, see the jagged edge? If I can get my feet free I might be able to topple it." He rolled on his back and swung his legs toward the small flames.

"No," Kadriya cried.

"It's all right. I have boots." He held his boots over the flame, eyebrows knit in pain. The rope caught fire.

He pulled his legs out of the fire, twisting furiously, but the rope held.

He stomped the small flames out on the floor. "It's looser. It's working." He crawled back to the fire and positioned himself again. Clenching his jaw, he plunged his feet in again. Sweat broke out on his forehead, and his eyes clamped shut in pain.

His feet trembled as he fought the instinct to pull them from the heat. The smell of burning flesh wafted her way and she felt faint.

Hoofbeats pounded. "They're coming," Kadriya cried. "Hurry."

He ground the burning rope against a fireside stone in a sawing motion, and the rope broke. John freed his feet and ran to the stack of chests, kicking them. They fell in a crash, but the noise of the arriving horses hopefully concealed the sound to those outside.

John backed up to chest with the jagged hinge and hooked his wrist ropes on it, sawing with frenzy.

Kadriya hobbled over to help.

The hoofbeats stopped. "Take me to them."

John's head shot up. "Eustace." He resumed his frantic sawing. The rope finally gave and his hands were free. He popped the latch of the top chest open and lifted the lid.

"Stop, monk. You can give better. More coin," said Rill.

Kadriya met John's eyes. "He bargains."

John dove into the chest, throwing clothes and tools onto the bed. "Miserable mercy," he groaned.

"What?"

"Look." He held up a large, antiquated dagger.

"Good. What's wrong?"

"It's older than sin, and dull." He grabbed her legs, wedged them between his and sawed madly. He put his full weight into it. "But it will do."

The raw rope scratched her skin, burning with each of his sawing strokes; Kadriya bit her lip to keep from crying out.

Outside, men came closer. "I have twelve guards with me," Eustace said, his voice cold and unyielding, "they witnessed my offer and your agreement. Show me the knight."

The rope gave way and Kadriya scrambled to her feet.

John slit the back of the tent vertically and pulled her out with him. "Quick."

They burst from the back of Rill's tent, racing for the darkness of the trees.

From the campfire Rill spoke in Romani. "Your knight is no match for Roma," he boasted, "Come, you can see how fierce he is." Laughter followed, then sudden silence.

A string of curses filled the air, followed by Rill's inflamed bellow, "Find them!"

CHAPTER 16
THE RIDDLES

John and Kadriya hurried back to the creek.

"Which way," Kadriya asked.

John considered. "There," he said, pointing to the creek flowing past the camp, away from the route they'd taken to get there. "Hurry." John hoped she could run as well as she could ride a horse.

Their feet sank in the soft mud. Kadriya struggled in her long gown, stumbling, gasping.

"Here," John said, surging ahead. "I'll go first. Follow in my footsteps." He strode, mindful to keep his strides shorter.

They rushed ahead some fifty yards. Behind them, men's voices shouted curses and orders, and horses whinnied as the guards mounted.

Think. Think, John. In this ravine, they were like eels trapped in a wicker basket. Eustace and his guards could simply run their horses along the upper bank until they found them, then move in. Ahead, the creek turned sharply to the left, and John remembered the brook meandering in large detours before the camp. They must get out.

"What now?" Kadriya asked.

"Climb that bank," he said, pointing to the right.

She scooped up the hem of her heavy wool gown, tossed it over her left arm and scaled the steep embankment.

John stripped his boots, unable to stop the grunt of pain from the leather scraping his burned ankles. He sank his feet in the cool mud at the water's edge and the moisture seeped into his hose, giving some relief from the burning. He pulled a rotted log from the water that someone had used as a makeshift bridge, and he dropped it on the bank, covering Kadriya's footsteps. He filled his boots with creek water and walked on the log to the rising bank.

"Here," he said, reaching up to hand Kadriya his water-filled boots and tossed the awkward dagger to the upper bank and climbed out of the ravine. A quick swipe over the embankment flattened the impressions of their footprints, and for good measure, he poured water, obscuring them. Though the moon was full, it would take sharp eyes to spy their exit point. He slid his muddied feet back into his boots. "Let's go."

They ran through the fields to another stand of trees.

Kadriya stopped. "I must catch my breath."

They heard men and horses below, in the creek ravine, and on the upper banks on the other side.

"Where to now?" Kadriya asked.

"Here. We'll stay here."

"But what about Buck?"

Above, the moon rose ever higher in the sky. "We can ill afford to miss him. What about Rill and his Gypsies? Will they give chase?"

She nodded. "They want Eustace's reward."

"It will be a long night."

She wrapped her arms around his neck and pressed her cheek against his, her eyelash fluttering like a butterfly's wing against his skin. "So long as you're with me," her voice thick with emotion.

John's heart surged. *She needs me. She needs me and trusts me.* The night's burdens seemed to lighten, and he took her in his arms.

Huddling together, leaning against a misshapen old oak tree, they waited. A chorus of crickets and frogs settled around them.

Kadriya had shifted her position and rested with her back against John's chest and her head resting on his shoulder. "How long have you known Buck?" Kadriya whispered.

"Buck squired at Middlebury, just north of here, near where I squired for Baron Brocherst—the abbot. Buck's liege was killed in Normandy and left no heir so Buck went to Poole."

"And how did you end up at the monastery?"

"My lord Brocherst was haunted by battle memories and became a monk there. Then abbot." John's voice grew tight with emotion. "He brought me with him to the abbey. He granted me a tract of land from his family's holdings."

A weight sat heavy on her chest. Their bond was strong. The significance of John's bringing her with him against the abbot's order settled in, and with the understanding came a new sweep of guilt for the trouble her insecurities had caused.

She could only find simple words. "What a good friend."

"Aye, and Buck, taking risks to help me."

"As you have with me," she said. "Loyalty works both ways. I'm sure Buck is glad to repay you." As for the abbot, she could not think why, other than John's defense of her, he would order John's arrest.

Some time later activity from Rill's camp could still be heard, but there were no sounds of pursuing horses or guards. A faint tolling of church bells sounded in the distance. "Nine of the clock, and Buck said to meet him at ten." John said. He rubbed Kadriya's tense shoulders. "Let's stay in the darkness of the trees and make our way back to Poole." He cast an anxious look at the moon's position. "Pray we reach the quay in time."

They took a path that led to the east of Poole.

As they walked, Kadriya translated the rest of her conversation with Bit. "It doesn't make sense," she said. "If Erol is a murdering thief, and if he had the tribe's horse money and the chalice, why would he follow Teraf and kill him? Why not just leave with all the money?"

"And live his life always looking backward? I wager Teraf wouldn't take betrayal with a shrug and a pardon."

She nodded.

Their steps made a soft *whoosh* sound through the tall, wet grasses. He took her hand in his. "Remember the loose gems. Whoever has the chalice is close. Let's get back to meet Buck and catch our thief."

Kadriya changed position, straightening her legs. Resting on the deck of a trolling boat hobbled by a broken mast and moored at Poole Quay, she and John waited for Buck's arrival. Her wrists were bruised from Rill's ropes, her gown was torn and stained with creek mud and she ached from hunger, but she and John were still together and ready to meet with Buck.

The full moon shone in the star-sprinkled sky like a glowing stone of amber. It painted the sea, turning the surface ripples into black pools of ink, landing, skimming, then disappearing in the reflected lights from dozens of boats moored throughout the harbor.

In years past she had crossed the channel under angry skies of grey, under cold, drizzling rains, and under pale blue skies, but she had never rested in a peaceful, splendid bay like this, held in her lover's arms. She snuggled against the broad chest of her knight, admiring his sharp features and blue eyes lit by moonlight.

He was a ruggedly beautiful man. At first she'd thought his masculine appeal a cruel joke, an attractive surface under which lurked a shocking mass of hatred. She had discovered since leaving Coin Forest that, though he might be at times stubborn and quick to judge, he also placed great stock in honesty and loyalty, and was proving to be more and more capable of looking beyond skin and differences to find truth.

A knight, violent, disciplined. Loyal to his abbot. Passion simmered just below his surface, ready to flare and overwhelm her. Yet when she was frightened or unsure, his presence gave her a calming steadiness. He was, by all her senses, perfect for her. Gelsey. Who was she, and how much of John's heart did this mystery woman still hold? By logic, she should not trust him. Her mistakes with not-so-gallant Englishmen and with Teraf revealed her lack of good instincts, yet from the depths of her heart she knew John was true.

His reactions to the Gypsy camp had been hard to understand. At first, she could have sworn he fell under the spell of the music. She had begun to sing, and the look of horror in his eyes had stunned her. She'd been told by many that her voice was lovely, but mayhap they were just being kind and her voice more resembled a frog's. She would not sing again in his presence.

Once they'd reached the harbor his affection and tenderness had returned and she basked in the simmering warmth of his presence. Maybe she was reading too much into his actions. He had much on his mind, and they were running out of time to find the chalice.

By the bell's tolls, it was nearing ten. The waves rocked the boat like a cradle and she let their troubling circumstances drift away. A gentle wind blew, bringing chill in the air.

He kissed her neck, his soft lips grazing her skin. A delicious thrill flickered down her body and she turned in his arms.

His mouth covered hers and she fell into his kiss, eager, needing his closeness.

What a path of magic she had taken when she gave herself to him. Uncertainty niggled at her brain, whispers of the abbot's disapproval, his wish to detain them, and the pending shame John would endure if the chalice was not found, of the considerable penalties he would suffer for having allowed her to travel with him against the abbot's wishes.

All this trouble because of Teraf. Because of her. She dove her hands into John's thick hair, deepening the kiss, welcoming the heat swirling through her, building the desire to a red hum in her ears, making her body as fluid as the sea around them, blotting out all thought of anything but this moment.

"Sweet heaven, Kadriya, what you do to me," he whispered, his breath ragged. "I vow, I will protect you. We'll get through this." He paused and pulled back, cupping her face in his big hands. "Can you swim if need be?"

A shiver of fear passed through her. "So long as there are no nets."

"Don't bring that to mind!" He tightened his arms around her. "If we must swim, I'll be close by. Where do you need unlaced to slip out of your gown quickly?"

She leaned forward. "Here, in the back—the sides—and here, on the sleeves."

He fumbled with a couple and gave up. "I think we'll make swimming our last choice."

A large, single-mast sailboat approached and they ducked below the portside so as not to be seen.

"Are you the dog who gave me this black eye?"

At the familiar sound of Buck's voice, they ventured a glimpse over the side. The sailboat carried Buck and an older man, visible in the light of the full moon.

Relief rushed through Kadriya, and John's muscles relaxed against her.

"Aye, and well deserved it was, too," John replied. The boat drifted next to theirs and John grasped Buck's hand and the men held the two boats together.

Stepping off the side of the hobbled boat, they climbed up the small ladder and onto the deck of the larger boat.

Buck's face was swollen like a melon from his cheekbone to his eyebrows, his left eye swollen shut.

"Oh, Buck, your eye," Kadriya said.

"You should see Henry," Buck said.

Kadriya hesitated. "Is he all right?" She had meant to stop the fight, not cause serious injury.

"He's fine. Let's just say his big head is even bigger."

She glanced behind them, at the wandering shoreline, dotted with lights and the darkness that could conceal the pursuit of guards. John's hand, calloused and warm, wrapped around hers, comforting.

Buck tossed a handful of black wool to each of them. "Hurry. Put this on."

Kadriya unfolded it into a black hooded cloak. She slipped it over her head, as did John, and they settled on the port bow on a bench wet with moisture.

"Get us out, Knobby. Fast as the tide and wind allow," Buck said.

The urgency in Buck's voice brought new fear. Ahead, the wide, harbor sprawled, the sea, boiling in sharp spikes of waves, a vast seacoast opening to a world she only vaguely recalled from her journeys as a child. She remembered landing in Normandy and crossing the wide plains of Champagne to the huge fair at Troyes. It seemed forever ago, her youth, enduring the physical discomforts of traveling, the grueling toil needed to survive on the road, on the sea.

"This is Knobby," Buck said, gesturing to a short man with thick legs, a tight-paunched belly and curly black hair tied back from his face. Busy with the rigging, Knobby gave a quick grunt and a nod. "Stay seated. No fights or you'll swim back, and keep the deck clean." He turned, revealing his profile and the knotted nose that likely gave him his name.

John looked uneasily behind them. "Where are the guards?"

Buck pointed two hundred yards down the shoreline where people shouted and swarmed in front of brightly lit, low-slung buildings. "The wharfside alehouse. The brawling continues, see there, and the guards were called to stop it. A few friends created the diversion we needed to slip away unnoticed."

"Much obliged," John said. "Buck, you look like you spent a little time there, yourself, my good man."

"If I hadn't asked for it, you would look the same, friend," he said with a wry grin. He patted a storage box underfoot. "I brought your bags and checked on your horses."

She thought of Allie. "How are they?"

"Taken by monks."

"They will treat them well," John said.

"But that means we won't be able to leave Poole."

The muscle at John's temple tensed. "We'll see."

The heavy night air weighed on Kadriya's shoulders. Few coins remained in her travel bag, her Allie had been taken from her and they were being hunted from all directions.

Knobby swung the boom, the sail whipped noisily in the wind then grew taught and they seemed to fly over the waves.

"Where are we going?" Kadriya asked.

Buck nodded discreetly in Knobby's direction, put a finger to his lips and lowered his voice. "I might have your man," he said, voice lowered.

John's hand tightened around Kadriya's. "What did you see?"

"A dark-skinned young man arrived yesterday, long black hair, stabling two fine Arabians. He's also sporting a fat purse and acting pleased as a bird after a rainstorm."

Kadriya's pulse quickened at the thought of finding the chalice. "Is he quiet? Reserved?"

"Not sure, but he was wearing a heavy gold chain at his neck and a cotehardie with gold embroidery and a lavish number of buttons."

"So he's proud," said Kadriya. Sudden wealth could do that to a man, even Erol. But the harbor was dotted with a hundred lights from a hundred boats anchored in this harbor. Her hopes dimmed. "How can we find him out here?"

"He's aboard the *Mary Bee,*" Buck said, "a ship scheduled to depart for Normandy on the morrow."

John leaned forward. "Good. We're close."

"Where is this *Mary Bee*?" Kadriya asked.

"It's moored out in the harbor, not far from the island," Buck said.

"Brownsea," John said in a sober tone.

Buck shot him a meaningful glance. "Just coincidentally."

"Thank you, my friend. I'm in your debt."

"Just where I want you." Buck slapped John's knee and gave him a crooked smile of encouragement. He walked ahead to stand next to Knobby and raised his voice to a conversational level. "Wind good tonight?"

"Brisk," Knobby said. "From the southwest. Strong tide, too."

"How long?"

"To the ship? If winds are constant, an hour, maybe less."

Buck returned and they settled into silence.

Kadriya's thoughts wandered to Erol, to what she'd observed during the short time she'd known him, to what Bit and the others had said about him. Erol, two years older than Teraf, had always been the serious one. While Teraf would tease, dance and sing, Erol would reflect, get lost in the fire's flames and drink himself into thoughtful oblivion. Was quiet, thoughtful Erol capable of stealing the tribe's entire fair profits, murdering Teraf and stealing the chalice? Was he out there now, on that ship?

"I have it. A saddle," cried Buck, drawing Kadriya back to the conversation on the boat.

John cursed. "I almost had it."

Knobby laughed. "I have another one."

"One what?" asked Kadriya.

"A riddle," Knobby answered. "Solve this one:

> Under the sea is where I toil
> Fighting the wind and wave
> Feeling the bottom, the sodden soil
> Struggling beneath the lave
> Should I fail I am wrenched free
> I must master the clutch to keep
> For if in the struggle my grip should wane
> In freedom I taste defeat. What is my name?"

"Easy," said John. "My name is '*Anchor.*' "

Knobby's eyes narrowed. "You were just lucky."

The words to the riddle echoed in Kadriya's head. *In freedom I taste defeat.* John's anchor was the church, and she had threatened his connection. Try as she might, she could not think of a way to fix it. They had no choice but to find the chalice, and—

"Hey," John said, nudging her chin up with a smile. "Cheer up. I have a riddle, and I wager you can solve it first. Listen:

> My house is oft cold, I am not loud
> God fated us together and proud
> I am the more rapid, the stronger
> My house travels hither and yonder
> I may rest though my dwelling still runs
> Within it I lodge and we are as one
> Should we be parted my death is swift. Who am
> I?"

Kadriya closed her eyes in concentration. A cold, running

dwelling, rapid. Death if parted. "My memory is still fresh from those treacherous long lines. You are a fish."

John laughed. "Right. See, I told you."

Conversation faded and the small waves jostled them about as they close hauled on starboard tack, nearing the western side of the island. *You are not welcome here.* Rill's words gnawed at her. She'd forsaken her home in Coin Forest, and her tribe refused her. Like the poor fish in the riddle, Kadriya had been parted from her home.

One more tack and the *Mary Bee* loomed twenty yards ahead. The ship was large, with three tall masts. Sails lowered and stored, the ship rocked gently on the water. Lights shone on deck, as well as below.

Knobby brought their boat in and a sailor appeared above. "Who goes there?"

"Knobby Ballinger, of Poole Fleet. Buck Penhale, harbor guard, is here to see one of your passengers."

A rope ladder was lowered and Buck climbed up.

John squeezed Kadriya's hand. "Wait here," he whispered. "If it's Erol, we'll take him and the chalice to Brownsea and that'll be the end of it." He gave her a parting smile and climbed up to the *Mary Bee*'s deck.

CHAPTER 17
SECRETS

The boat rocked at the side of the *Mary Bee*. Kadriya sat on the starboard side, thinking, while Knobby tinkered with the rudder and adjusted the boom. Their small sailing boat drifted toward the big ship, collided with its hull and shied away from it, only to be attracted again. Kadriya's thoughts jostled about as well as she waited. Each impact brought new, conflicting notions.

Until now she'd had one driving purpose, to help John find the chalice. The chalice, the chalice, all for the chalice. Now it could be here, on this ship. In moments John could come down that ladder, holding it in his hands. She could imagine one of his rare smiles. His joy.

So why this melancholy?

Because it will be the end of us.

The boat drifted nearer the massive side of the ship. *Bump.* Everything seemed bigger than her, this ship, the chalice, the bishop, the abbot. She had hoped to be stronger, for herself, for John, for her mother's people.

She shivered.

What if the chalice is never found? The incident would stain John's and Lord Tabor's names, bring misfortune to those she loved. The abbot would say she'd distracted John from his duty, stolen his loyalties. *John will ultimately regret he knew me.* She closed her eyes from the pain of that thought. She didn't want to be a regret in his life. She wanted to be a joy. *I want us to have a future.*

She looked to the top of the ladder where she had last seen John. *What if the dark-skinned man is Erol? The chalice will be recovered, and John's standing with the abbot will be restored.*

But what of us? If the chalice was found, the abbot would have no reason to be grateful for her help in regaining it. If anything, he would think she slowed John down.

How selfish, Kadriya. Why do you seek laurels with the abbot?

She shook her head. *I don't. But I do want a chance to prove that Roma can be honorable, that we deserve a chance.*

*That I deserve a chance with Joh*n.

Endless fears and a bell's toll later, John descended the ladder and boarded the boat, met her gaze, his face drawn. "It's not Erol."

Kadriya hugged her arms, chilled with disappointment and relief. "Are you sure?"

He nodded. "He's an Arabian horse trader." He met her eyes and nodded. "From Spain. Wealthy and deep in his cups, but not a Gypsy."

Knobby pushed off, found the wind and swung the boom. The sail on their small boat filled and the *Mary Bee* faded away.

They skimmed toward a dark, forested island. The boat bounced in the waves, causing splashes in the soft night mist.

John leaned forward slightly, peering ahead. "Take the channel until we pass the island, then follow the shoreline to the southwest side."

Several minutes later the island loomed, large, lush and inviting. Moonlight shone on the dense, tall trees; like silver ferns they hugged the creamy shoreline of sand spread below their trunks like so many yards of Sharai's lace trim. A vision of tranquility, but dangerous. This was the abbot's island. "Where's the abbey?"

John placed his hand on her waist and drew her near, lowering his voice. "There's only a chapel and monk's dormitory here, on the northeast side of the island, almost two miles away. Forest and a large lagoon separate them from us. You need not worry."

"Pray drop us there, Knobby." John pointed to an isolated, narrow beach backing up to small cliffs.

The boat skimmed up the beach with a soft sigh and Kadriya and John took their leave, carrying their bags with them. John walked far enough from the boat to gain privacy from Knobby and told Buck of Eustace's appearance at the Gypsy camp. "Where are they looking for us?"

"The channels, sandbanks and the small islands, but especially Poole Towne."

"Can Knobby be trusted?" Kadriya asked.

"I've told him naught, but to be safe I'm taking him to Dockside after this and I'm buying him as much cheap wine as he can drink and stashing him with a good, loose woman who—" Buck stopped abruptly and regarded Kadriya with an openhanded gesture. "Forgive me. I mean no offense."

Thinking of the pleasuring dancers she had spent her childhood with at the fairs, Kadriya almost laughed. She thought of Maud and the secrets women unearthed on the pillow, and she thought, too, of Prince Malley and Blackwater Point. "Distraction is an effective strategy. I take no offense."

"Thank you. I've asked the—woman—to detain Knobby until tomorrow afternoon." Buck surveyed the shoreline with narrowed eyes. "I'm still not convinced this is the best place to stay, friend."

"We would be caught in town within minutes of landing, and I know this island." John dropped his bag on the sand. "I need you to get word to the abbot. Can you do that without arousing suspicion?"

"The abbey's cellarer likely corresponds with harbor merchants. I'll ask one about messenger pigeons. What shall I send?"

"Just tell him this. 'Stones led here. Trust me. Call off guards. Mud.' "

Buck raised his brows. "Mud?"

"Mud. M-U-D," John answered.

"Is this whole business about jewels?"

"Don't ask. Your life will be simpler for it." John slapped Buck affectionately on the back. "You'll send a boat for us, come morning?"

"Bright and early."

"Good. Once the abbot receives my message, he'll call the guards off and we can all search for Erol."

"Why doesn't the abbot just close the harbor, so he can't escape?" Kadriya asked.

"He has his reasons. They must be compelling," John said.

The boat slipped away toward Poole Harbor, and they were alone.

Kadriya walked toward the cliff, her legs sore from the mad race from Rill's camp. She pulled her cloak from her bag, spread it on the sand and sank onto it, propping her back against the cliff. Small waves lapped the sand, their rhythmic sound calming.

John stepped out of his boots and removed his hose, washing the mud from them in the shallow water. He sank beside her on the sand with an exhausted sigh. He opened his bag and passed her a flask.

She accepted it and drank the cool apple and cinnamon-flavored mead.

"Here's some smoked mutton." He passed her a slice.

Her stomach growled in anticipation. "I'm hungry. Thank you." The meat had a rich tang, fully smoked and moist. "Mmm. Tabor would like this. He's always trying new woods for his smoked meats."

John scratched his chin in thought. "Your Lord Tabor is a long-time benefactor of the abbey."

She nodded. "He's a generous man. He's given me so much. I must spare him more scandal, but how can we find the chalice when we can't even face daylight without threat of arrest?"

"I will find it," he said, his voice hard with determination.

"We will," she said, pushing the doubts away.

Seagulls cried, and the splashes of feeding fish joined the gentling sounds of the lapping water. At various points on the shoreline bubbles shone at the surface, betraying the locations of buried sand eels.

"The ocean is so big," she said.

"Aye. Big, and fickle."

Light danced on the calm water, but Kadriya knew it could also be violent, tossing travelers into sickness with waves deep as ravines. She ventured the topic that had been worrying her since Henry's attack on the beach. "Fickle like your Gelsey?"

His wind-tossed hair brushed his shoulders and moonlight poured silver on his sharp features. "Aye."

"How long ago was it?"

"Several years, and not worthy of review." He took a drink from the flask and straightened.

His posture told her he didn't wish to speak of it, but her hand moved of its own accord, touching his arm. "Did you love her?"

"She taught me a lesson about loyalty," he said, his tone bitter.

"And now?"

He turned the lover's knot ring on her finger. "My faith is renewed. You have shown that a woman can be loyal, even under great trials, at great expense. You are a far better woman than she."

Her face heated. She had hoped for reassurances that he did

not still carry feelings for Gelsey, but she had not sought such a compliment. Now that he had given it, she carved it in her memory, his acceptance, his favor, his gift. "Thank you," she managed. "I feel sorry for Gelsey—" She paused. "But happy for me."

He laughed softly. "You are balm for a man's soul, Kadriya." He turned her face toward him and covered her mouth with his.

His lips, soft against hers, tasted of fresh mead. She turned to him, wrapping her arms around his neck. Desire grew from smoldering embers that lurked just below her skin whenever he was near, and she deepened the kiss.

He inhaled sharply and pulled her closer, and desire sparked between them under the stars.

He broke the kiss and returned for another, and her skin ached for the touch of his big hands, for the joy of lying next to him, skin to skin.

Groaning, he pulled away. "We have no privacy," he said. As if to prove his point, two small craft sailed by about two hundred yards offshore. John offered her his hand. "Let's go inland, and I'll make us a fire."

They climbed up from the shoreline and, finding a clearing, John whittled some kindling with his big dagger and sparked the fire to life.

His facial scar became visible in the growing light, streaking away from his cheekbone and disappearing past his left eyebrow, a sign of suffering, of survival. His blue eyes regarded her with a possessiveness that stole her breath.

She enjoyed the sight of his naked legs, lingering on the voluptuous muscles of his thighs. He broke branches, adding them to the fire, and shrugged his oak-colored hair from his face. It shone in the growing firelight, inviting her touch.

She came to him, her body heavy with need of his touch, of

the fire he could stir within her.

He plunged his fingers into her hair and pulled her to him, covering her mouth with his. He nipped her lower lip, sucking gently on it, then renewed the kiss, thrusting his tongue into her mouth.

She shed her clothes and he slipped out of his own and took her in his arms.

A gentle wind swirled around her and she sighed from the sensation of his hard chest against her breasts. Skin to skin, a fiery kiss from his body to hers, heating a growing need within her. Her tongue joined his and his mouth moved, wet and heated against hers.

He lowered her onto his cloak by the fire and settled beside her, rolling her over on top of him. Placing his big hands on her bottom, he pressed her against his arousal, rubbing against her feminine spot, and renewed heat seared her.

He skimmed the length of her with his hands, stopping to suckle on her nipples. She rose to meet his mouth, encouraged him to pull more invisible strings of desire from the depths of her body. A sharp cry, her own, met her ears when he nibbled gently, his tongue twisting, licking her to sweet madness.

I love you. I love you! The words pushed against her throat demanding release. She wanted to cry out the words, to swear her devotion to him, but she remembered the anchor riddle. Honor was everything to him, honor and loyalty to his abbot. Her vow would invite a reciprocal one from him, a vow that would clash with his loyalty to his abbot. "John," she moaned, reaching for him. She glided her hands lightly over his flat stomach, down to his erection, covering it with her hands. She caressed the velvet smooth skin, smooth, hard, hot.

He rolled over, supporting his weight, and his fingers found her, stroking knowingly, sliding inside, and she closed her eyes in rapture.

She wrapped her arms and legs around him, inviting him. His shoulders, wide, his muscles, fluid, as if sculpted like the saint's statues. She stroked them, traced them with her fingers, the fine hairs on his forearms soft like a feather's touch. He kissed her, a deep, passionate kiss, possessive and urgent, and she raised her hips, shamelessly inviting him. "I need you, John. Love me."

He started to enter and withdrew, teasing her just outside, his fingers stroking, he entered ever so slightly and withdrew, made a shallow entry again, a delicious, wet friction.

Each movement made her feel more empty inside, more needy. "Now, John," she pleaded.

His lips curled into a smile. "Almost. I want you ready so I don't hurt you." He entered a little deeper, sucking wetly on her nipples.

Her body felt as if it would melt, pulse into the ocean with the next wave. "John." She raised her hips suddenly, her legs tightening around his waist, forcing him inside her.

The sensation halted her heart and a small sound escaped from her throat.

John groaned and moved inside her.

A breeze came up from the beach below, lifting his light hair, and his eyes turned a deeper blue, his features stark with passion. He reached for her, his lips crushing hers with a devastating, throbbing message of passion.

He thrust with new desperation. "Kadriya."

She glowed from the sound of her name, and an intense hunger leapt to a higher urgency inside her. She clung to him, welcoming him, shouting his name, her voice ringing into the star-lit night.

Her body seemed to stutter. Suspended on the night breeze, she fell, fell from the cliff and into the inky darkness of the sea, a quiver working its way into shuddering waves within her.

Closing his eyes for a moment, he crushed her to him with one last thrust, gasping in release.

Her heartbeat rose to her throat, and she held him as the waves subsided. Covered with the warmth of him, she wished for the impossible even while knowing it could never happen. His abbot would never allow them to be together. The most she could hope for was to help him find the chalice and erase some of the damage she'd caused.

He slid a leg under her and cradled her onto his shoulder, stroking her hair and showering light kisses on her face.

I love you. She could not say it, but inside her chest, her heart pounded out the message.

Later, Kadriya cleansed herself at the water's edge and washed away the creek mud in the cool harbor waves. Her veil had been lost at Rill's camp, so she combed and braided her hair. At daylight she would see what she could salvage from her bag to cover it.

Returning to the fire, she slipped beside him on the cloak. Back in his tight-fitting green cotehardie and hose, he held the old dagger from Rill's tent. He sat near the fire, running his thumb over the ribbed steel handle. He grasped it with his big hand.

"It fits well in your grip," she said.

"The grip is thick. Poorly balanced. Here." He offered it to her. "See."

"It's heavy."

He laughed, then a look of loss entered his blue eyes. "After all this settles, I will get my sword back from Rill. It's my avowal sword. A gift from Lord Brocherst—the abbot." His expression darkened. "It was blessed to defend churches, widows, orphans. Servants of God. It does not belong in the hands of heathens." His voice grew thick with emotion and loss.

She had tried to convince John that Roma had honor but in the midst of her efforts, Rill had allied with John's adversaries to get the highest bounty for them. Though John's comments were directed at Rill and his tribe, Kadriya felt the sting of guilt, guilt born by the blood she shared with Rill, Teraf and Erol.

He stroked her face, gentle as the breeze. "I do not mean you, Kadriya."

He kissed her lightly, his touch gentle.

She choked back a cry of relief. "Thank you." She pushed her nagging thoughts about the chalice away. To redeem her mother's people, to help John and Lord Tabor, they must find it.

They must! But meanwhile, all she and John had was here, on this island, at this moment. She would enjoy it.

Slipping into the spell of love, she took him in again, the pleasure of his body, the promise of ecstasy in his blue eyes, the masculine, smoky smell of his skin, the surrender, the release. Afterward, they clung to each other, breathless and spent in each other's arms. The fire, the peace, the stars, a serenity that made them one with the sand and the breeze and the sea gull's calls.

She leaned back in his arms, facing the fire.

He nuzzled her neck. "What are you thinking of?"

"The abbot, the bishop. The chalice. Do you think we'll find it in time?"

He sighed his weariness into the soft night air. "I pray we do." He pulled the small bag from his pocket and held one of the emeralds to the firelight. "So beautiful, but, flawed. *Emerald silk*, indeed. What a tall tale."

"How much do you think it affects their value?"

"By a third, I would guess." He turned the stone, watching the fire dance on the cut surfaces. "Amusing how he tried to make it sound like it gave the stone more worth. How can a flaw be good?"

"By accident? In spite of itself, perhaps?"

He shook his head against her hair. "We pray to overcome our flaws, or find a way to succeed in spite of them. They're like a stain on our souls and ambitions. How can a stain be good? He was just anxious to sell the stones."

Kadriya shifted in his arms, turned to face him. "Sharai and Lord Tabor met when I was just seven summers. Count Aydin was our king at that time, and he wanted Sharai for himself. Sharai and Tabor were so much in love, and when Count Aydin found out he became furious. He stole her away, ripped her earring from her ear and cut her hair so no other man would want her. He was cruel and selfish—there was no redemption to his flaws."

"Aye. Virtue is the fabric of a man's soul. Either his vow is good or it is not. Good and evil cannot rest on the same blade."

She entwined her small fingers with his large, callused ones. "The jeweler was praising the flaw to make a sale, but he had a good point about how we look at things. Like autumn. It could be considered as a flaw. The earth offers her abundance, only to die in the process, leading to the bleak, cold winter. But without the death of autumn, there could be no spring, so is it a flaw, or just the process, like young turning old but making young in the process?

"The seasons are like the miller's wheel, turning around and around—cycles, one following the other. What the jeweler was talking about was a flaw and a strength existing at the same time. Like horses. Some are timid–a flaw for a destrier, to be sure, but a good thing for a child or mother's horse, sure-footed and cautious."

He laughed, a warm rumble deep in his throat. "Then look at Dover, so spirited he scared buyers away, yet with proper training he became the best in battle. He's ill-humored and difficult—but those same traits in battle make him valiant and fearless, a horse any knight would want."

"So the jeweler did think the flaws enhanced the stones' value?"

"No. I think it revealed his ambition. But the justice is that the flaw proved their authenticity so I was prepared to offer more for them, but his greed corroded his morals when he bought the stolen jewels. This left him in a compromising position with his guild so he couldn't bargain. In the end, the flaw did enhance the stone's value, but it was reversed—by his flaw."

"So good and evil *can* rest on the same blade?"

"No. The stone is flawed, but something good came of it. It brought us closer to the chalice."

"I pray to God we find it."

His jaw tightened. "We must."

Minutes later, she donned her cloak and shoes and rose. "Excuse me, I need to relieve myself. I'm taking a short walk."

John took her hand. "Don't go far," he said.

She walked past the glow of the fire into the trees. The dense growth of pines offered no path, so Kadriya stayed to the left. If she skirted the beach, she would not become disoriented in the trees.

Night-feeding gulls swooped along the water, their wings making minute changes to hover just above the surface. She thought of her doves and Prince Malley and hoped that Joya and Faith were caring for them. She hoped Sharai wasn't unduly worried about her. She missed them, but her heart was here, here on this island With John Wynter.

She shed her shoes and walked, her feet sinking in the sand, a cool, clean sensation so different from the muddy creek bed.

The ocean breeze blew fresh in her face, rich with the scent of fish and the earthy, fertile scent of rotting vegetation. The waves enchanted her, the waves and the silvery moonlight on the sand and the endless stars twinkling above. Warm with love, she wanted to savor this night, weave it into her memory forever. She could smell John on her skin, still taste his kisses. It was as if she had been awakened after a long, lonely dream, awakened in the arms of a strong, sensual man who shared her passion. Whatever the future would bring, she had found love, far from Coin Forest. She isolated one particularly bright star, so bright it didn't flicker, and she made a wish. She wished they would find the chalice in time, and that the abbot would soften, change his mind about her.

Finding a tree that afforded privacy, she relieved herself and emerged from the tree's protective branches, ready to return to John. Something to the left caught her eye, something white.

Her breath caught in her throat. A boat. She ducked back in the cover of the tree. She needed to return to alert John, but to do that she would need to cross twenty yards of open beach.

Flames from John's fire winked through the trees, at least two hundred yards distant. In her reverie she had walked farther than she thought. Whoever was in that boat knew she and John were here. Swallowing hard, Kadriya lifted her skirts and prepared to run.

A strong hand clamped over her mouth and another hand grabbed her by the waist.

Kadriya's scream died in the man's palm and she struggled. She thrust her elbow backward, but the stranger, short, with a muscular body, dodged it. She tried to twist free but he pulled her close to his chest, holding so tightly she could barely breathe.

"You have forsaken me, my queen."

She jerked her head around and faced a man with dark eyes and raven hair spilling carelessly to his shoulders and tied with a light-colored scarf.

Dread and disbelief numbed her. Certes the moonlight played

tricks on her vision.

"Teraf!"

CHAPTER 18
THE WEDDING

Buck stood behind the trees beside his assistant, Ditch, a stout tack of a man from the High Street guards.

Upon his return from Brownsea Island, Buck had reported to duty and had been present when a monk, posing as a pilgrim, alerted the guards to a Gypsy in the area.

Now he and Ditch peered into the night, observing the campsite from a distance before moving in.

Haz, a greying senior guard from Buck's unit, joined them, softly wheezing. "Hear anything?"

Just ahead, six miles outside of Poole, a half moon-shaped meadow provided a convenient stop for travelers on their way to the harbor city. Buck observed the Gypsy man who had arrived an hour ago.

The campfire light revealed a Gypsy too old to be the one John Wynter sought, too old and clearly poor, his faded tunic torn and soiled, his left eye bruised from fighting.

Buck focused on the Gypsy's hand, searching for rings or other signs of wealth. Couldn't tell from here, but the simple medallion he wore around his neck seemed unworthy of comment.

Jewels. His friend's plight involved jewels, a dead knight and two dead Gypsies. And the fetching Gypsy, Kadriya. Buck had thought the wedding story a sham, but John had shot a scorching glare of jealousy when Buck had taken her hand. Despite their efforts, the two of them could not resist touching and

274

stroking each other. His staid, intense friend was hopelessly in love.

But he was also in serious danger. Why had the abbot called for their seizure, especially after he had sent John here?

Voices brought Buck back. "—so if I was you, I'd avoid Poole," a plump man in a soiled linen tunic said. "They're looking for Gypsies, looking everywhere."

A flash of worry crossed the Gypsy man's face. "Who looks?" His voice was quiet as the midnight air. Buck strained to hear.

"Guards. Men from Poole," the man said.

"Thank you," the Gypsy man said, walking toward his horse.

Buck stood. He wanted to question the Gypsy privately but with other guards present, he could not. He also could not let the Gypsy go free. "Surround him," he said to Haz and Ditch.

The men went to their horses.

The Gypsy mounted his horse, grimacing while he did, and started on the worn path to Poole.

He covered several yards on the trail, then Buck emerged from his cover. "Gypsy," Buck called.

Haz and Ditch appeared at either side of him.

Buck advanced, meeting the Gypsy's even gaze. "Come with us."

A wooden mug crashed on the table, and Eustace jerked awake. Blinking and covering his head with his arm in reflex, he could not tell who in the crowded alehouse had thrown the mug.

Eustace stretched his neck, rubbing the stiffness away. Did these men never sleep? Drunk and vomiting their suppers, they kept on teeming their cups. Stinking fools. He had been here, just east of the quay, for hours. What else could he do? He had the abbey knights and harbor guards in pursuit, but neither John Wynter nor Teraf had been found. All he had found was Rill and his gaggle of thieving vagabonds up the river, leading him on a wild goose chase. Mayhap Teraf put them up to it.

Just thinking of the black-haired devil made bile rise in his throat. Teraf was a reckless lunatic with a dangerous secret. He must be killed this time.

The looming prospect of another failure brought despair. He had been here hours, and no one had spoken of a Gypsy man, nor of John Wynter and Kashiya, or whatever in burning hell her name was, the heathen. She had the priest Bernard fooled, but not Eustace.

Beyond the open windows, lights from the moored boats shone glowing tendrils of light like angel's hair from heaven. He wished he could weave it into a sacred net and cast it across the vast harbor and snare the thieving heathens, all. Damnation!

The sound of unsteady footsteps down the stairs from the whores' rooms drew his attention. "Come on, lover, stay a little longer. You're so good." One of the whores walked backward down the steps, apparently trying to stop a man from leaving. Her rump came into view, sumptuously rounded and barely concealed in an indecently thin linen shift.

Slim but well-muscled male thighs appeared and long-fingered hands cupped her buttocks in sin, rubbing her against him. "Little Emmie, you tease," a man said, his voice warm, young, vibrant.

And familiar? No, it was imagination. Lack of sleep.

The couple shared another embrace and he pulled away. "Stop now, Emmie, I need to go. Here's another coin."

Eustace knew that voice. His grabbed the side of the table to stop the sudden whirling sensation.

"I don't want a coin. I want you."

Another embrace. "Don't touch me like that, Emmie, I won't be able to walk. I need to get back to the ship."

"Stay."

"Get your hand out of there." He laughed, a sensual purring

lilt in his voice that shot to Eustace's stomach, making his gut tighten. "We leave for Normandy soon. Let go. I promise I'll come back." The man sidestepped the woman and passed her on the steps.

Eustace ducked his head, hiding behind his hood.

A young blond-haired man descended the steps. His cote-hardie, unbuttoned and carelessly flopping open, revealed his smooth, muscular chest and fit, slim waist, and his thin hose, haphazardly hooked, revealed his engorged penis and sinewy thighs.

Geoffrey.

The obscenity struck Eustace's eyes like salt and sand and acid, burning, scraping. Convulsions rocked his stomach and he bent to the floor, heaving his small supper of bread and red wine under the table as Geoffrey passed him without recognition.

"You come back to me, Geoffrey. I'll still be wet for you, honey."

Geoffrey paused just outside the door and his inebriated laughter floated back into the alehouse, lewd laughter from one who had been so dear, laughter in the face of Eustace's insurmountable pain. He'd risked his life to shelter Geoffrey from such temptations, but now the young fool rolled in them, reveled in them like a heathen swine in its own excrement. For this Eustace had risked his security and reputation at the abbey.

Eustace welcomed the anger. He drew up from the table and strode quickly to the door.

Kadriya froze in Teraf's arms. Flashes of memories impaled her: the funeral pyre, the leaping flames, the smell of burning flesh, Teraf's scarf and limp hand, visible through the blaze. The hand. Her gaze dropped to Teraf's long, slender fingers; she felt the uncalloused palm over her mouth. The hand in the fire was not

Teraf's. *We burned Erol. Teraf killed him so he could keep all the stolen horse fair money and escape with the chalice.* Horror and sorrow swept over her, making her knees weak.

She had defended a liar, a thief and a murderer, and brought shame and political crisis to her patron, Lord Tabor. All her efforts, ever since John Wynter and his knights had ridden into Teraf's camp, each thought and deed and sacrifice had been for naught.

Her thoughts hurried. Erol dead, Teraf alive, the chalice missing. Teraf had never lost possession of it. He had it now. *Teraf has the chalice.* New hope sprang within her.

She glanced toward the fire. John would hear her if she screamed. He would come to her. But Teraf abided by no rules when fighting and was known for his deftness with a knife, and she had just unwittingly become his captive. He could threaten her and John would disarm to save her. She could never live with herself if John were killed while trying to protect her. And if in the struggle John killed Teraf, they might never find the chalice. In that moment, she knew what she must do. *I'll go with Teraf and find the chalice.*

"Where have you been? And how did you find me?" She avoided addressing his funeral, which would lead him to conclude that she knew about Erol's death and his part in it.

"My ship's moored just out there," he pointed to a craft to the right of the *Mary Bee.* "I've been waiting for the captain to return and take us to Normandy."

"Us? Us?" She repeated it, forcing anger into her voice to conceal the fear. "You left me all alone at the monastery."

"You had your priest. I see he's gone and now you have a knight. Imagine my surprise to see people on this end of the island, and imagine when I came closer to see you, kissing the foul knight, John Wynter." His expression darkened.

The look of fury in Teraf's eyes lashed her. *He knows I've been with him.* She knew Teraf's temper. If she showed fear—

She struggled to get free. "Let go of me."

"So you can go to him?"

"How dare you!"

"I saw you lying with him on the beach."

She raised her chin in defiance and challenge. "Resting. Just resting. We're exhausted. He protected me. You left me after I risked my life trying to free you at Blackwater Point. I made an enemy of the abbot by defending you, and you lied to me. You said you hadn't been to the abbey."

"I hadn't."

"Still you lie," she growled. She hated him, and anger was easy to express. "The young blond-haired monk told me. For some reason he thinks you're his friend."

"You sinned with John Wynter, didn't you," he countered, "the very man who dragged me to the gallows."

"You're wrong," she said, stopping an eyelash short of a straight lie. "But yes, I came here with him. What else was I to do? Though I defended you, you were nowhere around to help me. Where have you been all this time?" She wanted to scream at him, condemn him for selling gems from the sacred chalice to buy pleasure women and God knew what else, but she bit her tongue. "The abbot ordered me to the nunnery."

"So you came here, alone, with the knight?"

"We're hiding. The abbot is upset with him. He's ordered Sir John's arrest, as well as mine."

Teraf's mouth thinned. "Lies."

"It's the truth. I swear on my patron saint." She placed her hand on his shoulder, testing him, and something, a look of hope maybe, flickered on his features. Encouraged, she continued. "I love you, Teraf. I've always loved you."

"So you went with the knight."

"He brought me with him. So long as I was with him I would

not be held at the monastery. The abbot wanted me to become a nun, don't you understand? I would be imprisoned at Cerne." She injected fear in her voice, not difficult, for her heart was racing, racing with fear that John would hear voices or worry about her absence and investigate. She needed to get Teraf out, fast. Somehow, some way, she would find the chalice.

She touched her silk purse, hidden beneath the folds of her torn gown. She still had some coin with which to buy help. Escaping from Teraf could not be that hard, what with all the sailors and guards in the harbor. "I was desperate to escape the monastery, and the knight has a position of power at the abbey. He's strong, but Sir John is just a *dilli* knight," she lied. "He's slow, easy to fool. He thinks I adore him." She forced a laugh. "A kiss here, a kiss there and he does as I say. I knew you'd find a way to escape, so I came here, trying to find you so we could return to France."

He stared at her, his dark eyes seeming to reach into her soul. "You still love me?"

She circled his neck with her arms and pressed her body next to his. "I never stopped, not for a moment. I brought my wedding gown. The English say, 'I love you' but I am Roma. Roma blood rules my heart." She lowered her voice, as if overcome with emotion. "*Kamavtoot*," she said in Romani. "I love you, only you, only you, Teraf." Her voice broke, her world tilting in sorrow that she was forced to say such words of endearment to this abominable, deceptive man, when she could not say these words to the man who owned her heart.

He hesitated, weighing her words. "You love me."

"Yes. Yes!"

She kissed him, feigning passion, careful to not be too demonstrative, for she and Teraf had never shared the type of passionate kisses she had with John Wynter.

He pulled her to him, returning the kiss, but ended it

abruptly. "You would make a miserable nun," he said, grabbing her breast and squeezing it as he would a flask, hurting her. "I hope you're not lying," he warned. "Let's go. Our ship's not far."

John waited, alarm growing like a tic at the base of his neck. He'd dressed again and slipped into his boots, but Kadriya still had not returned. His years as a knight had showed him the thin line between a reasonable amount of time and too much of it. *Kadriya should have returned by now.* He left the fire and hurried in the direction she had walked. The sound of voices, Kadriya's and a man's voice, reached him and he dropped on his knees, hiding behind a healthy stand of marram grass that grew above the four-foot drop-off. He caught sight of the sturdy Gypsy standing with Kadriya. *God's teeth, it's Teraf!* He grasped Kadriya. She couldn't escape him.

He drew the awkward dagger, intent on thrusting it into Teraf's heart to keep Kadriya safe.

Teraf released her, and Kadriya stayed of her own free will, so John waited, thoughts rushing. *Teraf, alive all this time. The chalice. The chalice!* Someone had died near the monastery and it wasn't Teraf. Who was it, and who had killed him?

He remembered Eustace, so worried about whether the dead man had talked. Somehow the tall monk had been threatened, and had protected himself. As before, John had only gut feelings, but they were strong. *God's bones.*

The sunken beach allowed John to get closer with little fear of being seen, and their words flowed clearly to his ears.

Kadriya fell into Teraf's arms.

John stumbled, clutching at branches to keep from falling, not believing his eyes.

"I love you," Kadriya said, followed by a string of foreign jabber. John didn't know the words, but their meaning was clear.

Her voice broke as she uttered them, her body pressed close to his, her hand caressing his neck.

Her lips touched his. "Yes. Yes," she cried out, joyous. The words punctured John's heart, ripping the air from his lungs.

She spoke something about nuns and prisons at Cerne, and tilted her head back to the fire, where she must have thought he still was, and laughed; said his name and called him a "*dilli* knight."

Dilli. John remembered Joya's reference to the slow-witted monkey, uttering the word, *dilli.* Slow-witted. *She called me a slow-witted knight.* She pointed back at the fire again, mentioned her traveling bag and something about a wedding gown.

The facts of all he'd seen and heard crushed him. He slumped back, made ill from the sound of her melodic voice forming the words that stripped all of the joy and beauty from what they had shared, leaving John exposed and alone.

John gripped the dagger tighter, a hot light burning behind his eyes and a vague, crushing pain filling his chest.

She kissed Teraf again.

Rage filled John, causing tremors, and he fought the urge to leap from his hiding place and rip out the thieving Gypsy man's heart. After all that had happened, after all John had done to help her, after Teraf had betrayed and abandoned her, she still loved him.

The image of Kadriya, soaked and almost dead from the river, came to him. She had risked her life to save Teraf at Blackwater Point. She had risked condemnation defending him at the abbey. She had to have known it wasn't Teraf they burned, yet she'd said nothing, and she had risked her life again for Dury. Her singing haunted him, the bawdy, sensual, spellbinding song of the Gypsies that had overwhelmed his senses and made him, what were her words? A "slow-witted knight," so love-struck he hadn't seen her true purpose.

His mind raced. She had never professed her love for him. He'd been a fool, a poor servant who cried in his sleep like a babe, and she had felt sorry for him and comforted him. She belonged in the Gypsy world, where she could sing her Gypsy songs and wander, carefree, as the blood in her veins had guided her thus far.

He refused to believe it. He glanced back at the fire. His gut heated with a need to know. He had to see for himself.

He hurried back to the fire. The wedding dress. It could not be true! He returned to the fireside and opened her travel bag. He removed her green wool gown, still damp from her ordeal in the river, and another gown. In the bottom a smaller bag was stored, a bag with a brass handle. He opened it.

A fine gown flowed through his fingers, bold with ribbons and bright colors of red and black, with small French coins sewn to the sleeves. Garish, yet the lines of the garment followed the English fashion, gathered beneath the b-spline with ornate lace. The fabric was silk. Very dear. This was a comely, special gown, and a mingling of two styles. *Gypsy and English.* The Gypsy woman, Sharai, was nimble with thread and needle. She would have sewn such a creation for Kadriya, who straddled the two worlds of Gypsy and English. *This is Kadriya's wedding gown.*

The happy colors taunted him, and the small garment reminded him of the lithe, slender body that could fit within its narrow pleats and tucks, the body that had so recently pressed in passion next to his in a convincing deceit born of desperation.

Fresh fury brought new tremors, and he threw the gown down in a heap on the sand and pulled his dagger. He pounced on it, a symbol of his loss, and slashed repeatedly at the fine silk, sending the foreign coins flying, piercing the red ribbon bows and trying to free the pain from his chest so he could breathe again, so he could forget the dainty woman with the green flecked eyes who had brought him such joy, and misery.

Her doves. He pierced the lace. *Faeries in the water.* He swung blindly at the fabric, cutting himself, but despite the pain and bleeding, he was helpless to stop. *Her pride, and a heady passion he had never known before.* He stabbed with renewed energy, stabbed until he could thrust the knife no longer.

Dropping it, he collapsed on the sand and lifted the battered fabric, profoundly sorry for the gown, for all the love with which it was made, for what he had destroyed. He held it close, smelling a trace of her exotic spice fragrance, and he wished for death to take him then to stop the pain, to stop the memory of holding her in his arms, the memory of loving her, her, not a Gypsy, but a woman he had trusted.

The sand enveloped him, pulled him into the womb of the earth, and he surrendered to it.

A distant movement caught his eye. Heavy with loss and exhaustion, he lifted his head, raised up on his elbows to see over the beach grass. A small sailboat slipped away from the island, its billowing sail under a red gaff growing smaller in the distance.

She'd left with him.

He jumped up, raced over the hard-packed sand closer to shore, splashed into the water to his knees. An unseen vice crushed around his ankle, and he fell to his knees.

I've lost her.

But from some shadowed spot in his soul he knew he could not embrace her songs, the distasteful connection to something foreign, so different from him and his world.

His uncertainty shamed him, but it was there, sticking like a thorn in his resolve to do honor to her. After all her sacrifices for Teraf, how could he destroy what little hope she had for finding happiness? Wild thoughts, weak thoughts of love and hate, honor and dishonor, tumbled in his head. He reminded himself that life at times made little sense.

The tidy boat slipped farther away from the island, blending in with the twinkling mass of boats in the harbor. The black terns flew in, settling on the beach. In the distance the shy water rails cried their pig-squealing calls. He was alone.

Teraf struggled with the boom, trying to change direction. The sail wilted, and they drifted. Teraf cursed and swung the boom the other way and the sail filled, ripping the boat along.

From starboard Teraf leaned into the rudder, putting his whole weight into it.

Kadriya sat with her back to the deck and her feet braced against the coiled anchor rope. "Tell me how you managed to escape from the monastery."

"There's a monk there," Teraf said. "Tall. Thin. Deep voice, with a belt laden with many keys."

"The Sacristan?" she ventured, careful not to call him by name. The less he thought she knew the better it would be.

"No, he's a guard for the church and the silver and gold pieces they use in their shows."

"Their masses," she couldn't help but correct.

"This monk, he hides dirty secrets. He thinks he's so clever, so much better than me, but I brought him to his knees. He helped me escape so I'd remain silent." He laughed. "He thought he was rid of me, but I came back."

"After you escaped? Why?" Had he tried to check on her? Had he felt any responsibility or concern for her at all?

"To torment him, mostly," Teraf said with a grin. "Plus he kept giving me nice things to keep me quiet." His grin grew wider. "The last time, I took something he loved dearly." He lowered his lids and gave her a sly, cynical smile that chilled her.

What else had he stolen? She was newly astounded at his greed and spite.

They reached a compact ship moored some distance from the *Mary Bee,* about twenty yards long, with two masts. Though small, it looked sturdy. Crowned with a complex maze of ladders and ropes, it reminded Kadriya of a snarled weaver's loom.

"Here we are. The *Adventurer,* our way back to Normandy."

She sneaked a peek backward at Brownsea Island. She had never swum that far before, and the island—John—looked distant, hopeless. John could never swim that far. She was alone.

Their small boat bumped into the tidy ship. The *Adventurer* didn't sit so far out of the water as the *Mary Bee,* so the boarding ladder had only six rungs.

Teraf tied up to the side, keeping his balance in the bobbing boat. A sailor's face appeared over the deck, recognized Teraf, nodded and disappeared.

Teraf hoisted her up to the ladder rope and they came on deck.

The *Adventurer* had three masts, a profusion of rope ladders running skyward, and a small deck with a round-topped door that led below.

On deck, the first sailor and two others greeted them, their faces and features round, their skin dark and leathered from exposure to the elements. They wore heavy blue tunics and spoke in a language Kadriya had never heard. She smiled and greeted them in English, then French then Romani, and received the same blank response from each effort.

"Don't try," Teraf said. "They don't speak any tongue we know. This one's Stammer," he said, pointing to the round-faced sailor, "this one Signers," he indicated the fat one with black teeth, "and here's Born," he concluded, pointing to a bald man with his left ear missing. "Ever hear such strange names?" Teraf looked upward at the main mast and gestured to a round-topped door. "Captain?"

Born shook his head.

Teraf cursed. "What can be taking so long?"

"What is it?" Kadriya asked.

"Mainsail's damaged," he said, pointing upward. "Captain was due back with it hours ago. He was battling with the harbor master over some new tax, but to be this late . . ." Teraf muttered, shaking his head.

She noticed that while the smaller masts were dressed with neatly folded sails, the horizontal tapering spar on the main mast was empty. Her heart skipped. Perhaps they would be delayed in sailing, giving her more time to find the chalice.

Teraf took her hand and opened the cabin door, leading her below deck. He knocked on the third door. "There's someone here I want you to meet," he said, his eyes lowered again and his mouth curved into a buttery smile.

He knocked again, louder, and the resulting silence sobered him. He opened the door and glanced in.

She looked over her shoulder, seeing no one in the cabin.

He slammed the door. "Bloody pox!"

It was the first time she'd heard Teraf curse in English. "Who is it I'm to meet?"

"A dim-witted hoopoe," he said, referring to the stupid birds that followed their wagons in France. "I told him to stay here."

He backtracked to another door and turned the latch. It opened with a loud creak. "This is our cabin," he said, drawing her through the narrow opening into a primitive cramped space. He pushed the door shut and shoved the bolt lock in place. "Now we have privacy."

Her heart started beating in her ears. Would the sailors come to her rescue if she screamed? She hovered near the door and swallowed hard.

He turned the wick up on a heavy, glass-covered lantern, and the growing light revealed a writing shelf and a crude box bed. He lit a second, smaller lantern, turning that wick up, as well, and the cabin grew light. His dark eyes glowed with a primitive knowing that chilled her.

The shelf held a collection of knives and a small chest just two hands wide, too small to hold the chalice. A new thought poked its icy finger down her back. *What if he's sold all the gems and the chalice is gone?*

Teraf sat on the edge of the bed and beckoned her with a crook of his finger. "Come here, my Kadriya," he said, his dark eyes locked on her every gaze and movement and his tongue swiping his lower lip in a lewd, suggestive manner. "Come show me you love only me, and that the knight didn't have his way with you."

Fear flashed through her. She dared not retrieve one of the daggers on the shelf and come running at him straight on. To offset his strength and size she would need the element of surprise.

She swallowed again. Could she use his own dagger against him? Out of time, she gave him a shy smile and walked to him. "I have missed you so," she said, and sat next to him.

Grabbing her shoulders, he pushed her back on the bed and fell upon her with his full weight.

Air whooshed from her lungs, but he had already covered her mouth with his.

He tasted of stale wine and his tongue invaded her mouth, writhing like a stripped eel. Afeared she would vomit, she moaned, and he took it as encouragement. He reached up her leg, the smooth palm of his hand reminding her that the man that held her captive was a murderer.

She panicked. The sailors would not help her. She was alone with a man who was about to confirm all her lies. Once he confirmed her virginity was lost, she suspected he would kill her, too.

Desperate and without any other idea of how to distract him, she closed her legs and pulled away. "We must wait until we are wed."

He laughed. "We are wed now, my sweet. The sailors above deck are our witnesses." He rose and reached for the lantern on the shelf. He brought the larger one close to her face, so close she could see the fibers of the wick. "See?"

He sank the wick, extinguishing the light, and struck the lantern hard on the floor. It crashed loudly, the brass parts ringing, and the sound of broken glass filled the small cabin. He held it up to her face, showing her the side where the heavy glass had cracked on one side and broken out on the other. "See? This is our tile, little Gypsy," he said, mocking the Romani ritual of breaking tile to signify the completion of the marriage ceremony. "We are now wed." He returned the broken lantern to the shelf and his voice became harsh and ill-humored. "Now lie down and welcome me."

"No." She kicked him and threw the cover over his head. Jumping from the bed, she lunged for the door, unlatching it.

He grabbed her by the skirt, pulled her back onto the bed and struck her twice on the mouth. "I know already, but let's just see where the big knight has been." He dropped his full weight on her.

Dazed from his blows, she growled at him, biting his neck.

He yelled, striking her in the ribs.

Gasping, she released his flesh from her teeth. He struck her again, and again.

From a fog, she heard the door creak open. "Mother Mary." A young man's voice cried out. "Leave her be."

Kadriya felt Teraf's weight being lifted from her. "Stop it."

Teraf shook the man off. "Get out or I kill you, stupid monk," he said, reverting to English.

"You're hurting her."

"She's whore, mumming as virgin. Get out."

Kadriya wiped the blood from above her eye. A young man with a full head of blond hair and a look of shocked indignation faced her. "Geoffrey." The young scribe from the monastery.

"Fool." Teraf cursed at Geoffrey. "This is how you do a woman. Do you only know men?"

Geoffrey's face reddened but he positioned himself between her and Teraf. "I just came from Emmie. She has no complaints." He glanced at Kadriya. "You've beaten her. A man shouldn't have to." He helped Kadriya to a sitting position. "Lord Tabor is her patron. He's a benefactor of the monastery and—"

"What? You left abbey behind. Want go back to Eustace? Maybe he's better than Emmie."

Geoffrey flushed past his ears. "You bastard," he growled, lunging at Teraf.

Teraf sidestepped easily and Geoffrey collided with the cabin wall.

Teraf's blade flashed up to Geoffrey's neck and Teraf laughed softly. "My, my, would monks know you now?"

The sailor, Born, appeared at the door, uttering a short foreign sentence and pointing above deck. "Deck," he managed, and pointed at Geoffrey. "You," he said, pointing at the stairs again.

The creaking sound of someone climbing the boarding ladder sounded from above, followed by the heavy thud of someone jumping onto the deck.

Teraf still held his dagger at Geoffrey's neck. "I told you not go to Poole. Who followed you?" With a careless scrape he withdrew his dagger and a jagged line of blood appeared on Geoffrey's neck.

Dagger still drawn, Teraf nodded to Born, pointed to Kadriya, then the lock. "Lock her in." He pushed Geoffrey through the door. "Get up. We see who is here."

CHAPTER 19
THE ADVENTURER

John awoke. The fire had burned down, perhaps three hours by the height of its flames and the rate of the moon's ascent. It still glowed, making the sea a throbbing silver soup, dotted with dozens of golden fires from lanterns on the ships and fishing boats. Unable to help himself, he reached for Kadriya, hoping it had all been a bad dream, but she was gone. He nodded numbly to no one in the moist darkness of deep evening.

You heard her. She still loves him. Love doesn't always make sense. That's why men struggle so with it.

He could think of nothing but her. He could cut his arm off and still feel the acute pain of her absence. She with her hypnotic eyes, flashing dark with the depth of her will, and hot with passion.

He recalled the sunny autumn day he had first seen her at the horse fair. She had lured him from the start, but he had resisted. No, not from the start, he decided on second thought, shaking the sand from the wool travel cloaks Buck had loaned them. At first glance, Kadriya had been leaning on Teraf, fawning over him.

She never fawned over me. At the time, John had thought her witless, indeed spiritless, the way she followed Teraf's every lead and deferred to him. Knowing her as he did now, he understood. Teraf had offered her a home, and her need for that, for a place to belong, combined with her gratitude, overruled her common sense. To her great detriment, he thought, a bitter taste in his mouth at knowing the extent of Teraf's duplicity.

It was Kadriya's beauty that initially caught John's eye, but it was her spirit that drew him. The real attraction between them had sparked with that game of stool ball. He remembered the look of challenge in her eyes, a dare-the-devil confidence that had inflamed him and made him want her like no other woman. He had won the game and the favor of her kiss but he had refrained, fearing her power. Until later, outside her chamber, when he could resist no longer.

She was wrong, he realized. Each time she'd mentioned John to Teraf, she had used an amused, unconcerned tone, dismissing John, but she had fallen under the spell, too, well before they arrived at the abbey. Where was the truth?

Slow-witted knight, Kadriya had called him. Gelsey'd called him blind. She'd left, too. He wasn't worthy of love. He was a good knight, but foolish with women.

He folded the cloaks, put them in their bags, and kicked the burned base off the trunk of a dead tree he'd added to the fire.

"I know you, John Wynter," she had said at the Seven Stars Inn, and there had been love in her eyes. He closed his eyes, saw her there, and he was struck with the truth of it. Words be damned, he'd felt it in his gut. He knew it, as well as he knew air was in his lungs, blood in his veins. By the saints, he had felt it. It had been real.

Alarm prickled, heating his skin. Her lovemaking had been real. John had been too shocked to realize it at the time, but now that he thought about it, when she kissed Teraf just yards from where he now stood, it held none of the sizzling passion John and Kadriya had shared.

A black tern's cry pierced his ears, as did new awareness, awareness of what he had learned way back at Blackwater Point but had forgotten in the shock of seeing them together.

Kadriya is no fawner. She's a fighter.

God's teeth, she was lying to Teraf. But why go with him, a thief who had abandoned her and betrayed her and her tribe?

The answer sliced him like a dull blade. *The chalice. She's trying to get the chalice!*

John paced in a fit of self-directed anger. How could he have been so stupid? Was he so exhausted he could no longer think straight? He was a slow-witted knight; that was the one thing she was right about. He cursed himself for being so frenzied that he hadn't seen it when it was right in front of him, when Teraf was standing right here, on this island.

Fear seeped in. What would Teraf do to her? *Why didn't she trust me?* Jesu, she probably determined Teraf had the upper hand and—his face flamed. She was protecting him, John Wynter.

He held his head, helpless as a wounded hare before dogs on the scent of blood. God's teeth!

She had helped him purge his nightmare, freed him from his hatred, helped him see. He loved her beyond words and he'd lost her. Nay, he had let her go. He was trapped on an island while the woman he loved was in the hands of a thieving heathen. *Who may have seen us together.*

Alarm bells rang in his head. Dawn was at the least two hours away. He couldn't wait for Buck's boat. Sweet saints, if anything happened to her . . .

He lifted the impaled rag that used to be her wedding gown. He folded it carefully and tucked the ruined garment in her bag, realizing how brutal he had been, not only with her dress but with the trust she had placed in him.

He kicked sand on the waning fire, stuffed their bags in a thick bush and raced toward the lagoon, the chapel and the boat docks that lay beyond.

Teraf and Geoffrey left the small cabin. The door yawned open, inviting Kadriya to bolt, but that opportunity was not what made her breathless with hope. Now, now, she thought, a chance to search Teraf's cabin for the chalice.

She would find it, tie it in the folds of her gown and jump overboard and swim, screaming all the way to Brownsea Island.

Born stood before her, his bald pate shining, his shorn ear poking out in dishonor and his eyes full of question.

Clearly he didn't understand Teraf's order that he lock her in the cabin. She frowned and pointed at the door.

His look of puzzlement disappeared and he left hurriedly.

She closed the door and bolted it. Her face throbbed from Teraf's blows, and her vision was blurred in her right eye. *No matter. Find it.*

From the shelf she retrieved the dagger, slipping it into her ankle strap, along with a small table knife that might come in handy. She tucked it in her purse in the folds of her gown. She swept the shelf, searching for anything that might hold a chalice or small gems. She probed beneath the shelf, finding a spool of rope, a shriveled apple and a bundle of candles. She lifted the thin mattress from the box, feeling in all corners, and explored the mattress for any obvious lumps.

Sweat breaking on her brow, she yanked open the doors below the bed box, checking all nooks, and examined the length of the floor, checking the floorboards for any signs of hidden storage.

She found nothing but rodent leavings. A voice screamed in her head, echoing her anxiety, "Find it. Find it!" She scanned the room, certain she had checked everywhere possible, and the voice became an impassioned plea.

She listened. Another voice was shouting, and the voice was real. A male voice, coming from the deck above—that and scuffling, the sounds of struggle. She left the cabin, running up the stairs, stopping short of the top stair so she could observe without being noticed.

The tall monk, Eustace, had come aboard. He faced Geoffrey on the starboard side of the deck. Teraf hid behind the central mast.

"You have sinned, Geoffrey, but it's not too late. You haven't yet taken your vows. Come back. Lead us to Teraf and I'll help you."

"It's you who sins, Eustace. You preach against sin, yet you wallow in it."

"How could you leave? How could you do this to me?" Eustace's voice rasped in agony.

Teraf stepped forward, revealing himself. "Sodomite. Back for more?"

Eustace turned, saw him, shrieked.

Laughing, Teraf stepped closer. "Alive. Stupid monk, kill Erol. Stupid monk." He approached Eustace, dagger drawn.

Eustace' eyes grew large. "Teraf."

"Yes." Teraf growled. "See, monk. See." Teraf threw his arms wide, posturing like a courting rooster, his tight pourpoint and hose revealing his sturdy build. "Me. I stole pretty Geoffrey from abbey. From you." In the shadow of Teraf's ill-humored laughter, Kadriya remembered the grey-haired monk with the inks who had come for Geoffrey in the stables when the horse was injured, the monk who had said Geoffrey was not allowed to speak to Eustace.

Teraf flashed his dagger in Eustace' face. "Now I kill you."

Buck held the side of the gig, the light ship's boat he had encountered on his way out to Brownsea Island, so it would remain close to his own boat. Hoping the Gypsy, Dury, could help John in some way, Buck had sneaked Dury past the guards and was bringing him to John and Kadriya when three men had waved Buck down as if to ask for help.

The three men in the gig jabbered on. They had caught

296

Buck's attention and he had stopped to hear them, but it was a wasted effort, for they spoke a foreign tongue, one that neither Buck nor Dury knew.

One of them, a bald man with a ragged left ear, slammed his fist repeatedly into his open palm, made the sign of the cross, held his hands as if praying and punched his hand again, pointing excitedly backward, toward the *Mary Bee*. Even more disturbingly, he kept pointing at Dury in between his other frantic signals.

Buck observed them for signs of drunkenness, but their eyes and movements seemed normal.

"Are you praying for power? Fighting for power?"

A string of unintelligible sounds flowed from the earless one, punctuated with the understandable words of "captain, woman, ship, monk."

The monks were probably becoming more aggressive in their search for John. All the more reason for Buck to sail forthwith to the island to help his friend.

Buck shook his head to the sailors with apology, raising palms to the sky to communicate he could not help them. He released their boat. These poor fellows would have to solve their own problems, and he must get to Brownsea Island.

Buck sailed past the *Mary Bee* to the island. Finding nothing there but a dying fire, Buck studied the lingering coals in the neat pit. Someone had kicked sand in the fire in a fleeting effort to douse it. The sand near the fire was stained with blood and deeply churned, as if a violent struggle had occurred.

Dury returned from his search. "No one," he said in his halting English. "No John, no Kadriya." They found at least two sets of footprints that led to the north side of the island and back.

"I think the monks took them," Buck said, returning to their boat. "There's still a good breeze. Let's try the abbey's docks, at the other end of the island."

John billowed the sail and tacked on the port side. Just as he'd hoped, the dormitory and docks were guarded lightly. The knights, John guessed, were posted in Poole City, checking ships. John had slipped undetected past a group of monks at the northern end of the island and stolen a boat from the monks' dock, an old sailing ship with a heavily patched sail, but solid and seaworthy. Not stolen, he reminded himself. He was working for the abbot, even if his actions might be puzzling to others.

John had checked two ships on the north side of the island, looking for Teraf's sailboat with its white sail and red gaff. No sign of it. So many ships, and dawn coming soon. Fear tore at his gut. He would try the other side, the side closer to Poole, the side where the *Mary Bee* was moored.

Eustace licked his lips. Fear tasted like old metal in his mouth. If he didn't find some way to distract Teraf, he'd soon be gargling his own blood.

A hiss sounded in his ears and Eustace looked skyward. Death whispered through the dense maze of ladders and hoisting ropes above, and beyond that, the stars, the heavens, the mysteries. Panic rose, clearing his thoughts. Eustace was not ready to experience those mysteries yet.

Geoffrey avoided his gaze. The young oblate had formed an unholy alliance with Teraf and was carefully keeping his distance, looking to Teraf for direction.

The Gypsy whore would be useful.

The heathen hid in the shadows, resting against a halyard on the port side of the deck, her face swollen, set in wide-eyed wariness. Eustace would sacrifice her to his cause, and he knew just how to pound the stakes in her heart. He would turn Teraf's anger away from him and onto her. So he could get the chalice. God would forgive Eustace for killing to preserve it. As Sacristan it was his duty, and Eustace always fulfilled his duties.

"I did not kill Erol," Eustace said, struggling to purge the tremor of fear that affected his voice. "It was the knight, John Wynter," Eustace said.

The whore stepped forward. "No! Lies!" she cried. "Swear it on the Bible, Eustace, and your soul will be lost."

"Tell more," Teraf ordered. He had sheathed his dagger and leaned carelessly against one of several barrels stored in the middle of the deck.

Eustace felt the weight of the slim dagger hidden in his black habit. *Patience. You will find the right time.* "John killed Erol by mistake, thinking it was you. But once he did, he found his error convenient. With you dead, the abbot would be satisfied, and Sir John would be free to do as he wished with Kadriya."

"Lies," Kadriya cried. "You killed him."

"Be not daft. Surely you found it suspect that Sir John was the one who found him dead?"

Her fiery eyes narrowed. "John said you were acting suspicious, worried that Teraf had said something before he died. Perhaps something like, 'I'm Erol, not Teraf, and the monk, Eustace, is the one who killed me.' "

Panic spurted through Eustace. *They can prove nothing.* "Sir John killed him. I heard him confess it to the abbot."

"No!" she cried.

"He did it for you." Eustace pointed an accusing finger at her.

Teraf's features twisted. "I know who lies. See, I give better trial from you. You talk your story. More than you give me." Teraf stepped toward him, dagger in hand and a cold, trance-like look in his dark eyes. "I come back to abbey get Geoffrey. I see silver cross again. Same cross you give me. Same cross I give Erol. Same cross you have now. You."

Eustace raised his left hand to block the blow and pulled the dagger from his habit with his right hand, thrusting it at Teraf.

Teraf twisted away, but Eustace felt the resistance of flesh as his blade found a home.

Teraf grunted softly.

Relief swept over Eustace, so intense he clenched his jaw from the power of it as it surged through his body. The heathen thief who stole Geoffrey from him would finally die.

A hot, searing sensation ripped through Eustace' chest, interrupting his reverie, heat and a punching sensation.

"No. Sweet Mary, no!" Kadriya's voice.

"Glory of God! What have you done?" Geoffrey's voice, on the edge of a scream.

Eustace looked at his chest. Teraf had homed his dagger up to the handle, his hand still pushing, now glistening with Eustace' blood. Eustace stared in horror and looked into the smug face of Teraf, King of the Gypsies and his own murderer.

"I have it, monk," Teraf said, an evil grin on his dark face. "I have chalice, here on ship."

Immeasurable pain coursed through Eustace, taking his breath. He reached to his left for Geoffrey.

"I'm here, Eustace." Geoffrey's voice, Geoffrey's arms, bracing him, holding him, lowering him gently to the deck. "Lie still. I won't leave you."

"*Brother* Eustace," Eustace corrected weakly.

"Brother Eustace," Geoffrey said. He held Eustace's hand and recited the Ave Maria, his voice breaking with emotion.

Eustace felt the love in Geoffrey's touch, and he succumbed to the light that engulfed him.

Kadriya glared at Teraf. "You killed him."

"Of course," Teraf said in Romani. "Or he would have killed me. But, then, that's what you've been hoping for some time now, isn't it?"

Geoffrey knelt beside Eustace's body and looked up at Teraf. "You bastard."

"What," Teraf asked in English. "He tried kill me." Teraf laughed. "Ah. You love him, pretty monk."

"I do," Geoffrey shouted. "Not the way he wanted, but I cared. He warned me about you, but he never mentioned murder. I know who killed Erol. You did." Geoffrey lunged at him.

Taken by surprise, Teraf fell on the deck beneath Geoffrey's body. He squirmed for the dagger, finding it.

Geoffrey grabbed his wrist, banging it viciously against the deck. The dagger skittered toward the bow. "Get it," he said to Kadriya.

Kadriya raced to the ship's front and grabbed it. It was a battle dagger, too big for her to handle, and Geoffrey likely had never held one, let alone knew how to use one. She tossed it overboard.

The men scuffled, arms and legs flying. Geoffrey smashed a fist into Teraf's face.

Teraf slugged back and kicked Geoffrey between the legs.

Geoffrey doubled up, grunting with pain.

Teraf glanced around the deck, his gaze resting on wooden barrel staves stacked on deck.

Geoffrey was bent over in pain and vulnerable.

Kadriya ran to Teraf, slamming her fist into his back. "Leave him alone."

Teraf spun and pushed her.

She fell and slid on the deck, crashing into the galley door.

Teraf raised a large stave and swung it. The curved oak struck Geoffrey's back with a sickening thud.

Geoffrey's head flew back from the impact, and he landed in a crumpled heap on the deck, unmoving.

"Now," Teraf said, advancing on Kadriya. "Wife."

John sliced through the water some two hundred yards west of the *Mary Bee*. He oared with all his strength toward the ship and the small boat with its white sail and red gaff.

Its galley was lit. A couple of cabins, as well. Three masts dressed, but the foresail was naked so it wouldn't be leaving soon. A movement caught his eye, a sailor, high above the ship on the rope ladder to the foremast. He arrived at the starboard side, and hastily tied his gig to the small boat.

At closer range he saw it wasn't a sailor at all but a woman, a woman in a gown, a woman with long hair. *Kadriya!*

Below, a slender man with dark hair. *Teraf!* He climbed behind her, trying to pull her down.

John's heart twisted.

"Get away from me," she cried out.

He started to call out her name, but let the sound die on his lips. Hiding his presence would give him the advantage of surprise.

Kadriya swung her legs away from Teraf and a momentary flash of light appeared near her hand. *She has a knife.*

Teraf shouted something to her in his foreign tongue. He climbed and grabbed for her, but either had no knife or chose not to use one. He caught Kadriya's foot.

Kadriya screamed, kicking at his face.

Where in God's name is the captain? Or the crew? John's heart hammered in his chest. Gypsy blood or no, life without her would be dark as an endless night. Slipping his dagger into his teeth he climbed the boarding ladder to the deck.

Kadriya had escaped Teraf's grasp and climbed higher on the top mast's rope ladder. Below her the ship rocked, making her dizzy and her balance uncertain. Terror clogged her throat like a lump of dry linen. She looked desperately about, hoping for other boats to pass by. Where were all the determined guards who were hunting John? Why weren't they out here, checking this ship?

"Help!" She screamed toward the *Mary Bee,* but it was so far away. Would they hear her terror, or think it was just the sound of drunken sailors?

"They can't hear you." Teraf climbed down to the deck and disappeared.

I will not let him take me. I will jump in the sea, even from way up here if I have to, but he will not take me. Then it came to her. *The knives on the shelf.* He could throw them at her. Sweet virgin! She climbed higher, past the horizontal spar and onto a solid, round platform she could use as a shield.

From her new vantage point she saw a movement from the starboard deck railing. A large, powerful man appeared. His dark blond hair was whipped back from his face from the winds.

John.

His eyes were narrowed, his jaw set, the fierce warrior's face that had terrified her when she had first seen him, but it was his face, his dear face, the face of the man she loved. A surge of joy made her weak in the knees. He had found her.

Teraf ran out from his cover, carrying the same heavy stave he had used on Geoffrey.

Fear rushed through her. "John. Watch out."

John turned.

Teraf struck John on the shoulder. John lost his grip on the deck and fell backward, away from the ship and down to the sea. A sickening thud sounded, and Kadriya imagined his body hitting the boat he'd come in. A splash followed.

Silence closed in. No swimming sounds reassured her, only the soft lapping of waves against the ship's hull. Her heart banged against her ears, thumping with a dread and a deep pain for his suffering, for the peril he faced.

She waited until she thought her soul would die from wishing, but no sound came from where John had fallen.

"John?" she ventured, and received no reply. "John!" she cried out, careless of Teraf's presence, of the sharp edge of terror that lined her cries. "John!"

Teraf walked to the bow of the ship so he could see her and laughed. "A true *Rom* would have guarded her purity. Too bad it was wasted. Now you'll have to hope you can at least make a good whore. Come down and I'll teach you some tricks."

Kadriya looked past him to the lights of Poole Quay. Teraf deserved no response. She would die up here, or she would fling herself in the waters and drown with John, but she would never go with Teraf.

Her dream was over. She'd made the wrong choice coming here, luring John to his death. Her heart's wish had been cast from the star. Waves slapped against the ship, useless sounds as her hopes sank under the dark sea's surface with John Wynter, the only man she would ever love.

Teraf continued to taunt her, but she could not move past her pain to care what he thought of her. He was a murdering thief and liar. That she had once thought more of him than John would haunt whatever time she had left of her life.

Eventually Teraf grew bored with her suffering, or perhaps he had better things to do. He disappeared below deck. Absently, she listened as his footfalls echoed down the stairs, and she heard the sounds of his strides as his boots slammed into the wood. One, two, three, four five, six seven. He sounded deliberate. A door below deck creaked open.

Kadriya studied the spar and the maze of ropes to her right, the starboard side. Should Teraf climb the steps to get her, she would have no steps to climb down on the starboard side. She would have to jump from where she was, about thirty-five feet above the water, and she would have to jump twenty feet away from her platform to avoid getting snared in the lines before she landed in the water. Fear no longer visited, however. Without John, nothing mattered.

A movement caught her eye, an agitation in the water at the bow. The water stirred, not from the waves, but in a rhythmic manner, a disturbance such as that a quiet swimmer would make. A cry of relief burst from her throat, but she recovered in time not to alert Teraf. John was alive.

From the bowsprit, the long mast that jutted out in the front of the ship to accommodate more sails, a series of ropes were visible, ropes that ran from the bowsprit to the base of the bow near the water's edge. John might try climbing that rope to board the ship. She would protect him by distracting Teraf.

Teraf appeared, climbing the steps to the deck. She stomped on the round platform to gain his attention and climbed down to the gaff, the tapered wood slippery and missing its foresail.

Teraf looked up. "What are you doing? Trying to kill yourself? If you fall you'll hang in those ropes."

His face no longer taunted, and he looked concerned.

"You care what happens to me?"

"You're a whore. I no longer want you, but you tried to free me at Blackwater Point. Come down."

"And trust you?" she scoffed. "Like Geoffrey did?" Geoffrey still lay sprawled on the deck, unmoving. Behind him, two big hands tied with strips of John's green cotehardie appeared, grasping the bowsprit.

"Do as you like," Teraf muttered, turning away from her.

She must act, or he would notice John. "I know who killed Erol," she said.

"So do I," Teraf said, without turning back to her. "The stupid monk." He turned as if to walk toward the foremast, but his gaze remained in John's direction.

John rose from the side, his upper body now visible off the bow.

"Look out, John," Kadriya cried.

Teraf pulled a chain from the deck and whipped it at John, hitting him on the head.

"No!" Kadriya screamed.

John flinched but held his grip.

Teraf pulled the chain back to strike again.

John retreated below the massive bowsprit, a wooden pole as wide around as a young tree.

Teraf lashed the chain and it landed with a clanking thud on the big beam. "So you come back, knight? Try kill me. Can't. Big, stupid knight." Teraf swung again. "Can't have Kadriya, Sir John," he taunted.

John retreated farther, beyond her view.

Teraf had gone mad and was swinging the chain repeatedly, trying to beat John off the front of the ship. Teraf moved his assault toward the starboard side, likely following John's movement.

Kadriya searched about in desperation, finding nothing she could throw at him. She remembered the footsteps during Teraf's visit below deck. Why would he find a compelling need to check below?

Swallowing her fear, Kadriya leapt off the gaff, grabbing a series of thick ropes that led to the deck below. She slid down the moist rope, and as she descended the rope burned fire in her palms and on her calves where her gown had drawn up. She landed in a thump on deck, but Teraf, still swinging and clanging the chain at John, didn't hear.

Racing down the steps, she reached the lower hallway. One, two, three, four, five, six, seven. Her strides took her to a cabin door. She put her hip to it and it popped open, unlocked. Inside, the bed was neatly made, with no personal belongings visible.

The space below the bed held no bags or boxes.

Her heart sank and she returned to the hallway. *I know I counted seven . . . his steps. They're longer than mine.* She raced to the last cabin and hurried inside. Another cramped area, but Teraf's personal things were here, his show saddle and reins on the shelf with his yellow cloak, and under it, two bags.

Two bags, each about two feet long and half that tall, both black canvas, oiled to repel rain, both filled. Which one? She grabbed both and lugged them up the stairs to the deck.

Kadriya ran to the starboard side, toward the stern, away from Teraf and heaved one of the bags up. "Here, John." she cried, tossing one of the bags over the railing. It landed in a silvery spray in the moonlight, just a yard from the ship, and bobbed in the waves.

"Li' ha' eer!" screamed Teraf. "By the gods. The chalice!"

Chapter 20
Ves' tacha

John jumped into the sea, swimming toward the floating pack in short strokes.

Teraf ran toward Kadriya.

She retreated behind the main mast to avoid him but he bypassed her.

Teraf ran, his muscular arms pumping furiously, his yellow scarf flying as he leapt onto the deck and jumped overboard. He seemed to float suspended in the air for a moment then dropped swiftly, landing in a frothy splash into the water, just inches from the floating satchel.

Teraf clutched the bag and spun away from John.

John swam after him. He grabbed Teraf by the hair and pulled him back. "Thieving dog." He slugged Teraf and reached for the bag.

"Mine." Teraf clutched the bag, striking at John with his elbow.

Locked in an awkward struggle, the men sank beneath the surface.

"John!" Kadriya screamed helplessly from the ship. "John!"

They resurfaced. John's hair glistened in the moonlight and a patch of red became visible. He was bleeding, and sinking deeper in the water. His strength was flagging, while Teraf, likely sensing John's weakness, grew stronger.

Sweet saints. John would drown if she didn't act. She snatched up the other satchel. A surge of power rushed through her body, and she was only vaguely aware that this one was heavier than the other. She ran to the stern and, bracing herself, she drew the bag past her left hip. "Here Teraf," she yelled. "This one has the chalice." A burst of strength rushed through her veins and she swung the pack. It splashed into the water fifteen yards from the struggling men.

Teraf looked from the bag he and John held, to the bag Kadriya had thrown. Giving an exasperated cry, Teraf released the first bag and swam to the other, heavier bag.

John struggled to the boat, swallowing water and choking from his efforts. He made it to the ladder, leaning weakly on the first rung. His forehead was split from the chain, and blood streamed in rivulets past his eyes.

"Oh, John, I'm sorry." Kadriya hurried down the rope ladder on the starboard side, reaching her hand out to him.

He passed her the bag.

Kadriya tossed it on deck and caught his hand in hers. "Hurry on board," she said, but John was unable to go on. He grabbed the second ladder rung and draped his arm around it. His breathing came, ragged and shallow.

Kadriya glanced nervously at the distant water. Where was Teraf?

John struggled to the next step, and the next, up all six steps to the railing, and together they fell onto the deck, spent.

She put her arm around him. "I love you, John," she said. "Please don't die."

"I love you, too. I should have told you before. And your dress, I ruined it. I—" He stopped. "Where's Teraf?"

They looked off the starboard side.

"There," she said, pointing to the spot she'd thrown the pack.

Teraf bobbed to the surface, clutching the bag. He coughed repeatedly, the sounds becoming distressingly wetter.

Kadriya stood. "He needs help."

John extended an arm, blocking her. "Don't go to him. He'll take you down with him. Throw out a rope."

Kadriya pulled a rope from a coil by the central mast and unwound it, leaving the first few coils intact for weight. "Teraf," she cried. "Here, take this." She flung the rope to him.

"*Gestena,*" Teraf gasped. *Thank you.* He grabbed the rope and Kadriya started pulling him in.

Teraf lost his grip of the bag and he let go of the rope to retrieve it, releasing tension on the rope.

Kadriya fell backward and the rope jerked forward, out of Teraf's grasp.

John struggled to her. "Here. I'll help." He reeled in the rope with fast, powerful movements.

Teraf resurfaced, making a gurgling sound. He struggled, his jaw sinking below the surface.

"Drop the bag," Kadriya called to Teraf.

Shaking his head, Teraf sank beneath the dark waves.

John hurled the rope toward Teraf, and it landed with a splash right where she'd last seen him.

An eerie silence settled around them. The ship rocked gently, as if to soothe them. Time passed, a sickening, hissing silence ringing in her ears.

Kadriya watched the water for Teraf to resurface.

The rope shimmered, a snake on the water's surface.

She waited.

Lights sparkled and split from the small waves, but he never surfaced.

Kadriya met John's eyes, blue and filled with compassion.

A dull despair settled in her heart. "I meant to help you, not kill Teraf."

John took her in his arms, cradling her head against his chest. "You didn't kill him, *Ves' tacha,*" he said. "Greed killed him. He made the choice."

Amazed, she looked at him. "You spoke Romani." She kissed him.

His face held a curious mixture of pride, and shock enough to render him speechless.

"Do you know what it means?"

"I first heard you say it to Joya and Faith. It means something about love."

"Beloved. It means my beloved." She rested in his arms, basking in the thought that he had cared enough to understand her language.

Her gaze rested on the bag still on deck, and she remembered. "The chalice," she cried.

They hurried to the forgotten pack. Their fingers collided as they untied the cord. They released the lacing and opened the flap.

John plunged his big hands in the bag and removed a bulky linen package.

She lifted the corners hesitantly.

The fabric fell away to reveal gold.

He pulled the chalice from its bed and held it high.

Its graceful curves sparked in the flickering pitch light. The cup swelled from its artfully swirled stem, of generous size for consecration of the wine.

John rotated the work of art and the cavities of the two missing emeralds became visible.

He turned it in the light and the remaining emeralds shone, silky and beautiful in the light, exquisitely set with a gold master's skill on each side.

"Your honor, John," she whispered. "You've fulfilled your vow."

"With your help." He pulled her tightly to him. "I feared I'd lost you." He kissed her with dizzying intensity. "I love you, Kadriya."

CHAPTER 21
HOME

Kadriya brooded at the window of her chamber in the upper level of the abbot's compound. Outside the morning sky was dark with clouds, the autumn trees dull red, buffeted by the wind, shedding leaves like tears.

Simply standing was tiring. She couldn't sleep. Memories of him whispered across her skin in the quiet moments after dark. She ached for him, yearned to look into his eyes, see his smile, feel his touch.

She hadn't seen John Wynter for five nights, not since they'd found the chalice. What a thrilling moment that had been. Holding it, cool and beautiful, realizing John's honor had finally been restored, that she'd helped redeem her tribe. Hearing, feeling the emotion in John's voice when he told her he loved her.

Just days after he'd wished her dead.

How could her life have changed so much in less than two sennights?

At first she'd thought him ignorant and violent. She'd learned that under all that muscle and ferocity was a good man, clever, faithful, devoted.

Honorable.

She hugged her arms. She knew him now, the light in his blue eyes when he saw her, the rare smile that caused a warmth to burst in her core. The smell of his skin, and how passion stirred deep inside him and erupted with a need so great it made him shudder and cling to her, a passion so rich he stirred the wild, untamed side of her. And after their love had been spent, she had known the warmth and security in his arms, relished the sense of wholeness only he could give.

I've been foolish, thinking of tomorrows with a man who will never have me.

She rubbed her forehead. How could she have lived so long and remained so simpleminded? It had been an adventure, filled with danger and desperation and passion. Those days in Poole she'd thought love united them, but it had been the chalice that had done so.

Just the chalice.

He cared for her, but he could never overcome her mixed blood. She knew that. Living under the protective wing of a baron in tranquil Somerset, Kadriya had never experienced the hatred of Gypsies from her own people. The English, she corrected. Sweet Mary, who were her people? How tangled it was. If she couldn't come to terms with her mixed blood, how could she expect it of John? Foolish to hope.

She had given herself to him. She would never regret that, for he had given of himself to her, too, in trust, in love, in need. He'd risked his position with the abbot. He'd risked death to save her from Teraf. His sacrifices reached all the way to her heart, tightening her throat and bringing a fresh wave of emptiness.

John Wynter was her knight. Her heart's dream.

And that's all he can be.

He must know that, too, for he had made no effort to contact her, had sent no word. From Poole, Sir Thomas had joined her, his shoulder still wrapped from his injury. He and a handful of monks had escorted her back to Cerne. She'd spent a fitful night at the Seven Stars Inn, sleeping in the same bed in which she and John had first shared their passions. Then four nights of cold loneliness in the abbot's compound. No longer held as prisoner, allowed to go freely, at least within the abbey walls, to ponder her fate.

She'd been willing to lie and blackmail the abbot, bargain for Teraf's life in return for the chalice. Now she hoped the abbot would consider her part in recovering the chalice and treat her with mercy.

The prospect of life in the nunnery worried her more with each passing day he refused to see her. She wished she could slip into his chamber and force his audience, but a half dozen monks stood guard between her door and his, belowstairs. What was he planning to do with her, and why had Sharai not come? Or Father Bernard?

She would never love anyone as she loved John Wynter. Would that she could spend her days helping Sharai at Coin Forest and live out her life as a spinster.

To be sequestered in cold stone walls with nuns! She had naught against them, but people were her connection to life— Lord Tabor, Sharai, their children. Laughing in the scullery with Maude, tending horses, running with Fang and Fool. Singing to her birds. The life she used to have, not the reflective, secluded life of a nun.

But Coin Forest was beyond her now. She'd brought shame and scandal to the Tabor demesne. Returning there would injure them even more. Wanting so much to find a home, she now had none but the cold walls of Cerne.

She dabbed at the plate of bacon and bread she'd been given to break her fast, unable to lift it to her mouth.

Someone knocked on her door. "Kadriya?"

"Father Bernard." She rushed to the door and opened it. Taking his hand, she repeated his name. "You're all right. Where have you been?"

His right eye was blackened and both eyes were bloodshot, as if he had suffered a fitful night's sleep. A dark crimson stain rose up his neck, making his white hair appear even more so. He patted her hands. "It's good to see you, too, child." He stepped into her chamber, leaving the door open, but lowered his voice. "Many details were left loose in Poole, decisions to make."

"Where's Sir John?" Dignity be damned; she was desperate to know.

"He's just arrived."

Her heart lightened, lifted by hummingbird's wings. He was close. The very air became softer, kinder.

"And Sharai?"

"Coin Forest. She sends her love."

"The abbot?"

"Here."

"Has he said anything more about the nunnery?"

"I hope I've given him sufficient reason to reconsider that." He took a breath. "Yesterday was a trial for him. Did you hear?"

"Hear what?"

"The bishop cancelled his trip here for St. Michaelmas."

John had told her about the preparations, the cellarer stocking extra food and wines for feasting, how the monks had prepared the grounds and guest rooms. "After all his worry about the chalice." She reeled at the news. After all the secrecy and sacrifice, the bishop was not coming? "Why?"

"He accepted the Bishop of Bath's invitation instead. Likely the healing springs tempted him more than this humble monastery. But speak naught of it to the abbot. The issue is still sore with him. Come. The abbot waits."

Downstairs, they heard a horse approaching, and Father Bernard opened the door. John was dismounting from Dover. His blond hair shone, freshly washed, and that unruly wisp fell across his forehead, just above his scar. His freshly shaven face revealed his high, pronounced cheekbones and the battered bridge of his nose. His blue eyes were clear and vivid, and welcome as sunrise.

She ran to him, placing her hands on his forearm. "I've missed you. You sent no word. I haven't known where you were, or what's been happening." She stumbled on her words, desperate to understand, to find answers to the questions she'd been asking in her solitude.

"I'm sorry. I was detained at Brownsea Island and had another commission."

"Where's Dury?"

"On his way to Normandy," John said. "He wanted me to thank you for saving him after Seven Stars. He asked me to give you this." He handed her the small silver medallion Dury used to wear around his neck.

"I went back up the river with Buck and his men." He smiled. "We found Rill, and I demanded my sword." He patted it, sheathed and strapped to his saddle.

She thought of Bit and the tribal women and children. "And the Gypsies?"

"The guilty are dead. The abbot returned the funds Teraf stole from them. They, too, are on their way to Normandy." He lowered his voice. "He did stipulate that they were not to return within fifty miles of Cerne or Poole."

"And Buck Penhale?"

"Forgiven. He'll receive a promotion, I'm hoping. But come; the abbot waits." He gave Dover a pat and approached the door.

Inside, the abbot invited them in and gestured for them to sit at benches by the fire. Kadriya sat on the middle bench, and John and Father Bernard sat on either side of her.

The abbot's grey eyes were tired, but with his ring, miter and hood, he maintained his dignity and grace.

"How is Geoffrey?" the Abbot asked.

"Several broken bones, but healing," John said.

"You told him he is welcome to return?"

John nodded. "A book merchant in Poole saw his writing. He's offered Geoffrey an apprenticeship."

The abbot took a deep breath and let it out, revealing relief. "Perhaps it's best." He turned his gaze to Kadriya.

She tried to settle the scrambling in her stomach and answered his gaze, chin held high. She must live with the consequences of her decisions.

"You used poor judgment, Kadriya, and complicated a delicate situation. You defied church law and put people's lives in jeopardy."

She lowered her gaze in contrition.

"I would that you join the nunnery to save you from yourself."

Her heart faltering, she raised her head to meet his gaze.

"But Sir John has given me no peace with this decision." He shot an accusatory look at his first knight. "He's argued on your behalf about helping to find the chalice. He's visited Coin Forest to confirm you are still welcome there."

"Sharai's forgiven me?"

"She's joyful at your safe return and asks that you hurry home. Godspeed."

The abbot rose and offered his hand.

She accepted it and stood, swallowing with difficulty.

"You have redeemed yourself. You're free to decide which path to take."

Kadriya blinked back tears that threatened. "Thank you, Father."

A troubled expression shadowed the abbot's features. "Tell me of Gypsy ways. Why would Teraf kill Eustace, an unarmed monk?"

"Gypsy blood does not bestow honesty any more than having French blood, or English blood . . ." She hesitated, fearing insult, but realized it must be said. ". . . or being a monk. Eustace was armed. He stabbed Teraf before Teraf stabbed him."

"Why?"

Teraf's lewd references to Geoffrey and Eustace rang in her ears. "I think they shared a dark secret," she said.

The abbot pinned her with his pale blue eyes. "Which are you, Mistress Kadriya? Be you a Gypsy, or an Englishwoman?"

His intensity sucked the air from the room, and Kadriya's heart beat rose to her ears. Thump. Thump. Thump. She had struggled with this question all her life. "I am not the only one who wonders about this, Father. What of you?"

The abbot's mouth fell. "Me?"

"Are you a baron, or are you an abbot? Each is unique to the other. You took your vow, you became an abbot, but there still lingers in you the baron, I dare say."

"Nonsense. My vows transformed me."

"Of course they did. But you use those parts of you that were a baron to fulfill your duties as abbot, do you not? Military strategies, your instincts with people, the knowledge you gained before your vows?"

The abbot's eyes narrowed. He raised his miter as if he would strike her.

She rushed on. "Your vows are sacred. You honor them. I do not challenge you on this, Father. You rejected the life of a nobleman to become a man of God. Your clothing changed, but you are the same man inside, pious, honest, fair."

"I asked about blood, and you speak of garments."

She released the breath she'd been holding. She had failed to make her point, failed to answer the question to herself or him. "I beg your pardon, Father, but I can't answer your question. I can only say that I am—just me. Kadriya."

The abbot walked to the opposite wall, faced an ornately carved wooden cross on the wall. He remained still, thinking. After a time he returned to them. "Gypsies started this, but they also helped end it." He held up a tied parchment. "This is my court register. The bishop was to have taken it with him. I fear Brother Eustace was as involved as the Gypsies with the chalice's theft. I would that this incident not make it into the bishop's register." He turned to them for a response.

"No one but Kadriya and I saw the chalice in Poole," John said.

"I know naught of any chalice," said Father Bernard.

" 'Tis best left to the ashes." With a short, silent prayer, the abbot tossed the parchment into the crackling flames.

Kadriya, Sir Thomas and Father Bernard passed the gates of Cerne, taking the well worn path that would lead them to Coin Forest.

A few hundred yards from the gate, Sir John approached on Dover and reined to a stop by Kadriya. "I would have a word with you."

Father Bernard nodded.

She slid off Allie and John led her under the protective branches of a large oak tree, its red leaves sheltering them from the fine, late morning. He spread his travel cloak on the lush, leaf-strewn grass.

She glanced at the black wool, remembering the passion they'd shared on Brownsea Island.

His gaze met hers and his eyes turned a deeper blue, his lips parting slightly, and she knew he recalled it, too.

She sat, leaning against the trunk.

A muscle worked at his jaw, and he held her with his gaze. "I've missed you, too."

This is where he'll leave me. This is his good-bye. Her throat went dry. She didn't trust herself to speak.

"From Poole I returned to the jeweler in Dorchester. Because of his fear for his reputation, he was the safest one to repair the chalice and not speak of it."

She nodded.

"Then I went to Coin Forest. I needed to see your family, apologize for the disparaging things I said. I begged Lady Tabor's forgiveness."

He unstrapped a bag from his saddle and returned to her. Dropping on his knees, he placed the bag in front of him. "In a moment of madness when I believed you still loved Teraf, I ruined your wedding dress. Sharai was gracious enough to repair the damage." He lifted the dress, his big fingers gentle with the ivory and red silk. "This is a fine dress. English, but Gypsy, too."

The colors, the coins taunted her. She could not decide who she was. How could she ever expect him to accept her if she could not accept herself? She could not find her voice.

He wiped her tear away with his thumb. "I'm sorry for the pain I've caused you."

He was leaving her. She covered her mouth to stop the cry that would escape.

He took her free hand. "At the first I saw only the color of your skin, then I began to see you. I love your strength. Your courage. Your loyalty. All of you." He swallowed. "Even the Gypsy part."

She shook her head. "It's all right. I know how you really feel," she managed.

He nodded. "The music still stirs you. I saw that in Poole. You're free to rejoin your tribe if you wish."

He would send her away from him, back to the Gypsies. She had shown them such loyalty, it was understandable, but the pain made it impossible to breathe.

"I would escort you there for safe passage, but much as I love you, I could never join you there."

He stroked her hand, and she laced her fingers in his, unable to let go, even as he banished her from his life.

"Will it end like this? What of your English blood?" His voice broke, and his eyes mirrored the pain she was suffering. "Is there no hope for us? You could decide to live with me. Here." He cupped her face with his big hand. "I love you, Kadriya."

"But I'm a Gypsy."

He smiled. "The abbot's ears are still ringing from your speech about blood and duty. It will take him some time to see the wisdom of it. But me? Some say I'm a slow-witted knight, but I knew what you were trying to say."

"Oh, John, you know I was bluffing about that."

He nodded. "You're just you. Kadriya. You have your flaws and God knows I have mine. It's how we choose to live our lives that counts. Live with me here in Cerne. My lands aren't grand as Lord Tabor's, but they're well tended, fertile, with a clear stream. Room for horses."

"What of your duty to the abbot?"

"He's not convinced our marriage is right. He will be troublesome at first, but he knows how I feel about you, and has given his blessing. And I will defend your honor all my days." He paused. "What say you? Will you be my wife?"

She lifted the brightly colored silk with the prim lines and shining coins. "I can wear my dress?"

He smiled, warming his eyes. "I would that you will."

"And sing Gypsy songs?"

Discomfort weakened his smile, but he recovered. "As loudly as you wish."

She laughed. "You're so gallant. Yes." The word danced past her lips. "Yes."

He kissed her, his mouth hot and intense on hers, and she fell into the warmth of John Wynter's arms.

BOOK CLUB READERS' GUIDE

1. Roma (Gypsies) fear assimilation with *Gorgio* or *Gajikane* societies because they dread being corrupted by those societies' influences. America is known as the land of immigrants yet, when viewed in terms of historic continental migrations, European countries have also received waves of immigrants. Is it possible for a people to integrate in a new country, without assimilating?

2. It's been quoted that only about 5% of the estimated 10–12 million Roma worldwide can really be called "peripatetic nomads," which suggests they are traveling due to economic reasons. Because of their lack of permanence, can any statistics about Roma be relied upon?

3. In the early fifteenth century Gypsies enjoyed a type of "honeymoon" in Europe, accepted as nobility on pilgrimage at demand of the Pope. By the sixteenth century, French mobs threatened to hang any Gypsy who refused to leave. In the eighteenth century, Empress Maria Theresa (violently opposed to entertainment) passed a law under which Roma children were stolen from their parents and given to Christian farmer families for "civilizing." Any Roma parents trying to recover them were accused of child theft. In the nineteenth century Gypsies came to represent freedom and self-determination. Today, is their biggest obstacle to integration the prejudice that

comes from conceiving a stranger as an enemy? If so, what can they do to address this?

4. *Love Will Find a Way, by Janet Lane*

> Breached by ignorance, fear, mistrust
> Like puzzle pieces splayed
> O'er cities, states and continents
> Discrimination made
> Us separate and hostile; can we e'er its stain
>   allay?
> With open hearts and open minds, love will find
>   a way.

In cases of intercultural and interracial love, do you believe love opens the mind and lessens prejudice, or do you think it's simply a matter of one person seeing another person behind the skin, or religion, or age?

5. Romantic relationships aside, is education the key to understanding different cultures and races? Or must we have the "melting pot" influence to bring it beyond textbook theories to flesh-and-blood reality?

ABOUT THE AUTHOR

Janet Lane writes about affairs of the heart in the medieval romance and contemporary women's fiction genres. She graduated with honors from the University of Colorado, where she completed the creative writing program. She leads writers' workshops, facilitates an online critique group, and created *Romancing the Tome*, a monthly column she's written for seven years for RMFW's *Rocky Mountain Writer*. In 2006 she was presented the Gold Nugget award for service to RMFW.

Her debut novel, *Tabor's Trinket*, received critical acclaim and made the Denver bestseller list. Her short story, "It's About Time," will appear in RMFW's second anthology, *Tales from Mistwillow*.